Th Laughing Bear

A Novel by
Diane McBain

Cover illustration by
Francis Burras

BearManor Media
1317 Edgewater Drive #110
Orlando, Florida 32804
www.bearmanormedia.com

Hardcover: ISBN 978-1-62933-567-4
Paperback: ISBN 978-1-62933-568-1

Printed in the United States of America.
Book design by Brian Pearce | Red Jacket Press.

Done is better than perfect...

SHERYL SANDBERG

Foreword

When I left Los Angeles, I left behind a life that had been filled with many unbelievably wonderful things. I had a successful career in film and television-making that was fulfilling; I had the honor of rearing a wonderful child (quite alone); and I had gathered unto myself many divine friends. Why did I leave? It was all Los Angeles was able to offer.

I landed in the beautiful California mountains of Los Padres National Forest, in a tiny village where I found all sorts of new friends, fulfilling activities, love and loss, and opportunities I had never found before.

At first, at a loss of what to do with myself, I went to a meeting of quilters and found in the midst a bevy of delightful women and an occasional man who were friendly, helpful and generous beyond my fondest expectations. There, I learned how to make quilts of all sorts — blankets, table runners, pot holders, jackets and not least of all, wall-hangings that looked like paintings. Each was a patchwork of textures, colors and visions that made my heart sing. I learned about templates: the shapes of circles, squares, rectangles and octagons that helped me create the most wonderful images. Later, I took up water coloring doing wonderful paintings that again were patchworks of textures, colors and images. The templates I used in this endeavor were photographs — some that were taken by me and some that were the offerings of others. At some point, I took up my computer and began writing stories that seemed fascinating, again using templates. These templates were the people and places I had come to know, some very intimately and others more casually. The story of The Laughing Bear emerged from this endeavor, the templates finding their own textures, colors and images which eventually became a novel I felt I could be proud of. Just as the quilts no longer bear resemblance to the templates from which they sprang, or the paintings only resemblances to the photos that gave them shape, nor do the characters in the story any longer bear resemblance to the people who initially gave them birth.

So come, join me in Dancing Bear Springs at the Laughing Bear B&B with an occasional divine meal at the Singing Bear Bistro where we can laugh and cry together.

CHAPTER 1

Wally

Early Fall, 2015

There was a low growl. The sound pierced his sleep like a sharp knife. Wally Wharton had gotten precious little nods lately reacclimating himself to sober life. There had been ten months of rehab — that is, the rehabilitation that Wally could manage. His mom had left him in a sea-side town near San Luis Obispo, California, taking his dog, Buddy, home with her to Dancing Bear Springs in the mountains nearby. She arranged to leave Wally at a rehab center his dad had located. He went through 72-hour lockup to do 'detox' and stayed at the facility for a couple of weeks. That had been the worst of it. He never wanted to suffer that way again. It wasn't that he hadn't expected it be rough, but the detox had turned out to be far worse than he ever thought it could be. The trial had been severe, his insides torn apart. He couldn't breathe, couldn't eat, couldn't function. The depression was the worst he had ever experienced and hoped he would never experience again. At one point, he had wanted to kill himself. He was exhausted most of the time, had mad mood swings, difficulty concentrating, and at times, extreme anxiety. He wanted to run shrieking from the facility feeling as if his heart would jump out of his chest if he didn't.

And now he would do anything to stay away from methamphetamines. He had joined the homeless community while staying at a shelter walking the hills and dales of the area finding places where a soul could pick up a meal. For ten months, he struggled successfully to overcome his addiction. He had plenty of help. Folks he would run into on his way around town gave him good advice and sometimes stayed with him while he went through a tough time. Without that help he would have never made it. He was grateful for them but he overcame the addiction to meth mostly on his own.

Wally heard the growl again. He did not want to open his eyes to see what was causing it. He didn't want to think. He just wanted to go back to sleep. Then he felt it, a warm, sloppy tongue on his toe. It felt like a warm kiss.

"Hmmm," it felt so good he couldn't help but think about Lana, the woman who would come all the way up the mountain to see him. Lana, who lived in the San Fernando Valley, did not want any involvement; all she wanted was good sex. That he could provide. They would rent a cheap motel room down by the freeway for a night and spend the time fucking their brains out. It was always a good time and it always had an end, a definite end until the next time she came to visit. She would not call and carp about how little attention he paid to her; she would not follow him around town as one young girl had never saying anything, just spying on him; she would not call and hang up on him without a word as another girl had done when he lived in Los Angeles; and she wouldn't go before the town meeting and rat him out on something he had never done like that badass, Sally Oliver, did when she got mad at him. The sex was not worth the trouble.

Again, the sloppy kiss was accompanied by the low growl. He opened his eyes and his dog, Buddy, a small black lab mix lying next to him growled yet again. "What's up, Buddy?" Buddy's black eyes were fiercely focused on Wally's feet which were hanging precariously out the door of his car. It was late summer and he had slipped out of his sleeping bag during the night to catch some air. There he had remained with Buddy sleeping next to him.

"GRRRR," the dog's growl suddenly burst into sharp barking and Wally knew something was up. Looking down at his feet he could see a nose and a tongue, neither of which belonged to his dog.

Startled, he jumped up and discovered he was facing a four-hundred-pound Black Bear.

"Yeeeeeee!" He screamed.

The bear jumped and, fleeing wildly, ran as fast as his four legs could carry him. Buddy chased him back into the woods nipping at his butt. Wally stood just outside his car astonished as he watched the terrified bear, his butt tucked under him, scramble away. And he couldn't stop laughing. It was the funniest sight he had seen in a long time. Imagine, a scared bear. At least he still had his toe.

"I guess the bear was looking for some breakfast," he said, still laughing. Buddy had run after the bear for a few feet, then stopped when Wally's piercing whistle warned him to halt. Buddy knew his master inside and out and would never willingly leave his side.

"There is no way I would have thought I'd be waking up to a bear kissing my toe. That's a new one."

Wally's life in Dancing Bear Springs had been replete with odd experiences. He and his woman of twelve years, Shanna Bradley, had moved to the remote mountain community nestled in the California mountains several years ago. They had been through a lot together.

When he and Shanna first started their relationship, they decided to wait to get married so they would have enough money to raise a small family. They were starting from scratch and worked hard in their respective occupations — he had his own moving company and she worked as a barista — to save up for the down payment on a cabin. Once they purchased the tiny cottage in the mountains, they had lived part time there and part time with his mom in her West Hollywood apartment. Both had to work in the city. There were few substantial jobs available in Dancing Bear Springs.

The only vehicle they had was a Honda Reflex 250 Scooter. It was a big scooter but hauling the two of them up the mountain week after week had been a stress on the machine. Nevertheless, they had made it every single time despite rain, hail, snow, wind and weather of all kinds with the help of his mom's prayers to a God she didn't know if she believed in, except one late night rescue when she got out of bed, drove up the mountain to help the pair get home. His mom had never let him forget waking her in the middle of the night to drive the ninety miles up the mountain. They had continued this practice for two years until finally it was time to buy another house and another vehicle. His mom told him she thought they had been very brave.

Soon, they could buy a big house in Dancing Bear Springs where they were going to accommodate Shanna's mother and siblings. Shanna's mother didn't know how to be grateful and worked her way out of the situation and back to West Hollywood within the year taking Shanna's siblings with her.

Wisely, Wally's mother had taken the little cabin they moved out of and made it her own. That was long before Wally and Shanna had any problems. They had worked hard for everything with much to show for it. By the time the 2008 economic crash came along they had acquired three properties in the remote valley and Shanna had earned her real estate license. Life in the mountains of California made all the sense in the world for them. Everyone seemed happy and content for the first time as they cobbled their lives together to create a new family.

The enterprise worked for several years even as he and Shanna borrowed heavily to expand their property holdings. He and his woman had a love that looked solid and long-lasting. He felt whole and was headed toward the kind of life that would keep his mom, Shanna and any children they might have together, safe. That was before trouble in the form of methamphetamines entered their lives.

The drugs arrived in the satchel of a man, Juaquin Brody, a gang member who had a reputation as a killer. Juaquin, a name Wally did not believe was his, proved to be big trouble. Shanna had turned cold toward Wally after she met the meth dealer. Suddenly, she was spending a lot of time — she said — showing properties to potential clients. There were clients Wally knew. The real estate market was hot before the recession and she worked very hard to rack up some sales. Nevertheless, the amount of time away seemed inordinate to him. He didn't like it.

He learned later she had gone behind his back and borrowed another $60,000 against one of the houses they owned together leaving them over-leveraged on the houses. She left Wally holding the financial bag on the back of a Harley with her arms around Juaquin, the phony meth dealer, just as the economy was crashing around their heels. It had been a cruel thing to do and Wally fell into a deep depression that only got worse as he dove into the world of drugs. Shanna might as well have shot him through the heart — he thought that would have been merciful.

As the economy faltered, the houses went to seed as they sat under-water. No one ever came to look at them for sale. The bank foreclosed and his mom had to move from the house she had rented from them. This was when Wally began to doubt himself. He had always had a great deal of confidence that had been cobbled together from his skateboarding days, his early days in business, running his own moving company and his recent purchase of the properties he now owned. He felt entitled to be successful if he worked hard and he did work hard, proudly.

As always in a small community, word had gotten around about Wally's drug use and the village made it nearly impossible for him to live a normal life. Not that he could anyway. He was too far gone to be good for any-thing. Though he was a hard worker, he would leave jobs unfinished and angry homeowners would end up hiring someone else to complete the work usually at a greater cost. He ended up with no money and nowhere to live. His anger was relentless and finally it had affected enough people in the village that a friend got a hold of him and talked him into admit-ting his addiction and getting help.

CHAPTER 2

Danie

"Thank you, thank you all very much for your generosity." Daniela Wharton's eyes teared. "Seventy-five today and here you are to help me celebrate this auspicious moment."

The dulcet tones of an operatic tenor wafted through the restaurant's back room. The Bistro, owned and run by a former Italian opera singer and his talented daughter, was the only good restaurant in Dancing Bear Springs. Their European menu sported items that were out of this world. Daniella loved the tiny space decorated with Italian wall tapestries, low hanging lights and antique Italian tables and chairs. None matched but that was the charm.

How many times had she visited the Singing Bear Bistro; how many meals had she shared here with friends? It had been enough to have tasted everything on the menu. Each dish was a reminder of special moments. They were wonderful memories and…she couldn't help thinking about the nagging question on her mind, the one thing that darkened every good moment.

Despite the cheery mood in the room, Danie's head throbbed. She resolved to go on as she always had. Feeling the need to say something she rose and spoke to the group gathered at the table: "I'm not sure I am ready for seventy-five; I don't even feel like I am seventy-five. Physically, yes — you know, the aches and pains. But inside…every time I glance into a mirror, I feel like I am looking at someone else. Oh yes, I am of course me…Oh never mind, I look older than I feel. So be it!" She laughed.

Appreciative amusement erupted from the small crowd. Her friends had similar experiences even though most were younger than Danie. Those assembled were book club members from Los Angeles.

"So, thank you," Danie continued. "You have been generous with your thoughtfulness, since I didn't want *things* (her voice emphasized the word 'things'). I have enough *things*." The crowd smiled. "Nevertheless, you have presented me with wonderful gifts. Thank you very much for coming." She sat down heavily.

Aside from Danie's book club friends, attending the small birthday celebration were new friends from the village she lived in, the local newspaper owner-operators who were becoming good friends. They had done an impressive job helping her promote her recently released autobiography, *All That I Am: A Hollywood Memoir*. Formerly a minor movie star in Hollywood, she had disclosed her life story — her life stuff and the true story of a failed career. There had been a lot to say about that, as it turned out, and she felt she had made a small dent in the publishing market.

It had not been easy. She had made a good career for herself — for the first ten years but her fame slowly dwindled in importance as time went on. As the culture changed, her style became outdated and she was unable to shake the stereotype she had acquired during earlier times. Danie knew she had not been good at making business decisions and had squandered a small fortune on clothing and the kind of digs she thought she needed to present herself well in the public eye. She would later lament the misspent money she could have used to buy desert land that would later become worth millions or even billions had she been smart. Who knew? Well, in fact, many people knew, but she had not. Lamenting what could have been was a useless occupation; that she knew.

The close friends who surrounded her now made everything worth it. She valued these relationships more than life itself. She dearly loved her son, Wally, too, of course. But he was often the source of her stomach and headaches — there had been far too many bad times; the tears again stung her eyes.

"Hey, what's the matter?" Samantha, her closest friend from LA, reached her arm around Danie and hugged her close. "I hope those are tears of joy." Sami was shorter and a little plump, pleasantly so, and she had the biggest most generous heart on the planet. Her short strawberry blond bob bounced around her sweet face like autumn leaves falling briskly in the wind.

"Sami, I wish I could say they are. They are certainly a mixture of joy and sadness. I'm being evicted!" she blurted. "That woman moved in and after that everything just deteriorated."

"'That woman'?" Sami asked.

"Oh, you know; the interior decorator I told you about. Bernadine is her name — the 'one-name-wonder' of interior design!" she exclaimed. "The landlady, Mrs. Seward, recommended her, said she found her running a little furniture shop in town. The woman was looking for a place to live since she's new up here. She seemed so nice, but the way things have gone since she moved in, I can't be sure Bernadine's there for the reasons she said she was."

"What do you mean?"

"Well, when she moved in — interior decorator, you know — she moved all of her stuff in and all of my stuff out to the corners and out of the way. I had to fight her for the couch. I love that couch and I wasn't about to let her move it from the living room. It's where I spend most of my daytime hours!"

"You told me she wanted to hang an over-sized painting of a sexy woman in red above her blue sofa?"

"She did it!" Danie reflected in dismay. "Now, every time I come into the house there it is, a gigantic painting of a woman with blue eyes, dark hair, surrounded by deep maroon folds of a flowing dress that gently caress her breasts. Good god, it's intimidating!"

"Oh Danie, did you do something to the painting? Tell me that isn't the reason you're being evicted!" Samantha said it a little loudly and got the attention of the others.

"What?" A chorus of voices asked the question as if on cue.

Danie cried again. "Oh, it's just stupid! I can't believe this is happening but after That Woman moved in the owners came in for an inspection and found a hole in the wall of the room that Wally used."

"A hole?"

"He was never supposed to live there." Danie was trying hard not to whine. "I never saw it and of course I never did anything about the damage because I didn't know about it." She shrugged. "Now the owner is on my back about the repairs for which I am responsible since I know Wally did it." She took a deep breath, "I agreed to pay of course, but…"

Everyone was looking at Danie with that odd quizzical expression people have when they can't put the facts they know into a coherent logical reality.

"It's complicated," she continued, "but I had plenty of money on deposit in her bank account that was to cover any damages and the last month's rent. I thought Mrs. Seward could use that money for the repairs and make a new lease with me based on the new rent I was paying with a roommate."

"She didn't agree with that?"

"No, she did not. She said, 'All right then you're out. I don't want you in my house anymore.' "

"What?"

"I was stunned. It's not what I expected at all. The woman repeated herself and said, 'You're evicted! Get out!' "

"Oh no!" The chorus of guests intoned.

"I have no choice but to move and I have no idea where." Tears ran again. "I thought I would live in the little house forever, for the rest of my days." Danie's running mascara blackened her eyes. "Maybe I'm being silly." She wiped her eyes with a tissue and blew her nose. "I'll find another place. I'm sure I will."

The party was over. They had eaten birthday cake, chocolate of course and paid the check. Danie led the way to the parking area and said her goodnights. Her friends had been sympathetic and she knew everyone was solidly on her side but that didn't change anything. She would have to find a place to live and maybe get storage space for her things. Most of her friends of the birthday evening, as caring as they were, would go back home to Los Angeles. She would solve the problem on her own — no one could ever say she was less than a 'strong independent woman.' She wondered if Wally would take any responsibility at all. He had not been inclined to do so in the past.

As she swung the car onto the road and made her way home after the party, she thought about the day she first met the owners four years before. They were making some small repairs when Danie moved in. Mrs. Evilyn Seward was a tall woman and seemed terribly nervous. Her most distinctive feature, her chin, had an enormous dimple right in the middle of it. She was plain and dressed in bland colors that matched her brown stringy hair. She sat perched on a folding chair like a bird ready to take flight, fidgeting with her hands and picking her short-trimmed nails. Danie had a hard time thinking of what to say.

Thankfully, the woman leaned into her bag and drew out the ream of papers Danie had to read and sign. She knew the routine; she even knew everything written on the pages. They were always the same.

Danie perused and signed the rental agreement as the woman chattered on about what was in it. "And," she finished, "in the addendum you'll find a couple of restrictions with which I would like you to comply."

Danie, taking note of her stilted, super-correct English, looked at the added page. The restrictions had to do with her son. He had a reputation in town that had hampered practically everything Danie tried to do. He was wild, angry most of the time, narcissistic, and he hated the people and the village they lived in. But Wally was still her son. She loved him and it hurt that his actions had so distanced him from most people. He was defensive about it of course but she knew it must hurt him, too.

"Wally is likely to visit me on occasion," she told the landlady. "I hope there isn't any objection to that."

"Well no, not exactly. He has a right to see his mother, but you know he has a reputation and I am concerned about safety and insurance issues."

Danie wondered if it would be worth telling the whole sorry story about Wally. Would it do any good? Could she employ her sympathy?

"Ms. Wharton," Mrs. Seward interrupted her thoughts. "I want us to get off to a good start, but frankly your son is unwelcomed here."

"But you just said he has a right to see his mother."

"He does," she said reluctantly, "but he is not welcome to stay not even temporarily. That's all I am willing to say."

It wasn't long after she moved in that Wally asked to join her and Danie had to tell him he couldn't when he had been so generous toward her in the past. He was destined for a homeless existence and her hands were tied. The situation lay heavily on her heart and she had not known what else to do. Eventually, Wally did move in. Danie was hard put to prevent it. And now she had a week before she had to move out and had no idea where to go. It was little wonder she had these damned stomach and headaches, both of which plagued her now.

These were her thoughts as she came home to the dormered house, slowly climbing the steep stairway to her room and removing her clothes. She got into bed cuddling with her cat, Dusty, and fell into a fitful sleep.

The sparkling blue eyes came to her in a dream that awakened her with a start. It was the same dream. Stress brought it on. She knew what it was. The baby she had given up to adoption when unmarried and in the middle of a rising career. He was the product of rape at a time when women were reluctant to talk about such things. The memory plagued her now as she tried her best to sleep. She had been unable to keep the baby boy and it was a deep regret.

CHAPTER 3

Wally

The next day, after the birthday party the whole town had heard the news about his mom's eviction. It was impossible, even as a minor person of note, to keep a lid on the gossip and his mom was a person of note; people loved to talk about her.

After some consideration, worried about how she would react, Wally called her. Her cell phone answered on the third ring. "Hi Honey," she said in her usual cheerful tone.

"You mean you're not mad?"

"What should I be mad about?"

"You know."

"Sweetheart, I love you but I am not a mind reader."

"You're being evicted."

"Oh, that."

"What do you mean, 'Oh that?' You have to move."

"Well yes, that would be true. So, who told you?"

Her question caused a problem. He had heard it through the wait staff at the restaurant. Wally didn't want to cause them, friends of his, any troubles. "Mom, you know how word spreads in this town. Everyone knows!"

"Oh, great. Now I am the new homeless person everyone can talk about. It just gets better and better."

"Mom," he chuckled. "I'm homeless. It's not so bad."

"It's horrible for anyone to be homeless!"

"I just called to say I'm sorry."

His apology obviously caught her unprepared.

"Well, I can't say it was all your fault. I must have done something to tick Mrs. Seward off." She countered. He could tell his apology surprised her, that she had accepted responsibility, too. She sighed. "I never really trusted that Mrs. Seward. She seemed a little too nice at times — yet she didn't do the repairs I wanted. She refused to do anything about the woodpeckers attacking the side of the house. You'd think she would want to save the wood, but she just sat on her hands about it."

"I put that hole in the wall because those nasty birds woke me up from a late afternoon nap."

"Oh." She responded flatly. "When you were doing meth, you would sleep for days on end; I'm surprised you woke up at all.

"I'm sorry I didn't tell you."

It was rare for words of contrition to leave Wally's lips. He was uncomfortable now as he said them. Regret was an unfamiliar feeling and he was always unsure just how sorry he was. But here he was apologizing. Seeing how she reacted made expressing regret more attractive. At least, there was something to be gained from it.

Wally Wharton knew he was the one who had messed up. The meth, he was convinced, still jumbled his head and there were times when he did things, even now, that afterward he wished he had not done like putting the hole in the wall. He did love his mom. Nevertheless, he would go on tangents that would lead to wrong thinking and suspicions that led him to do things to her — unfair things. He would storm and rage in an argument with her that would lead to damaging tirades on the house. He had learned a long time ago that raging on people, especially his mom, did too much harm, yet sometimes it was hard to stop. Therefore, he would rage against things. He destroyed possessions that would have been worth something in the future. His mom had pointed out that he was only destroying his legacy. It had been one argument with her he could not counter. She was right. Many of the things his mother possessed were worth a good deal, money that might get him through when she was gone. He did not like to think about that; at her age, it was an ever-present possibility.

Since he had been off the meth, Wally had tried hard to make his life better. He was a good worker. He did yard and clearing work with great gusto whenever given the chance. He was developing a craft turning pine trees into furniture. He had a few sales and those who had bought his furniture were very happy with it. It photographed well too. He advertised his pieces on Face Book and Craig's List. He thought his chances of getting orders were good. It would just take time.

"Mom, I'll help take care of the damages."

"You will?"

"Yeah, it's my fault…If the fucking landlady had done her job, I might not have gotten so mad."

"Please Wally, your language."

"Come on Mom. You've used the "f" word before!" His voice boomed as it always did when he was trying to prove something.

"We aren't talking about me now. Let's just agree the word is strong and I don't like it."

"But Mom!" This was where their conversations went south. She would criticize him for some small infraction and his mood would turn like a hot knife buried in his brain.

"I know I have used it too much in the past. I'm trying to get beyond that time in my life," she added.

Wally knew his mother was so over her time in West Hollywood, struggling to make ends meet in high cost LA County. He was too. They had lived there for twenty-two years after her divorce from his dad while she competed in the film business for jobs in a world she no longer recognized. Her career had begun in the early 1960s and it was during that time that the world turned upside down. The movement away from traditional film-making was mystifying to her generation.

He had heard the story many times over the years. Wally had been very young then, and the "F" word had reached his mother's lips often during that period. Life had been tough for her. There had been tremendous challenges rearing a young son alone. He knew that now though he had been clueless then.

His dad had pretty much abandoned him. He was a deeply religious man, a Zen Buddhist, and he let that obsession lead him to a life of solitude. When his dad met his mom and fell in love, he allowed his mind to turn to worldly things like sex and comfort. His mom provided both.

In fact, his dad had spent a good deal of her money at a time when it was harder to come by. Her popularity had suffered when she married an outsider, a person who lived below the radar and wanted to stay there. At the time, people thought Buddhists were weird and when his parents were required to venture into public life his dad demurred. Public life was eschewed for long periods of solitude and meditation. His mom's career dipped into a downward tailspin as she tried to draw some normalcy out of her marriage. Nothing worked and divorce was inevitable. Wally recognized that his entry into this mix had been a big mistake. He knew they loved him — they said that — but his dad had left and it all felt like abandonment to him.

Her voice pierced his thoughts, "Anyway, I would appreciate some compensation. I need to find a place and put a deposit down. This has really caught me off guard without anything in the bank."

"Don't worry, Mom. We will make it work no matter what."

His mother wouldn't have to wait long for Wally to keep his promise. "Mom!" His voice was excited over the phone. I think I have found a solution to your problem, at least a temporary one."

"Temporary?" she queried hesitantly.

"These are friends of mine." Her first reaction was to moan — she did so almost inaudibly but Wally heard her; there was not even one of his friends that she would want to live with or rent from for that matter.

"Mom, these are wonderful people." He knew his voice sounded defensive and critical.

"No doubt they are, Wally. Do I know them?"

"You might."

"Okay, so who are they?"

"I'm afraid to say because you'll find a reason…"

"Wally, who are they?" She said wearily.

"The Neumanns."

"Oh." Her voice sounded relieved. "I've been to the Laughing Bear Bed and Breakfast for parties and yes, of course I've met them, though I don't know them well." She switched gears, "How do you know the Neumanns?"

"I've worked for Darwin Neumann now and then and he has mentioned he could rent a room to me if I had enough money. I never did. It's a little high for me."

"So, he doesn't just rent by the night?"

"I don't think so. You could call or go over there and talk to them. They like me, Mom. I've been very good to them."

"Okay. Maybe I will. That Mrs. Seward is going around to the rental agencies in town telling them that I didn't pay my rent."

"Why is she doing that?"

"I'm not sure. Maybe since I'm leaving by using up my entire deposit to pay for the damages *and* the last month rent. I don't trust her to give me my money back whatever I have coming. She must have spent the deposit money. Maybe she's resisting by claiming that I didn't pay my *last* month's rent — a technicality to be sure," she added. "It's still a lie and it really doesn't matter," she sighed. "People will believe it no matter what I say or do. It just means that I won't be able to rent a place up here at all!" She was on the brink of tears. "I mean, where am I supposed to go?"

"But you can prove that you paid by showing them your bank statements, right?"

"I've tried that already. The rental agent had to believe me because there it was in black and white. When I tried to rent a house, the owner of the house said, 'No'. It was a real cute one too. It was perfect and it had a pretty good price."

"I didn't know you were looking."

"Oh, yes. I started right away." After a moment, "I've done all my homework and talked to a lawyer. So, I'm on top of it, Wally."

"Good, Mom." He said condescendingly. He was always accusing her of failing to do her 'homework.' He thought the criticism was justified — she didn't usually.

"I guess the Laughing Bear is a possibility. I'll have to talk to Mrs. Neumann. She seems like a very nice person."

"Good, Mom." His irritation and impatience would allow little improvement in the tone of his voice and he knew it.

CHAPTER 4

Danie

After the early morning phone call with Wally, Danie showered and dressed, adding her favorite perfume, Magi Noir, hoping for a good effect, then wondered if Rose could be allergic to perfume. Oh well — too late; she didn't want to take another shower. The tan corduroy pants went well with the mist green shirt she chose. She added a peach and green striped scarf for warmth and a little fashion. She rarely bothered with make-up anymore especially after her birthday when she had cried dark mascara down her cheeks. Her blond hair had turned a golden white when she was sixty which complimented a clear complexion. She had wrinkles; somehow, they didn't look as bad to her as she once thought they would. Her features were very light too and all she needed to do was apply a little lipstick. Red was her favorite color, but it bled when she tried to wear it, so she had settled on a light peach to match the scarf. The color was delightful next to the green. When she glanced herself in the mirror on her way out the door, she saw a deliciously fuzzy and pluck-able peach. The image made her smile.

On the way to the inn, Danie was nervous and thought she would be okay with Rose but didn't know if the cost would be prohibitive or what to expect. The inn was a bed and breakfast but she didn't want them to cook for her and she would offer to clean her room and the bath she would use. That way she hoped to keep the cost down. Of course, she wanted to use the kitchen, but Danie didn't know if that would be okay. It would be impossible to eat out every night. She couldn't afford that even with the royalties coming in from her book which were inexplicably meager.

The car radio turned to the news. It was a National Public Radio station and she trusted the news she heard there. The commentator was announcing something about the presidential primary. In Danie's opinion there were far too many contestants running for the Republican nomination and she thought it was very much like a circus.

Her mind was a-buzz with questions that had no answers which just ramped up the anxiety she felt. The things happening in politics seemed to reflect the insecurity she was feeling now. What would she do if the

Laughing Bear didn't turn out? How would she find a place that would rent to her?

As she drove, Danie's mind kept coming back to the house she would have to leave. She loved it. Her little two-story cottage in the woods was perfect. The tiny house situated in a grove of tall pine trees was shaded so that it never got too hot in the summer. The problem with the house was the Woodpeckers. They had driven everyone mad who tried to read or sleep in the afternoon when the red crested black and white birds were busy pecking little worms into the outer wall. Still, her heart ached thinking about having to leave.

Danie felt a fool letting the situation get out of hand. When Bernadine moved in, she had been a little too gracious at first. The decorator was going to make the place a dream house and we would all be very happy about it. Now, Danie wished she had recognized the warning signs. It should have been obvious to her what was up, especially when the woman had made such a big fuss over the hole in the wall. If she had just kept her mouth shut the owners may not have noticed the problem before Danie had a chance to fix it. Instead, Bernadine had pointed it out to them. That was a shocker and Danie should have known something was wrong.

It still didn't make a whole lot of sense. Why did Mrs. Seward turn on her so abruptly? She had always paid her rent on time; she liked to dress the place up and purchased items to make it more attractive; she had worked hard to maintain the house in good order. The yard in the back had been a problem, especially in the rocky terrain they lived in; yard work was a bit too much for her. Mrs. Seward hadn't complained though she had extracted a promise from Bernadine to get the yard work done. Bernadine was younger.

Danie wondered if she had complained once too many times about the noisy birds. The whole eviction thing was just incomprehensible.

There was the time — when Wally was at the house — the owners came by to do some tree trimming. Although he had given up the meth, he was often haughty, narcissistic, full of rage, destructive and just plain mean. The word demon was appropriate. He had sauntered up to the husband with his usual condescending attitude and told the man he could do a better job. Mr. Seward was using a small handsaw with a slim blade and Wally was right; he had an electric saw that would do the job in seconds. Mr. Seward's way would take an hour instead of minutes. Wally was not right in the loathsome way he presented his line of reasoning. He had been so impertinent and spiteful about the way he handled the situation that the owners took an instant dislike to him.

They apparently thought her son was the product of a poor upbringing; it was Danie's fault Wally had turned out so badly. Their opinions were just one of those things about which you could do nothing. People would think what they wanted to think no matter the underlying truth. She had not been a perfect parent — who was? But she had done her best.

As she arrived at the bed and breakfast, she settled on a spot for the car in the designated parking area and quietly approached the large two-story, wood-frame house. It was a softly quiet morning; the forest surrounding the house was very still except for the soft chirps of birds and the barking of a small dog; it's yip also sounded like the chirping birds. The combined calls resonated like a small symphony of piccolos. She wanted to be as still and peaceful as the setting.

The entrance, gated with a small wood frame portico trimmed in a deep forest green, sported a sign that read, "The Laughing Bear B n' B." The creamy-beige, two-story wood frame residence looked enormous with large windows also trimmed in forest green, and lovely decorative pieces leading up the long porch to the huge double doors. The oak entryway was inlaid with two ornate windows. There was a rose design etched into the frosted glass.

Danie couldn't find a doorbell and wondered how she could possibly knock loud enough to let anyone know she was here. Just then, the door opened and there stood Rose Neumann bundled in a red-checkered bathrobe. The early morning autumn air was chilly and Danie suddenly wished she had a cardigan to wrap around her shoulders.

"Hi Rose," she said hoping Rose would remember her. Danie had been to a few events at the B&B during her time in Dancing Bear, but whether Rose remembered her she couldn't be sure.

"Daniela Wharton! Good morning!"

"Good morning, Rose!" she replied surprised. Danie had been an import from the city for some time now but she didn't think Rose knew her last name. Most of the people who lived in Dancing Bear Springs called each other by their first names. It was easier and there were few enough duplicates that it was the practical thing to do. The locals were mostly those who had grown weary of city life — the crowds of people, the noise, the traffic, the complications of getting from one place to another, parking without getting an expensive ticket, not knowing or even caring about one's neighbors. They felt a bereavement for a time of simplicity and innocence, an innocence that may have never existed but had once permeated the lives of the city's residents. They were here in the remote village because they *wanted* to know their neighbors by their first names.

"I'm here because I'm looking for a place to stay."

"Come on in." Rose answered softly, her German accent carefully subdued. "Do you think it suddenly got chilly this morning? I hope you don't mind that I am still in my robe. I decided not to get dressed all day."

"I feel like that sometimes too." Danie replied, wanting to build familiarity.

Rose led Danie to the lush couches placed in a conversational array. The pine-paneled great room was warm and inviting. Large, comfortable pieces of furniture dotted the open space and a huge wood-burning stove decorated with big iron figures and giant claw feet warmed Danie as she passed by. She chose to sit in a cozy spot on the couch and snuggly sank into the pillow behind her.

Danie noticed a statuette of a dancing bear perched on a windowsill. Looking more closely, she could see the bear shape was the natural form of the wood that looked like a dancing bear. It was magical.

"I'm wondering," she said as she tried to sit up a bit, "if it would be possible to rent a room here for the long term, that is more than one day at a time. And of course, I need to know how much that would be monthly."

"I heard about some trouble you were having." Rose responded. Danie figured she would want more of the story. In the small village nothing was secret.

"Yes, my landlady decided quite unexpectedly to evict me. It's a long story but it had nothing to do with my ability to pay the rent. I did every month and I can prove it with my bank statements."

"Would $650.00 per month be too much for you?"

"Heavens no. That would be quite nice. Does that include the utilities?"

"Oh yes. The television and Internet service too."

"I am quite willing to clean up after myself."

"That will be quite a change." She laughed. "I am used to cleaning up after everyone, even Darwin."

Danie had met Darwin quite separately from Rose when they worked together in his recording studio doing a voice promotional for her memoir. She knew him professionally and he was a delightful person, full of fun and silly jokes, easy to be with and to work with. "Okay," Danie smiled at the implication of Rose's claim, "When can I move in?"

"Let me show you the room — make sure you like it. It has its own bathroom; that is, it is a half bathroom. You will have to shower in the guest bath upstairs."

"Okay. I would like to be able to cook my own meals, too. Would that be possible?"

"That will work out fine if we time it around the breakfasts I make for guests."

"No problem."

The room was a cozy, welcoming space with quaint features and fabrics. Danie knew quilting and she could see several handmade pieces placed around the room — one hung over a rack on the wall, one was thrown across a chair, another graced the daybed. Tiny crystal balls rimmed a decorative burgundy lampshade and delicate lace curtains adorned the windows. The morning sun shone through the windows casting lovely light and lacy shadows over the entire suite. A private door led out to the garden conveniently close to the parking area. Everything took on a warm hue — Rose called it the Tea Rose Room — and the daybed was inviting with a lush comforter and plenty of feathery pillows. Danie felt like she could live in this place forever. She hoped she would be able to find her own house soon but the room and the situation here at the B&B looked like a good interim solution. Her heart warmed as she could see herself settling in.

When Samantha called the next day, Danie told her she would be staying at the B&B.

"Isn't that the same place we stayed at a couple of years back?"

"Yes, you did, and I think you told me that Rose, the proprietress, went to school with you in Santa Monica."

"Gosh, that's right! I remember her well although she didn't remember me at all." Sami said with dismay.

"It was a long time ago."

"But I remember her *very* well. She was tall and serious. She spoke with a German accent to die for."

"Who would want a German accent?"

"Me. Heil Hitler!" She said playfully.

"I have a feeling Rose would not take your comments with much amusement. It's my understanding that she spent her earliest years in the middle of the war."

"Hell, the war was over a long time when I knew her."

"I'll have to ask her about her time in Santa Monica."

"She should remember me. I did have the biggest knockers in the whole school."

"Oh, you think everyone is going to remember that."

Sami whimpered. "There wasn't much else I was known for." She played the "dumb blond" role to a tee; she believed it herself.

"But I'm glad to hear you have a place to go. I was worried, my friend."

"Oh, don't you worry about me. I can take care of myself," Danie declared.

"I worry because I care about you. You are like a sister to me, Danie, and I worry. Okay?"

"Okay, okay! So, worry. Have it your own way."

CHAPTER 5

Rose

On moving day, Rose ran around frantically cleaning up after the weekend and readying Danie's apartment. Her mother, the notoriously spoiled Mercedes Parets, had lived in the Tea Rose room for several years before going to the nursing home. The room looked different now mainly for the lack of medical equipment.

Her mother had turned quite ill toward the end. Rose felt terrible sending her away to the home — "Hitler was a better provider!" she had said. The woman was horrified that she would spend her final days and hours in such a place — but it had become a life-saving measure for Rose. Her bladder cancer had appeared for the first time when Mercedes took a turn for the worse. The burden of the illness along with her mother's constant need was unbelievably unfavorable to her cancer treatments. Living in the mountains didn't help. Rose was sentenced to three-hour-long trips four times a week to get radiation and chemo treatments in the San Fernando Valley. That meant she had to leave her mother's care in the hands of her husband who would do his best to be helpful when needed. However, Darwin's nursing skills needed up-grading as did his patience with her mother.

Darwin hated Mercedes. She had constantly criticized how he lived his life. In his opinion, he didn't need to be nagged. He thought he was good about keeping up with chores around the house. His standards were lax, but he was sincere in his efforts to make Rose happy. Rose knew that, but it was hard to counter her mother about him. She would tell her he was wonderful in other ways, ways that were important to her. She had been looking for love and comfort. Darwin had provided both abundantly. For this, she was grateful she had found him.

That did not keep Rose from complaining to Darwin after Mercedes had been tucked safely into the home. Rose took up her mother's mantel and criticized Darwin's sloppy habits. Now that mother was dead and gone her voice constantly reverberated through Rose's head. In fact, she was always tempted to nag Darwin as her mother had. It was a mostly unconscious wish that often seeped into their relationship. She was irritable like her mother; she felt it in her genes.

Danie was moving in before long and Rose hoped the woman would be okay to live with, even on a short-term basis. She had proffered an excuse when she told Danie that the room was licensed only for short-term overnight use. Rose could ask her to leave if Danie proved to be bothersome, a drunk, a slob, a sleepwalker, or something awful like smelling bad. No. Rose thought Danie would be a very nice roomer; she would just have to be firm if things did not turn out well.

The perspiration trickled down the sides of her face as she hurried down the stairway, her arms filled with bedding that needed to be laundered. Rose didn't mind laundry as much as she minded doing dishes. In some weird way, she had grown to like doing chores around the house. She liked the way it felt to see everything in good order and clean. The constant chores filled time she might have been drinking alcohol instead. She had been an alcoholic, following obediently in her mother's footsteps and "the AA program" had taught her to stay busy. When she complained about the abundance of work around the B&B, and when Darwin had taken over a chore for her, she only ended up adding something else like yard work to her busy schedule. She lived in horror of free time. It was her enemy and she would not have it.

This was truly the only source of trouble between the couple. When they bought the B&B, they had agreed to split the responsibilities so that neither would end up taking the whole load. It was an agreement that usually worked even though Mercedes hadn't seen it that way. The one thing Rose had trouble accepting was Darwin's focus on screenwriting. He was an actor and that she had to deal with. However, this screenwriting business was far from a hobby he could engage in occasionally. It had become an obsession and he believed he would sell one of these scripts to a moviemaker. She didn't see it happening. She thought it was just a 'pie-in-the-sky' idea and she was adamantly against it. The constant writing and re-writing took up much, too much time and she hated seeing him on the couch with his lap-top punching away at the keys like a mad reporter typing out his article in time for publication the next morning. This was the source of her anxiety about the inn. She was afraid the screenwriting would take over and she would end up doing all the work. Rose's worries made her heart pound in her chest and she thought at times she would die from it.

CHAPTER 6

Wally

It didn't take long to get Wally on board about moving his mom. He had been a pro in the moving business at one time and it hadn't been that long ago. He was one of the best moving van packers around. His skill would come in handy today. His mom had called the local moving truck rental company and they had to run down the hill to pick up the U-Haul. Part of the job today was to move his mother's stuff out of the house, take most of her belongings down the hill to pack into a storage unit by the freeway, and then return the truck to the rental agency. The rest of her things, the items she was taking with her, were to be packed into the Subaru Outback. It was a simple move and he expected to have it done early in the day. His mom was exacting about time and the cost of the truck rental. She wanted the job done so that she would not have to pay extra for the van. She was operating on a strict budget. He understood the anxiety but he hated to be rushed.

He hired a friend, Joey, to help. Joey was a hefty dude who could pick up a refrigerator and carry it on his back. He would not have to go that far today. The heaviest item on the list of movable pieces was the couch. It was heavy and ungainly.

"Fuck, man…I'm hungry. When does a dude get food for his empty stomach?" Joey's voice boomed from the back seat of the car.

Danie and Wally looked at each other knowing "the dude" would have an enormous appetite. Shrugging her shoulders and peering in the rear-view mirror, she said, "How does In 'n Out Burger sound?"

"Oh, ho, ho, ho. I'm on board for that!" his voice bellowed.

After two sessions feeding Joey five burgers and three bags of fries each, they locked up the storage rental, returned the truck, and headed back up the hill to get Danie's carload tucked away in her new room.

It all went fast and efficiently. Wally prided himself on his moving skills and knew he should try putting a moving company together up here in the mountains. He just couldn't get the motivation he needed to do all that work. It wasn't that exactly now that he thought about it — the mountain community wasn't that fruitful when it came to work. Senior citizens didn't move that much and if they did, they moved to the city, so they would hire movers from the city. Most businesses in the town had failed within two years. He was afraid he would be unsuccessful. It was too big a risk.

When he and Shanna were together, she had been the real fire in his belly. He would do anything for her. Since she'd run off with the meth dealer, Wally couldn't get inspired about anything. The whole incident had shot him through with a deep sadness and an unwillingness to create anything worthwhile. He was depressed.

Women had become a source of great pain and disgust. He had natural desires he knew. The women available to him on the mountain were 'skanks' and he didn't want to soil himself with them. He stayed away from sex pretty much now. There was the woman, Lana in LA, who was willing to come up from the city and hook up with him. He liked Lana — she was not a girl to get too close — or married. And there was that Sally Oliver who'd ratted him out at the town meeting. He hated her for it.

It must have been the time he got some Meth for a friend of his, a woman. She had paid him back when he brought the drug to her. Maybe Sally thought he was making a profit. But there was no added value there. What if he had gotten baby diapers for her little girl? Would Sally accuse him pushing baby diapers? He had to smile at the silly thought. But Sally sure didn't help. Everyone avoided him after that town meeting which made him want to do more drugs instead of quit. He felt lucky he hadn't fallen into that disturbing trap.

The job was done; his mom seemed content to have everything in her new room though nothing had been put away. She would have to do that herself and Wally figured she'd be up all-night working on it. But he'd done the move on time and within budget.

CHAPTER 7

Danie

Good morning, Neighbor!" Darwin Neumann's voice boomed over the early morning quiet. He was tall, handsome in a Germanic sort of way with clear blue eyes, a square jaw, broad shoulders and a barrel, football-player chest. His hair and goatee were light brown turning white. Danie felt safe in his presence. She recalled the time they had worked together when she needed a promo for her book. He had fashioned a small sound booth deep inside the garage shrouded in black soundproofing to record for voice-overs in commercial work and promos as Danie needed. Darwin's strong suit was voice character work. He could do any accent, any tonal quality, any age group that a voice could produce — that is mostly for men. As an actor, he had played roles as a woman but only in comedy. His body type made it impossible for him to look feminine, yet he did the amusing female roles in the local theater group. Uproarious laughter and applause would always follow these humorous efforts. Darwin was all man and though he walked with a limp, he looked like he could take on an army. Now, he lingered in the living area of the main room off the kitchen.

"Good morning!" she replied fairly shouting across the room to match his energy. "I didn't expect anyone up this early."

"Oh, I get up pretty early especially when I have to cook breakfast."

"You don't have to cook for me. I plan on cooking my own food."

"We have four others beside you this morning and I have to cook for them."

"I hope I don't get in your way."

"I hope not too."

Darwin bent down to pet his dogs with a "good morning," and now the two dogs and the man lumbered toward the kitchen. "We have our break-of-day rituals." He said referring to the dogs. He opened the doggie cookie jar on the kitchen counter and his enormous hand reached in to get the biscuits for the drooling dogs. They both sat as instructed and received their "Good dog" treats. Danie would soon learn that was the extent of the "good dog" behavior.

The Dalmatian called Pepper was pretty with doe-shaped eyes and a slender pointed nose; she had the attitude of a spoiled princess. She would turn out to be the "perfect" dog — she never barked, was never in the way and she didn't beg. The other dog, Heidi, was a hound of medium size and short brownish hair. The animal, a cattle dog, was rather ugly, the kind only a mother could love. Her eyes were small and she had one ear that would not stand up straight. The ear, which folded over, was her only endearing feature and she had a quixotic expression; it appeared that she was always asking a question. According to her master, the only question on her mind was food: *Where is it, and why isn't it in my mouth?* Otherwise, the dog was obnoxious with a constant sharp bark that pierced the air and made Danie cringe.

"Shut up, Heidi Hound!" He threw her another treat. "That's all she wants — FOOD."

Danie took note of the reward tendered for the barking behavior. When compensated for barking Heidi would continue to bark. It was simple as that. Simple or not, it was always harder to extinguish a behavior. Rewarding a dog for not doing something was far more difficult than rewarding actual behavior. She wondered if Heidi could be trained not to bark. A sign on the wall said: "Bark Less, Wag More."

Darwin headed for the dog food bin and scooped up two large servings of dry food.

"GRRGLEGRUMBLE, GRRGLEGRUMBLE, GRRGLEGRUMBLE," the hollow sound came from deep inside the garbage disposal. "GRRGLEGRUMBLE, GRRGLEGRUMBLE."

Danie had opened the refrigerator door and was peering inside looking for cream for her fresh-made coffee. "Umm, do I hear an *odd* noise?" It was a disturbing noise and it seemed unnatural.

"Oh, the garbage disposal. I know. It has a mind of its own. I have to get in there and figure out what's going on."

"GRRGLEGRUMBLE."

After attending to the dogs, Darwin headed out the back door to feed the birds. There seemed no end to the morning rituals. He must have been out there for fifteen minutes because she had her entire breakfast fixed and on her tray by the time he came back in.

"Well, enjoy your breakfast and Rose will see you after." He chimed. "She should be up and awake by then."

"Will I see you later?" She asked.

"I have a gig at school this morning. I'll be gone all day teaching."

"Really? You have a busy schedule."

"I have to teach. It's necessary to augment our income."

"Well, have a wonderful day."

"Thanks. I will." He grabbed a spatula and expertly flipped some pancakes.

A thunderous noise descended the staircase at the front of the house — the noise heralded the footsteps of a couple of Hispanic children and their parents who had stayed at the inn the night before. They had smelled the frying bacon and pancakes which called them from their slumber and down to the great room.

Danie headed down the well to her room where she settled into a morning breakfast ritual that would become her habit while living at the Laughing Bear B&B. This was going to be fascinating, she thought.

CHAPTER 8

Darwin

His children had not been his own though he had reared them to maturity with his second wife. Connie came with a boy and a girl. The boy, only four when he married Connie, had responded well to Darwin's masculine guidance. The girl who was a year and a half older responded with anger. Darwin was not going to replace her daddy. He understood how she felt and didn't mind that she rejected him most of the time. When he and Connie divorced, it was not seeing the children that he regretted most.

It was because of this experience that he went back to school and got his teaching credentials. He liked the job well enough when the children were not problematic. Therefore, he chose to teach the earlier grades before the kids had a chance to become "hoodlums," as he preferred to call them.

Now, with the B&B to take care of, he didn't have time to teach every day. He signed up for substitute work and ended up spending as many as five days in a month careening down the mountain in the early morning traffic as he was doing now trying to get to a teaching gig. When the class he was to teach was older than ten-years-old, he was always a little dismayed with the behavior. He muddled through using his sense of humor getting the kids to laugh often enough during the day. They seemed to respect his attitude; he was willing to create laughter rather than to scold. His acting experience came in handy amid a bunch of children, some of them from dysfunctional homes. He would 'grin and bear it,' as his mother had been fond of saying, because the work brought in extra needed income.

The Laughing Bear Bed and Breakfast was no laughing matter when it came to expenses. Beyond operating expenses, there were repair and maintenance costs. Just the food they had to provide was an enormous bill that had to be met. He and Rose often charged the credit card and the debt was beginning to mount. Being a tolerant educator was simply necessary as Rose had gently reminded him.

He was glad too, that the woman, Danie Wharton, had moved in. Her regular rent for a while was welcome. It wasn't always possible to rent the Tea Rose room every week and sometimes it went empty too often especially in the wintertime. Her arrival just now in the fall at the beginning of winter was something of a miracle.

His long hair flew past his ears in the breath of wind that came through the Jeep window. At sixty-four years, he was still something of a hippie. He would have to remember to tie the graying wisps back into a neat ponytail before he entered the classroom.

The school was in the San Fernando Valley and he was quite familiar with the route to get there. It was a hot day in the unremitting dry heat of the valley, something he truly hated. With no air-conditioning in the Jeep, he perspired profusely whenever hit by the oven-like temperatures. Dripping from his fine hair, the perspiration rolled down his shirt and stained the back with sweat. His armpits had acquired stains and he hadn't arrived yet. He hoped he could catch a breeze on the way to class.

When he arrived in class the room was empty. In a panic, Darwin, with his bum knee, ran to the principal's office. "Did I make a mistake?" He bellowed as he entered the office and made his way to the clerk standing behind the counter. His voice carried farther than he intended and everyone at their desks looked up to see who was roaring through the room. He turned red-faced as he realized how thunderous he was. "Sorry," he mumbled. "I didn't realize I was being so loud."

The clerk, a kid of about sixteen, looked up with sympathy. Darwin had grown cynical about teenagers and the boy's expression was surprising. Teen boys always seemed out of control and spiteful. Of course, Darwin could not be too judgmental remembering how he was when he was that age. Nevertheless, a sixteen-year-old boy was usually a challenge. This one sported glasses. He was one of the unfortunate souls who had a long neck, no chin and a protruding Adam's apple. His eyes seemed to bulge a little too, even without the glasses. Darwin's attitude softened. Moderating his voice, he said, "Did I get the wrong classroom number?"

"No, sir," the young man answered respectfully. "They are all gathered in the assembly hall. You have time to set up your room before they come back to class."

"Thank you, young man." Darwin said quietly. He was impressed by the boy's response and thought that teaching a class in this school might be okay after all. He hoped they were all well-behaved. It was a thin hope. He knew that public schools had their hands tied when it came to discipline. The children were largely unmanageable.

The day did go smoothly. He had taught math which was not his favorite subject. He even made a couple of mistakes and wiggled comfortably out of his errors with his usual humor. "I'm not Steven Hawking after all." He exclaimed, crossing his eyes for effect. "I can make a mistake and he can't!" They laughed. "But you can't either." He added. "You have to be just as good as Steven if you are going to graduate and go to Harvard." They roared, most of the class knowing that in their socio-economic situation, Harvard or any other college was out of the question. Most of these kids were either Mexican-American or African-American. Their aspirations, as sincere as they might be, would get them nowhere. Even the white kids in this neighborhood would have a tough time.

When he arrived home, he cried in his wife's arms. His mood had crashed during the long ride back up the mountain thinking about these children, many rather bright, and how their lives would likely turn out. They would graduate high school and go on to work at a place like Wal-Mart, Costco or MacDonald's. If they were lucky, they might rise to the position of manager but that would likely be as far as they could rise in the game of capitalism. It was a dead end, Darwin knew. It tore his heart out. Rose was understanding and felt the same. She did not cry about it because she couldn't have more sympathy for Blacks and Mexicans; their plight wasn't any different from the way women were compensated for their hard work and sometimes extensive education. Darwin knew how she felt. There didn't seem to be anywhere to go in the world anymore unless you were a well-connected, rich white man.

Darwin certainly met the second criteria — he was very white — and never the first. He wasn't entirely sure he would want to be a part of the so-called "One Percenters." He would be inclined to give his money away. One thing Darwin knew, he was happiest when he was giving and giving big.

CHAPTER 9

Danie

It was a lovely day that was destined, she hoped, to become a wonderful memory. The day had gone well so far. Wally and Danie drove back from a shopping trip in town. They always tried to make their monthly shopping trips together to save money on gas.

The first time they tried it after he came back from rehab, they were not successful at all. Although he had overcome his meth addiction, he was still depressed and angry. Danie was angry too, at Shanna. She had always had reservations about the girl her son was marrying; they had gone together for twelve years waiting until the right time. Shanna had matured during that period and had become a successful real estate agent. She had done a lot to assuage Danie's fears. However, her actions of running off with the Meth dealer were proof to Danie the girl had issues.

Nevertheless, Danie had grown to accept Shanna and hoped the girl would produce a family. Wally loved her unequivocally and for reasons unknown and unfathomable, she ran off with a man who fed her methamphetamines.

"Mom, I'm in trouble. I've been using methamphetamines for months. I am so strung out and I need help. I was talking to a friend of mine who's been through this before and she told me I had to quit or die. I don't want to die." This, a rare occasion when Wally and Danie could communicate honestly, "I mean, I almost did die, Mom." This was something she never wanted to hear.

"I don't want you to die either, Sweetheart. What can I do to help?" Danie was hardly surprised by the announcement; she had wanted to talk to him about his drug use and she was grateful for the friend who had told him to quit or die.

It had been a surprise to her. He had not listened to anything Danie told him since he was thirteen years old when he decided, while having his picture taken, he would never do anything his mother asked of him again. The photograph said it all; his stubbornness, like the photo, froze him in time from then on. Any positive influence others might have on him was always profoundly welcomed because he never listened to her.

"I thought you'd be mad at me," Wally continued.

"Honey, not mad, just disappointed that you chose to do drugs. They are so harmful. But I am relieved and proud that you want to face this squarely. I only want your success." He was silent. It had been the first time in years she could finish a whole paragraph without his angry, accusing interruption and she was stunned.

They called his dad who lived with his new wife in a seaside town down by the Pacific Ocean. His father found a plan that suited Wally and Danie took him down the mountain to the treatment facility. It didn't seem like a very warm place but the people were very nice and accommodating. Danie felt good about the situation and its inhabitants; Wally was less enthusiastic but was willing to try.

She left him there heading home with his dog and praying that Wally would do what he had to do. He did but not the way she had hoped. He disappeared from the facility and for ten months he struggled to overcome the addiction on his own. And for ten months Danie worried.

At last he called. Danie collected Wally at a shelter and watched as dog and master reunited. She cried. Wally came to the car and hugged his mom warmly saying, "Thank you for taking good care of Buddy." He looked good and much like his old self though she noticed he had lost a little hair in the front, like his granddad.

When Wally overcame his addiction, it had been a miracle in Danie's life, so she was open to his request to come to the house for a few weeks. Letting him stay, even for a short while, was the wrong thing to do. The drugs though no longer ingested, stayed in his system for a long time. His behavior changed dramatically. He no longer spent days on end sleeping and he wasn't nearly as violent. Still, there were times when he was filled with unpredictable rage.

At last, Danie felt she needed to have him leave. She had done for him as much as she could and she was done putting up with his moods, habits and quirks. Mrs. Seward was pressing her about him staying at the house even if it was temporary. Danie froze him out the only way she knew to make him leave. It felt awful and she hated herself for having to be so cruel. She knew however that he was becoming too dependent on her and he had to get out on his own even if it meant he had to sleep outside for a couple of months. It was that warm and sunny time of year so there was little to harm him weather-wise but she worried about the wild animals — mountain lions, bears, and coyotes — that populated the area.

She needn't have been concerned because Wally was good at couch surfing. Though he had spent a few weeks out in the forest, he often managed to find a friend with a place to stay if only temporarily. Wally was a very charming person — when he was in his right mind.

And there was the rub. He often didn't have his 'right mind' available. Coming home without a drug addiction to occupy him, he turned to conspiracy theories. A high school dropout, he didn't have training in logic and discernment and he tended to believe much that was incredible. The Internet was truth according to him and he believed most of the messages that were impossible for Danie to accept. People who were not his relatives had less patience. The result — he was asked to leave the place he had found because the folks there were turned off by his conspiracy theory rantings. Danie lamented having to freeze him out and he was very angry with her. She had to move on despite the pain of separation and the guilt of sentencing her son to life in the forest.

Thankfully, he finally found a permanent solution to his homelessness by moving in with a friend, Richard, new on the mountain.

"I sure will be glad when they solve this problem," Wally said breaking the silence on their way down the mountain to grocery shop. "Of course, they won't. Not enough money in it." Wally's eyes scanned the horizon through the windshield.

"What problem is that?" Danie queried.

"You know, energy."

"You know?" She smiled. "I don't *know* what the hell you're talking about."

"Mom, you really should do your homework. I sent you an email. You were supposed to read up on it."

"Really? I don't remember anything I was supposed to research."

"I sent it to you yesterday!" He said with an accusatory tone in his voice.

"Sorry, Sweetheart, I didn't see it," she lied.

"Really? It was the most interesting thing I've found on energy!" The sound of his voice began to grow. "The 'quantum vacuum zero-point energy' theory. It could make our travel to the city like cost nothing! For little or nothing we could drive across country if we wanted to. But it's being suppressed by government."

"I can't imagine such a thing would be suppressed. Why would they do that?"

"Oh mother, you don't know anything."

"Excuse me? I think I know quite a lot. I have at least 33 years on you, you know!"

He was 44 years old now and Danie was sure he was not yet an adult. In fact, it seemed that emotionally he was still stuck back at age sixteen when young people go through the 'know it all,' stage. He still thought he knew everything and there was nothing he could be taught; maybe it had been the pot he smoked beginning at that age or thereabouts.

Danie wasn't sure when he'd acquired the habit, but she knew it had helped him get control of a spasm in his neck that caused him to shake his head constantly.

This time Danie wisely let go of arguing with Wally about an energy system that likely wasn't real. Wally had spent some time taking cell-phone pictures of the streaks of exhaust left behind by military jets seeking to land at nearby Air Force bases. "Oh wow!" He would exclaim. "They are really out today." Danie didn't dare ask just what was 'out,' though she had some idea since Wally had told her before the left-behind jet streaks were 'chem-trails' designed by the government to 'snuff us out.' His 'smartphone' contained "lots of evidence" of the travesty against the people endorsed by the very rich and the politicians. Those were issues she could get behind, but she was sure that Wally would have a very different view on how this was all taking place.

It had only been the last few miles that he began to complain about being hungry.

The silence in the car had lain heavily between them and she was glad it had finally been broken even with complaints about hunger. Their long silences were a defense against the rancor that could and did occur between them if they dared broach any subject other than where they were or where they were going. What they were going to eat was another acceptable subject but not much else was broach-able. 'Chem-trails' were not broach-able.

Now Wally and Danie were miles from any food, but they were also just a few miles from the top of Mountain of the Pines. They decided to ignore their roiling tummies and drive the ten miles to the summit.

The forest was thick with dense pine trees of various shapes and kinds. The Jefferson Pines, the tallest, had been trimmed to the same height by wind and lightning strikes — the towering trees had raw stumps on top. Groves of irises grew wild too, quilting the area with the assorted colors of Lilac trees in the springtime. Now of course in the late autumn, the groves were bare of blooms.

They hiked to the campground tables. Danie was delighted to sit down at last. They occupied a picnic table isolated from the few campers in the park and it was dead quiet except the birds.

"Heavenly," she thought. Surely heaven could not be any more divine. What more was there in life than to sit idly soaking up the sun in any entirely natural setting? When she and Wally spoke, it was to exchange thoughts about the beauty they were fortunate enough to enjoy.

As suddenly as a meteoroid splashes through the sky, a lone Monarch butterfly flitted into view. Its butternut wings threaded with fine veins of black, flapped up one way and down the other, seeking the sun one moment and the shade another. As the insect came closer, details of her body and enormous wings were more easily recognizable.

Danie marveled. "Oh, you are the most beautiful sight!" she nearly sang. "Hello, pretty thing. How are you today? Are you enjoying the sun as much as we are?" The creature which had passed by them suddenly did a U-turn and flitted back to where Danie sat. It perched momentarily on the brim of her hat and then flitted back onto its previous path.

"The butterfly said 'hello' to you, Mom!" Wally marveled. "It really did respond to the sound of your voice. You could see it!" he exclaimed.

"Yeah." She turned to watch the butterfly go just as surprised as he was. "So long, pretty thing. Thanks for stopping by," she chimed.

It was memories like these that kept her frustration with Wally down to a manageable level. Well, almost.

Then within moments, the subject they had managed to avoid came up. Conspiracy theories abounded. "Look at that, Mom!" He exclaimed. "Look at that giant streak of chemicals invading our skies." She looked up and saw for the hundredth time a so-called chemtrail. "The chemtrails are going to diminish our crops and make us sick. They want to get rid of us."

"Sweetheart, those exhaust trails aren't any different…"

"Mom," he loudly interrupted, "military jets contain poisonous exhaust intended to kill things!"

"All jets contain poisonous gases. They use jet fuel, for heaven's sake."

"Mother, you are so stupid. You should do your homework. Didn't you read that thing on 'chemtrails' I sent you last week?"

"Yeah I read it this time and I don't agree."

"Then why do the trails stay there? You know they never did that before." He was adamant.

"Honey, they fly higher than they did before and the contrails freeze up at that altitude. That's why you can…"

"Don't you remember the few days after 911 when we had clear skies because no one was flying then?" he asked.

"All planes have poisonous gases and…"

"Mother! You are not seeing reality! That's when they realized they could change things to their advantage by contaminating the jet fuel and creating death machines."

"Well, I can see why *they* might be experimenting with seeding clouds to create more rain. We sure have needed it. And anyway, why would *they* want to kill us all?"

"So, they can have it all to themselves!" He screamed. "Haven't you noticed? There are far too many people on the planet!"

"But Wally, they need us to buy their products. And won't the so-called chemtrails kill them, too?"

"Oh Mother, you will never understand!" He had said repeatedly that she didn't have the brain power to get it.

Danie decided it was useless to argue and she fell silent. Her son had said it all before. It was the Illuminati, the Free Masons, and the United Nations that would take over the world and before we knew it, we would be following them like blind sheep…if we survived.

We already were, according to Wally. We were sheep just following along without a criticism in our heads. And with some ferocity Wally asserted the history we had been taught was false. When Danie brought up historical facts he discounted them as fantasy. He had never studied much history or any other subject to any degree; he took his information from the Internet believing nothing there could be untrue. She tried her best to inform him of the reality that nothing on the Internet had to be vetted. News organizations though imperfect, at least had to investigate and verify information they received before allowing it to go out to the public. He argued that the very few people who were taking over the world owned all the news organizations. He was not exactly wrong about that.

She had argued that none of the information he was seeing on the Internet was verifiable. The people who put the videos together where mentally ill, extremely gullible, or just plain stupid. She even argued that these people were likely making money on their postings. Or they were just plain crazy.

It saddened her deeply that her son's brain had been so fried with drugs that he could not see something like these videos and understand how false they were. She worried constantly about what to do now. Perhaps her methods of upbringing had been inadequate. She had made important mistakes. She and her mom had been best friends and she thought that was the best part of her relationship with Dorothy Wharton, the woman who chose to bear only one child; the depression in the thirties had determined her choices as an adult amid World War II. Having more than one offspring seemed careless in the early 1940s.

The fate of World War II had changed everything, of course. And Danie wondered if it was the fate of the Viet Nam conflict that had ruined her chances at true love. She fantasized that her 'soul mate' had met his premature death in that conflict. And now she regretted divorcing before having a second child if there was to be one. Wally had ended up without any attention from his dad and no brothers or sisters. Feeling guilty, she had turned Wally into her best friend when in fact she should have simply been his mother with a lot of strict rules.

Danie wondered if she had made the one mistake that made all of this so unfortunate. She could have had two children, but she had given up a baby at birth to adoption because he had been a child of rape. It was a decision that plagued all of the choices she had made since.

She felt she was much better equipped to be a parent at this point than she had back when it was the time. "That's it!" She exclaimed aloud. "I'll…!" Danie stopped her words just in time realizing she was still in Wally's presence.

"You'll what, Mom?" His words were barely courteous.

"Never mind. It was just a thought…Nothing important," she lied.

Ha! She thought. It was very important. Inside, the idea stirred. She felt a little twinge of excitement, something she had felt little of since Wally was an adult. Was it possible she wondered to re-parent a person? Didn't she remember Dr. Phil saying something about reparenting? It was something she would have to try. He was too old to be running around the way he was and she hoped she could stop him somehow.

The day had been nearly miraculous except for the late afternoon argument. Danie decided to go with the good feelings as they made their way back to Dancing Bear Springs and something to eat.

CHAPTER 10

Rose

She was inspired. Her artwork was about to take another turn. For years she had focused on animals and birds. Her paintings were wonderful representations of animals in their habitat. She had sold most of the work and was making money — especially doing projects for industrial clients with her graphic design business.

She felt successful in her artwork, much more than with the B&B. The house was beautiful and she was very happy even when the house was full and there was more work for her to do than she had the time. The burden fell on her — though Darwin tried to help, her hyper-critical mother had never thought so.

Her mother, Mercedes Haber, who later became Mercedes Parets, was part Jewish. She had led a messy life in Europe mostly on the run from the Nazis. In the wake of that disastrous lifestyle, she had two children from different men. The boy, Rose's half-brother, ripped from her mother's arms, was the son of a Jewish man. The Nazis removed him to a death camp. They learned later that the boy died. He was only three years old. Rose considered herself lucky that she didn't end up with the same fate. She and her mother had reached America by the time they learned the fatality of the child, but the news was devastating. She had been too young to appreciate what had happened to her little brother, so she hadn't understood the enormous trauma her mother endured until much later.

Mother changed. The lifestyle that had produced the two children came to a screeching halt. It was 1947 and they ended up in California. Mercedes became primarily reclusive. She rarely emerged from the house they lived in down by Venice Beach near the ocean. Rose had become the main breadwinner in between the small payments from a trust fund her mother's family had provided. Rose would pack up her paper, pens, pencils and paintbrushes for the trek down to the Santa Monica pier. There she would set up her easel and draw caricatures of anyone willing to pay her a few coins. In her spare time, she would shoplift food for their larder. She hated that she had to steal — otherwise they would not eat. In the meantime, her mother became an obsessive house cleaner and a drinker.

Mom had never lifted a finger when they lived in Europe. When Rose was a baby in Germany, they had lived with Mercedes' mother who did all the housework.

Rose was very little, and her first memory was that Nana let her sleep in her bed. In the afternoons as Rose tried to nap, she could hear the small single engine airplanes flying overhead buzzing about like bees. Later the bees would drop bombs. She was bigger then and was allowed to play among the rubble the bee-bombs made. She remembered trying to rebuild the houses that had been destroyed. She'd had friends who had lived in those houses and she wanted them to come back and play with her. They never did.

Mercedes had finally married a man of wealth which meant the house staff did the housework. Rose and Mercedes had lived for a short time in the lap of luxury with the entrepreneur industrialist, Victor Parets. It was wonderful for her mother. She was finally able to live the kind of lifestyle she felt entitled to.

For Rose it was a disaster. The man could not be satisfied and he came after Rose who was tall for her age. She was only seven-years-old when he began touching her in inappropriate ways. First it was grabbing her and bringing her close so that he could touch her bottom. He would act as though he was playing with her but she knew this was not just innocent fun. Soon, when they were alone, he would tell her she had to sit on his lap. She could feel his hardness protruding from his lap and poking her in the bottom. It was very uncomfortable and she never knew what to do. She just knew it was wrong.

Thereafter he began his litany of sex. According to Victor it was natural for a father to teach his daughter about sex. It was his job to show her what to do and how to do it. She hated "the lessons" as they came to be called. He would corner her in various parts of the house and make her take off her panties. The assaults continued until they left Europe when she was nine. The relief she felt in her body when she finally escaped Victor's "lessons" was radical. She felt human again except for the nightmares. They were persistent for many years after.

Her mother had been the one to change the most. Perhaps she was trying to make up for the life she had lived before. The guilt she must have felt about the child who had been ripped from her arms in his infancy could not have been easy. She had made a terrible mess of things and she was trying to atone by being the best housekeeper there was. In the process Rose's sense of cleanliness was challenged constantly. A young teen, she didn't have much interest in keeping the house clean and her mother insisted that the floors be tidy enough to eat off. Somehow Rose knew it was excessive cleanliness, but she was too young to appreciate the source of her mother's obsession. It was only later that she realized what her mother's difficulties had been from that time in Europe and she forgave her. Now that Mercedes was gone, her voice loomed large in Rose's consciousness. Her mother's obsession became her compulsion.

Some of her lineage turned out okay. Rose's biological father had been a caricature artist of some note in Germany where they were from; she had inherited his artistic abilities, so mother had chosen well. Nevertheless, her father died during the war and she had never gotten to know him.

Rose had been a "love baby." But her mother's relationship with Victor was purely survival. Before she died, Mercedes admitted to Rose that she was aware Victor was molesting her but she didn't know what to do about it because starvation was on the other side of the mansion walls for them both and she couldn't risk it. She justified her husband's "despicable behavior" by thinking survival was worth whatever had to be endured and the regrets were huge when she realized the damage the abuse had done to her daughter. That of course was much later. She had tearfully apologized and Rose by then was old enough to understand.

Now mother's death only brought her closer. The entire family history blended into Rose's desire to become a more serious artist. Her abilities, a given, and well-practiced, were a huge asset and she wanted to give herself more freedom to experiment in abstract forms. She wanted to explore the human body, experience it in a way that she did not yet know. She just knew that something was cooking beneath the surface of her creativity.

Maybe Danie Wharton would be willing to pose for her. It was a brief inspiration but not a bad one, she thought. The woman was beautiful even at her age. Except for the arthritis that caused her to walk with difficulty she would be picture perfect. Rose felt positive that exploring the form of the older person might be an interesting and unusual form of art. She wasn't quite sure yet how she would accomplish her goal. Enlisting help from the woman who was now living under her roof seemed like a very good idea indeed!

A brief thought, almost too brief to remember, crossed Rose's mind. Danie was beautiful and all men appreciate beautiful women. How did Darwin react to Danie? She quickly tucked the nasty little jealousy away so she wouldn't notice it. She liked Danie and didn't want to smear that with some conjecture, some silly supposition. That would be something Mercedes might do but not her. Rose was careful not to play that game as tempting as it sometimes was.

The phone rang. Her doctor announced his news briefly and Rose hung up stunned. The cancer was back. This time a small spot in her lung the doctor had been watching was enlarging. What she would do now she could not imagine. It was all too much. Darwin was due to have surgery on his knee. The operation had been scheduled in two weeks. She would have to nurse him back to health before she could schedule anything for herself. She prayed the cancer would not grow too much in that time. She decided Darwin should not know about it until after he had recovered from his surgery. Otherwise, he would cancel and she felt strongly that he had been through too much already planning for the operation. No, it would be better for her to wait. Darwin would be her first consideration.

CHAPTER 11

Wally

He was in a foul mood. Turning 45, his life was bereft of anything one could call success. If he tried to conjure up something he had done, that could count for him in his current situation, it would melt in the fog of illusion. Sure, he took care of his mom sometimes and this last time was a success. She seemed happy in her new digs even though they were temporary.

The people at the B&B were as kind as he thought they were. Knowing that was always a relief. So often he would put his trust in someone, then he or she would turn on him suddenly without any warning. He had been with a woman, Sally Oliver, for a short time after Shanna left only to have her turn on him and announce at a town meeting that he was a meth dealer. He had never sold anyone a single dose of methamphetamine and the lie socked the wind out of him just as he was coming around to trying treatment. Leaving Dancing Bear Springs at that point was the only thing to do. No one would have anything to do with him.

His time living homeless had taught him a lot, mostly to stay away from skanky women. They always betrayed; it was in their blood. Women had become such a puzzle to him — he couldn't figure them out. His usual keen senses would fail him whenever he met a girl who would meet his gaze. He was good looking; his mom said he looked like a Viking, tall with a full head of light brown hair, a trim beard, blue eyes, a strong jaw and a sexy smile, so girls flirted with him often. He knew intellectually that a certain woman could be trouble, but if she met his gaze at that precise moment, he was helpless to resist her. His mom said it was his hormones, that his reactions to women were nothing more than a chemical consequence of being male. She said there would be a day when the attraction to women would wane and he would be able to have a normal conversation with one without getting a hard-on. It felt differently to him — like he was being corralled by looks, senses, and an attraction to a girl's essence. He could smell her scent, he could feel her hair without touching it, he desired her legs around him and that indescribably amazing feeling of being inside her.

Since that time, he had not hooked up with a woman on the mountain no matter how desirable she might be. He would resist, walk away, or pick a fight with any female who dared to flirt.

The lack of a sexual outlet did make him feel odd, out-of-sorts, peculiar. It put him into a foul mood and that is where he was now on his way to the fancy restaurant in town to celebrate his 45th birthday with, of all people, his mother. He had come to call himself a 'Mama's Boy,' yet his mom had never coddled him or expected anything of him except he be himself. At times, he thought he knew himself; at other times, he felt a stranger in his own skin. Now, he knew he didn't want to be anywhere near mother.

CHAPTER 12

Danie

Danie was mystified. Wally had walked out on her. Her conversation had nothing whatever to do with either him or the server he seemed to think she was mocking. He had completely misunderstood her point about overweight in the general population. She did not mean to imply anything about Lisa, the server whose bottom was arguably chunky. She only meant to comment on the way our food is grown on industrial sized farms, mono-crop farms, and how it is processed which causes people to gain so much weight.

However, his focus had been on a world that was as incomprehensible to her as hers was to him. They skipped past each other completely on every subject. His world was that of the Internet. Of course, it was apparent to her, as it was to anyone with any history behind them, that much of the Internet postings her son read or watched were as phony as the egos of some politicians. Not to her son though. He was a true believer in the extreme sense of the word.

Her son was complicated in ways she could never understand. He had done well in the world of business when he owned his own moving company. He later engaged in real estate, acquiring property, and made a bit of money with the US distribution of alcohol made in Mexico. Ultimately, he had lost everything after his woman of twelve years left him for another man, and just after he put the engagement ring on her finger. Essentially, she killed Wally, his soul and his faith in love.

He had fallen off the deep end and got himself totally out of control. There had been many times when he was so out of it that he lost everything. He would get high and stay up for three or four days. Then he would crash unable to take care of a current crisis, occurrences that eventually took away everything including the moving truck and the car he was living in at the time. The cops had confiscated them only because they were parked in the wrong place. Had he been awake he could have parked the vehicles somewhere else.

He had survived several crushing blows; he would never be the same again. That much Danie knew.

She had splurged by taking Wally to the Singing Bear Bistro, the best restaurant in town. She felt he deserved to be treated to a nice meal. The waitress was the owner's daughter. "Lisa is a sweet girl and a terrific waitress." Danie was eyeing the girl's rear end as she moved to the next table for their order. "It's too bad her diet isn't better."

"Why? What's wrong with her diet?" He asked as he dove into his crispy salad swallowing the butter lettuce in whole chunks. Danie always marveled at the sight of entire bites of food moving down his throat as he swallowed. She couldn't fathom how he digested his food without chewing it.

"I imagine she eats a lot of processed foods."

He came up for air from his salad as a swimmer's head pops up from the pool, "What's that got to do with it?"

"Industrial farming."

"Really Mother?" He dove back into his greens.

"Yes, I've always believed in eating farm fresh."

"Gosh Mom. You are sounding like a commercial."

"I've done a few of those."

"I know. So, where are the cameras now Mom?" She took note he was mocking her.

She decided to ignore his punch. "Well Sweetheart, you read the Internet. You must know about those industrial giants who grow most of our foods now. The best way to grow food is on a multi-purpose farm where they grow all kinds of food including livestock and planted food together."

"I haven't read anything about that."

"Really? Talk about conspiracies! Now there is a conspiracy we should all know about."

"What's wrong with the food?"

"I'm shocked you aren't up on this. It's the reason Lisa's weight is out of control."

Lisa was finishing up her orders and heading back to the kitchen. Wally watched her go. What's wrong with her weight? She looks fine to me."

"Nothing really. I mean if she chooses to eat processed foods even while surrounded with the good food her father serves here, then maybe it is simply her preference and she doesn't care about the results. To me she is making the wrong choices and she would be better off eating fresh only.

"Mother, what do you know about her diet anyway?" His fork dropped onto the plate with a clang. "Do you follow her around taking notes?"

"Of course not!" she countered. "I'm only referring to her chunky bottom."

Wally got up and walked out taking his birthday present with him — of course — leaving her with the bill, the birthday cake, and the embarrassment of being stood up, left behind in a small community.

She paid the bill even though they had only managed to eat the salad and quietly gathered her things. She wanted to cry but managed to hold back the tears until she was well on the way to the car. She never meant to hurt him, certainly not on his birthday. He was as mystifying to her as she was to him and she would have to admit the fact and get on with her own life. Maybe re-parenting him was just as much a fantasy as the space aliens Wally insisted were among us. She would love to meet one just in case the E.T. could help her with her recalcitrant offspring. If they were intelligent enough to get to earth, maybe they would be smart enough to turn around Wally's life.

Arriving back at the B&B, she unlocked the door to a room that was bereft of anyone except for her cat Dusty. The grey and white feline who loved to roll around in the dirt, thus his name, had taken it upon himself to claim a spot on the bed just where her knees usually took up space. He knew her favorite spots and he would be there snuggled right on top of her legs when she climbed in. She smiled knowing she accepted her kitty friend because he was a cat and she could not expect him to be more than that. It was a lesson she had to learn repeatedly with Wally. He was who he was and she would have to accept him the way he was.

However, the disrespect had to go. It was the one thing she didn't feel she deserved. She was far from perfect but Wally expected her to be Mother Therese. That she would never reach the level of sainthood did not mean she was undeserving of some positive acknowledgement. She wasn't a mean person. She had done everything she could to avoid being dismissive of her child while he was young and still lived with her. She had never called him names; she had never told him he was bad or wrong or not good enough. That she followed these rules had been like a creed of motherhood, almost a religion she had adopted. She would never let Wally feel bad about himself.

Perhaps she had gone too far and thus the disrespect. Maybe she should have been more critical when he had deserved critique. Instead, she had gone to extreme lengths to do otherwise, to never take the wind out of his sales. She came to realize she had been too indulgent with Wally. That was why he could walk out on her now. He had never learned respect.

CHAPTER 13

Darwin

The pain in his knee led to the pain in his hip, which led to the pain in his back, which led to the pain in his neck. He was hopeful the surgery would help. It was scheduled at the end of the week and he had a lot to do to prepare. First, his doctor told him to lay off the aspirin. It was a blood thinner; he did not want to lose too much blood. There were other things he would have to do. He was supposed to starve himself eight hours before the surgery which meant he could not eat the way he liked. He had to ingest a major antibiotic 24 hours before arriving at the hospital. The doctor warned him to have plenty of pain medication on hand at home when he was released from the facility. Living so far away from town, the preparations had to be done before hand — they could not just up and run to the 24-hour pharmacy since the closest one was over an hour away. Rose insisted he get some laxatives too. They would be needed when he started the other medications.

If nothing else, he was a thorough man. When he knew what he had to do he did it with tenacity until it was done. He did not like to leave any detail unattended.

He knew Rose would say differently. She never seemed to be satisfied with him. Rose had a different idea of a job-well-done and she never seemed to like what he contributed to the house and the business. That bothered him a lot. Though he was confident in himself as an actor, as an intellect, as a man, she could make him feel completely inadequate.

He had never been a huge success in his acting endeavors, not the kind of success he thought would be enough. He had been a character actor so the success of stardom eluded him. There were times when the odd jobs he had to do for survival took over and the acting jobs seemed to melt away like ice cream on the sidewalk of a hot Hollywood day. Much of the survival work had eroded his sense of self and his ambition.

He always wanted to act. He would do anything and would go anywhere to do the jobs offered him. But there were times he felt defeated. That is how he felt now as he faced the surgery. He wondered if he had done all he was supposed to do. He didn't know if he could handle another defeat.

The knee was crucial. He could not see himself wandering around in life like a gimp. He felt vital inside; he felt strong and youthful even. The gimpy knee didn't fit his image of himself.

The new woman in the house emphasized these feelings of inadequacy. He wanted to strut around like the vital human being he knew he was. Yet, Danie was probably looking at him as done, over, worthless. How could it be otherwise? That is what he saw in the mirror when he had the nerve to look. His hair was a grayish, white, wispy concoction; his face was all whiskery and flabby; his body wasn't bad except for the belly he'd developed sometime during his forties. It hung low over his belt now. How could any woman find him attractive?

Of course, he had to remember he was a married man and other women were of no consequence to him. Yet, he wanted to think of himself as attractive — not old. He was far from being vane but he did think haircoloring would be useful. He wondered if a light brown shade would look good on him. Rose colored her hair. Why shouldn't he? It was something to think about.

He liked Danie. She laughed at all his jokes in the mornings. Anybody who would find him funny was on his 'A' list. She was always up early in the kitchen making her breakfast when he wandered in with the dogs. He figured she had developed the early morning habit when she was an actor in Hollywood. They wanted her in the make-up chair at 6:00 a.m. for an hour of adornment that would make her look like a Greek Goddess. She'd told him earlier that her total time in front of the make-up mirror these days was all of ten minutes. Darwin wondered what she had eliminated.

He had his morning chores — feeding the dogs was first on his list, feeding the birds out by the fence was another. He loved the wild birds as they gathered around him waiting for the seed he would toss and the millet he would put into the feeders. The pigeons and doves would coo, the small wrens and sparrows would chirp their insistent song and the medium sized black birds with their red, white or yellow wings would squawk at him. He loved the feeling of the birds fluttering against him demanding their due. And when they flew off in sync, it was magical.

He quickly ascertained that Danie was a political junkie who watched far too much television. She would enter the kitchen with a new political factoid that could be interesting or slightly radical. He, Rose and Danie occupied the same corner of the political spectrum. That was a blessing. Political arguments were off his list of things to do in his spare time. He refused to engage in the kind of righty-lefty stuff that some folks found so invigorating. He didn't think that kind of talk was useful at all. However, discussing what might be better for the people in a democracy was always interesting to him. The way the presidential campaigns were shaping up worried him. He noticed things in the primaries that were disturbing. He was becoming obsessed with the results and found the television more alluring than before. He didn't want to become like Danie though, attached to the TV all day long.

Danie was a complicated woman; that was certain. But he appreciated her intellect. She challenged him to think more deeply and he like that a lot.

"What are you thinking about?" Rose asked as she entered the kitchen. She was fully dressed and ready to cook for the guests.

"Oh, nothing important. Just wondering about my surgery next week." He was glad she couldn't read his mind thinking about Danie the way he was.

"You are not worried, are you?"

"A little." He was very worried and felt vulnerable.

"Come on, Darwin. I know you. 'A little' doesn't really describe what's going on in that brain of yours."

"Oaky, a lot." He replied defensively. "I'll be okay. You don't need to worry too."

"Oh, I will. You know me."

He grabbed her around the waist and hugged her mightily. "I love you, Rose. You are my favorite person in the whole world."

"Why? Because I worry?" She laughed.

Just then Danie entered by the service pantry. "Oh dear, I'm sorry. Didn't mean to intrude."

"You're not intruding. We're just having a 'a little' moment." He laughed. "Rose here was tickling my insecurities."

"You don't look like a man with insecurities."

"Thank you, Danie. You said the right thing. Keep it up and you can stay as long as you like."

Rose agreed. "Likewise, I am sure," she smiled.

CHAPTER 14

Rose

"I am reading Danie's book." They were relaxing in the living room right after dinner. Rose had the book in her hand and held it up for Darwin to see. A beautiful early photograph of Daniela Wharton filled the front cover along with the title "All That I am," and her name as the sole author below it. "She borrowed the title from a song that Elvis Presley sang called 'All That I Am.' I wonder if he sang it to her." Rose giggled. "Do you think she had an affair with him?"

"I guess you'll find out in there." Darwin answered pointing to the book and rising to take the dinner dishes to the kitchen. "Is it a 'tell-all' Hollywood memoir?"

"I think so. She starts out with a big tragedy in her early life."

His expression was one of derision. "I don't put much stock in those Hollywood stories, you know."

"I know, Darwin. Why would you? You have heard them all, haven't you?"

"Yeah, I guess." He opened the freezer door and found the carton of chocolate ice cream. "They just seem like such — God, that's cold — cheap stabs for attention. She had a career — so what?" He jabbed the hardened ice cream with the spoon. "She didn't change the world, she didn't discover a cure for cancer, she didn't journey out into space. Where is the story? She did some acting jobs. That's all."

"Honestly, I'm not sure, Darwin. But I certainly hope I am not wasting my time. I don't have that much to waste."

"Well, I guess since she lives here, we should know more about her life, I mean the parts that didn't make it into the press. She did generate a lot of that when she was active."

"Yes, I remember something about an affair with a married actor. She upset that applecart. I remember the incident because I was infatuated with the actor myself. Do you remember MacDonald Desmond? While I could understand the attraction, I couldn't understand how she would just break up a marriage like that. The wife was pregnant too."

"She didn't marry Desmond, I know," he reminisced. "Did she ever marry?"

"Yes, she married some non-actor. That is how she had Wally. The man wasn't a professional of any kind if I remember correctly. I don't know where she found him or why she married him." Rose paused for a moment with a thought. "Maybe he got her pregnant." The thought made her smile.

"Well get reading and keep me up-to-date on the important things. Okay?"

"What do you think is important?"

"Truth is, I haven't a clue. I like Danie and I really don't know what I would want to know or not know."

"I like her, too. I hope the story has a positive outcome."

"Hollywood stories don't get told unless there is a positive outcome. Believe me."

"I suppose you are right. Why would they?"

Rose thought again about asking Danie to pose for her in a painting. "I wonder if she ever posed nude."

"That I do remember. I saw the pictures in *Playboy* Magazine. They were mighty racy — excuse me, they were 'hot'." He smiled wryly as he returned with a dish of ice cream for them both. "I'm trying to update my language. The kids I teach look at me funny when I say things like 'racy'."

"I look at you funny when you say things like 'racy,' Darwin. I hope you know that." She spooned her ice cream and shoveled it into her mouth while smiling at him. "Gosh, that's cold!" The ice cream sat on her tongue in a cold chunk as the hair on her arms stood on end. "Brrr."

"Gosh?" My students would laugh at 'gosh' too, you know."

"What would you have them use instead?" She replied through the muffle of the melting ice cream on her tongue.

"They don't mince words. They say 'God!' with a capital 'G' and an exclamation mark. Of course, they wouldn't know where to put exclamation marks in a sentence, but they sure do know how use them in their speech."

Rose looked up at him with her brows raised. "After reading the first couple of pages of this book, I think it is going to have a lot of exclamation marks."

CHAPTER 15

Danie

Danie tried to be prudent about her trips off the hill, especially for visits to doctors and dentists. She made all the appointments on the same day. Of course, this meant the day would be long and she never knew exactly what to expect. Would she be able to drive home without concern after such an appointment or would she find herself too weak or disoriented to get behind the wheel? It was always a dilemma.

This time, she was on her way to the periodontist because she had cracked a tooth right in front. The tooth had been removed and a temporary made to take its place until the implant could be inserted. Today she would get the stem for an implant; it was a procedure she was dreading.

It was also the day she would spend at the skin doctor's office getting a biopsy from the tip of her nose. She must be a glutton for punishment she thought. Neither of the procedures would be pleasant and Danie guessed she would feel awful by the end of the day.

As she descended the mountain traffic began to slow. Enormous big rigs that appeared to her like huge dinosaurs herding through the canyon, formed a long line in the slow lane. Of course, she hadn't lived 65 million years ago, so she would not know what a line of herding dinosaurs would look like but she surmised her imagination was competent enough to feel accurate about what she was watching. The big rigs were herding dinosaurs, each one more gigantic than the last. They took up a lot of room on the freeway even though they stuck to the outer side of the road. That was the law. Yet their presence slowed everyone down. Jockeying for position in those two outer lanes kept other cars from speeding down the highway though they certainly tried. Danie felt unsafe here. She wanted to scurry away like a tiny bunny in the way of a pack of coyotes.

Like a coyote, she took note of the lack of water, the extreme dryness of the flora along the divided highway. The California drought had taken a toll on everything, not just the land. Danie herself felt dry and brittle, her skin a thin barrier against the extreme famine of moisture in the air. She worried about the animals that depended on the water they found for their sustenance. It pained her heart to think about a mama bear seeking enough moisture for her cubs to survive. How would she do that in this dry, barren wasteland? She could picture a weary mama with her two lively cubs trudging from one dry watering hole to another without finding a single drop. These forays into her imagination usually produced feelings she didn't want to deal with, feelings of frustration and despair. She knew how a mama bear would feel — the worry, the dread, the hope that the next place would produce something, some small something for her cubs. These feelings often produced tears.

Finally, Danie arrived at her destination. The efficiency of the dental office felt good, certain. This was one place where she felt she had safety, enough power over the direction of her care that she could relax and feel confident in the results. She had been here many times, often enough to know the periodontist well and to trust him.

First the dentist removed the temporary tooth he had fashioned from an impression he had taken the last time she was there. Once the Novocain wore off, she would re-insert the temporary so she would not look toothless — a blessing for sure.

The surgical procedure took a while and Danie hoped to have a bite to eat before going for the biopsy. She found an attractive lunchroom and ordered a chicken sandwich. Concerned about the numbness in her mouth, she ordered an iced tea instead of hot coffee, which was what she wanted. Despite the care she took in eating her sandwich, she managed to take a bite out of her inner lip. She was too numb to feel the nip she'd taken but she did get a small hunk of something she couldn't chew. She swallowed it quickly hoping it was just a bit of gristle from the grilled chicken. A headache began to needle its way into her head and she wondered if it had to do with the numbing agent the dentist had used. Maybe, as it wore off, this headache would subside.

She arrived at the Dermatologist's office just as the numbness was wearing off and she could feel the wound left by the chunk she had eaten from the inside of her mouth. It wasn't exactly tiny and it hurt a lot, as did the headache. After the long requisite wait in the doctor's depressing outer office, she was ushered to an examining room by the nurse.

Danie's arms were cold and she shivered with a chill as she awaited the dermatologist's arrival. Goose bumps arose on her arms and the cold of the small space seeped into her bones. A feeling of foreboding took over and Danie wanted to leave this room and never return.

The idea of having a nose removal terrified her. The red mark on the tip of her nose, she had to admit, was not huge, just a tiny irregular point on the end. Its presence however was a threat as big as Godzilla.

The blemish took on proportions that shook her from her complacency about the disease.

Danie had been lucky. She had never had much wrong with her physically. The arthritis was the worst of it and though her joints were sore most of the time, the disease was hardly life-threatening and she didn't expect to give up any limbs to it. Cancer was different. This was her first run-in with the life-threatening disorder and when she thought about it, this little smudge should not be much of a problem. Nevertheless, the terror lay just beneath the surface of her usual calm.

At last "Dr. Dreamboat" entered the room. Taken aback by his looks, Danie was suddenly rendered speechless. This was her first encounter with him; he was young enough to be her grandson. His age didn't dampen her imagination however. As she was floating off into a sexual fantasy which included him mounting her on the examining table, he asked without emotion, "What is your complaint?" She was about to learn he was a man of few words.

Danie didn't expect much sentiment but she sure would like to feel like he cared a little. She pointed to her nose and he attacked it with intensity. "Yes, that's cancer alright." The nurse who had entered the room with him tendered a hypodermic needle. He took it and before Danie could object, stabbed the needle into her nose.

"Ouch!" she screamed.

"Sorry," he said unceremoniously. "I have to numb you a little so I can take a biopsy."

"Okay…I guess." She responded uncertainly wishing she had retained more of the Novocain effect from the periodontist. "What comes next?" She asked wondering if she could have a warning before he started in again.

"The biopsy. I'll be back in a minute when you're ready." He left without another word.

Slowly the numbness grabbed her nose and she felt as ready as she ever would. He didn't return to the room for another fifteen minutes and by then her headache had disappeared. She was grateful for the relief. However, by this time, she was thoroughly cold and her skin crawled with a chill.

"I don't mean to complain, but it is very cold in here."

"Less chance of infection that way." Again, the doctor, his real name was Dr. Thomas, took to her nose without ceremony with a scalpel.

"Ouch!" She yelled. "That hurts still."

The skin doctor's ministrations felt assaultive; he went at her face with a fervor she didn't appreciate.

"Sorry. It should have been numb." After a moment he was done. His manner never changed. "Too late. I have what I need."

He headed for the door. "Make an appointment as soon as possible." With that he was gone.

Danie wasn't sure she liked him.

The nurse smiled sheepishly. "His good looks are deceiving. He's really a total jerk."

Danie laughed. "Maybe you shouldn't say things like that. People won't want to return."

"Oh, they do. I'm going to dress your wound." She proffered a small aluminum container. "This is an antibacterial ointment and you must be sure to clean the wound with soap and water, then apply the ointment regularly."

Danie took the tiny package and applying her glasses read the instructions. "Just snip the top and squeeze, huh? It doesn't look like much."

"It does the job." The woman was trying very hard to make Danie comfortable. Evidently, she had plenty of practice assuaging the fears left behind when "Dr. Not-so dreamy-after-all" left the room. With that she applied a small round Band-Aid to the end of Danie's nose. "You will return in two weeks for your surgery."

"Surgery?" Danie was startled. "Surgery is a big word. What is he going to do?" She laughed nervously. "He can't have my nose."

Now the nurse laughed. "No, I don't think that will be necessary. The procedure is called 'Mohs.' He just scrapes a little off, then sends the sample to pathology to check it. You could be here for a while if he has to take any more than one scrape. Each one takes about a half-hour so be sure to bring some reading material."

"I will be awake?"

"Yes. Very awake. He only numbs your nose."

"I hope he does a better job next time. That biopsy hurt."

"Don't worry, he will. The spot doesn't look that bad. I think you caught it early enough."

When Danie left the office, she was warmed by the 'Indian Summer' air that hugged her body. She would have to wear a sweater for the surgical procedure and she hoped she could find a good book to read, maybe a non-fiction about someone who lacks a nose.

"What happened to your nose?" Rose looked more closely. "That looks like a bad wound." On this particular morning Rose was preparing the breakfast and Darwin was off the hill doing a teaching gig.

"Oh, it's just a biopsy. I'll be okay. The operation — it's in a couple of weeks — the doctor should take just a tiny bit off…Or so the nurse said."

"The important thing is that you need your nose."

"More important than you can imagine. I can earn money because of this nose."

"How is that?"

"Sometimes, I do autograph shows and people want to have their picture taken with me. They pay me to do that and they won't if I don't have a nose!"

Rose laughed. "I know it isn't a laughing matter, but that is funny."

"On top of that, I can't find my temporary bridge with the tooth. I've look all over and I can't find it."

"Could it be anywhere else?"

"No. I never take it out unless I'm here. I've checked the wastebaskets too. It looks like I'll have to go without it until I get my new implant."

"I'd be more worried about my nose."

"Frankly I'm terrified. What if the doctor finds more cancer than I think he will?"

"You will be told before the doctor has to take more off."

"Sure, but I still won't have a nose!"

"You'll be fine." Rose was sympathetic. "Better to not have cancer don't you think?"

"Frankly, I'm not sure." Danie knew she was being silly. Cancer was not something to take lightly and whenever she thought about how serious it was, she felt weak inside. More immediately she felt ridiculous without a tooth in front and a bandage plastered to the end of her nose.

CHAPTER 16

Rose

"I have read the book." Rose announced. "Actually, I drank it. She is a good writer and her story is a page-turner."

"What book?" Darwin was concentrating on his screenplay. The monitor of his laptop computer reflected a blue glow over his face.

"You know Danie's book, 'All That I Am.' She claims that Elvis Presley sang the song to her in a 'private setting'; that no one else ever knew this about her, that she *knew* Elvis and..."

Darwin looked at her with a blank expression. "You are interrupting my train-of-thought with drivel about Danie and Elvis?"

"Excuse me!" Rose felt put off and stomped into the kitchen. "Well, she did!" And, she was a marriage wrecker! That woman is living in our house and she is a home wrecker!"

"What?" She had his attention now. "You don't think she is going to wreck our home, do you?"

"Well no. Not so far." She said with a little hesitation.

"Rose. You don't really think that at *our* age..." He paused.

"You didn't finish your sentence, Darwin. Do you think it is somehow impossible to have feelings at our age?" She arched an eyebrow.

"Well I wouldn't worry about it if I were you. I haven't seen any reason to believe that she is currently a home wrecker."

"She's really attractive, Darwin. Don't tell me you haven't noticed."

"Her earlobes could use a little ironing and she could lose a few pounds." He murmured using his best puppy dog look. "And...well, she waddles like a penguin which takes away from the whole Hollywood glamor thing."

Rose had to giggle at his observations.

Encouraged Darwin continued. "She has nutty little ways of expressing herself, too — like the spoon she just used to serve the cat food calling it a 'doggie lollipop,' or that silly 'kitchen dance' she does...Oh, and she says funny things like 'Golly, Gee' and 'Okeydokey'!"

"Sounds to me like she's pretty special to you, Darwin."

"She is attractive and I've notice how beautiful you are, too." He lowered his voice pushing to convince her and whispered, "You are more svelte than she is. You are tall and slender with exotic good looks. I'm not blind, you know."

Rose smiled.

"You do a pretty good 'kitchen dance' yourself, the way you swing your hips to avoid a collision." He smiled that sweet sexy way again.

Maybe Darwin could be trusted after all. She had never had any reason to believe otherwise so Rose decided she would trust him. Trusting Danie might be another matter. She liked the woman a lot. They had even shared life experiences that drew them closer…

"I had a child out of wed-lock when I was too involved in my career to take care of him." Danie admitted one morning while she watched Rose cook breakfast for some guests. Danie leaned against the counter with her arms locked around her. "You and I were both a bit reckless when we were young. Have you finished reading my memoir?" Danie asked as she unfolded herself and hauled some heavy dishes from the dishwasher into a cupboard.

"Oh yes. Your story about MacDonald Desmond reminded me of a boy I loved. He was so romantic and I was madly infatuated with him. "Did you give the baby up?"

"Yes, I had to. At least I didn't get an abortion. Maybe we all have those moments when we lose our good sense and forget everything our parents tried to tell us. I plainly forgot that some men can't be trusted."

"I would agree with that entirely." Rose responded. "How would we ever learn otherwise? Of course, my mother was a whore in Europe. I guess she had to be — it was survival for her then. We had a hard life until we could come to America. I didn't get the right kind of lessons from my parents. My step father, Victor Parets was his name, abused me sexually from the time I was seven-years-old when my mother married him."

"That's awful, Rose! Danie exclaimed. "Why would your mother allow that?"

"She had her reasons, which I came to understand and forgive later." Rose grew silent as she opened the oven door and slipped in a metal tray of croissants needing baking. The oven was in grave need of cleaning. Avoiding the tears that choked her, she made a mental note to get it done.

Danie peeled a banana. Then, "I'm very sorry you had to go through that, Rose. I can't think of a good enough reason to expose a daughter to that kind of abuse." She took a bite of the peeled banana.

"You might be surprised. The choices we had to make in those circumstances were extreme. She didn't really *do* anything. She just ignored the signs, which is pretty common in those circumstances."

"Yeah, maybe…I'm glad to say my parents were both pretty wonderful. My dad was a gambler and that caused problems but basically, compared to other people I know, my parents were ideal."

"Your problems turned up later, right?" Rose asked.

"Yeah, when I got into the business. I was very naïve. My mother tried to warn me but of course, I thought I knew what I was doing and…Well, you read the story. I got raped."

"I'm sorry."

"I'm sorry about you." They regarded each other with the camaraderie that souls who are like each other share. Mutual sharing Rose noted was usually special between women.

"We have something else in common," Rose announced. "Our boys. Wally and my son, Jason, are very much alike. Reading your account of rearing your son on your own sure did resonate with my situation. Jason is doing well now but there was a time when I didn't think he was going to make it in this life. When I divorced his dad, he became a real handful, a lot like Wally."

Danie's eyes teared. "I find Wally to be so difficult…Sometimes, I really don't know what to do about him." She paused to take a nibble of the banana. "I thought I might try re-parenting him as I might have raised him up a long time ago if I'd been better equipped at the time." She wiped the damp from her eyes with her sleeve.

"I've heard of people doing that but I don't know if it is possible when they're over thirty."

"He isn't stupid, you know, just uneducated. If only I could get him to take up course work on the computer. He could complete a college education that way if he was diligent enough. I wish he would read books, novels, well written history books, science books. Somehow, he just didn't get the basics. He went to school but some way or another it passed him by and I don't know how that happens. I wish the Internet had been developed when he was in school. It came up right after."

"There are so many things people can do today that we couldn't. I suppose it is redundant to say that, but it sure is true." Rose commented. "Maybe you could get him to log onto a college course or two."

"If only he would go after his GED. He could do a lot after that."

"Did you say he is 45 now?"

"Yes; just had a birthday."

"Whoa. A lot of traffic has passed over that bridge."

"You have no idea."

She told Rose about Wally's breakup with his woman of twelve years, how Wally's life had been one tragedy after another. He had never had it easy. He was the child of divorce with a father who stayed away and he had a grandmother who was paranoid-schizophrenic. Though he tested high on the IQ scale, the drugs had taken a toll on his mind and Danie wasn't sure he didn't suffer from some mental disorder. On top of all that he was in the deleterious position of being the son of a 'movie star' — "never a good deal unless you planned to be one yourself." Danie added.

"I married at the ripe old age of 30," she said, "hoping to have a child or maybe two. My biological clock ticked loudly when I chose to marry Wally's dad. It was a huge mistake," she continued after placing the banana peel in the trash. "I always *thought* I knew what I was doing. On the way to the temple (he is a Buddhist, you know), my car died on the freeway and it took an act of God to get to the place. If only I had known what I was doing, I would have taken the vehicle stall to mean I was making a mistake and should turn my car around and head out of town."

After a moment she said, "I was determined to get the ring on my finger and I refused to heed the warnings and forged ahead. After the ceremony I learned the real reason my mother-in-law couldn't attend the wedding. Mom was interned at the State Institution for the Mentally Ill. That honeymoon information turned me cold and it was a month before I could consummate the marriage. That one act did the job. Wally was born nine months later. I filed for divorce a couple of days after he was born. I have to admit, I'm embarrassed to tell that part of my story to you — you are such a new friend, Rose."

She paused for a moment, "I must have been crazy to divorce so soon. Maybe I could have made the marriage work if I had been more willing to compromise." Danie's tears resumed. "It's been really hard rearing Wally on my own."

"It might have been harder with a husband you did not love."

"Maybe. No way to know that now."

"When I adopted Jason, my marriage turned sour too. I kept wishing it was different. My husband was abusive, demeaning. I couldn't handle it after Victor."

"I couldn't save my marriage and you couldn't prevent divorce."

"We were too independent." Rose smiled. "You couldn't have stayed with your husband any more than I could."

The conversation between the two women was a bonding experience for both. Rose felt she had a friend for life.

CHAPTER 17

Danie

The morning after her nose surgery Danie wandered into the kitchen hoping she was early enough to miss everyone — Darwin, Rose, or any guests. She was feeling self-conscious and hated that her nose looked so ridiculous.

After five hours the previous day in the icy examining room, Dr. 'Not-so-dreamy' at last announced that she was 'clear' and she could go home. The nurse had patched up her nose, which was feeling very sad and sent her on her way with instructions to be careful to clean the wound and to add the antibiotic ointment each time. They sent her off armed with plenty of the tiny aluminum packets.

The nurse had thankfully added a nice bandage, but the covering had come off in the middle of the night. Danie tried to fix it and failing that had tried her own dressing. Mostly, the problem was that everything — cat fur, dust, the cold morning air — stuck to her nose because the salve and the bandage were sticky. The effect was a constant tickling of the end of her nose.

"You don't look happy this morning." Darwin came up behind her, his deep voice boomed in her ear.

"Oh, you startled me!" She exclaimed as she jumped.

"I promise not to hurt you." He said as he backed off with his hands up.

"My startle-response is exaggerated. Sorry." She laughed.

"Oh, oh. What happened to your nose?"

"Cancer."

"Shit."

"Yes, that would be one of my responses."

"It's on the end and it doesn't look too big. Are you going to be alright?"

"So far. The good doctor hasn't removed my nose yet."

"Gosh, I hope he never does. That's a pretty impressive nose."

"Thanks. It tickles."

"Tickles?"

"Everything — cat fur, dust — sticks to the antibacterial salve. It's driving me mad."

He sidled up closer so he could see. "Oh, I see what you mean. That looks nasty."

The end of her nose sported a funny bandage and a little gray cat fur stuck out. She blew at the offending fur and the bandage end flew up while the other end remained stuck to her nose.

"Look at the stitches. Wow!" Darwin loomed over her to see if he could get a hold of the tiny piece of fuzz. "Do you think I can get it off?"

She cringed as his huge hand headed for her nose. "Just don't hit my nose please. I couldn't deal with the pain."

His eyes nearly crossed trying to get a bead on the end of her nose. "I can see it!"

Just as his hand was about to clamp down on the fur Rose entered the kitchen. "My! What have we got here?" She asked with a little suspicion in her voice.

Darwin jerked his hand away guiltily as if he had been caught with it in the proverbial cookie jar. "Oh nothing! Just trying to solve a problem with Danie's nose."

"Her nose? What's the matter with her nose?"

"It's nothing, Rose." Danie interjected. The salve the doctor gave me is gooey and Dusty's fur is sticking to it. It tickles."

"I was just trying to get it off." Darwin added awkwardly.

"Your face is red, Darwin," Rose said accusingly.

He lunged toward her and swept her into his arms. "My face is only red for you, dear."

Danie could see a smile creep onto Rose's lips. She was trying to suppress her amusement.

"You never have to worry about Darwin, Rose. He is a lover only for you."

Danie had feared this situation more than her nose, her missing tooth, her relationship with Wally, or anything else plaguing her life right now. She simply could not do anything to threaten Rose's marriage to Darwin. It was a line she would not cross no matter what else happened.

She had learned her lesson well. After driving too many wedges into the middle of the unions of some of her co-stars, she had decided long ago never to do anything like that again. It was her eleventh commandment. 'Thou shalt not steal life-mates' — committing the act of adultery was a small matter compared to the actual theft of a person's heart.

"You know, Rose," Darwin added breaking the spell, "Danie doesn't look quite like the movie star she used to be. I mean, just look at that nose, and she's missing a tooth right in front." He turned to Danie and winked to indicate he was only kidding. "You look pretty ridiculous. I hope you aren't planning to go out anytime soon. People will laugh."

Danie chuckled. "You bet I'm going out and I plan to go to the club tonight for a drink and dinner. My plot is to embarrass my friends." She said conspiratorially. "I wonder who will be the one to break the silence and say something. Do you think they will notice the stitches or the missing tooth first? How long to do you think it'll take?"

"Are you taking bets?" Roared Darwin. "I bet it will take at least twenty minutes."

"Rose, not wanting to be left out wagered "twenty bucks on a thirty-minute wait."

"Maybe they will say nothing…ever!" They all laughed wondering if anyone would care.

Danie felt relieved that Rose was so easy-going. They both were. She was beginning to feel truly comfortable with these two-improbable people.

CHAPTER 18

Wally

She did it again! His mother insulted him. She had flung a statement at him that made him feel bad about himself. The cat, Dusty, on his way to the vet, was meowing pitifully in the back of the Subaru, locked into a cage that was ample enough for a medium size dog. The cat hated cages and his mom had finally found one that was big enough for Dusty to be very comfortable. However, he meowed louder and louder all the way down the hill. Apparently, comfort was not the issue.

"It's okay, Dusty. Wally will stop farting any minute now."

How the hell did she come up with these things? "Really, Mom? Why did you say that? I have not been farting!

"You did once. I could smell it."

"That was Dusty! I wish you would stop insulting me."

"I wasn't insulting you, Wally. I was just teasing. I was trying to be funny."

"Well, it wasn't funny, although the end of your nose looks pretty funny."

"Oh, thank you. I'm pretty proud of it." She changed tack. "Look, I'm sorry if you feel insulted. But why do you take it so personally?"

"You did say my name, Mother. How else am I to take it?"

"This is a problem we've had *like forever.*"

Was she trying to be funny again? "You said it. You are *always* insulting me."

"I'm teasing. This is something you missed out on because we don't have a big family with a dad and siblings. If you had had brothers and sisters, you would have learned…"

"I would have learned to insult people!" His voice rose to a fevered pitch. "That's what I hate about this country. Everybody is out to insult…"

"Maybe teasing is only a tactless way of telling the truth, Wally. I'm just trying to explain that you missed out on…"

"I missed out on garbage. I hate the way people treat each other. Everybody is so nasty. We are all like alienated from each other and…"

"Alienated?" Her voice formed a question mark. "Honey, teasing, when we learn how cultural it is…"

"I don't care about culture. I don't like being insulted!"

"You aren't really being insulted. It is a way for families to help each other grow up and become adults. When we don't have to face family ridicule in our upbringing, we tend to become conceited and self-absorbed."

This couldn't be what she meant. "Mother, you don't really believe it is better for us to be made fun of — for us to constantly compete playing this one-up-man-ship game that hurts people."

"You know; I actually agree with you. It's lousy being alienated from other people."

"You bet it is."

"However, there is…"

"You are always trying to wheedle out of being wrong. I know you, Mom, and you are just trying to make excuses for yourself."

"No, that's not what I'm trying to do. I'm trying to inform you about something that you missed out on when…"

"I missed out on nothing!" Wally's voice was adamant now. He didn't feel like his mom was listening. "You're trying to make me feel stupid!"

"No. You missed out on family. And, families help each other to become humbler through joking…"

"Everybody's always telling me I'm too sensitive. I am not too sensitive! And, that humility thing. Who wants to be humiliated?"

Danie almost laughed. "Well, no one. But…"

"I'm tired of everybody trying to humiliate me all the time."

"Do you really think that's what they're doing?"

"Yes!"

"Sweetheart, when someone else can humiliate you, maybe it is because you don't have enough humility yourself."

"I don't want to humiliate myself!" He charged on.

"Being humble means, you can't be humiliated."

"Why should I be humble?!"

"Well, the Bible says the meek will inherit the earth." Her voice trailed off like she didn't believe it herself.

"Right Mom. Like that's really happening." This was very confusing to Wally. He wanted to feel good about himself like he was worth something. People his entire life had told him to have self-confidence, but his mom was telling him he should be humble. It didn't make sense.

"Have you ever heard the story about Narcissus?" She asked.

"No. Who in the hell is Narcissus?" This was where she would insult his intelligence by trying to tell him something he didn't know. He hated her when she did that. But she was going on as if she thought he should know.

"Narcissus was a Greek God, a hunter. Apparently, he was very good looking, even beautiful. Maybe they didn't have mirrors back then but Narcissus quite unexpectedly glanced his image in a pool of water. He fell in love."

"Good. People are always telling me I should love myself."

"The problem was that he loved his *image* so much that he was always looking down at his *reflection,* unable to see or care about anyone or anything else, even himself. In fact, he died from the absorption he had with his image. He couldn't get past it."

"Mom," Wally groaned.

She pressed on. "What if he'd realized that all he was in love with was an image, a reflection, not the real person?"

"Mom." He whined. "What does that have to do with me?"

"Well nothing exactly."

Now she was lying outright. "Then why are telling me?" He was growing more frustrated.

"I don't know. Just maybe Narcissus didn't have a family to help him grow up either."

"Mom, I had you. You raised me just fine."

"Maybe; maybe not."

"Mother, do realize how insulting that is?"

She grew quiet then. Dusty resumed his incessant mewing as the noise of the car engine and the cat replaced their argument. She thought he was stupid and he resented her deeply for that. Wally didn't think he was stupid at all. He read information on the Internet and he was far more up-to-date than she was, in his not-so-humble opinion.

CHAPTER 19

Darwin

Darwin was doing his favorite thing hanging out in his "man cave." It wasn't much of a cave located in the back of the garage. He had hoped it would be a room suited for music and vocal recording, to be an attraction to people in the area who wanted to do recordings for Internet advertising or personal and professional use. He didn't think it was a bad idea. Unfortunately, few people on the mountain needed such things. Danie Wharton had been different. When she wanted to promote her book, she called and he was happy to accommodate her.

She came by at the appointed time. He had come to expect this kind of punctuality from most actors. Small and curvy for a woman her age, she seemed very authentic for an actress. Danie didn't seem to have any affectations unless she was pretending to be a character of some kind, which she would do while telling a story or relating a joke. Her laugh was infectious and she seemed to bring light into the darkened room.

When they settled down to the work, she did a good job on her first try. She made a couple more recordings until she was happy and left. The whole thing took no more than a half hour, most of it just gabbing and joking with each other. He had given her a couple of suggestions which she managed to incorporate into her reading quite easily. She seemed a delight to work with and she was self-deprecating with a terrific sense of humor. So naturally when Rose had come to him about Danie moving into the 'Tea Rose Room', he happily agreed to let her rent the room for as long as she wanted. Rose had told the woman there were licensing laws they had to follow; she didn't want Danie to think she could stay forever. *Women!* He thought.

Probably Rose was a little jealous of Danie's looks, although the two were way past the age when there needed to be any competition. Rose was a handsome woman too. She was tall and dark, almost exotically Asian in her appearance. And she was strong, hardy, unlike Danie who was soft and a wisp of a thing. His wife had nothing to worry about as far as he was concerned.

Danie had fully intended to move out the month after she moved in, but life happened and when it came time to pay the rent, she came forward with her check explaining why she would be there for another month. He and Rose had decided she was a delight to live with and if she needed the room, it was hers.

Finished with his current project, he closed the sound room door behind him and headed out of the garage area.

Just then Danie's car pulled in to park. She yanked up the brake and set the gears on the manual shift. The windows were open; it was such a lovely early autumn — 'Indian Summer" kind of day. Beautiful music, the sound of a weeping violin emanated from her car.

She didn't turn the radio off, just sat there almost in a trance. Her golden white hair rustled in the wind and her clear blue eyes filled with tears from the sound of the composition. He watched her for a while as the music filled her face with amazing emotion. At last the piece ended and the cold sound of the announcer's voice that followed caused her to turn the radio off and get out of the car. It was at this moment when he noticed the little bandage on the end of her nose and remembered the spot of cancer there. She grabbed her bag of purchases and headed for the door all the while cooing greetings to Dusty, her cat, who sat waiting behind the screen door, ready to spring to freedom.

Darwin stepped back so Danie wouldn't see him. He didn't want her to think he was stalking her but he was entranced with the vision he had just witnessed. His mind was treading on dangerous ground. First, he was far too old to be thinking the thoughts that were cropping up in his brain. Second, and no less important than the first, he was married, happily as far as he was concerned even though it was sometimes tough to make Rose happy. And, if there needed to be a third reason, these thoughts had nothing to do with the way Danie felt about him. He had no idea how she felt, but he was sure, after having an affair with MacDonald Desmond and Elvis Presley, she wasn't interested in a love relationship with him.

Darwin did not count himself among the Lotharios of the world. He was one of the "nice guys" who were so thankful that a woman was willing to play with him that he would buy a house and marry her out of gratitude. He had done it three times. Had he been the "bad boy" that women seemed to go for, he would have kept his money and his properties for himself. Instead he had forfeited the houses each time. Divorce had rendered him a poor man who ended his youth living on church grounds as the sexton, the maintenance overseer. He had squandered a fortune and he knew it.

As it turned out, he had the good luck of meeting Rose there at the church and when the time was right dwelling in a fine home as partners in a business that allowed them to live well in this breathtaking environment. He was happy and he would do nothing to jeopardize his relationship with Rose. He was getting on in age and had no plans to wander.

So why did his thoughts wander so recklessly? Surely, he had more self-control than this. Danie was limping because of a case of sciatica. Why would he be even a little attracted to her? She was old and he was old.

No, their coupling would be embarrassing for both. Two old flabby bodies slapping together trying to get excited. Rose had put an end to that when he had gained a little too much weight. After he lost the weight, he never lost the floppy stomach. He was a strong man and felt he could manage a good time with a woman. However, Rose had gotten cancer of the bladder, which had to be removed, and now she had to carry the surrogate bladder, a colostomy bag, on the outside. It was an impediment to sex more on her part than on his. It was she who was too self-conscious. He would have accepted any condition because he loved Rose.

"Okay." He said out loud, "I can do this." He headed for the house hoping to find Rose to tell her he loved her.

CHAPTER 20

Rose

Darwin nearly knocked her over. He ran into the house as if on a mission. He grabbed Rose and drew her to him the way he used to when he was feeling amorous.

"What's up? She asked, wondering if she was going to have to put out.

"Oh, nothing." He said a little guiltily. I was just thinking about you and wanted to hold you.

"What brought that on?" She smiled. "You haven't wanted to hold me for a while."

"Come on, I always want to hold you. You don't want to hold me or I would be holding you all of the time."

"Go on." She pulled away. "You know how I feel. I love you but I'm sensitive about love making."

"We don't have to make love, Rose. It's okay. I understand."

She knew he understood and she loved him for it. "But you want to, don't you?"

"Oh well, if I take my Viagra maybe." He smiled that silly, dreamy grin he used to disarm her.

He grabbed her again bending her back so that he could kiss her. "I love you, Rose. That's all" Then, he planted one of his best on her.

Rose crumbled into his arms receiving his kiss with a bit of fervor she didn't know she had. His mouth was smooth and wet, his tongue probing, and his passion overwhelming. "Whoa!" She said as she came up for air. "What is this all about if you don't want sex?"

"Oh, did I say that? Well maybe a little." He let go of her realizing that he was showing a lot more passion than Rose's comfort zone could take. Suddenly he felt overwhelmingly guilty, realizing that he was trying to conquer some thoughts he shouldn't be having. That woman, Danie, had caught him up in a way he did not want. He blushed.

"You're red, Darwin Neumann." She accused. "What are you thinking?"

"What could I be thinking? It's been a long time since I've thought anything at all!"

"You are being silly now. I know you want sex a lot more than you let on."

"Well, it comes up now and again." He smiled sheepishly.

Rose blushed feeling a bit more excited than she had in a while. Why not, she thought. She took Darwin's hand and led him up the stairs to their bedroom where she slowly disrobed taking the urine bad off as discreetly as she could. She took a pad and plastered it to the wound so the urine would not leak. It was a source of embarrassment but she knew Darwin didn't care.

The late afternoon sun shone through the paned glass windows creating shadow patterns across the bed. The dust in the air shone in sun streaks making the room in which they spent so much time seem different — warm, romantic, soft.

Afterwards she lay in his arms the way they had when they first met reveling in the amazing feelings that Darwin always managed to awaken in her. In fact, it was times like this when she couldn't remember why she didn't want sex. Why didn't she always want it? Her lack of enthusiasm did have something to do with her bladder problem but in the back of her mind there still lingered the horrible feelings she'd experienced with her stepfather, Victor.

"I'm going to have that surgery tomorrow. Remember?" Darwin's voice interrupted her thoughts. Back down to earth with a big thud she looked up at him to see how he was feeling. His face was contorted with worry. "I'm not looking forward to tomorrow."

"You'll be fine. This is not a life-threatening operation you know. The worst part is the anesthesia. You are a big man, healthy, and I am sure that won't be a problem."

"I know I'll get through it." He mused without conviction.

"You will." Rose smiled at him wondering if she should let him in on her news about the cancer in her lung. He was too close to his surgery to cancel it so she thought maybe the time was good. She could see him through the worst of his recovery and schedule her surgery then. "I have an issue that may be a bit of a problem."

"What?" He sat up abruptly.

"Don't sit up so quickly, Sweetheart; the blood will rush from your head and you won't be able to think." She placed her hand on his chest and pulled him down next to her. Then, wanting to smooth her way into the subject, she cuddled him and kissed his forehead.

"The doctor called — my oncologist." He struggled against her trying to sit up but she was strong enough to keep him on his back. "The X-ray indicates the cancer has returned. It is in my lung."

"Rose! No!" Tears sprang to his eyes. "Lung cancer is not an easy diagnosis. Did the doctor say what he wanted to do about it?"

"Yes, he wants to remove the part of the lung where the cancer is located."

"When?"

"As soon as possible."

"I'll cancel my surgery and we'll concentrate on you then." He said it with such finality, that she sat up straight and said: "Oh, no you won't! You are going to have your operation and then I will have mine. There is still time."

"When did you learn this Rose?"

"A couple of weeks ago."

"What? You've had this problem for that long and you didn't tell me?" He sat up straight now too.

"I didn't tell you because I knew you would react this way."

"Well of course I react this way." He reached for the phone on the bed stand.

"Darwin Neumann, don't you dare cancel your surgery. You are going to have that operation if I have to drag you kicking and screaming into the surgical theater myself."

"But Rose, it will take another month, at least, for me to recover enough so that you can take the time off. I can't let you wait that long."

"Yes, you can and you will. This spot has been there for a long time and for all that while they have been watching it and it did not grow. It is not a fast-growing tumor and it isn't a metastasized cancer, so we do have time." The doctor had told her that a cancer tumor originating in the lung was not as dangerous as a cancer that had metastasized from another part of the body.

His taut bulk relaxed a little against her and he cried. "Rose, I can't live without you. You must be okay or I won't be okay. Do you understand that?"

"Of course, I do, Sweetheart. I know how you feel because I feel the same." She thought for a minute and said: "I don't know how we are going to do it but we must die at the same moment." She smiled.

"You think God will make the arrangements if we ask nicely?"

They hugged each other and laughed; they could always find something funny to laugh about.

CHAPTER 21

Darwin

He was grumbly, just like the garbage disposal he hadn't gotten around to fixing. He felt like he needed fixing too. Indeed, he was on his way to get fixed.

On this cold foggy morning Darwin's knee hurt more than usual. His things were packed in a small valise by the door and all he had to do was get out of bed, get dressed, brush his teeth and leave. He couldn't eat or drink anything and he was afraid that a stop in the kitchen would cause him to snack on something. A banana would be good. He thought about the soft sweet creamy flavor of a fresh banana and wondered if it would be so awful if he snuck one.

As he reached the bottom of the stairs, he considered the possibility of that banana and began to veer in the direction of the kitchen.

"Don't even think about it!" Rose's voice arose out of the dense quite of the early morning house. She was sitting in her chair as was her habit every morning. It was a kind of meditative practice she had adopted to get her days started. She would sit quietly with a cup of warm coffee in her hands and stare out the window at the array of pine trees just outside. It was a beautiful sight — peaceful, restful — and it put her in a good frame of mind, usually.

This morning was a little different. Darwin surmised she hadn't had enough time to meditate and it was foggy outside which caused the trees to seem like ghosts…No, more like zombies marching through the mist. Her voice was stern and she sounded like her mother.

"I haven't done anything yet. Give me a chance."

"The car is warming up so all you have to do is take your bag and get into the passenger side."

GRRGLEGRUMBLE, GRRGLEGRUMBLE, GRRGLEGRUMBLE… As if on cue, the garbage disposal announced its neglect.

"Oh, shut up!" Darwin intoned trying not to make too much noise. He didn't want to rouse Danie who had announced the night before that she intended to sleep in. So, he took Rose's command seriously, grabbed his valise and marched out the door to the car, still wishing he could eat a stupid banana.

"You haven't fixed the garbage disposal yet." Rose said as she got in and put the car in gear. "What happened? I thought you were going to do that yesterday."

"Rose my darling; I was busy making love to you. Don't you remember?"

She softened. "Oh yes, I do." Deftly Rose backed the vehicle out onto the road. "I remember very well." Her ponytail flipped jauntily around as if to emphasize the recollection.

"Careful. The haze is pretty thick." He laughed. "Believe it or not I would rather have the knee surgery than have an accident in this fog."

"Yes, an accident would be much messier don't you think?"

"Rose, I love you."

CHAPTER 22

Danie

She had the list. It was small, but the amethyst bracelet was going too far. It had been missing for a short while since Bernadine had moved into the house. Danie had asked about the bracelet a couple of times and decided she would have to wait until after the move to figure out whether it had been misplaced or if it had been taken. Naturally, Bernadine said she did not know anything about it. Danie expected that response whether it was true or not.

Another issue was a non-issue. Danie was down to the bottom eighth of a bottle of Magi Noire perfume when Sami and the book club members got together and bought her a new bottle for her birthday. However, the old bottle was gone and she hadn't moved it herself. The cost of the good smelling stuff, even just an eighth of a bottle, was arguably worth the value of an oil well. The price of the bracelet hadn't been that great but it had been a favorite and it matched her amethyst earrings. Danie missed having it and she was at the dormered house to retrieve it, if she could.

The third questioned item was a glass cake plate with a delicate etching of a hummingbird lingering over a fluted flower. It had been a gift she had bought for herself right after she had given her baby boy away, the one she couldn't keep. Within that glass cake plate were the memories she had tried very hard to expel, a gift she had given herself for being so responsible and grownup. She had given it to Bernadine to sell in her village shop because it was such a sad reminder. Now she wondered why she had done that. The woman never said whether it had been sold or not and Danie wanted to know; she wanted it back because she missed having it in spite of its sad meaning.

It was later in the evening than she intended; the quilt meeting took longer than expected. The group had an expert speaker talking about landscape quilting, a subject that fascinated her. Danie loved to create hanging quilts that looked more like paintings. The woman had taught some techniques that could be useful. However, the evening was later than planned and she was concerned about arriving at the dormered house after dark.

Slowly she approached the cottage wondering if Bernadine was home. Remembering a time, a while ago when Wally was still living in the house, his late-night arrival with car headlights ablaze had highlighted the most amazing confluence of events. She had been sleeping in her room with Dusty nuzzled next to her feet keeping them warm. Suddenly a bat flew in through an unscreened window. Dusty, awakening her with his movement, sprang from the bed and caught the rodent in his teeth mid-air bringing it down to the floor. Wally's headlights had caught the whole event highlighting for Danie in her bed and Wally outside the remarkable feat accomplished by the cat.

"Wow, Mom! Did you see that?" He bounded up the stairs to her room excited about the cat's startling feat. Dusty was beginning to eat his catch which was dead in his paws. "Come on Dusty. You don't want to eat that. Not really." Wally gathered up the creature from the disappointed feline, "Good kitty," he said and took the dead bat to a trash receptacle wrapping it in a wad of tissue.

It had been a staggering achievement by the cat, and now Danie was reminded about the headlights lighting up the room so brightly. If Bernadine was home, she didn't want her presence to be known just yet.

Turning off her headlights Danie pulled her Subaru into the dirt parking area outside of the house. There weren't a lot of lights on; those that were cast a warm glow over the porch and down the driveway. She could see the blue-glow of the television in the darkened living room. Bernadine had a habit of sleeping there with the TV on all night, but it didn't seem late enough for her to be asleep. Danie hoped this would be a good time to drop by. Only one thing was out of the ordinary. There was a car parked in the driveway mostly hidden behind a tree. The car looked familiar but it was obscured enough by the tree that Danie couldn't be sure who it belonged to.

She tapped lightly on the front door. A glance through the door's windowpanes revealed movement on the blue corduroy couch in the living room. They were the quick movements of being unexpectedly discovered. She could see a body — two *nude women's* bodies! Embarrassed, Danie quickly moved away from the porch and headed down the driveway. The unrecognized car suddenly gaining recollection in Danie's stunned mind. It belonged to Evilyn Seward!

Danie could hear a voice now; behind her Bernadine called out. "Is anyone there?" Deciding her car was parked too far down the driveway and partially hidden by some bushes that it could not be seen, Danie crept quietly toward it using the broad California Oak trees to conceal her hoping she would not be discovered. She reached it and climbed in as the front door of the house closed. No one had come out to investigate and no one had seen her or the car's interior lights when she opened the door. Danie was surprised. She was sure there would be more investigation. Bernadine probably thought it was a creature outside making a disturbance. Black bears and raccoons, both noisy visitors, were not rare.

Danie hesitated to start her vehicle too soon and sat there ruminating about what she had discovered. Just exactly what was it she had exposed? Her mind raced. The situation had been weird to begin with and now the eviction suddenly made all the sense in the world. Bernadine and Evilyn? Oh my god, she thought. This was why Evilyn had suggested Bernadine as a housemate. She intended all along to get rid of Danie so she and the decorator could have a love-nest all to themselves. "Oh my god." Danie exclaimed quietly. That poor man, the husband, was a patsy of the first order.

His wife was far more cunning than Danie imagined. She had orchestrated this whole eviction so she could have an affair with Bernadine! It was just too amazing to contemplate.

Sitting there pondering, Danie had to wonder if there was anything she could do. Evilyn had been truly mean going to the town's rental agents indicting her as a poor tenant who didn't pay her rent.

Looking back at the time the woman tossed her out, Danie realized Mrs. Seward clearly had a plan. She had called one day and said, "I know the rent is a little high for you. I met a woman who is an interior decorator and she is looking for a place to live. Would you be interested in having a roommate?"

It was a great idea and Danie felt like this was a bit of serendipity — this woman showing up at just the right time to share the expenses looked to her like a miracle.

At first Danie liked the designer, thinking she was being sincere. She quickly realized that was not the case. This move into her home, her space, would become a thorn in her side rather than the miracle she was seeking. She had hoped instead for companionship, someone with whom to drink wine during quiet evenings on the porch. Instead, things turned almost immediately. Bernadine didn't care for Danie's decoration and though she had been nice about it, she began to demand that her furniture replace Danie's. In some cases that was fine. However, when it came to her couch in the living room, that was off limits. They argued but stubborn Danie would not budge. The couch was very comfortable for sleeping as well as sitting; it was also beautiful with gentle, flowing lines and, she thought, much nicer than Bernadine's. Hers was an ordinary blue corduroy sectional, faded in spots, and much too big for the room. Danie had seen the exact same couch in several of the homes she had visited of late. It was a popular style and far too common.

When Danie discovered that Bernadine had spilled the beans to Mrs. Seward about the hole that Wally left behind, neglecting to mention them to Danie so she could do something first, she began to see this was far from being a miracle. The new roommate always played the cheerful, never anything wrong in *her* life, self-absorbed act. Her attitude apparently fascinated Mrs. Seward because Bernadine sure did curry favor from the woman. Bernadine prevailed in the end because Mrs. Seward evicted Danie and hired the decorator to redo her home while she lived there — alone.

Now of course, the whole plot was exposed. Could Danie be just as vindictive and let the town know the truth behind the crafty eviction? This was out of her league. Danie did not feel the least bit adequate outing someone who didn't want to be 'outed'. It wasn't something she could easily do. In fact, she didn't think she could expose the lovers at all. Could she save herself by being revengeful? That was doubtful. In the end she could only make matters worse; of that, she was certain.

The beautiful glass cake plate would have to wait until a better time. Danie hoped she wasn't too late to retrieve it.

CHAPTER 23

Rose

The low-level roar of the sliding pocket-door and Danie's entrance didn't stop Rose who was in the middle of playing with Darwin's hair. The couple, joking around with his long, flowing white mane, looked very much like two people in love. Darwin's thinning hair was cropped into a ponytail on top of his head, the wispy strands hanging in his face. Still recovering from the knee surgery, his bandaged leg rested on the coffee table.

Danie's presence had not yet registered. The sight tickled her and she giggled.

As always, Darwin noticed Danie before anyone else. He swung around almost like a girl and asked, "How do you like it? Don't you think it's...fetching?"

"Well..." Danie tried to suppress her desire to laugh.

"This is what I wake up to every morning!" Rose said with droll dismay.

"You mean, he goes to bed like that every night?" She said incredulously.

"What's the matter? Don't you think I'm just adorable?" He removed the hair band with performance flair and his long flimsy locks flew all over the place lifted by the static electricity in the air. He adopted a feminine posture and batted his eyelashes like a girl.

"Oh, I can't find the words..." Danie answered, chuckling as quietly as possible.

"You look irresistible."

"Well you never know." Rose said under her breath smiling.

"I guess there is reason to believe your hair is a real turn-on." She added.

GRRGLEGRUMBLE, GRRGLEGRUMBLE, GRRGLEGRUMBLE.

"Oh Darwin, when are you going to fix that awful garbage disposal?" Rose's voice turned cold with disgust. She got up dashing to the sink to run the faucet for a moment. The garbage disposal had become the eternal reminder of all that was wrong.

Rose had been complaining to Danie about Darwin while he was still in the hospital. He didn't work hard enough. He didn't try hard enough.

"He spends a fortune feeding the birds — and the squirrels are growing fat eating the leftovers. He spends an inordinate amount of time writing his screenplay about Zombies when he has never sold a screenplay yet. Doesn't he know how hard it is to come from the outside and sell an idea to those on the inside? You know how that business is, Danie. And, why doesn't he notice that he never lands a professional acting job even though he spends plenty of time in his sound room practicing voice-overs and too much time doing plays here in the village?"

"He's a good actor so he should be able to land something." Danie weakly offered.

"Frankly, the whole thing about screenplays is mystifying to me too." Danie said. "He should know how difficult it is. Insiders don't breach their ranks too often; when they do, it's usually with a young person who has exceptionally fresh ideas and more than one concept in mind."

"There are other jobs that he takes on occasion; he can substitute teach or he can work for the road crews here. Those jobs are undesirable for the low pay and the hard work." Rose added.

"People from the community mention they have seen Darwin out on the road crew..." Danie said. "...working in the hot sun on his feet all day and not looking very well. They say he shouldn't be working so hard."

"Well I feel differently. It is good exercise. Darwin is a hardy soul and he is years younger than I am. I do more than anyone else even with my health problems."

However, Rose had trouble accepting Darwin's lax attitude. Her mother had been a taskmaster; she had pushed Rose until she was imbued with an unstoppable work ethic. She had nagged Darwin just as her mother had endlessly complained to her.

Rose confessed to Danie that her mother had come to live with them in the room Danie was staying. During that time while her health began to deteriorate, "Mother became more and more critical of Darwin and his sloppy habits." Though Rose was disappointed with her husband's poor routine, she saw many of the good things too. "I married him for love and affection which I have gotten in spades. And I love his sense of humor." She exclaimed. "Who wouldn't?

"Nevertheless, Mom was right and I took over the criticism after she went to the nursing home." Her eyes filled with tears. "She just passed away not long ago."

"It's hard to lose your mom. Is your dad gone, too?" Danie asked.

"Oh yes, my real dad passed away when I was very young."

"Then you are an orphan. I am too — have been for a long time."

Rose smiled. "I have Darwin." Her response was a little smug and she was right to be happy with her choice. No one is perfect after all. "Darwin has many wonderful attributes." Rose knew she was foolish to be so critical. Sometimes, she forgot how lucky she was to have him.

GRRGLEGRUMBLE...

CHAPTER 24

Danie

At last, it was time to get her tooth. Since she lost the temporary, Danie had been running around with that center tooth missing, which made her look a little daft. Although her experience with the people on the mountain had taught her that most folks do not look and don't care. Her years in the movie business made her especially sensitive to the way she appeared. A lot had been expected of her when she was in the public eye. Her appearance mattered little now. However, as philosophical as she could get about it, Danie was anxious to have these problems of the tooth and the nose finally over. Other people may not care about a funny looking nose and a missing tooth, but when she studied herself in the mirror, she found she cared, a lot.

Her concerns were mollified when she discovered at the club that many people were walking around with missing teeth. Until hers was gone, she had never noticed that half the population of Dancing Bear Springs were missing teeth. Most of them were seniors waiting, as she was, for an implant.

The inlaid tooth was a process in two parts. The periodontist did the surgical part of implanting the metal stump to which the false tooth would attach. Part 2, the tooth, would be completed by the dentist. Her office was in the village. At least, Danie wouldn't have to drive all the way down the freeway into town to get the tooth. The drive was always harrowing.

Two problems arose almost as soon as she entered the dentist's village office. Right off the bat she was faced with a conundrum. Wally's former girlfriend, the one who ratted on him at the town meeting about dealing meth, was staffing the front office. Sally Oliver who had dark brown hair and eyes and sported two adorable dimples in her cheeks, was otherwise indistinctive in her looks. However, she was quite memorable for her decoration. Danie's sense of propriety which was not exactly conventional, felt offended. The woman was dressed more for a late-night date than for an office setting. The tight midnight jersey dress clung to her ample body with tenacity and the cleavage between her hiked up boobs rivaled the gulf between the Grand Tetons. So, everyone would notice, she had strung a long chain of deep blue baubles from her neck that formed a tributary between her huge breasts. A pair of earrings added a touch of spray.

Danie stopped in the doorway not confident she could enter the anteroom. Afraid of what she might say or do in this woman's presence, she hesitated just long enough to evoke a "Come on in, Ms. Wharton. I won't bite."

Embarrassed, she tried to imply she was only hesitating to catch her breath. "Those stairs are a bitch. I'm getting too old for climbing." She smiled secretly hoping Wally's old girlfriend couldn't read her mind as she worked at not staring at the woman's mountainous boobs. "I'm here to see Dr. Erlich."

"Come in and sit down. She'll be with you in a moment — finishing up with another patient. I don't think she'll be too long." Her voice was cheerful which Danie felt was helpful.

"Thank you." She sighed as she sat on a small love seat set against the wall adorned with cheap wallpaper. She looked around and noticed a huge picture window behind the desk that Sally occupied. The beautiful peaks that surrounded Dancing Bear Springs were cuddled with white clouds that looked like a comforter tossed upon the mountainous ridge as if warming a sleeping giant. Aside from the sound of some crackling paper as Sally worked, Danie could hear the intense silence of the village, so unlike the incessant noise of the city.

"I read your book." Sally added shortly. "I liked it a lot. You were very honest."

"Thank you. Have you ever wished you could be in the movie business?" It was a question she often asked when someone mentioned reading her memoir.

"Gosh, doesn't everybody?"

"Well no, not really. I get a lot of different answers to that question."

"I've been doing plays here during our Shakespeare Festival in the summertime. But, I'm probably too old to get started in Hollywood."

Danie was tempted to tell her she should consider going to Hollywood and giving it try, just to be rid of the woman here near her son. Thinking better of it she softened. "No one is really too old. It depends on what you want to accomplish."

"I guess if I wanted to be a super-star, I would be a little too late."

"Probably." Danie fell silent wondering if she should speak to this Sally Oliver about what she had done to Wally and how wrong she had been to do it when the dentist came running into the anteroom.

Dr. Erlich was short and thin with officious looking glasses poised on her nose. "I can't believe it!" She screamed in an accent that sounded Eastern European that Danie couldn't identify. "The lab sent the set without the correct instrument. The one they sent is too short. I can't get the tooth out of its little slot. I don't know what we can do."

"Oh no!" Sally offered. The office erupted into a small storm of activity as the dentist and her assistant went to work figuring out what to do.

Danie knowing what the outcome would be — she wasn't getting her tooth today — picked up a magazine. No use getting upset she thought. The situation will not be resolved until the lab sends the right tool.

At last the dentist left the room once she was satisfied the problem was resolved. The new implement would be delivered in a couple of days and then they would finish the job. Danie got up to leave and stopped at the door.

"Sally, is it alright if I call you by your first name?"

"Of course." She answered hesitantly.

"Please, feel free to call me Danie. I just need an answer to a question."

"Shoot." She said.

"Why did you lie about Wally at the town meeting?"

"I like you Danie. But your son is a piece of work."

"We can't argue about what my son is like. I'm asking you why you lied."

"I didn't lie."

Danie drew herself up. Not good in confrontations, she hadn't expected to have to defend Wally. "He was a user. That was established when he got the help he needed and quit the habit."

"I'm glad to hear that."

"I'm surprised you didn't know. This is a small town."

"He used and he sold."

"No, he didn't sell." Danie said in measured tones.

"What's the difference?" Sally turned obstinate.

"Oh, come on, Sally. Big difference. However, whether he was guilty or not I find it reprehensible that you would rat him out like that, especially since he has straightened himself out now."

"I was warning the community." Her voice wanted to rise in anger. Nevertheless, she was wise to remain controlled.

"And, you think that justifies you?"

"Yes, I do." She answered emphatically.

"I have a situation myself that may warrant an airing. Since you think what you did was justified, maybe you'll think what I want to do might be justified too." Danie replied.

Sally was surprised with this U-turn on the conversational road. "Shoot."

"I was evicted recently from my home; it was the home I loved in which I expected to spend the rest of my days. The landlady was malicious and lied to the real estate people up here telling them I didn't pay my rent when in fact I did. I paid her every penny she had coming. Yet she chose to be deceitful."

"That's awful. Have you found a place to live? Didn't I hear you are staying at the Laughing Bear?"

"You did. And I have been blocked from renting any property up here because of what she said."

"Wow!" Sally exclaimed.

"That's not all. I have recently discovered she evicted me because she is having an affair with my former roommate. Apparently, she — they — wanted privacy."

"That's a pretty complicated situation. You were living with a man and she took him from you while evicting you at the same time?"

"No, I was living with a woman. She and I were friends, nothing more."

"Oh… My god!" Sally seemed as stunned as Danie had felt when she discovered the couple. "Did you know your roommate was gay?"

"No, I didn't. She told me she had been a firefighter when she was young. I guess that should have been my first clue. She was also highly competitive like a man. I'm not sure those are indicative of homosexuality, but I never thought about it until I made my discovery. I didn't have a clue about the land lady."

Danie continued in a different tone. "I would love to go before the community meeting and rat this woman out. I'm furious with her. Do you think I should?"

"Sure. It's what I'd do."

Slowly Danie responded measuring her words. "I know her husband and he's a very sweet person who doesn't deserve to discover his wife of many years with whom he has reared children is having an affair with a woman." Danie turned to the door to leave. Then: "I'm fairly sure it would be a terrible shock to him. And there are the kids, old enough now to understand the situation."

"So, what are you going to do?"

"The man will have to find out some other way. I can't do it to him." Danie was about to leave, changed her mind and turned back. "Let me be clear; if I did tell him, it would be a vindictive action and it would seem that I am homophobic, neither of which I am. Well, I do feel vindictive Sally, but to act on that would be reprehensible, in my own opinion."

Danie walked out of the office noting the clamor of silence she left behind in the room.

CHAPTER 25

Rose

The person standing on the front porch waiting for someone to answer her knock was Rose's age of seventy-nine, yet she looked much older. Her hair was a dark shade of steel gray which emphasized the wrinkles on her face.

"Eugenia Steinholtz!" Rose barely recognized her when she answered the door. She was tall like Rose although she had a good deal more weight on her. Two suitcases sat on either side of the woman.

"Are you going to invite me in Dear?" she said in a markedly German accent. "It is a bit icy out here." Her words were sharp and biting like the cold wind coming through the entrance to the B&B; the hoot of a lone owl penetrated the usual silence.

"My god of course," Rose replied backing away to allow her friend through the door. "I would answer you in German but I barely remember anything. My mother and I never spoke it again after we came here." She opened her arms to welcome Eugenia; the woman lowered her bags and stepped forward to hug Rose. She felt like a hunk of lard in her embrace. "How wonderful to see you again. What brings you here to the Laughing Bear B&B?"

"I could not come all the way from our homeland and not look up my good friends."

Rose remembered the woman as a German sympathizer she had gone to school with just before she left the country of her birth. Eugenia had been much thinner with an impressive auburn mane and gorgeous big brown eyes. Rose felt suddenly saddened to see this woman after so many years. Time had not been very kind to her.

"Please come into my home." Rose murmured. "Stand by the fireplace and warm yourself. Let me have your coat — I'll hang it up in the coat closet right here," she said indicating the correct door.

"This is your home? I thought it was the inn here in town."

"It is. My husband, Darwin, and I own it, live in it, and run it. We have a good thriving business here. Do you need a room?"

"I do. Thank you." She said. "I hope you have suitable quarters for tonight."

Rose thought suitable or not there were few other choices in the village. "I have three fine rooms. They are all upstairs. One is the Lilac room, there is the Pine Valley room, and finally the Round-up room."

"Wieviel kosted das Flieder zimmer?" She asked in her best German.

Rose understood her, "It's the same as the other rooms. They are all $100.00 for the night."

"The price is extremely reasonable compared with what I have seen in Los Angeles! I am surprised."

"But, Eugenia. You are a good friend from home and I want you to have the room on me — for tonight." Though she was glad to see her friend she was beginning to hope the woman's stay would be short — like one night.

Just then Danie emerged from her room marching through the kitchen to the great room. "Hello," she said, "My name is Danie." She had made a habit of welcoming people to the inn whenever she was around. "I'm Daniela Wharton." Rose noticed that Danie was good at advancing her book and she liked to establish relationships with the roomers so she could sell her memoir which she promoted unabashedly.

"In fact, I am a big fan, Miss Wharton." Said Eugenia as she took Danie's proffered hand. "I certainly did not think I would be meeting one of my favorite celebrities right here in Dancing Bear Springs." Eugenia's face miraculously lightened.

"Thank you." Danie responded wincing from the handshake. "You are German. You must be a friend of Rose's from there."

"Ja. Guilty as charged," she said trying out an American cliché. "I say it right, Okay?" It seemed to Rose that Eugenia was uneasy meeting Danie. Her perfect English seemed to fail her for a moment.

Danie had become a huge asset for the B&B with her greetings and subsequent offerings of a card advertising her book. It seemed to make the customers happy that they had met an actual movie star. And of course, it helped book sales. When Danie wasn't in the room the guests would often go on and on about the stories they had heard about her 'back in the day.' The excitement made it easier for Rose to run the inn without having to constantly entertain the folks.

Darwin was good at the entertainment part. When he was around, he would chat people up with flair and with the certainty that what he was saying was acceptable. It was always a huge relief when he stepped up the rhetoric. Rose felt inadequate in this regard. She had a hard time thinking of things to say when Darwin just talked and talked without a single thought at all. His mind worked fast and he filled in any lulls at the breakfast table with an amazing amount of information always imbuing the time with robust facts, opinions, witticisms and retorts that would bring on uproarious laughter. It was truly a talent he possessed and she did not. When she spoke, the guests would smile politely but rarely laughed out loud.

Eugenia wandered further into the great room examining the furniture, paintings on the walls, which were mostly Rose's, and the breathtaking views outside. "This is very nice Rose. You have done well."

Rose didn't know why but she suddenly felt like she was back in the presence of her mother.

"Eugenia," Danie interrupted. "Did I pronounce your name correctly?"

"Ja. You do fine."

"If you are interested in reading my memoir, I have a card here that tells you the details about how to order your copy." She offered the woman the card which she took and read.

"Oh, very nice. But do you not have a copy here that I could buy?"

"Well yes I do. I don't usually sell from my stash of books, just at autograph shows. But I'll make an exception since you have come from so far away. Would you like it signed?"

"Oh, very nice, ja, ja," she replied excitedly.

For a moment Rose could swear she saw the girl she used to know. Eugenia's eyes again became large dark pools like cups of black coffee. Danie told her the price of a signed copy and left to get one from her suite.

"Let me show you to your room." Rose interjected. "The Lilac room is lovely. I am sure you will be very comfortable. The bathroom upstairs is shared by the three rooms." Rose started up the stairway. "No one else has reservations for tonight so you won't have to worry about that."

"It is not a problem. I am used to sharing."

"You must tell me all about your life in Germany now. I haven't talked to anyone from there is ages. Needless to say, I was thrilled when that horrible Berlin wall finally came down."

"That was such a long time ago." Eugenia responded a little surprised. She seemed to have a bit of trouble getting up the stairs. Arthritis, Rose assumed.

"I know, I know. It's just that I am bereft of news from home. When we left — my mother and I — no one else from our family was there. Most of them were dead by that time — the death camps you know."

"Many people believe that about the so-called death camps."

Rose heard her words but could not believe them. Was the woman saying she didn't believe in the gas chambers that had killed six million

Jews? She decided to drop the subject because she wouldn't know what to say if Eugenia was in denial.

"Yes, they certainly do here."

Eugenia entered the offered room and began to inspect it. She looked into drawers, under the bed, and behind the antique washbasin. Rose was surprised she didn't strip the bed and inspect for bed bugs.

The room was her favorite because of the Lilacs. Dancing Bear Springs was famous for its Lilac bushes in the springtime. They blossomed abundantly almost every year. The room depicted the blossoming beautifully.

"Everything is in good order." Rose said a little defensively.

"Yes, yes, I can see for myself."

"Well I'll leave you to settle yourself in. Darwin, my husband, will bring your bags up in just a minute."

"Danka."

Rose closed the door and stood there staring at it when Darwin, still hobbling from his surgery, came up the stairs struggling with Eugenia's bags. "These stairs aren't getting any easier." He said.

"My Darling. I am so sorry." She turned realizing how heavy the suitcases were. "I should have done that."

"No, no. I'm not a cripple."

"You are still healing! You shouldn't be doing anything this difficult." She grabbed one of the suitcases and dragged the heavy piece of luggage across the floor to Eugenia's door. "Eugenia, your bags are here already. Darwin is trying to impress me with his manhood — he brought both bags up despite his recent knee surgery."

The door opened just as Danie arrived at the head of the stairwell with a copy of her book. "Oh, I was not expecting the whole family." Eugenia said as she stepped out.

"Danie isn't really family," Darwin noted. "She is our resident movie star."

"Yes, I have heard, and I am thrilled to meet her. She is bringing me her book. It is signed, no?" She asked Danie.

"It is signed, yes." She responded with a big smile. "I hope you read it and let me know what you think."

"I will. Be very sure."

"I am Darwin Neumann." Darwin held out his enormous hand. "We haven't met yet."

"Eugenia Steinholtz." She took his hand. Darwin grimaced.

"Very nice to meet you, Ms. Steinholtz. I hope you enjoy your stay here," he said trying to cover his reaction to the pain.

"Danka. You are German too, ja? Neumann is very Germanic."

"My ancestors were. I am an American." He said proudly.

"Ah yes. America today remind me of my homeland. There are those here who call this country 'The Homeland' as well. Do you suppose they will elect the blond business man?"

"Oh, do you think he will make a good president?"

"He reminds me of the Fuhrer…before the war." She added.

"You could not be old enough Eugenia," Rose declared. "We are the same age."

"My family loved the Fuhrer. I heard all of the stories and I saw him once when I was very young." She pondered for a moment. "His eyes were cold but he was very handsome." She smiled.

At that moment, each of the three said a collective "Oh… Goodnight, Ms. Steinholtz, and dispersed down the stairway. The door thankfully closed behind them as they slithered away.

"Did you hear what she said?" Darwin was the one to break the silence. "Rose, where did you find Eugenia? It appears she never got over the Fuhrer." He said 'Fuhrer' with his best German accent. Then when he was way out of earshot, he broke into a hardly chuckle.

"I went to school with her briefly." Rose answered. "My mother and I lived in Berlin and we escaped to Brussels — it was just in time, otherwise I would have ended up speaking Russian." She laughed. "Eugenia and I became fast friends when I started at the academy; then she cooled. She may have learned that my mother was part Jew. I've heard of Germans who loved the Fuhrer and who never gave up on him. Some actually believe he survived and ran to Argentina."

"I've heard that." Danie interjected. "A lot of German nationals ended up there didn't they?"

"I believe so. Maybe Eugenia should have gone with them!"

Just then another knock at the front door interrupted the three as they commiserated on their new 'neighbor.' Darwin answered as Danie headed for her room.

"Good evening, Sir." He boomed his best greeting to the new guest. "Welcome to the Laughing Bear Bed and Breakfast."

CHAPTER 26

Darwin

The sudden appearance of Eugenia Steinholtz was unsettling. Darwin wasn't sure why, but he had a dread about the woman. She was big and ugly even though Rose swore she was beautiful as a young girl. She had ample breasts and her clothes, mostly suits, fit like a condom. Darwin was uncomfortable, guilty really, with this image of a condom wrapped tightly around her. It was the only impression that came to mind.

Rose seemed nervous too. He didn't like the effect Eugenia was having on her. She became obsessively clean and neat even though her normal habits were quite fine. She seemed to think she had something to prove. She doubled her laundry load and made sure to rescue the sheets from the dryer right after the buzzer signaled the items were dry. Unlike her usual attentiveness she became compulsive about wrinkles in the sheets smoothing them especially at the edges where they tended to curl up. If a sheet was too wrinkled, she ironed it. She tackled the kitchen with her cleaning materials and when she was done the room was genuinely sterile enough to eat off the floor. Her mother would be proud.

"Good evening." Eugenia appeared coming down the stairway.

"Good evening." Darwin responded politely.

"I am reading Ms. Wharton's memoir. It is fascinating. I should finish it by morning."

"You will be reading all night?" He said it as a question, truly curious.

"I am fast, even in English. It is one of my talents."

"You must love to read."

"In many languages." She said. "I am retired now of course but when I was active, I was a translator of every kind of book into German."

"That must have been very interesting. What do you think of Danie's book so far?"

"She is a good writer. I think it is worth reading. Have you read it?"

"Hollywood memoirs are not my thing though I plan to read it anyway. Rose has read it and she liked it."

"Memoirs are not my think either." She said mistaking Darwin's reference to 'thing.'

He decided not to mention the error; he was pleased that she had put a chink in his perception of her perfectionism. Eugenia looked more human to him now.

She continued. "I like that she is so honest. That alone makes this an unusual memoir. Most people when writing about themselves tend to 'polish the apple' so to speak." Eugenia seemed to appreciate American sayings, especially the trite ones.

"Your recommendation makes me curious. I'll have to read it soon."

"She had quite a reputation back then. She does not try to cover it up like some people would do."

"Rose thinks she's too honest, that she could have softened some of the edges. I guess I'll find out what she means by that."

GRRGLEGRUMBLE, GRRGLEGRUMBLE, GRRGLEGRUMBLE...

"Sorry, that's the garbage disposal. I've been putting off fixing it hoping my knee could heal before I have to get down on the floor to tackle it."

"Ah, procrastination." Eugenia said with a certain glee. "My mother would say it is a bad habit."

"Your mother would not be the first."

Darwin resented Eugenia's reminder. It wasn't that he didn't want to do the work or that he was too lazy; it was that he hurt. His knee wasn't sufficiently healed to bend down enough and get under the sink. He wanted to explain this to her but he knew it would sound like a weak excuse.

"Yeah, your mother would not be the first." He added irreverently.

CHAPTER 27

Danie

"Good morning Neighbor!" As always, Darwin's voice rose from out of the early morning light.

"Good morning Darwin. Didn't we have a guest last night? Someone other than Eugenia. I heard someone leave early this morning."

"Yup. He left at 5:00 a.m."

"Before I went to bed last night you mentioned he was drinking. That was pretty early."

"Sure did. He came by about six and said he had bought a house up here and was out celebrating. Smelled like liquor then. He rented the Round-up room upstairs and promptly returned to the bar to resume his celebration."

"What time did he get back here?"

"It was morning about one."

"One a.m.? He'd been drinking the whole time?"

"I believe so. Kept me up."

Shocked by the news she asked, "What does he do for a living?"

"Said he runs the fuel rods for a nuclear reactor." He chided.

Danie's amused hoot was loud enough to awaken the whole household.

"Shhhhhhh! He said grabbing her mouth instinctively. We have a guest — Eugenia, remember?"

Danie froze. "My nose still hurts." She reacted grimacing.

"Gosh, I'm sorry. I didn't mean to."

"I know." She held her face cupping her nose to protect it as she contorted in pain. "I'll be okay in a minute." Darwin hovered over her like a mother hen.

"Good morning." Another voice, this one with a German accent, emerged from the dim front room. Eugenia was fully dressed and coiffed making Danie feel self-conscious in her morning robe with her hair tied up in a knot.

"Is there any coffee available?" Her voice expressed an undercurrent of disapproval.

Danie suddenly felt compromised as if she had done something wrong. "Yes, there is some brewing at the coffee service over there," she said pointing in the direction of the dining area.

"I hope we didn't wake you Eugenia." Darwin interjected. "I was joking with Danie here about our other guest last night. I hope he didn't keep you awake."

"No, I sleep like infant. No problem for me." She headed for the coffee maker to pour a cup.

Darwin and Danie suddenly felt the need to get busy. They scurried around the kitchen in a mad fury to fix things.

"Eugenia, do you like eggs and bacon for breakfast?" Darwin inquired. "We also have pancakes and fruit — your pick."

"Pancakes and fruit sound very good. Do you have yogurt too?"

"Sure do." He was being cheerful to a fault.

Danie felt awkward, though she wasn't sure why. Eugenia cast an odd pall on the house. Her presence was chilling. She wondered if all Germans were like that. Danie had never been to Germany though she had ancestors from there. She had heard the German psyche was cold because of the weather.

Rose was far from cold. She was one of the warmest people she knew. She recalled the afternoon recently when Rose had asked Danie to pose for her nude. She had been enormously embarrassed to ask the question. "Danie, I am going to ask you a question that is very uncomfortable for me."

"Oh dear, you want me to move."

"Heavens no!" She had responded. "That is the last thing I want you to do. I am hoping you can agree to pose for me. I want to do a painting of you."

"Rose, I'm so honored."

"Nude." She looked embarrassed just suggesting such a thing. She turned a deep red.

"Oh." Danie responded startled." After recovering from her surprise, she answered, "Rose I am not the young thing I used to be. My body is old and lumpy. Maybe you should consider someone younger."

"No, I want old and lumpy." She stopped suddenly hearing what she just said. "Danie, I am sorry. I didn't mean that quite the way it sounded."

Danie giggled and looked at her perplexed. "Well gosh Rose, if that's what you want."

"I want to explore the older body. Everybody does young and gorgeous. How many nudes out there are of elderly people? Not many and I want to help break the mold.

I really see the elder body as being quite beautiful and I think I can express that, if you will let me."

"Rose thank you. That is a wonderful idea. I will be happy to accommodate you. When do you want to get started?"

"After my cancer surgery."

"What?"

"I suppose no one told you. I have lung cancer."

Danie's eyes stung with tears. "Rose. Lung cancer! That's awful." Lung cancer was practically a death sentence. One of her best friends had died within months of such a diagnosis.

"I know it sounds really bad, but this tumor has been there for a while and they were keeping an eye on it for all that time. It just started to grow recently so they are very hopeful the surgery will take care of it."

"When will you do this? Have you scheduled the operation yet?"

"Yes, I have. End of next week. I'll go into the hospital last of the month. I'm pretty optimistic."

"Rose, you are one of the most positive people I've ever met. If anyone should be okay it's you." Danie wiped her eyes embarrassed that she had reacted so viscerally. "But, what about the inn? Will Darwin be up to the job while you are recuperating?"

"He will do his best, I am sure." She answered with a little dismay in her voice.

"I'll help. Don't worry. I'll make sure everything looks clean and neat." She declared. "And we will do this nude posing thing as soon as you are well enough."

The expression on Rose's face softened — knowing that her needs would be met, she was able to release a great deal of tension.

That was a day before Eugenia showed up. Danie wondered how long the German woman intended to stay. No matter how private the sitting would be, she would feel completely exposed if that woman was still in the house.

CHAPTER 28

Rose

As it turned out, Eugenia stayed at the B&B for two nights threatening to stay longer which threw Rose into a funk. Her surgery was scheduled for the end of the week and she wasn't certain the woman would leave by then. She cleaned the morning breakfast table with a flurry she hadn't known in a while. Eugenia's standards were overwhelming and Rose felt like she had to work twice as hard as she did before just to meet unspoken expectations. She practically threw dishes into the dishwasher.

"Whoa Rose." Danie came into the kitchen just as one of the plates cracked with the pressure. "Everything okay?"

"No, not really. I never liked that plate anyway." As she tossed the broken pottery into the trash, she lowered her voice hoping Eugenia was out of earshot. "I am due to go into the hospital and Eugenia is still here. I can't tell what her plans are. She doesn't respond when I ask how long she intends to stay."

"Oh, oh." Danie matched the quiet of her voice. "Do you suppose she can afford to be here indefinitely?"

"How do I know? She claims to have been a single professional woman all these years. I suppose she made some money. She probably saved if she didn't have any children. I don't want to be rude to her, but I sure do wish she would make some indication that she is leaving soon."

"Maybe I can throw a hint in her direction."

"No don't. It will be fine. I am probably over-reacting."

Later, Rose discovered Eugenia sitting on the couch knitting a sweater. The afternoon light was fading and she turned on a lamp next to her so she could see.

"Danka."

"You are welcome," she responded as she sat on the settee opposite her guest. "Eugenia, I am due to go into the hospital at the end of this week for surgery."

"Oh, my goodness. I hope it is nothing too serious."

"It is lung cancer but I am hopeful the problem will be resolved with the surgical procedure."

"Lung cancer is not a good diagnosis." She lowered the knitting to her lap.

"No, of course it isn't. We have caught it early."

"Das ist gut." Eugenia sounded truly sympathetic. "Perhaps I should stay on and help out here at the B&B. I certainly wouldn't mind."

"No, no. That won't be necessary. Darwin and Danie can handle everything," she responded trying not to indicate her alarm if Eugenia should stay. "Where is your next destination?"

"I am planning a trip to San Francisco then on to Seattle. But Rose, are you sure you want to leave Darwin and Danie alone in this house? Together?"

"Why wouldn't I?"

"Well, I wouldn't want to speak out of turn but I have witnessed things here between them."

"Oh no Eugenia. I can't believe there is anything…" Rose hesitated.

"To worry about?"

"GRRGLEGRUMBLE, GRRGLEGRUMBLE, GRRGLEGRUMBLE."

"Lord, that garbage disposal! I wish Darwin would just fix it." Rose covered trying to skip the subject. She didn't want to raise questions about Danie, especially right now when she needed her so much.

"Yes. I don't believe that at all!" Rose stood up to warm her suddenly chilled skin by the fireplace. "They are fine here together. It is just a lot of work that needs doing. I am only a little worried it won't get done the way I like it. Like for instance that garbage disposal!"

"Darwin needs guidance. He needs to be told what he should do, right?"

"Yes, that seems to be true. If he has a definite list, he will accomplish it."

"I am good at making lists." Eugenia smiled. She smiled so little, Rose felt like she'd received a warm splash of water.

"GRRGLEGRUMBLE, GRRGLEGRUMBLE."

"I think you should go to San Francisco. Enjoy your trip. I am sure that will be better than staying here making lists. Danie will do what needs doing."

"Isn't she more used to being waited on? Eugenia added carefully. "After reading her book, my guess is she won't be much use waiting on others. She must be spoiled by her life in Hollywood."

"I like Danie. She is even-tempered; she adds a great deal to the life here at the inn; she even buys products to add to our pantry. She is very generous." Pausing only to think of something else Rose added, "And she pitches in now and again with dishes, laundry and gardening.

"She is very likeable. In addition, she is a whore."

"Not really a whore; she was…sexually active. That was before. Remember, she had that epiphany so to speak and decided she could never do that again?"

"I do not believe people change. What is the saying? I love American sayings. A tiger can't change its spots — something like that."

"It is stripes, but that is good enough."

"Oh yes of course, it is stripes." She demurred.

"Nevertheless, I do believe people can be redeemed." Rose added.

"Redeemed maybe. Changed, I don't know."

"Isn't being redeemed the same as being changed?"

"I don't think so. I think a person can make amends for something and then go out and do the same thing over again. Temptation can be overwhelming."

"Have you been overwhelmed with such temptation Eugenia?" It was impossible for Rose to imagine Eugenia in love.

"Oh yes." She suddenly took on the essence of a young girl. "It was when I was very young of course, but I did have one affair I never got over."

"Never?" Rose questioned. "You said you were 'very young'. Isn't that kind of temptation reserved for the very young?"

Her demeanor changed. "No Rose. You need to think twice about leaving her here with him alone."

When Rose awakened from her lung surgery, she found Darwin by her bed holding her hand. He seemed to be praying. She felt the old leaden arm of disappointment well up. "Darwin Neumann, what are you doing here? You are supposed to be at the inn taking care of things." She barely had a voice.

"You don't have to worry. Danie's taking care of it."

"She isn't supposed to *run* the inn. She is a guest." Just then a searing pain attacked her lung. "Awhhhhhhhhgh." She screamed.

"Rose! My god what's happening?"

"Awhhhhhhhhgh!" She screamed again.

Darwin hit the button to get help. "Rose, baby. Please, are you okay?" He knew it was a stupid question and she looked at him out of her pain with that derisive expression she had so perfected. "Rose, I can't stand to see you in pain!"

She knew he couldn't.

A nurse came running. Her first action was to check the intravenous lines to make sure they were clear, then she looked at the bag of medicine being pumped into Rose to see if all was working properly. "This is fine. She may need another sedative — something a little stronger. I'll check with the doctor."

"Please hurry. I can't stand to see her this way." Darwin added as if the nurse would not know that.

The pain took over and exploded Rose's body. "Awhhhhhhhhgh." She could barely breathe.

"Rose darling. Try to take deep breaths and relax."

She couldn't speak and she thought that she hated Darwin just then. It wasn't that she didn't want to breathe or that she wouldn't breathe if she could. The pain in her chest was searing and was just too much. She was beginning to panic. What if this was it? What if this pain was the harbinger of her demise? Tears stung her eyes as she tried her best to stop screaming.

The nurse unable to do anything for her rushed out of the room to call the doctor.

"Rose please try to relax. Tensing up around the pain doesn't help."

"Darwin Neumann, I caaaaaannn't!" she shrieked.

He dropped her hand and ran from the room. She could hear him even in the midst of the pain: "Nurse, nurse! Please, you must do something!" He grabbed the first official looking person he could find walking by and pulled the man in. "You have to help my wife!" He insisted. "She is screaming in pain."

"Yes Sir. I can hear her." The man, a lab technician, was obviously help-less to be of service. "I can't help you — it isn't my job."

"Awhhhhhhhhgh."

The hapless man raised his voice in an effort to overcome the sound of Rose's scream. "The nurse will be here in a moment, I'm sure."

"She just left!" Darwin shouted. "She didn't do anything but look at that thing."

"She was doing her job!" The man shouted back. "She can't do anything more Sir."

"Awhhhhhhhhgh." Rose screamed again helpless to do anything else.

"I can't stand to hear her like this. Do something! Somebody has to do something for my wife." Darwin was panicking which Rose knew, even in the midst of the throbbing pain, was damaging to her cause.

"Darwin," she croaked. "Please, the man can't do anything." She gagged out the words. "We will have to wait for the nurse to return."

The unfortunate man faded from the room taking his cue from Rose. "Sorry Ma'am. I hope you feel better very soon."

Rose moaned a response. As he left, Darwin mimed a knife attack on the man's back. "He's wearing a white jacket. He should do something." He whispered to Rose.

Just at that moment, the nurse returned with a hypodermic needle in her gloved hand. "This should take care of that pain very soon." She quickly inserted the needle into Rose's IV. The agonizing pain in Rose's lung overcame everything. She couldn't think, so she groaned instead. "Oh God, please help me." She prayed.

Darwin's eyes were filled with tears. Rose could do nothing for him and she wanted to stop everything that was happening at this moment. "Darwin, please go home." She croaked.

"I can't go home until I know you're alright." He tried to steady his voice but it was hopeless. He was just as distressed as she was.

"But you know you can do nothing here. At least, at home — awghhhhh — you can take care of the guests."

"I would only worry and be useless."

"Darwin please. Do as I ask. I can't bear to have you here now." Her voice faded with that and she dropped off into a Morphine-induced slumber.

CHAPTER 29

Darwin

Dejected and feeling inadequate, Darwin headed home. He couldn't help his wife in the hospital or out. He felt totally laughable as a man, as a helper, as a lover (well, maybe not so bad a lover), or as husband to take away all of Rose's pain, her anxiety, her obsession with hard work and the need to prove herself. He thought she was perfect. Why couldn't she see herself that way?

All she seemed to do was worry and get upset with him when everything wasn't just right. She needed perfection...even in her paintings. Instead of drawing or painting freehand, she would take photographs she had found and cut them out like the cutouts little girls loved to do. Then she would use the pattern as an outline. He had seen her cut out a photo — the eyes of an owl — and trace the opening in the picture to make the size and the placement of the eyes look perfect. It was a technique she had refined to make the work go faster and to achieve the precision she felt about so strongly. Absolute perfection was her goal.

He wasn't sure about the technique because he wasn't an artist. His introduction to fine art had been the movie about Vincent van Gogh, "Lust for Life." The movie about van Gogh's decent into madness had impressed him deeply. Rose had managed to be an artist all these years without going out of her mind, though Darwin wondered how. She could not accept imperfection in any form even though she had managed to accept him. Well, she had married him — acceptance had come harder in their relationship and he wasn't sure she did accept him. In fact, the more he thought about it, the less accepted he felt. He could never live up to the image she had of the husband she wanted. That man would be perfect in every way; this he knew.

Eugenia had thankfully left on a day before Rose went to the hospital for her surgery. His wife had seemed so relieved to see her go that Darwin wondered about some of the conversations that had gone on between them. In fact, Rose had acted strangely in the course of those days. It wasn't something he had thought consciously about, but now on the long trek up the freeway to get home, he had time to ruminate about how things had been before the woman left. He had started to feel observed. It wasn't exactly like being spied on, but there seemed to be an awful lot of scrutiny of him, his schedule and plans.

Rose had suddenly found it necessary to write lists of things for him to do when she was in the hospital. She didn't seem to want Danie involved at all in any of the jobs that Rose did normally. She was fine if Danie greeted the guests but she wanted her to be uninvolved in anything else. It was weird.

The next morning, he awakened to the sound of the aging washing machine which had a bad habit of vibrating madly when it went into rinse and spin mode. It made a huge racket. Danie had gotten an early start on the laundry. It was time to get up anyway so he put on his robe which was not his habit — he usually got completely dressed — and meandered down the stairway to the great room. The dogs scurried awake suddenly aware their master was up and on his way to the kitchen. They romped down the stairway right behind him saving their stretches for later.

There she was standing over the sink, washing dishes that couldn't be cleaned in the dishwasher. Danie's white luminous hair was caught up into a knot on top of her head and she almost glowed in the light of the lamp just above her.

They scampered to the kitchen, he and the dogs, and Darwin suddenly realized he was feeling those funny feelings for the woman he'd had previously. This depressed him. He thought he had better self-control than he'd been experiencing lately. Nevertheless, he was drawn into her glow as if the universe was pushing him and he had no restraint at all. He wanted to grab her and hold her. He wanted to weep in her arms and be soothed by her warmth.

"Good morning!" His voice carried and he was suddenly aware of how loud he must be. There were no guests so being quiet wasn't necessary. His guilt, piling up in his mind, made him feel like he should whisper. He stood there speechless knowing that anything he might say now would be wrong — just wrong. He didn't remember being speechless ever before in his life.

"Good morning. I thought I heard you and the dogs coming down the stairway.

How is Rose doing? Is she okay?" Danie asked.

"When I left last night, she was passed out in a drug induced slumber which she needed more than anything else."

"Good. Then she didn't have too much pain…" His expression said otherwise. "Or she did?"

"She had pain alright. Apparently, it was extreme the way she was reacting."

"Oh no!"

"Her screams must have awakened the dead in the morgue."

"It was that bad?" Danie asked perplexed.

"It was that bad." He responded with a definiteness that expressed every feeling he had had in the room with Rose after the operation.

"Gosh, I'm sorry to hear that. But they were able to drug her enough?"

He felt reassured by Danie's calm. "I hope she's okay this morning. Maybe I should call the hospital and ask."

"That's a good idea." Danie was always right there with the right answers. Before he could reach the phone, Wally came through the front door with a load of firewood in his arms.

"What are you doing here?" Darwin asked astonished.

"Oh, I meant to tell you." Danie responded. "I asked Wally to come by and help. He is happy to do so."

"Hey there Mr. Neumann. I'm happy to do chores." Wally interjected.

"I can't afford to pay you."

"No need for pay. I could use a place to stay for couple of nights if that's okay."

Shrugging his shoulders Darwin headed for the phone and punched the numbers for the hospital. After the usual transfers from one department to another he managed to get the nurse's station in the ICU where he had left his wife the night before.

"She's been moved." Was the nurse's response. "Mrs. Neumann is in room 312."

"Does that mean she isn't in anymore pain?"

"She still needs medication but she is out of difficulty surgically. That's why she was moved. She should be fine now."

"That's a relief. How can I get in touch with her?"

"Ask the operator for room 312."

"Thank you."

When the operator came back on, he requested his wife's room. Able to ask for what he wanted and get it made him feel in control again.

Rose was in tears when she answered the phone. "I can't breathe it hurts so bad," she cried.

"Have you asked for some medication to relieve the pain?"

"Of course, I have!" She thundered into the phone.

He had to hold the receiver away from his ear. He wanted to be able to dive through the phone and land right there next to her. "My god, honey."

He knew she was frustrated beyond words and needed him there. "I'm on my way." He said with alarm.

"NOOOOOOOOOOO! You will just make things worse." She said with great finality.

"Worse?"

His intention had always been to make things better. Darwin was dismayed by his wife's rejection. "How could I make things worse?" Before he finished his sentence, he was sorry he'd asked the question.

"Darwin, you get so angry and then you get everyone upset and unwilling to do anything." With that she repeated last night's excruciating wail. "Awhhhhhhhhgh!"

"Honey, it sounds like you need me."

"Please stay at home. I'll manage on my own."

"How are you going to do that when you're in such pain?" He was trying very hard to stay calm even though he felt a huge panic building in his heart.

"I can manage on my own!" she yelled and hung up.

He stood there staring at the phone. The busy signal came through loudly and it was obvious Rose was no longer on the other end of the line.

"Oh, oh. Do I hear trouble?" Danie asked.

"Yes. Now I don't know what to do. Should I go down there?"

"We can handle things here if you need to go."

"I have no doubts about you, Danie. I only have doubts about how effective I could be down there. She doesn't want me."

"She doesn't? That's extraordinary. Why doesn't she want you there?"

"I don't think she wants me at all." He lamented. "She told me I would only make things worse."

"Darwin, I'm sure she didn't mean it that way." Danie came toward him and he felt like he had to back away; he was afraid of what he might do. He grabbed the kitchen counter to steady himself.

"She's in a lot of pain and isn't really herself. I'm sure she'll feel better soon and everything will change." Danie placed her hand on his. It was cool and soothing.

He felt reassured by her words and the comforting tone of her voice, which was deep and soft. She seemed to know the mood of the moment. He couldn't fathom how she was always so calm and happy.

Maybe she was the devil in disguise. Didn't the preachers always warn of the underhanded way the devil seduced his victims? Embarrassed, he moved his hand away. Then, he said to himself, *Really, Darwin? Really, when you don't believe in those things?* He remembered the quote in the

Bible that defined the 'evil one' as 'legion'. Didn't it mean that the malevolence was in everyone and that he needed to be careful to reject anyone who was tempting? That seemed right but he wasn't about to reject Danie. She was just too nice and he could never imagine any malevolence in her sweet face.

There you go again, Darwin Neumann. Be careful.

Danie's voice was so reassuring that he decided he could do as Rose asked and stay away. After all, what could he do at the hospital? He would call regularly and make sure she was okay as Danie suggested. If the situation with the medication didn't resolve, then he would drive to the hospital and make things good for Rose. In the meantime, he would worry. Wasn't that what good husbands did, worry?

He stood there staring at the floor wondering what to do next.

"Are you okay?" Danie asked.

"Well I won't go to the hospital but I am discouraged by what Rose said. She honestly thinks I make things worse because I get angry and I guess I say things that are not helpful. Maybe I do make things worse." He looked down at his attire. The threadbare robe was dirty and dingy, something he had never noticed before. "I think I should go upstairs and get dressed for the day."

"Sure. That's a good idea. You'll feel better if you shower and stuff." He could tell Danie was trying her best to make him cheer up and he was grateful. He just couldn't succumb.

Passing Wally as he started a fire to rid the house of the early morning chill, Darwin slowly staggered up the stairway hoping a shower would change his mood. When he got to his room, he couldn't think of a good reason to keep going and climbed into bed. He knew there was a list he was to follow but he couldn't focus on anything more than the words Rose has spoken to him — "You will just make things worse."

That was it, wasn't it? He would just keep on making things worse. They had all said that, each of his wives. It must be true he thought. I make things worse. With that, he fell into a dream-laden sleep during which he tried and tried but was mired in a thick black tar-like muck and could not get anywhere.

CHAPTER 30

Danie

Thanksgiving was on the way. Wally and Danie had decided to celebrate the holiday with a small day-trip. They planned a trek down the mountain to Morrow Bay where they intended to have a very nice meal in a restaurant by an inlet watching the sun setting over the water.

They piled into the car looking forward to having a fun time together.

"Mom," Wally said after the seat belts were fastened, the car warmed and backed out onto the road. "You will never guess what happened."

"No mind reader here." She replied. "What gives?"

"You remember I told you about Sally Oliver? I told you about what she did to me at the town meeting."

"Sure, I remember. She works for Dr. Erlich here in the village. That's where I got my tooth." She pointed to the tooth in her opened mouth.

"Well, she apologized to me about what she did. Said she was really sorry she had hurt me that way."

Danie smiled inside. She didn't want to let on about the conversation she'd had with Sally at the dentist's office. "That's wonderful Sweetheart. I'm very glad to hear that."

"I wonder why she suddenly feels sorry."

"Oh, you know how it goes. She realized that what she did really harmed you."

"I don't know. She may be setting me up for something."

"I'm not sure you should come to that conclusion. You aren't planning on dating her again, are you?"

"NO WAY!" He stated emphatically. "I still don't trust her."

"She really isn't your type."

"What *type* is that?" He asked sarcastically.

"Gosh, you're putting me on the spot. I don't think she has much...class."

"Mom, what is that supposed to mean?"

"Oh, nothing too awful. She's just a little 'fast' for you."

"Are you saying that I'm 'slow'?"

"Heavens no." She laughed. "I'm talking about her style. She dresses like a whore."

"Mom, why do you say things like that?"

"Because I think them."

"Well I don't. And, I don't like it when you say stuff like that."

"Well she does."

"Mom, she looks fine. She isn't a whore. Why would you say that?"

"I suppose she isn't. She works for the dentist and she's making an honest living. I'm just thinking about what she did to you at that town meeting. That was whore-ish, if you ask me." His mood was crashing and Danie was sensitive to his irritations. They often erupted into rages that could ruin a whole day.

"She thought what she thought and now she doesn't think that anymore." He said. "That makes her upstanding in my opinion."

"You are absolutely right, Wally." Danie knew he would respond well to anything positive she had to say; especially when she told him he was right.

"Well," he mumbled surprised at the turn she'd taken. "Yeah, Sally's okay."

Danie was relieved the long ride would be peaceful if she managed to keep the mood light and happy. There had been a time when nothing would mollify him and he would erupt into rages that could take a week to subside. That had been when he was drugged up and out of control. She was happy to see him accept a new turn in the conversation without spending the whole day ranting on about all the dissatisfaction he'd ever experienced. There had been a time when he could go on for hours, even days, ruining any chance for a decent time.

Wally had changed a lot. She only wished that other people in the village would see him the way she did now. It was hard for Wally to catch a break. He'd done the hard work of changing his life around but would have to wait for the rest of the people he knew to catch up with him. It was unfair but she understood how folks were. Everyone in her experience had been a combination of good and not-so-good, shadowy things that tripped folks up along the way. No one was perfect. Imperfection was desirable as far as she was concerned.

Danie's mind turned to the inn. Rose had come home after three days in the hospital and was still recuperating. Wally had stayed for the few days to help out. Darwin was in a funk of a mood. He had taken to heart what Rose said to him and he was doing his best to make things better for her.

She knew that Rose still loved Darwin but she had done some damage when she told him he made things worse. It was hard to be around

Darwin when he was sad. He still made jokes but they weren't as funny and sometimes he didn't mean to be amusing. Danie wanted very much to do something to make things better. She just didn't know what.

She was also concerned about the effect that Eugenia had had on Rose. Something had taken place between them that had changed the mood around the house. Danie couldn't put her finger on it, but Rose seemed a tad suspicious whenever Danie and Darwin were in a room together. She hoped there was nothing serious going on in Rose's mind. Danie decided to be a little less available to him just in case there were any suspicions developing. Rose had become a good friend and she did not want to do anything that might upset that relationship. And she was looking forward to seeing what Rose would do with the nude portrait sitting. Once they got to the point when they could sit down and work on it, Danie thought things would smooth out and anything Eugenia might have said could be easily dismissed.

The long trek down the mountain took them through California's Earthquake country. Danie was familiar with the Carrizo Plain in the Central Valley and its sizeable grassland seemed unending. Only a few hours from Los Angeles, folks had a rare chance to be alone in the wide-open spaces without people, traffic and buildings, often exclaiming, "You can hear the silence!" It was like that in Dancing Bear Springs too.

"Have you ever noticed this area and how interesting it is Wally."

"What area?"

"The San Andreas Fault moves through the Carrizo Plain."

"I know all about earthquakes, Mom." His mood was sullen. He hadn't gotten over his earlier resentment.

"Good. I'm glad to hear it." And, she grew silent hoping his mood would eventually catch up with hers. She was looking forward to dinner by the ocean because she knew it would include a beautiful watery sunset and she looked forward to watching the seals and other marine life romping in the bay. She was determined to make this a nice day.

There was a little mood changer lurking in her mind. Lately, she had been regretting an action she had taken early in life that had taken a toll. For some weird reason the baby boy she gave up for adoption kept coming up. She hadn't really thought about him very much until not long ago and his little face, which she had only seen for a minute, kept invading her memory. It was astonishing how such a brief memory could be so persistent. He'd had a shock of black hair just on top of his little head and his eyes had been blue. She heard that newborns' eyes were always blue so she wondered if they had stayed that way. She felt like she would recognize those eyes anywhere. "Oh well..." she said thinking there was nothing to be done about it now.

"Oh well, what?" Wally asked.

"Nothing really. I was just thinking out loud for a moment." She had never mentioned this baby to Wally. It had simply never come up and there was no need for that now.

The shoreline was beautiful as they made their way up the coast. All the towns and their respective home developments stretched out along the way. Few places were left that didn't contain some fabricated structure. Danie thought that was unfortunate. She remembered the days in her childhood when her family would take long Sunday drives up the coast. Back then groves of orange trees, olive trees, almond orchards, and vast stretches of land were the norm. Today, she couldn't see anything natural growing, outside of the endless grape orchards that lined the coast. It was pretty, just different.

Entrances to wine tasting grape farms dotted the long stretch. Had she not been driving she would have liked to try some wine tasting. That sounded good and she wondered if a little wine would lighten Wally's mood. But on they drove passing up all the little stops that might have made the day easier. Danie knew it was better that way.

CHAPTER 31

Wally

Thanksgiving had given him a lot to be thankful for. Wally's experience of the drive up the coastline was focused on the ocean. He didn't care that much about wine orchards or endless housing developments. He didn't even care that much about the Carrizo Plain his mother seemed so fascinated by. Earthquakes could cause a lot of rumbling and noise but his experience of them so far was mild.

The biggest one he'd ever experienced was back in the 1990s. The '94 Northridge earthquake happened early in the morning. The movement of the quake wasn't what awoke him; it was rather the noise of all the car alarms going off at once. The shaking had caused a lot of damage and some deaths and injuries but Wally's experience in West Hollywood was more of astonishment. The worst part of it was that he couldn't get anything to eat or drink. Everything was closed down since there was no electricity to run homes and businesses. Their apartment had suffered little damage. He was glad because he hated the landlady and hoped that she would not come nosing around. He had a few things to hide such as the bedside drawer-full of condoms and his stash of weed.

Of course, he wasn't totally crass; remembering the Northridge earthquake as being tolerable, he didn't want any big earthquakes to shake his little village in the mountains, though the San Andreas ran right through the town. He had straddled the earthquake line and thought that was kind of daring even though there was little fear of an earthquake happening just then. Even if it did, he would be outside and there wasn't much harm being in the open if you could avoid falling trees, or unless you were near a rocky overhang or lose ground. Some people thought the earth would open up and swallow anyone close enough but Wally thought that was movie-stupid. He had seen some of the old films about fantastic earthquakes, people running and suddenly disappearing into a crevasse with their arms raised in fateful surrender.

He was much more worried about getting swallowed up by some woman. Now however, Sally was looking better to him. She had apologized. He had never received any apology in his life other than the little ones his mother offered for minor infractions of his time and space. This was an important apology and he felt it must have taken a lot of guts for Sally to say she was sorry. In fact, he was wondering if she would go out with him again. He had declared to his mom he wouldn't date her, but he didn't have to tell her he was seeing the woman again. He would just keep it under wraps. First, he had to ask Sally and that would be hard.

As it turned out it wasn't that hard at all. Sally accepted with a bit of excitement in her voice.

She was pretty in her mid-thirties. She wouldn't tell him exactly how old she was but that was his guess. If she'd said she was in her twenties he would have thought she looked old for her age. He supposed that women kept their age a secret because they were embarrassed about their looks. He thought that was silly. There were few datable women he thought needed to lie. They were all beautiful to him. They didn't even have to get made-up. All he cared was that they showed up when they said they would. Getting stood up was unacceptable.

His mom had told him once that his dad had stood her up on their first date. That surprised him. He wondered how his dad had managed to get her to go out with him the second time he asked when he had failed to turn up the first time. He guessed that his dad had posed a problem for his mother that she could not refuse to solve. She had resolved it by marrying him and then divorcing him almost as soon as Wally was born. The whole marriage had taken all of eighteen months. Wally was only eight months old when his mom split taking him with her. She said she wasn't the marrying kind — "too independent for a man to control," were her words.

Wally was born too late to have any knowledge of the so-called 'plight of women,' so he didn't understand what she meant, except the time she had tried to explain to him about how women had been repressed by men. He knew about the women's movement but he couldn't fathom why a woman would give up staying at home and taking care of children for the independence the working world was supposed to give them. He would be happy to give up the working world to take care of a house and children. He thought that would be a great way to live.

Especially today. He had worked hard all day starting at 8:00 a.m., working out in the sun and wind clearing a property of anything flammable, packing it all up and taking it to the recycling center. The day had been long and hard. Tonight, he would pick Sally up at her place and take her to dinner at the Singing Bear Bistro. He figured Sally would like a romantic meal in a restaurant with candle light and the singing owner-waiter. He assumed the dinner and wine would cost him his entire wages for the day but it would be worth it because he knew Sally would put out.

He was promptly at her door at 7:00 p.m. Night in the village came early and ended early since everyone went to bed when the sun went down. There were no street lamps in Dancing Bear Springs, only a few strung Christmas tree lights hanging over the village itself. Taking a few steps outside of the main street, the dark was foreboding. Tonight, they were lucky because the moon was full. It would light their way home after dinner.

They had shared a bottle of wine at the restaurant and Wally saved a little money when Sally suggested they share a dish instead of ordering two plates. His stomach was tied in knots anyway so he hadn't missed the extra food and she had shared a little more of her half which he thought was really nice. The servings were always very generous at the Italian owned restaurant.

The evening had gone well. They hadn't argued as they had so many times before they broke up, so Wally was feeling very positive about how things were going. And now that he wasn't strung out on drugs, Sally seemed kinder. Maybe she had been this better person all along and it was the drugs that had caused the problems. He was willing to concede that. It was also true that Sally was open to some of his conspiracy ideas like the Free Masons and the Bilderberg Group which had gained a reputation for wanting to take over the world and meetings of secrecy with big government and business leaders. Sally didn't argue with him about it like his mom did. Yes, it was all good.

"Do you want to come back to my place?" Sally asked as they were leaving the Singing Bear. "I think we have more to talk about, don't you?"

"Awesome!" He stated, "I'd love to tell you about the ancient civilizations I've been researching. I know things that will amaze you."

They didn't have to walk far in the moonlit dark which in the thin mountain air lit their way nearly as well as the sun. Wally had brought his flashlight with him just in case. Moon shadows deeply outlined the tall pine trees on the path along the way and when they looked up at the sky, they could see the Milky Way despite the full moon. In Dancing Bear Springs, one could always see the stars.

When they arrived at her door the cat was there just outside waiting to greet them and to claim a warm place by the fire. There were coals left in the grate so Wally took to the job of adding wood and stoking the fire as Sally went into her bedroom to "get more comfortable." Wally's mood brightened with every step they took toward making love. He'd been Jones-ing to be with Sally — she was super in bed and he hadn't had an opportunity in a long time since Lana hadn't been up to see him. This was going to be good.

When Sally returned, she was more comfortable all right; she was dressed in her sweats. He was hoping for something a little sexier. But you get what you get and he wasn't about to complain.

She also had a stash of weed with her and a pipe. He hadn't done any drugs in a while except the sleeping pills he'd obtained from his black-market connection. He had been cautious about taking them reserving for himself the nights when he just could not get to sleep. It wasn't often, but when it happened the sleeping medicine worked well. This would not be one of those nights. He was getting sleepy already which he fought mightily.

"Hey Sally. I was expecting something a little more inviting than sweats."

"It's too cold. We haven't had an early December this cold in years. I wonder if it's because of that El Nino they keep telling us about. I thought it was supposed to be about a lot of rain. I hope that pans out; we sure could use the water."

"Can I fill that pipe of yours?" He asked. "I hope we won't be spending the night talking El Nino and the California drought!"

She laughed. "No, we won't be spending the night like that." She handed him the pipe and bag of pot and sat down in front of the fireplace to warm herself. "Fill the pipe and keep it filled." The cat climbed into her lap and made itself a nest. Kitty-kneading followed as the feline turned around and around finally snuggling into the crux of her lap.

"Nice cat." Wally said with a bit of sarcasm in his voice.

The pipe was the glass-blown artisan type with a teal blue base and curly-ques of red, yellow and purple. He stuffed the bowl and handed it to her. "Greens." He said. "Please, be my guest."

She took the pipe. "Excuse me. It appears to me that you are *my* guest."

"Well yeah, but I couldn't take the greens for myself."

She shoved the pipe at him. "Oh, go ahead. It doesn't matter to me."

He thrust the pipe back into her hand. "Please, be my guest," he insisted. Smiling she took it and lit the top. Her lungs captured an amazing amount of smoke. She held it in a good while and when she let it out, there were four exhales to expel the fumes from her lungs and the room filled with the smell of delectable weed. The cat purred loudly. Wally was amazed by Sally's lung capacity.

He took the pipe from her and filled his lungs. It had been too long and he coughed, choking madly.

Sally laughed. "I guess your mom was right. You've been clean for a while, huh?"

"My mom? When did you talk to her?" Wally was alarmed. He didn't know Sally and his mom had had any opportunities to discuss him. And it was obvious they had talked about his drug use. He wondered if there was anything else they had decided was okay to gossip about behind his back. Angry now, he got up and started pacing.

"Wally sit down," she said as she stroked the slightly stoned cat. "You have nothing to worry about. Your mom and I had a very nice chat about you."

"Oh, I bet." Wally's head was throbbing from too much wine. He hoped the marijuana would take the pain away. He drew another deep hit and this time was able to keep it down.

"Wally," she took his hand and tried to draw him down next to her. "Please sit down and forget your mom. She is very nice and we just chatted a little about you when she came in for an appointment where I work."

"I know. She told me you work for her dentist."

"It was all very innocent." She lied. "I was glad to hear you gave up the meth. I'm starting to warm up. How about you, Wally?" She removed the sweatshirt over her head. Her enormous breasts popped out as if thrilled to be free of the confinement.

He liked that she didn't need a lot of encouragement for sex. He wouldn't have to spend much time getting her in the mood — she was already there. That was good because he suddenly felt dead tired. After one more long hit on the pipe, he nestled in with her on the couch close to the fire.

"Aren't you a little warm there, Wally?" As he removed his sweater and shirt, the cat leapt from the couch.

"I'm just right," he said as he snuggled down into her ample breasts… and promptly fell asleep.

When he awoke, he was naked in her bed. She was naked too, but had fallen asleep apparently waiting for him to come to. How she had gotten him into the bed without his clothes was a mystery. Maybe he had gotten there on his own. Wally was immensely embarrassed. He had never reacted to marijuana this way. That stuff she had must have been powerful product, he thought. He wondered where she got it and if it was spiked with something extra. He wasn't ready to wake her up yet so he decided to let her sleep and nodded off again. In his dream, he was floating in a pool of warm water, naked and hard. A shadowy figure stroked him and took him into her mouth.

The next time Wally awoke, Sally was on top of him. She'd gotten him hard while he was asleep dreaming, and she was mounting him. He didn't mind. She felt that good and he was ready to come. It took everything he had to stay with her and to bring her to orgasm. He remembered her orgasms and wanted to go with her if possible.

As she rode him, she bent down so her breasts would touch his mouth and tongue. He buried his face into them and rolled over so she would be underneath. The rhythm of their bodies together was perfect and Wally came all over her stomach as he tried to pull out. He had no protection and didn't know what Sally had done to protect herself. Wally hoped it had been enough and in time. It occurred to him that he had never gotten a girl pregnant, with or without protection, so he dismissed the worry easily.

CHAPTER 32

Darwin

Winter, 2015

Christmas was coming. Rose was better, finally, although she had a bad cough that kept her from feeling at the top of her game. Darwin's knee was pain free too and he was into planning mode for the holiday. He removed the Santa suit from his closet and upon examining it realized it needed a good cleaning. The last kid to mount his lap had hurled all over him and the suit hadn't been cleaned since. He needed a better beard and new gloves as well, so a trip to the Valley was in order.

Darwin was one of those fortunate or unfortunate souls (depending on how he was feeling that day), who were big enough, old enough and portly enough to pull off the Santa gig. He'd been hired by several parties to play the jolly old man. He looked more like Santa than anyone he had ever known either on the TV screen or in person, on the streets or at the malls. Even though he would never admit it, he loved the job playing Santa Clause more than any of his other gigs, especially riding in the town parade in Dancing Bear with all the children and their parents attending — it was his best chance to shine like the star he longed to be.

At last, the dry-cleaning job that had taken a week was ready. Darwin was anxious to get the suit out of the cleaners and try it on again. He hoped it would fit as it had before. No weight gain had occurred over the year; nevertheless, his body was changing. It seemed to be falling. Everything looked like it was an inch lower than before. He was alternately embarrassed by his body and proud he could pull off the Santa gig so well.

"Good morning!"

A small, nice looking Chinese lady stood behind the counter. His voice boomed as always and he startled the poor woman. "Oh my, Sir! What can I do for you?" She said trying to cover her astonishment. He was dressed in a red and black plaid flannel shirt tucked into his work pants with a warm scarf wrapped around his neck. The outfit was completely appropriate for his mountain home but here in the city, he looked like a lumberjack seeking a tree to fell.

He handed her the ticket for the suit and smiled big. "This is my time of year." He said proudly.

She took the ticket not understanding his reference and unceremoniously switched on the conveyor belt that would bring the item forward. As the belt delivered the red suit, she took it from the hook and swung it over the counter for him to see. "We did a very good job on your suit." She said with great pride. That will be $35.00 Sir.

For a moment, his astonishment rendered him speechless. It had been years since he'd had any use for a drycleaner. "What did you say?" His tone had lost it usual blustery confidence and his words fell weakly into the space between him and the clerk. "Did you say thirty-five *dollars*, Ma'am?"

"Oh yes. A very good price."

He pulled himself up to his full stature, "Madam, do you not know who I am?" He said it with such great authority that the woman drew back to look at him with more perspective.

"Oh, well…Santa Clause comes to mind." She said trying not to laugh aloud; her Chinese sensibilities would not allow her to insult him.

"Doesn't Santa get a discount?" He said trying to sound indignant.

"Can I sit on your lap?"

"NO!" Darwin feigned alarm.

The clerk, despite her Chinese manners, broke into a laugh unbecoming the proper lady she normally was. Faced with this laughing bear of a man, she couldn't help herself. "I am not the owner here," she said as they both broke into giggles over their happy banter. "But maybe I could give you a ten percent discount — just because of who you are, of course."

"Of course, Ma'am." He said smiling. "I wouldn't expect a discount unless I was the *real* thing." He pulled out his wallet and produced some cash, "How much will that be then?"

"I will charge the 'Big Account in the Sky,' Sir. You should not have to bear the cost of cleaning the most special suit there is." She smiled back. "I couldn't let Santa Clause pay for his own dry-cleaning, now could I?"

"Oh Madam. I can't thank you enough. The elves will be dancing in the streets tonight when they hear the news. Mrs. Clause will be happy, too," he winked.

He took the suit by the hanger and bowed to her. She bowed back. "Have a very Merry Christmas, Sir," she said.

"That's my line." He laughed and reached out his hand; she took it. "May your holiday experience bring you great joy, Madam," he said with all of the sincerity in his soul. When he left, he looked back to see the little Asian woman grinning from ear to ear.

On the way up the hill Darwin mused about the day's happenings, especially this last special moment with the dry-cleaning lady. She had made his day. These small happenings occurred often enough in his life to keep him going despite his shortcomings. He had been doing a thorough search of his character lately, something he'd learned to do when he was in AA years ago. It was useful then and he felt it would be useful now. He realized his ambitions to be a working actor were unrealistic because of his age. That didn't mean he could never get a job in the business acting, but the likelihood of such an outcome was statistically out of the question; and, one gig would not a whole career make.

He also realized that his anger was his excuse for being lazy and a little forgetful. He wasn't physically lazy, but in some instances, he was unavailable to his wife because he didn't feel like doing what she wanted. He was doing his own thing, like writing a screenplay and didn't want to be disturbed. Then, when the consequences arose, he would get angry and lash out trying to dissipate his dissatisfaction with himself. He could see, too, he was extremely fearful of losing Rose. The fear had driven him into inappropriate behavior with the doctors and nurses who cared for her. It was illogical but sometimes he couldn't help himself he was so frightened. He had never thought of himself as scared, but now he had to admit he was terrified. Losing Rose was out of the question. It just couldn't happen.

These thorough inventories of his psyche were always humbling and he wasn't sure he liked it, but he knew it was necessary to acknowledge his flaws and get on with improving himself. He was doing it for Rose and she was well worth it. He had to change to give her what she needed to survive.

His mind turned to Danie. She had volunteered for the Community Reading Program in which the young children got personalized help learning to read. Danie was perfect for this job and he had actively encouraged her to volunteer. She was a writer and, as an actor, she had learned the power of story. The children he had worked with needed the kind of input she could provide. So many of the kids read the words without any comprehension of what they were reading. He was anxious to get home to hear how her first day had gone.

When he finally arrived, Rose was at the grocery store. Some unexpected guests had shown up and she needed breakfast food for the next morning. Danie was there warming herself near the hearth and once the fire had been properly stoked, he sat down next to her on the couch and asked about her experience.

She was just as excited to tell him about her day as he was to hear it. "Thank you for encouraging me to do this because I had a *great* time." She said "great" with a lot of emphasis. "Maybe I should have been a teacher instead of what I did."

"You would have deprived the world of your great talent." He insisted.

"You flatter me, Sir. But today was much more satisfying. I had many conversations with these students. I was astonished. They just come up and start talking. They don't seem to have any filters and will say anything on their mind."

"You're right, they do that don't they? What age were they?"

"Around seven; they were in the second and third grade and so open. I loved talking to them. The students I worked with were wonderful. They struggled with words but they seemed to be very willing to do the hard work. I thought I'd have trouble getting their attention but they were fine."

"You've told me that Wally had Attention Deficit Hypertension Disorder. These students would seem very different to you."

"Yes, they did. One girl was pretty antsy, but she did well anyway."

"ADHD doesn't mean you're stupid."

"No, of course it doesn't and she was very bright. But another girl that I didn't work with talked to me out of the blue. She was sitting alone at another table so I walked over. Honestly, I was stunned she would speak so openly to a perfect stranger about her problems. Her brother was in the military. He was training somewhere in a foreign country and one of his buddies shot him by mistake. She told me he died just yesterday. I was so saddened by what she said. I sat down next her and asked her about her brother, how old he was, what he was like, things like that."

Danie sat there silently for a moment, then, "I remembered when I was about her age my grandmother died. It was not a surprise to me. She was old and she often talked about wanting to go home to Ohio where her husband, my grandfather, was buried. She wanted to be buried next to him. One day she announced she was going home to visit some friends in Cleveland and I remember saying 'goodbye' to her at the airport. I watched as she walked, waddled really, across the tarmac all the way to the steep steps leading to the airplane. It must have been very painful for her to walk up those long stairs to the aircraft. She had terrible arthritis, as I do today, and believe me it was painful. I never saw her again and I knew I wouldn't. When the news came that she had died in Cleveland, I was unmoved because I knew she wouldn't come home.

"The next day I went to school and felt dismayed that I couldn't cry. I loved my grandmother very much. She had been the one to raise me because both my parents worked. I missed her but my heart could not feel anything. I guess I was in shock. The feeling was numbness and I am told today it is a common reaction to losing someone close. I didn't know that then, of course. Anyway, I was sitting outside at the lunch tables when my teacher walked by. I sniffled a couple of times wanting to get her attention and she stopped asking if I was okay. I said 'No, my grandmother is dead.' The teacher wasn't a sentimental person but she sat down and talked to me. I don't remember the conversation but I will never forget that woman's face as long as I live because she sat down and talked to me when I needed it most."

Danie started to cry. Darwin was sorry for her. The child today had awakened some long-buried feelings. He put his arm around her shoulder to comfort her and she fell into his embrace as naturally as if she'd been there her entire life.

"The girl," she added, "her eyes were dry just like mine were."

He was completely taken by her sadness and wished she didn't have to cry, but he understood her need. "It's hard to lose someone like a grand-mother. It probably feels fresh even today."

Suddenly, Danie stiffened. It was very slight but he noticed she was uncomfortable. He let her go just as Rose walked through the front door.

"Hello!" Rose said rather loudly. "I am home!" Her mood seemed very bright. She nearly glowed. Rose was far too cheerful — she had to be faking it — Darwin thought she must have seen them in the embrace. It was a tiny thought, almost imperceptible, but down deep he knew Rose was jealous.

Danie swiped her eyes with her hand, "Rose, Hi. I was just telling Darwin about an experience I had when I was seven-years-old." She arose from the sofa. "You are lucky to have such a sweet person for a husband. Darwin was being very comforting."

"He can be good at that alright. It's why I married him," she said dryly.

"I bet." Danie said. "I was teaching the kids down at the school today and my experience was very touching at moments. "A girl there had just lost her older brother in a terrible gun accident."

"Those guns!" Rose exclaimed. "When will people realize it is the guns that are the problem."

"Well dear, in this case it was a military situation." Darwin interjected. They were training."

"Oh. I don't know if that makes a difference. Gun violence is gun violence. Guns kill. That's what they're for."

"Honey," Darwin added patiently, "They have to train so they will be ready on the battlefield."

"They were training with live ammunition?" She asked astonished.

"Look, I'm tired." Danie said. "I'm going downstairs." She headed for her room. "Later."

As she left, Darwin was able to take a much-needed deep breath. "I'm taking the dogs for a walk," and headed for the door to get the leashes. The dogs, always ready for their walk scampered to attention and headed out the opened door.

"I'll go with you." Rose said putting down her groceries and heading out.

"Oh. Sure, come on." He held the door for her as he donned his warm jacket.

As they headed up the street, she asked tersely, "So, what was that really all about?"

"Nothing!" He objected. "It was exactly as Danie said it was. I was comforting a crying woman. What would you have me do?" He fired back.

"Nothing!" She said. They fell silent for the rest of the walk.

CHAPTER 33

Danie

This was bad. Danie knew her time at the inn was coming to a close. It was the moment that she had been dreading. Why did it have to happen this way? She was very fond of Darwin and had paid him a lot of attention, she knew. But she felt she had paid Rose as much consideration and felt they had a strong woman-to-woman bond. Danie was still looking forward to their nude portrait session. Nevertheless, the mood had changed since the time Rose asked Danie to pose. What had happened? She wasn't sure. But since the time the German woman, Eugenia, arrived nothing had been the same.

And now things were definitely worse. Rose had walked in at just the wrong moment. It was all very innocent with Darwin. But how was the woman to know that?

Good god, aren't we too old for this? Danie wondered. She had to admit the feelings were the same no matter how old she got. They would come in a rush during an unguarded moment. Suddenly, her body would want to do all the things it used to do and without the least provocation. That is, even though she felt she could rise from a chair and run across a room without any trouble at all, when she tried to do that nothing happened. Everything hurt too much. She thought it would be like that in sex too. She would feel like she could make love all night, but when it came to doing it, well…

No matter — Rose would think what she wanted to think no matter how true or untrue. Danie's heart sank. It meant she would have to move. She looked around the room in which she had been so comfortable. She had made a few changes so the place would work better for her. The décor was feminine and old-fashioned; it always felt warm and inviting.

She looked out the window. It was starting to snow. At first the sheets of sleet driven by the wind slanted across her view. Then as the flakes became larger, the snow was heavier, wetter, and they floated down. She awaited this scene every year with great anticipation. The white stuff drifted in big flakes like chicken feathers covering the ground first with a dusting, which looked like white lace carpeting the pines and the earth. After a while, the dusting turned to a blanket that sparkled like diamonds when a sliver of sunshine managed to peek through. The scene was glorious.

She cried. Danie knew her time at the Laughing Bear Bed and Breakfast was in jeopardy and it would be painful to leave. She picked up the newspaper and riffled the pages until she found the rental ads wondering if any of the rental agents had gotten past the gossip mongering Mrs. Seward had so blithely left behind. Then — she couldn't believe her eyes — there was a picture of the little dormered house in the middle of the page. It was for sale!

Hurriedly she picked up her cell and dialed the real estate agent's number. The agent who answered wasn't anyone she knew. His name was Ed and he sounded nice; he was happy to help of course. He quoted the price on the house and asked if she would like to see it.

"I know the house like the back of my hand," she replied. "There is someone renting it though, isn't there? I thought it was rented."

"Yes, there was but they moved."

"Really?" Danie was astonished. What had happened? Where had Bernadine gone? Tons of questions cropped up in her mind that had no answers. Had there been a break-up? Did the husband learn the truth about his wife? Was there going to be a divorce? Did the house need to be sold and divided up?

After Danie hung up the phone she calculated what she would need for a down payment. She wondered if she had saved enough. She had been here a few months and had managed to save some money. It had been the first time in her life when her expenses fell short of her income; usually it was the other way around. Saving had become a game she played every month trying to gin up the sum each time.

She checked her account on the computer. It was just short of the amount she needed. Would the house sell out from under her? The area had been under water for a while and the house prices had come down considerably since the 2008 housing depression. However, the homes here had not been selling even now that the recession was over. It was hard to know exactly why, but Danie guessed it was the drought.

Dancing Bear Springs had not been spared the extreme dryness the state of California was experiencing. Fire was the biggest enemy. It was nearly impossible to get fire insurance in a place like this and it cost a fortune. People were afraid. However, El Nino was on the way and if today was any indicator this would be a wet winter.

She looked out the window again as the snow piled on top of the tree branches weighing them down. The winter was off to a good start, but summer was a different matter. Their village was right in the middle of an area that had been spared fire for over a hundred years. Statistically, they were sitting ducks waiting for the gauntlet to fall on that dry, windy day when there would be no protection against the ravages of an enormous blaze. Their little village could be wiped out in minutes. It was a terrifying prospect for anyone already living here and happily settled. For a stranger, no price was low enough to chance that horrifying possibility. The result could help Danie take a little time to save up. But time was short. She would have to act fast even though the house was priced a little high. Maybe the next royalty check for the book would put her over the top. It was due any day. If she got a decent check, she would immediately make an offer, an offer the Sewards would not be able to refuse.

CHAPTER 34

Darwin

Lucy was due tomorrow. She was the best news Darwin had gotten in a very long time. Lucy Hayes Johnson was a dear friend from college days. He remembered her as Lucy Hayes; she had since married a man named Ted Johnson. The couple met in the final months of school and had been together ever since graduation.

Darwin, because of his huge frame and his prowess on the football field, had earned himself a scholarship to a HBCU, a Historically Black College or University — a 'Negro College', as it was known then. Virginia Union University in Richmond, Virginia, had been bold and today the school was more integrated; back then it was primarily black students. His scholarship was an experiment at a time when schools and colleges were being challenged to accept integrated student bodies. Before, the law had allowed what was called separate but equal education for both blacks and whites. However, in 1968 the Supreme Court ruled "actual desegregation of schools is required." He would never forget the first time he viewed Pickford Hall, a stately mansion that would become like a home for him.

The integration was something he welcomed. He enjoyed his time getting to know people with a different background. There was a lot to learn from them and he had been excited to be a part of the process of integrating society. He had recently read a Gallup poll taken in 1958 that showed only 4 percent of Americans favored interracial marriage. By 2013, that number was 87 percent. In that there was a lot to be proud of.

The friends he had gotten to know there were terrific people. He was surprised the color of their skin could vary so much. Some were black as night and others simply looked like they had a good tan. One of Darwin's friends who was studying to be a doctor told him we are all pink on the inside. He liked the idea and pursued a relationship with the girl named Lucille. Lucy was wonderful.

Now Lucy, a girl he might have married if the time had been more propitious, was on her way to the inn to spend a couple of days catching up. His memory of her was special. She had been the most luscious coffee 'n cream color and her deep black eyes were pools of mystery. Her body had been slender and well curved. Best of all, Lucy and Darwin were best friends. Having an intimate relationship with your best friend was almost a guarantee for a successful marriage. It had certainly worked that way with Rose.

Lucy taught him a lot about himself and his prejudices which he didn't realize he had. Darwin had to admit that back home he would cross the street rather than face the fears he had toward black men he didn't know. It wasn't that he felt unequal in strength to the men he tried to avoid; he had no reason to be fearful physically because of his size and strength. But he did feel inadequate in what he perceived to be the 'menace' of the 'black mind.' He had no basis for thinking such things; he had to assume he had learned it along the way, though the learning had been unconscious. He was also shocked to learn about the depth of prejudice blacks had to endure at the time. The names they were called, and that *he* was called because he had a black girlfriend, were beyond demeaning.

Shockingly, people believed blacks were animals, sub-human and not worth trying to educate. Supposedly, they didn't experience pain the same way white folks did. The people he got to know proved that to be completely false. They were smarter than he was and his black friends on the football field endured more pain than he had. Had he known the future would be better for blacks and mixed couples, he would have stayed with Lucy, if she would have had him.

That was then; this was now. What would Lucy be like now? Older, wiser, he was sure. What would she look like? Would he want to hold her as he had those many years ago? She had been a mother of several children. He couldn't remember them all but he was sure there were at least five. They were all grown of course and Darwin was certain she had done a fine job rearing them.

Best of all, Lucy would be a distraction from the issues raised recently between him and Rose. His wife had developed a formality with him and he knew he was in trouble. He was honestly innocent, yet he had had those pesky thoughts about Danie. Certainly, thinking wasn't a sin, was it? If that was so, thinking would be the biggest sin of all. Most people never actually did the most enticing things they thought about.

Anyway, his feelings about Danie had been mostly innocent and he would never act on them. Furthermore, he loved his wife. Rose was the perfect woman for him. If not for her mother and the effect she had had on Rose, she would be a perfect human being. And there was the secrecy about her stepfather, Victor, a silence she had rarely broken. That hush-hush had always kept the situation mysterious, though Darwin knew her step father had raped her. He wondered if the man had been unfaithful to her mother with other women too, which would cause Rose to be suspicious about men now.

Danie was sweet and she laughed at most of his jokes. He had very fond feelings for her and he would never ask her to move out. She added a great deal to the inn and its activities. She was a bright light amid some of the dreariness that came with ordinary life and the way it was lived. Her personality was what had made her a movie star.

The tasks and chores one had to do to keep things going were often monotonous and boring. When Danie was around, the ordinariness of a day could flip in a moment's time. She brightened things up. And Lucy would enliven the day, too. He remembered she was the kind of person who could make the sun shine brighter.

Rose on the other hand, often brought tension and tedium into a room. She would try to be bright and cheerful but her underlying mood would be one of stress. She added pressure because there was always something else that needed to be done. Darwin was sensitive to her moods — they were often dark and brooding.

Here it was, time to get ready for Christmas and every box and crate stowed away in the basement had to be brought up to the living room. The mountains of decorations Rose had amassed over the years had to be released from their temporary tombs to grace the house with holiday cheer. This was a reason to hate Christmas: the ruckus that was made every year with unwanted presents, fattening eggnogs, and enough food and sweets to send a person to the emergency ward.

All he wanted to do was to sit by the window and watch the snowfall, preferably by a warm fire. Here in California, snow was such a rare occurrence that taking the time to watch it seemed like a ritual that couldn't be missed. He loved it and moving to Dancing Bear Springs had been the best thing he had ever done with his life, outside of marrying Rose of course.

Now Darwin's biggest concern was how to fete Lucy while keeping Rose happy doing chores around the house. Rose seemed to be okay about Lucy even though she knew the relationship between them had been intimate. But Rose never seemed to mind the women from his past. It was the current woman living right under their noses that seemed to be a risk to her. Somehow, he couldn't blame her for feeling threatened.

Maybe Lucy would add some sensibility to the situation. How that might happen he couldn't fathom. He just had hopes, those capricious things that flitted here and there like sparrows in his mind. Actually, they were more like gnats ready to fly up his nose or into his mouth only to be spit out again. As good as they could look, hopes were never something you wanted to ingest. His hope that Lucy could influence Rose was best left untouched.

CHAPTER 35

Danie

It was Christmas card time. Danie's habit was to send a personally signed card to everyone she knew who was still living. Her address book was filled will names of people who had already died. It seemed like the expiration dates for most of her friends came in waves. Occasionally, she would get news all at once about three or four people she had known, some well and some just acquaintances. However, every Christmas she faced an address book with names of people who no longer existed in the flesh. It was a sad time to think of those who had passed. She would say a little prayer for each one as she intersected their name. She marked the name with a check and moved on to the next one, often with regret. It felt like she was abandoning her friend to the grave and a feeling of despair accompanied it. She would prefer to send a card instead.

And, there was the "name" of a little one who had to be given up. She had placed it at the end of her address book as if there would be an address someday to send a card to. She called him "Little One" though she knew he would be a grown man today, fifty-five years old. It was impossible to believe it had been so long.

For a moment, she sat back to take a deep breath. It was natural she supposed to think about her future amid writing Christmas cards. Her fear oddly enough, was not about dying. She figured that would happen at some point with or without her permission. Her worst fear was living beyond her means — her financial means, her physical means or her mental means. Any one of these would be a countdown to her demise. She honestly did not want to survive any one of these possibilities. Each would mean a hardship for which she was unprepared. Who would want to live in poverty, poor health or mental degradation? People did she knew. She would not willingly sign up for any of these possibilities. She supposed no one did. Maybe God could be more co-operative when it came to death. Danie supposed the Almighty could arrange timely demises for his children, but these days the medical profession had more of a say in the matter than God did.

One thing she would not tolerate was living in a body without a mind or without hope. As far she was concerned lingering was out of the question. She had placed these notions into her 'living will' and she hoped that Wally and her friend, Sami, could work together toward a solution that she would want should anything place her waning life into the hands of an overzealous doctor.

Enough! She said to herself. Dwelling on these issues did no good. She just hoped that her demise would occur without a lot of fuss.

There was always a lot to live for and Danie's thoughts turned to the school and the little girl who had shared the story about her brother. Knowing she was there for the child at just the right moment gave Danie the warmest feeling she had ever known. She was sincerely looking forward to returning to the local school the following week to check up on the girl and to resume the new reading program. It was the best part of her life.

And it served to take her mind off the possibility that Rose would ask her to leave at any time. She was surprised she hadn't already. Danie had naturally done her best to stay to herself in her room hoping to stay out of the way. 'Out of sight, out of mind' was as good a maxim as she could think of. She kept busy with quilting get-togethers, potluck parties, art projects and other club activities as they came up. There was plenty to do but she missed being more of a part of the B&B, the people and the activities there. She had become a part of the 'family,' as Darwin would readily tell her from time to time. And now, feeling estranged, she felt saddened and lost. What should she do?

Her best hope was to buy the little house she loved. Her funds were short but she hoped beyond hope that the house would still be there when she was ready. Knowing where one might be at the end was comforting. Having a home where she could live or convalesce became her main focus. Having such a goal caused her to feel in control even though she knew beyond a shadow of a doubt there was no such thing in life. People thought they had control but Danie was certain that no one really did. Having control was an illusion people entertained with great faith. One hoped life would cooperate when one made plans. But that was the best one could do. In any case, that was all Danie felt she could do; make a plan.

As she thought about her plan, a headache cropped up. It was one of those tension headaches she was beginning to get used to.

CHAPTER 36

Rose

Life had turned into an endless round of cleaning rooms, doing laundry, making breakfasts and getting ready for Christmas. Amid all her chores, Rose wanted to stay active in her social groups, playing paddle tennis and keeping up with art projects. Her graphic arts business remained healthy even during the holiday season. And she wanted to get that nude portrait of Danie done. In fact, despite all the other things on the list to do, she wanted to get the portrait done more than anything else. She had developed a burning desire to have it done before Christmas. Rose wanted to loosen her style, to become freer with the paints and make an original piece of artwork. She didn't want this painting to look like a copy of some other artist's style. She wanted it to be her own, all her own.

They had to figure out a good time to do a sitting. Rose intended to figure out how to place Danie and just how much of her body should be exposed. She had no idea how Danie would react to her direction, but Rose figured with her acting background she was up to the job.

Once the decision was made to use one of the upstairs rooms and a place where Danie could sit looking out onto the pines, the two women went to work on the positioning. Danie suggested to Rose she should be draped with a towel so her upper body would be all that was exposed. She didn't want to feel posed; she also didn't want to look clumsy. Rose suggested that the mood would be pensive but not somber. And she wanted Danie to be comfortable enough to allow her body to be relaxed and un-posed. She also wanted Danie to do something that she might have done as a child sitting looking out a window. Danie went back to her room to reflect on her youth and think of something that would work for Rose.

While Rose awaited Danie and her decision, she set up her materials. She planned a large painting but her sketches could be much smaller. Finally, Danie arrived at the room and came in. She seemed a little hesitant. She had come up with a couple of suggestions and wondered which Rose would prefer. First, she thought of eating or sucking on a Popsicle or an ice cream cone.

"I actually remember sitting at a window once eating an ice cream cone. It was vanilla which was my favorite flavor at the time. Now it's chocolate." She laughed.

"But I could also be writing, say in a diary or a letter. That's something people don't do anymore with email. How many postage letters do you get Rose?"

"Not many come to think of it. Just bills and announcements. I do get Christmas cards now and again during the season. While she posed looking out the window, Rose thought about a letter she had found in the mailbox recently. Even the 'to and from' addresses carefully handwritten on the envelope were a surprise. It had been the only handwritten letter she had received in a very long time, probably as many as twenty years since the last one.

"Are you comfortable, Danie?" Rose draped her with the towel and used the lace curtain hanging next to Danie to touch her head lightly as she glanced down at her writing. It caused Danie's hair to ruffle a little and Rose thought that was a good touch. Both worked to get the pose to look as natural as possible. "Danie, can you slump a little so you will look relaxed." Rose suggested. "This is good and we may go back to this pose but you are looking down and not out the window as I had hoped you would. Let's go with the ice cream cone idea. Of course, we can't use real ice cream melting down your front." Rose laughed "That would look kind of nasty, especially if it was vanilla." The naughty thought caused the two women to chortle.

Danie got into position at the window and pantomimed eating the ice cream looking out at the pines. The towel was draped satisfactorily and they settled down to the sketching and drawing. Rose liked what she was seeing. She squinted to soften the scene and started drawing.

"You know, I did get a handwritten letter recently. It is from a dear friend from school days who lives in Colorado with her husband. Her kids are grown of course. She is like me, older, and her handwritten letter is written in cursive — to perfection, mind you. That wasn't the surprise. It was her news."

"What did she say?" Danie asked.

"She told me that she and her husband of fifty years had been going to couples counseling for some time trying to work out their problems. It seems her husband was involved in an affair with some woman. Can you imagine, at our age? He was supposed to stop the relationship with the other woman as an agreement during the therapy; but my friend got suspicious and discovered that he was still seeing the woman and had been all along. Apparently, the other woman was much younger. Typical, don't you think?

"My friend is the nicest person you would ever want to meet." She became silent.

"And, he did that to her. What a shame."

"Yes."

"Do you think she will divorce him?"

"She said she had already started the separation process which is a pain!" Rose exclaimed. "I know since I've been through it."

"Oh yes, divorce is one hell of a process." Danie responded.

"My friend said in her letter: 'I'm done.' "

"Oh, so there's no more room for compromise then."

"Nope." Rose looked at her sketch holding it out for some perspective. "This will due for now."

"You're finished? That was fast."

"Yes. I want to keep it simple and now I will transfer what I did here to the larger canvass. I hope you like it when it is finished."

Rose suddenly felt awkward wondering if Danie would find the painting to her liking. Then she decided that would not matter. Rose was determined to make the painting to her own liking, not Danie's. The painting was becoming something of an obsession though she would not admit it to herself. But Rose was certain this painting would change her entire emphasis on artwork. Perfection had been the focus in the past and she was anxious about perfection now, though she could not think of a reason why. She just knew she had to loosen up and give herself permission to be free. So what, if the painting didn't turn out right? She could always try again. She would do the painting in watercolor and it was unlikely the result would end up in the Smithsonian, however it turned out. And if she messed up, it wasn't as though she couldn't afford more paper. Or paint, for that matter.

Her frugality had come from the days when she and her mother first came to America. In those days, she scavenged paper from trash cans. Rubbish cans always had plenty of paper in them and a few pieces would be adequate for her purposes. The projects she had then were for art class and the teacher was impressed with her finds telling her she was clever to seek out unusual mediums for her work. Rose took that to heart and it had stayed with her up until now. She couldn't think of a good reason why she should save paper today. It was silly really. She giggled. Rose felt good suddenly, like she had discovered a precious metal or something of great value. She was discovering something new about herself that she liked and it made her grin from ear to ear.

CHAPTER 37

Darwin

Lucy arrived as Rose and Danie were upstairs doing their painting. Darwin was deep into his screenplay about Santa Claus and zombies. He had decided if Rose could do her artwork that was unrelated to running the inn, he could do his project too. He had settled onto the couch after stoking the fire. The computer screen and the fireplace provided the only light in the early evening dusk.

Heidi and Pepper barked; a knock at the door startled him from his work. "Come in, come in." He said before he arrived at the door. As he grabbed the handle, Lucy opened it and they fell into each other's arms. Her scent caught him — it was apples and cinnamon. The memory of her scent brought back feelings he'd thought were gone forever.

"Oh dear, hello!" He laughed embarrassed as they disentangled themselves from each other. "Lucy! My god, it's you!"

"Yes, 'old fool.' I told you I'd be coming."

"Let me look at you."

"Well, don't look too close. I've gotten old too."

She was right. He would never say, but she had gained weight and tried to straighten her hair. Back then, she would never have thought of doing that taking pride in her African origin. Now her coif was plastered down and short.

"Oh heck, everybody gets old." He said covering his astonishment. "Look at me. I look like Santa Clause."

She laughed. "You know, you do."

He took her coat and bag and showed her to the room. Lucy was staying in the Lilac room. He explained that Rose and Danie were working in the Pine Valley Room across the way behind a closed door. He silently wondered what they were doing in there. He knew Rose had a project in mind but he had no idea what it was. He mentioned them to Lucy and said, "Take your time, relax, and come down about six. We have reservations for dinner at the club, just the two of us. Rose isn't in the mood to go out."

"The club? That sounds fancy."

"Well, it's nice and the food's good. They have a bar. I don't drink but it's there and you can if you like. It isn't dressy here on the mountain. We're all very casual."

"Good. I'll wear pants then."

"Fine. Let me know if you need anything."

Just then the lights went off. The house went dead. "Oh shit!" Darwin's expletive was justified. A line was down from the storm. "My apologies Lucy. I'll get you a LED lamp before it gets too dark."

"What?" She laughed. "No kerosene lantern in a place like this?"

"Are you falling for her?" Lucy asked after a martini and a strange explanation from Darwin about what had been going on at the inn. They were sitting near a window in the dining room of the club overlooking the golf course. It was turning brown because of the drought, but the pines and birch trees, now bare for the season, softened the blow.

A generator moaned outside providing electricity for the club. The room was crowded because no one had energy at home and came here to find warmth and food to eat. Candlelight illuminated their table and drinks.

Darwin didn't want to go into the whole thing about Danie, so Lucy had only a sketchy idea of what he was saying. "No!" He objected. "I don't have feelings for Danie."

"Come on 'Buddy.' I know men."

"No!" Then he demurred embarrassed. "Well, not anything serious."

"What is that supposed to mean?"

"Okay, she has caught my eye on occasion. But it's just moments. It really isn't serious at all...Just moments."

The whites of Lucy's eyes grew larger before they crumpled into a hearty laugh. "Well, if you say so, Darwin. You were never very smart about women."

"You don't have to rub it in." He said sipping his coke through a straw. "It's times like this I wish I could drink again." He eyed her martini wishing he could take a swig.

"No, you don't and I'll send this back if it's bothering you," she said referring to the drink.

"It's just that I don't know what to do." He lamented. "Rose is cold toward me because she has a notion in her head that is completely unfounded."

"Unfounded?"

"I would never leave her."

"Do you know how this 'Danie-girl' feels?"

"Of course not. We've never discussed anything about it. This is entirely between Rose and me."

"Surprise!" Danie had snuck up behind the two amid their deep conversation. She placed her hands over Darwin's eyes. "Guess who?" She intoned.

Darwin, startled, could feel the delicate cool of Danie's hands over his eyes. "Gee, I can't imagine who you could be!" He laughed.

"Gosh, you got 'a at least try."

"Danie," he turned to her, "I want you to meet my best friend from college days, Lucy Johnson."

Danie extended her hand to Lucy. "I am very happy to meet you. Darwin has been looking forward to your visit for weeks. I hope you have a happy stay here."

"Thanks," Lucy replied. Glancing at Darwin with those challenging eyes, she said, "You are Daniela Wharton. I remember you from 'Gracie's Garden.' I loved that movie. It's one of my favorites."

"It's one of my best — a 'chick flick' through and through. I'm glad you liked it. I wrote the screenplay you know."

"No, I didn't know that. I don't pay much attention to movie news."

"Yes, I woke up one morning with an entire story plot developed in my dream. I had to sit down right away and write it."

"You did a good job. The scene in the end with the old woman and the young man holding each other in a hospital bed as he died was a tear-jerker."

Just then, the sound of the generator died and the interior lights went off. A collective inhale and a stunned silence arose where people had been chatting loudly only a moment before. Within a second or two the lights resumed with a collective sigh of relief.

"Thank goodness," Darwin exhaled deeply. "That was fast. Usually they take a full twenty-four hours to fix the problem."

Momentarily, Danie's attention was drawn away, "My friends are arriving and I'm joining them as I do every Friday night. It's our ritual. Have a great time you two. Nice meeting you," she said to Lucy, and she turned away waving to her friends.

Lucy watched her go with an expression aimed at Darwin that would make a zombie feel guilty. "So, you're saying that Rose just walked in on a couple of incidences that *looked* funny but were completely innocent… with *that* woman?"

"And come to think of it, it was only once but Rose reacted strongly." He said ominously. "It was all innocent." He felt defensive.

"And exactly how is she supposed to know that?"

"We told her — we explained it to her."

"Maybe she has seen more than you realize."

"What would she see?" He looked at her perplexed. "There hasn't been anything!"

Lucy looked back at him like he must be kidding.

"There was another incident when another guest walked in." He thought he may as well get the whole thing on the table. "Eugenia was her name and she was an old friend of Rose's — from Germany," he added ominously as he remembered Eugenia and her Third Reich loyalties.

"Okay, now you have a reason why Rose is giving you the cold shoulder. Eugenia probably told."

"It wasn't anything. There had been a customer the night before who had been drinking heavily before leaving early for work. I joked that he ran fuel rods for a nuclear reactor.

"That is funny," Lucy said.

"We were laughing about it a little too loudly in the kitchen. Worried about the noise, I tried to shut Danie up by putting my hand over her mouth. It turned out badly because I hit her nose. She'd had a procedure on the tip recently and I hurt her. She was reacting… That's what happened when Eugenia walked in."

Lucy looked at him like he was crazy.

"Well, you asked."

"You didn't think that your hand on Danie's mouth in that way was provocative?"

Darwin stopped for a moment. He was suddenly struck by her logic. "Holy shit! You know Lucy, you're right. It looked bad!"

His mind flashed back through all the small moments that could have looked bad to anyone. Rose tells me I always make things worse even though I try very hard to make things better."

"You're probably trying *too* hard."

"Too hard to please her? I don't know, Lucy. I try, I really do but nothing I do is good enough."

"Is she critical?"

"Not exactly, not out loud. It's that she's never satisfied." He heard himself repeating the old mantra and he hated himself for complaining. Rose was the one with the cancer and having half her lung cut out. "Look Lucy. Forget about it. I never said anything, okay?"

"Darwin, it's okay if you feel you need to talk about it."

"I don't." He cut her short with a question about her marriage. "And, children — didn't you say something about five kids?"

"So, you are wriggling out of your problems by turning the tables on me?" She laughed. "Look Darwin, Danie is an attractive woman — in fact, she's beautiful even at this late date. Any woman would be jealous of her."

"But she is so nice and she doesn't flaunt her looks. She's quite modest. She doesn't even wear much make-up; most of the time she walks around completely natural. The other day I told her how I admired her and she demurred to my praise saying that her family had always impressed upon her humility in the face of high regard. They apparently told her that beauty began on the inside, not to put too much stock in outer appearances."

The waitress came and served their dinner.

"Her family was wise to tell her that," Lucy said as she took her napkin into her lap.

"I don't know; I think she should be proud. She has accomplished a lot and she deserves to feel good about herself."

"She obviously has plenty of self-confidence. I wouldn't worry." Lucy paused, then added, "I think her family was right and it sounds like your friend took those words to heart. That's admirable."

"Danie is a bright woman, a good writer and an even better actor."

"Maybe you admire her a little too much."

"Maybe a lot too much." He smiled. "Lucy, I get it. Just a hint of interest is going to set Rose off."

"Ya think?" They laughed and dug into their meal while Lucy ordered another martini.

Once she had been served, Lucy took a sip and said, "I have something important to tell you, Darwin."

"Sure, what is it?" His hunger had taken over and he was deep into his food.

"This isn't easy for me, but my eldest son is light skinned, unlike his father. However, I decided to raise him completely black like his siblings. I felt it was the right thing to do."

"You've never talked much about your kids, Lucy. Why is that?"

"Because my eldest isn't Ted's." Lucy put her fork down and stopped eating. "Darwin, he is yours."

Darwin dropped his fork on the plate with a big thunk. "What?" He could barely get the word out; his voice utterly failed him. His entire body seemed to deflate.

"I'm sorry Darwin. I know this must be a shock. I should have told you a long time ago. I let it go too long and then I couldn't find the right time to tell you."

"I have a son?"

"Yes Darwin, you have a son."

Tears filled his eyes. "I thought I was childless. All this time I thought I was childless."

Lucy reached across the table to touch his hand. His stomach suddenly turned and he pulled away. "No, I can't. Excuse me. I have to use the restroom." — he got up quickly and stumbled to the men's room holding the storm of pain that wanted to escape his lungs. When he reached the men's room, he gasped with sobs that had caught in his throat. His dinner didn't want to stay down and he ran to the toilet to throw up.

Leaning against the washbasin to steady himself, he looked into the mirror, "I'm a father?"

The idea seemed so ridiculous he laughed. It couldn't be true. He had tried with his wives and had never produced a scintilla of a pregnancy. All this time Lucy had his son and he didn't know. This was unfathomable. He couldn't wrap his mind around it. How could she have kept it a secret?

And why? He would have been a good father. He would have loved to know his son. He felt cheated and the sobs came in waves. Why?

Lucy was at the door knocking. "Please Darwin. Come out. We need to talk about this."

"Ya think?" he grumbled still crying. He opened the door to her and wiping his face with his sleeve, he strode to the table as he took money out of his pocket and slapped in down.

"Come on," he said. "I have to get out of here." Lucy grabbed her jacket and purse and followed him out of the club.

They found the car and wanting to escape — he knew not what — he took off to the top of the mountain. During the ten-mile drive he was silent. During the ten-minute hike toward an active campfire, using his keyring flashlight to illuminate the way, he couldn't think of anything but his question. Why? But he was silent.

They came up to some people sitting around the fire.

"Mind if we sit down for a minute and warm ourselves?" He asked the group.

They all nodded and indicated their acceptance. Darwin sat and stared at the fire deep in thought. Lucy sat next to him quietly waiting for him to sort it out. The rest took their cue and remained silent, uninvolved in what was obviously none of their business.

After a while he took the flashlight and said to Lucy, "Come on, we need a place to talk."

They walked a little further into the campground and found a picnic table. Placing the tiny torch on the rough, sun beaten surface he said, "Maybe you should have brought that unfinished martini with you. You might need it."

"Darwin, I can't say how sorry I am."

"Phew!" he exhaled. "Not nearly as sorry as I am. My entire life I have wanted children. I would have had a gaggle of kids given a chance. It never happened. I thought I couldn't have them and you are telling me that *we* had a child together?"

"He is a beautiful man. He has your build and manliness." She smiled. "Loves football."

Darwin wiped his nose on his sleeve. "I just can't believe this right now. It doesn't seem real to me. You must have pictures."

"Oh gosh, yes. I have my phone right here." She rummaged through her bag and produced the promised photos on her cell.

The glow from the screen shone on his face and a stream of tears flecked his whiskers. Darwin peered at the screen seeing a stranger. He was handsome and manly as his mother said, but he was a stranger. Ted, her husband, stood with his family around him, all black as night except for his son who was a beautiful coffee color.

Then Lucy produced another photo of his son with his wife and children. All were black, of course, except for one light-skinned girl who took after her father.

"His family is handsome; don't you think?" Lucy said. "They are wonderful kids, too. All bright just like you are."

"I have grandkids." Darwin marveled. "Lucy, I am sorry, but this is such a shock. I don't think I'm handling it well. I'm angry, sad, really pissed off and really sad. On the other hand, I feel so blessed." He stopped and shook his head. "I can't tell you how I am feeling; it is too complicated and too overwhelming." He got up and walked into the deep black of the forest. Lucy wisely let him go to think.

CHAPTER 38

Danie

She was utterly surprised that Rose hadn't creamed her during the sitting. Danie was expecting a dressing-down, not having to do with towel draping. At least she thought Rose would take the opportunity to warn her to stay away from Darwin.

Surprisingly, the woman had been cheerful, even warm. Of course, she had brought up that issue about the friend who was divorcing her husband because of an affair. Danie wondered if that was some sort of object lesson meant for her.

In any case, Darwin had been scarce in the kitchen lately. He didn't show up as often with a brain full of jokes, and Danie found it harder to laugh when he did. The mood of the house had changed from Christmas-like joy to Crucifixion and she found it impossible to do anything about it but simply stay out of the way.

She had to work on her Christmas shopping; she wanted to find something appropriate for her hosts. It was difficult to think of anything that the two of them would appreciate receiving as a couple. Rose loved to shop and anything she didn't have one minute she bought the next, so it was difficult to think of anything she might want.

One thing she needed more of was help; Rose needed help with the cleaning, laundry and the endless cooking and tending to the kitchen. Danie marveled at Rose's energy. She was older but still could do many things that Danie had given up on for some time. She didn't know how Rose could keep up with all the work.

Most of Danie's older friends had hired people to do housework. Perhaps she could hire a person to come to the house and do some work for Rose. She decided to check with Darwin first before hiring someone they didn't know. He suggested a young woman with two kids who could use the work. Danie got in touch with the housekeeper immediately and made the arrangements.

But what could she get for Darwin? Danie could think of nothing.

Danie hoped no one would go to too much trouble for her. It would be nice if Wally found something because it would be a meaningful gift.

Wally's gifts had been very poor in the past. He always got something for her that *he* wanted.

Christmas, a holiday she loved and hated at the same time. Danie couldn't help being a little envious of her friends who loved to buy for their grandchildren. Now that would be fun to do, she thought. There were tons of things in the stores for grandchildren and children always needed something new. Then, Sami told her she was having a horrible time finding something her grandchildren hadn't gotten already — that didn't cost more than the national debt.

Having grandchildren was an idea Danie had to give up on noticing that Wally and Shanna had never had a child nor a pregnancy in the twelve years they were together. Had it been a purposeful intention? Danie didn't know but she suspected Wally was infertile since Shanna had had two babies since. It had been tragic for her — the babies were adopted away because of her addiction to methamphetamines. The girl's love for the meth dealer was incomprehensible.

Love wasn't supposed to be harmful as it had been for Shanna. The love Danie had for men in the past had been harmful too. Perhaps it hadn't been real love at all, but an ego need gone unmet. Love had been elusive to her as an actress of some note. She was 'arm candy,' an obnoxious designation that meant men loved to go out with her in public to show off. When it came to committing to a marriage after her divorce there were no men to be found. Danie could be 'arm-candy,' but she would never make a good 'trophy wife' — she was too independent.

She thought it had been a sad time for lovers in general. Love and marriage needed to be re-thought in her opinion. Pondering the subject more deeply, she thought perhaps romantic love had been an illusion. Now that she was no longer plagued with hormonally driven urges, she could have a normal relationship with a man without sexual complications.

Gifts — for men, for women, for children, or for the elderly — they were a conundrum and she wished she could think of better possibilities.

CHAPTER 39

Rose

She noticed Darwin and Lucy were spending a lot of time with their heads together. They went for long walks and spent significant time talking. The conversations between them seemed intense and Rose couldn't figure out what was up. Darwin though happy to see Lucy, was distant and preoccupied. He was acting strangely and she couldn't put her finger on the problem. She had been a bit frosty toward him because of the thing about Danie. She still didn't know exactly what to think about it. She only knew that he was acting very odd even after seeing Lucy and having opportunities to talk with her. In fact, now that she thought about it, he was acting very strange. Jealousy, an emotion she avoided like the plague flirted at the edge of her consciousness, like a stream of smelly unwanted cigarette smoke lurking just outside the window threatening to seep in.

This turn of events was troubling since Rose needed Darwin to do chores around the house preparing for the holidays. She was waiting for him to go down into the basement and bring up the decorations for the house, something she would do herself if there weren't so many spiders down there.

She had awakened from a disturbing sleep in which she dreamed about her nutcrackers coming alive getting loose in the basement and wreaking havoc with her favored assortment of glass ornaments. The collection of giant-sized nutcrackers gave her a great deal of pleasure during the season while they were out lining the stairway and placed strategically around the house. They were beautiful and differently designed; represented many cultures and lifestyles. Her favorite was a tall beautifully dressed New York model with long sleek legs covered in black net stockings, a silky, hip-clinging dress made of a spotted leopard fabric, long black gloves and a hat with wild red feathers sticking out. In her dream the New York model became a jealous witch bent on destroying every prized ornament Rose possessed.

Darwin lightly snored next to her and she rolled over to face him and wake him up. She kissed him on the forehead. "Darwin baby, wake up; it is another beautiful day in Paradise."

She knew better than to hit him first thing with all the chores she wanted done so she asked a question hoping to bring him gently to consciousness. "I am so curious to know what you and Lucy have been talking about lately. It seems very important the way you two put your heads together."

"Good morning. You aren't jealous, are you?" He asked groggily.

"No, not exactly. She has been taking a lot of your time and I have needed you to do things around here."

"Oh. Sure. I know. You want me to get into the basement and bring up the decorations. I'll do it this morning."

And suddenly he broke into tears.

"Darwin what is the matter?" Rose asked bewildered.

"Sorry. I didn't mean to…"

"You didn't mean to what?"

"Cry. I am a man after all. I shouldn't be crying like a baby." He turned away from her.

"Darwin what is it?" Rose was worried now. She had no idea Darwin was so distressed.

"Lucy. She came here to tell me something she should have told me years ago."

"What on earth?"

"What could be so terrible that I would cry?"

"Yes Darling."

"It isn't so horrible; it's wonderful except that she neglected to tell me." As he spoke, he was growing angry again. "I am furious with her; she should have told me when it happened."

"The suspense is killing me. What the hell is it?"

"I am a father. I have been a father all along!" He rolled out of bed energized by his fury.

"My god Darwin; what happened?"

"She got pregnant with my baby just before we broke up."

"Your baby?!"

"Yes, my son is a grown man now with a family. I have grand kids, too." He grabbed his robe and threw it around his shoulders while he slipped his arms into the sleeves with some difficulty.

"Oh Darwin, that's wonderful! Aren't you happy?"

"Rose, I am conflicted. I was never able to produce a family and now I find that I had one all along and didn't know it." Angrily he tied the robe around him. "I feel cheated."

"Of course, you do. Why didn't Lucy tell you until now?"

"She says she lost her nerve on many occasions. Then as time wore on, she couldn't find a good way to tell me."

"Why didn't she tell you when it happened?"

"She had just started dating Ted, fell madly in love with him and couldn't tell him she was pregnant. She rationalized that telling me I was a father then would be tantamount to giving up on Ted. She knows it was selfish but she didn't have the smarts to know the right thing to do, or so she says." Darwin's fury caused him to tie a knot in his robe instead of the bow he was attempting. "So, she let him think the baby was his born a little early.

"My god. But she wasn't just a teen, was she?"

"No, she was twenty-one, graduating from college. We broke up because back then we couldn't see our way through a mixed marriage. Well I should admit, I was warier of it than she was. You know there was a time not long before those days when you could get killed if you were just seen with a black person."

"Oh right. She's black. It is hard for me now to remember how bad it was at the time."

"I think Lucy was right to raise him as a black person and not in a mixed situation. He is light and he has a light-skinned daughter. They are handsome kids. She says they are smart too, like me." He added proudly.

"I'd love to see pictures of them." Rose said softly. "Maybe we should think about a trip to see Lucy and her family."

"Rose that would make me very happy. I want to meet my son and his brood. Lucy says that Ted was furious with her too, when she finally admitted her eldest was mine. But in time, he got used to the idea and realized he was as much a father to him since he'd reared him. And that's why I feel so cheated. I would have been a great dad."

"You know, you have been a great dad to a lot of people, especially Connie's children. You were great with them and with Jason. You have helped every soul you could, even if it was just a word or two of encouragement. Why do you think you are so great at being Santa?" She chided him. "Santa is the greatest dad of all!" she declared.

"Lucy is going home soon and I want to let her know how accepting you are of the situation. I wasn't sure how you'd feel."

"I am happy for you Darwin. I can imagine how important this is to you. I'd be concerned if it were not."

"Rose, I love you."

CHAPTER 40

Wally

Wally had seen Sally twice since the first time they were together. He was shocked that she was so different now from the time before when they were dating. Maybe it had been because he moved in with her too soon. They should have dated longer. Or maybe it had been the drugs. He had been doing meth and everything in his world had turned bad during that time. Whatever. This time was very different with Sally. She was far more cheerful, upbeat. The critical words she had used were replaced with respect. Respect was something he liked. Before she had been mostly crabby with nasty moods that ruined everything. After the first week they had spent living together, which had been cool, he couldn't remember a time when they had been happy. Their relationship had quickly turned sour and they separated.

The difference had caused Wally to think about how he was then. He justified it with self-absorbed precision, of course. It had always been Sally who had been obnoxious and caused him to do the things he did. He thought it couldn't be any other way. He blamed her for being depressing and oppressive. He couldn't live under her thumb very long and now he was uncertain that living together would be any different. He had thought of asking her to consider the idea again but decided to wait.

He had yet to mention Sally to his mother. He wasn't sure how she would react to the idea of Wally and Sally together again — after what the girl had done. However, he had told his mom that Sally apologized and he knew that impressed her. His mom's attitude toward the dental administrator had begun to change over time, yet he knew she did not like the way Sally dressed. She did behave sexily and the things she wore always showed her breasts off to enormous advantage. Wally loved it. She had a full figure and he couldn't think of anything better.

He had told his mother that he would be over to her place to help with some heavy lifting she needed done. Wally drove the truck he had borrowed from his friend Richard who had a new car, and felt fortunate that the man trusted him with the vehicle.

Just outside her door was a stand that held a small living Christmas tree his mom had purchased at the town nursery a day or two before. The clerk had told her to leave the tree outside for as long as possible because the living tree would not do well inside. His mom intended to decorate it; she wanted to give it to Darwin for Christmas.

"If you need to hide a Christmas present in plain sight, what do you do?" She asked rhetorically. "You decorate it." She wanted the tree brought inside now that Christmas day was only a week away. Once that was done, he left to do some errands and promised to come back to help with some other chore.

When he arrived back at her suite the tree was decorated, the lights were on and it sparkled in the happy way Christmas trees do.

"How do you like it?" She said with pride.

He didn't answer right away just getting his bearings inside the space where she lived. He felt too large for the room.

"Or, I guess you couldn't care less." She added.

"Mom, why do you say things like that?! I hate it when you say things like that."

"Well, the expression on your face…"

"You have no idea what I am thinking!" He was roaring now.

She tried to hug him.

He pushed her away. "You always do that! You are always second-guessing what I'm feeling. I hate it! The fact is I like the tree. It looks really nice."

"Please, let me apologize."

Barely taking a breath he continued: "You have been treating me like this ever since I can remember. It isn't fair. I am a man now and you treat me like I am still a kid."

"Yes, you've said that before, and I am sorry. I don't mean to…"

"And what about the other day when you walked out on me."

She paused for a moment as if trying to remember, "I felt uncomfortable."

"Yeah? Well, that was rude too!" He had asked his mother to help him make the first batch of Christmas cookies he intended to produce for his friends. They had made a plan and she tried to help him in the beginning. But Wally thought she was doing it all wrong. She focused on the recipe instead of giving him the instructions. He just wanted her to tell him what to do. He didn't read the instructions and made a mistake almost immediately rendering the batch spoiled and had to start all over again. He was so mad he screamed. He not only blamed her for letting him make such a mistake, he also wanted his mom to accept him for who he was, not the person she wished him to be.

Her face was screwing up into a mask of wrinkles. "I was feeling abused; that's why I left."

"Abused?!" he screamed. "Fuckin'-A! You abused me!"

"Wally, you don't realize…"

"You don't realize how you treat me!"

"I was trying to help."

"Then why didn't you just help?"

"I thought it would be better if you learned how to read the recipe and follow the direct…"

"I'm not stupid Mother. I can read instructions."

"Of course, you're not…"

"You treat me like I am stupid; I can read directions; I just wanted you to tell me what to do."

"Wally honey, if you read the recipe you would know what to do. It tells you."

"Oh, I give up. You will never understand me!"

She threw up her arms and said, "I guess not. I guess I will never understand."

He walked out disgusted. Loving his mother was the hardest thing he had to do in life and he didn't understand why. After her, Sally Oliver would be a piece of cake.

CHAPTER 41

Rose

Her son Jason was coming for Christmas. Rose was more excited this year than she had been in a long time. The holidays were shaping up in a way that brought anticipation to a head.

It wasn't all good. Darwin was still brooding about his missed opportunity to be a dad and she felt bad for him. But he was still on her list. She was feeling suspicious and betrayed because of what Eugenia had said about Danie and what she had seen subsequently. If her relationship with Danie hadn't been so meaningful, she would have asked her to leave right after the initial incident. However, Lucy was staying at the inn and Rose thought the woman would have a positive effect on her husband and the situation. At least that was her hope. Failing that, she knew what she had to do.

Jason was on his way to spend the holidays with them. He would fly in from Honolulu on the day of her birthday and she would pick him up at LAX that night after spending the day shopping for the guests coming for Christmas. There was a lot to do and she was anxious to pick up the painting at the framers. It was important to have it done as soon as possible. She was nervous about how it would look in the framing she had chosen. The painting had to turn out just right.

Because she had been in such a hurry to finish the work, she had painted quickly never stopping to be too critical. Having decided to do the work in watercolor, she couldn't tarry over it too long. At first, she worked primarily from the drawing she'd made that first day, and then she asked Danie to pose once more for more detail. Nevertheless, she had spent very little time agonizing over it. She had learned long ago to let the paint settle and to go back and look at it at least a whole day after finishing. It was fascinating how, miraculously, the paints took on aspects in the second viewing that she hadn't notice at first. She liked it and felt proud.

Jason was tan and gorgeous. He was tall like her. His features were sharp and his eyes looked almost Asian as were his mom's, except they were an astonishing blue color. Neither she nor her husband at the time had blue eyes, so it was the only trait he didn't share with his adopted parents. His hair had started to recede, which made her feel old.

But Jason could always make her feel young again when he picked her up in his strong arms and swung her around to say hello. He had carried all he needed on the plane in a duffle bag and was ready to pile into the car and go home. He considered the B&B to be his home, too, since he had been instrumental in designing and building the Tea Rose Room Danie now occupied. He was home for Christmas and Rose couldn't be happier.

"So, how are things at the B&B?" He asked as soon as he was settled in the car. She applied pressure on the peddle under her foot, and the Volvo took off almost floating onto the road. Rose knew this was the result of her good frame of mind. She felt light and happy. The car's action reflected her mood perfectly.

However, his question had put a dark note in her memory. "They are okay."

"Just okay?" He asked. Jason knew his mother well. Mostly reared as the only child of a divorced mother, he could read her as well as he could his wife. She was transparent. Something was off and she knew he would keep asking until he got an answer. So, right away, she told him the area of her discontent.

"I am not sure about Darwin." She said.

"Jez, Mom, what does that mean? You've been married almost twenty years. How can you be unsure now?"

"Oh, it's really nothing."

"Come on. With you it is never 'nothing.'"

Rose was reluctant to involve her son in her marital problems, but she continued anyway. "You know that Darwin is lax in the way he does things. That has already been a problem for some time."

"So, that's not it."

"No, not exactly. But I am wondering if he is becoming lax in his personal life, too."

"Uh-oh, that doesn't sound good. He isn't having an affair, is he?"

"Oh, I don't think so."

"Come on, Mom. It's something like that, isn't it?"

"Well, yes. There is that woman staying at the inn, Daniella Wharton, who could be a threat. I just haven't decided if it is a real threat or something else."

"Wow! That really clarified the situation."

She looked at him with a wry expression. "That doesn't mean something isn't happening. Something is definitely happening. I'm just not certain how serious it is. That's all."

"Alright, explain to me exactly what you are talking about. That is, if you feel you can, Mom."

"I can." She proceeded to tell him all she knew, and felt better when she had conveyed it all to her son.

"Mom, I love you and I love Darwin. I can't imagine that he would be interested in any other woman."

"I hope not. However, you haven't seen her yet."

"I remember one of her old movies. It wasn't that good. She was beautiful, I'll give you that, but she seemed phony to me."

"She isn't so phony anymore. In fact, she is very different from what you would expect, not like other actresses who are so overly self-involved. I mean she hasn't even had any 'work' done on her face. She is very natural, the kind of woman that appeals to Darwin. You'll meet her and then you can tell me if he would be interested. I'd like your opinion."

She changed the subject quickly, "That's not all." She added. Darwin recently learned he is a father. After all this time thinking he was childless, he now knows that a girl he loved in college had his baby without ever telling him until recently. It has knocked him off his game and he is furious with her. He always wanted to be a dad.

"But that knowledge about Darwin having a son and not knowing until now must give you something more sensitive to feel about him. I mean, how can you be mad at the guy now that you know he is so troubled?"

"Oh, I am not exactly mad at Darwin. I think he may be a little weak toward Danie but you're right. I am more concerned about Danie. She may be flirting with him when I am not looking."

"I can't wait to meet her. She sounds like some kind of a witch."

Rose laughed. "You know I've had dreams lately about witchy women destroying things of mine."

"Wow Mom. I hope you aren't creating something you might regret."

"What on earth could I be creating other than the painting I've done of her?"

"You've done a painting?"

"Yes, using Daniela Wharton as a model. That's impressive don't you think?"

Jason made Rose's day. Just having him there at the inn made her happy.

She remembered the first time she ever saw him. He had a shock of dark hair and the most intense blue eyes. They were still like that. She remembered holding him at the adoption agency, this little bundle of a baby so tiny and helpless and telling herself, *he is mine, all mine.*

Jason had slept late. Jet lag would take him away for a morning or two until he adjusted. Once he was awake, he took up chores for her as if he had been doing it all along. He was a good man and Rose was proud.

Danie made herself available to do laundry for the week and ran into Jason for the first time in the laundry room.

"Good morning. I'm Jason, Rose's son."

Rose stood off to the side watching as the two made their acquaintances. "Of course, you are. You look just like her!" Danie smiled and he warmly hugged her. "How wonderful to meet you." Danie continued before he could respond. "She doesn't stop talking about you. I can see why she is so proud."

"I am proud because he is a good person." Rose stepped up to make herself known to the pair. Have I told you he took on the rearing of his step-son?"

"Andrew is my wife's boy and he's sixteen now."

"How old was he when you married her?"

"He was three."

Rose interjected, "It hasn't been a smooth road Danie. Jason has had his hands full with the boy."

"He is challenging Mom. That's true."

"My son is challenging too," Danie interjected, "only he is a lot older than sixteen. Wally is like forty-five going on sixteen." She laughed.

"Andrew has ADHD and it has been hard for him to concentrate on studies." Jason added.

"I understand. You have to love him for who he is even when it's hard to do."

"My wife has a harder time than I do. She wants him to do better. It's hard for him to live up to her expectations." He continued thoughtfully. "It turns out I am the stern parent insisting that he do his studies, chores, etcetera. Oddly, she has become more of a friend."

"I'm sure she could take some pages from my playbook. I made the mistake of making my son, Wally, my friend. Parenting sometimes took a back seat to the relationship. Big mistake."

"I think I could impart some of that wisdom to her. She might benefit from your experience."

Rose watched her son and Danie put their heads together and relate as if they had known each other all along. He obviously liked her and talking to her was easy. Maybe he would be able to impart to Danie something about her concerns. No, that would not work. If there was something going on between Danie and Darwin, Jason would not be the person to do anything about it. It was up to her to fight and win her own battles.

CHAPTER 42

Danie

The invitation had been clear. Rose and Darwin asked Danie and Wally, with his dog, Buddy to come for Christmas breakfast and gifts around the tree, and to spend the big day with them and the other B&B guests who would be there. Darwin's friend, Lucy, had gone home for the holidays and the current guest list included Jason and any Laughing Bear visitors who happened to need a reservation on the Eve of Christmas. They expected the inn to fill up long before any stragglers arrived at their door, so it was likely the foot-draggers would have to go somewhere else.

Darwin didn't like to turn people down and on Christmas Eve he was especially reluctant to turn anyone away. There had been times when he offered a couch or two to sleep on when all the rooms were filled. That offer had stood mainly because of snowstorms.

This Christmas would not prove to be an overflow but the reservation list was filling up fast. Danie extended the invitation to Wally with great enthusiasm. It was the first Christmas in many years they had a good place to go for the day. She thought he recognized how excited she was to have such an opportunity — if Wally noticed anything about anyone other than himself.

He knew that Christmas was her favorite holiday. She had told him of her memories of family gatherings when she was a child. She'd had a decent sized family then. There were her father and mother, her grand-mothers, her aunt and her cousins — two boys. With a couple of visitors added, Christmases were often the best days.

She remembered how her cousin who was ten years older and a young teen at the time would perch her on top of his knees and tease about when he would let her fall to the floor, which he did with delicious, startling regularity. She loved the feeling of losing his knees holding her and sud-denly, unexpectedly releasing her to fall to the floor. She would squeal in delight and beg him to do it again.

Christmas presents were a source of great mystery and hope of course. Santa was sure to bring the best presents. Her family didn't have a lot of money then but they had supplied enough under-the-tree gifts to make her happy. Anxiety arose only when she learned she was expected to give gifts herself. She didn't have much money, only a small allowance every week, but she diligently saved up so she could buy something for her mom, her grandmothers and her aunt. She wasn't expected to get the men or boys anything just yet. This was the first Christmas when she would have to produce a gift for each woman in the family.

Her mother had taken her shopping at the local Five and Dime Store where she could buy certain things for pennies. There they found some facial powder puffs Danie knew the women could use; her mom told her that. They bought four which had cost her a whopping 20 cents. It was almost all the money she had. Her mom had let her use some of her wrapping paper so Danie could cuddle the little puffs into a bit of tissue covering to hide them until the moment when, with all surprise, the women would open their gift and see with enormous excitement a fresh little powder puff to use for the year. That was the time Danie learned the joy of giving. Each of the women had received her gift with such excitement and elation that she would never again worry about how much a gift would cost if she could get the recipient to react with such joy.

That never turned out to be an easy chore but she engaged in it with enthusiasm at the beginning of each new opportunity to find the perfect gift.

With or without gifts, Danie was nevertheless excited this year in the way she had been as a child. She and Wally only had each other when it came to family. Her family was gone and Wally's dad's family didn't care much. So, a chance to celebrate the holiday in a family atmosphere even with strangers was exhilarating. She hoped Wally felt the same.

She was also excited that Rose's son was aboard for the holidays. Jason's arrival had put a cheer into the doings at the inn. The Christmas tree went up quickly once he arrived. And the season was looking very good indeed. She liked Jason a lot. He had the most gorgeous blue eyes, eyes that looked familiar to her though she couldn't put her finger on why.

Somewhere in the middle of preparing for the holiday Wally got it in his head to provide a good Christmas for a couple of his homeless friends. They were deserving, however, asking the Neumann's to include these homeless men was going too far. In Danie's mind it was best to invite them another time. But Wally was resolute. He left a vague message with them to call him because he wanted to extend this invitation to 'some of his friends.' Busy with holiday preparations, neither Rose nor Darwin got back to him and didn't know how to answer because they couldn't tell how many men there would be. Danie took matters into her own hands and told Wally 'no,' at which point Wally decided to have his own party on Christmas morning with his friends and 'oh, yes,' Danie was welcome to come if she wanted.

It felt like another slap in the face and it wasn't as if this kind of thing hadn't happened before. In fact, Danie had privately predicted Wally would do what he did; it felt like a power play and she felt devastated that he had done it again. Yet, she didn't want to engage in some control game of one-up-man-ship.

It hurt and she wanted to be able to express that feeling. She knew she would get a ton of blowback if she tried. Was it worth it or should she let it go? If she let it go, he would continue through life never knowing how hurtful he could be. Or maybe he did know and telling him would only feed into his sense of control over her. She wanted to be the adult in the situation; it didn't feel right that he should get away with his insult.

He had stood her up just as his dad had so many years ago. Now of course she wished she had let that go as well; life would be so different now if she had not taken the second invitation to go out with Wally's dad. She might have married someone else who could be more reliable, someone with whom she could have had many children and reared a family the old-fashioned way with both parents present and available. At this stage of life, she knew that was naïve. Most of the people she knew who had remained married all along — making it into retirement with the same partner with children and grandchildren — were only just coping with the results. Perfect loving families were rare. Happiness was no longer expected and was elusive. The whole idea of love and marriage had hit a wall in the general society; that is, the earlier infatuation with true love and marriage had all but dissolved — all but the wedding part. Weddings continued on unabated with glowing brides and reluctant grooms standing before a preacher or a judge getting hitched the old-fashioned way. Well, it was what it was and there was nothing to be done about it now but to live graciously with the results.

Her mind took up an old nag. Danie wondered what life would have been like had she kept her first child. Maybe her biological clock would not have ticked so loudly. Perhaps having a child all those years might have given her less reason to fret about having a family at all. She had chosen her husband because he was available just when her biological clock was ticking the loudest. He was all wrong for her and she knew it, but she had forged ahead believing she would not have a family at all if she waited any longer. It was a big mistake from the beginning and she wondered what might have happened had she not married and had Wally.

She wondered what life would have been without Wally. That idea was just as unacceptable as any other.

She warmed herself by the fire ruminating about their life together. She thought about the influences in Wally's life when he was growing up. She of course was his greatest influence but it occurred to her that he had been reared during a time in American culture when movies like *Star Wars, Close Encounters of the Third Kind,* and *E.T.* were gracing the big screen. This was a time when they would go into big darkened theaters that had huge screens on which to project their movies; sometimes you would spend an entire evening going to the movies long before big-screen TV. It was easy to see how these spectacular films could influence a small boy. Perhaps those movies had taught him to believe in extra-terrestrials. It was a plausible theory, as plausible as anything else.

She didn't have a clue how to handle Wally. She never had because it was true, tragically she didn't understand him at all. Danie had thought it would be easy to re-parent him but it wasn't turning out very well. She had to decide, since there were no other options, to let it all go. When she thought about it, she couldn't be offended about Christmas because Wally was doing something very nice — inviting homeless people for a holiday breakfast was a very kind thing to do. How could she be critical under the circumstances? Wally was being a generous soul; what could be better than that?

It was hard to do but Danie decided Wally would have to learn from someone else how rude he could be. He could have handled the situation better and there was no doubt that he was absent on the day manners were taught. He was too old now to parent him in any way. She felt a failure as a mother and there was nothing she could do. Lost opportunities where just that — lost. There were no do-overs.

As predicted, snow began falling in the early evening before Christmas Day. Those who were going to church left early so they wouldn't have to rush through the ice and snow. The Christmas tree that Rose, Jason and Danie had decorated days before sparkled with clear and colored lights, shiny glass balls and strings of popcorn. The stairway up to the bedrooms was lined with a variety of decorative Nutcrackers that Rose had collected over the years. There must have been a hundred of them strewn around the house. Giant wreaths adorned the walls of the great room and beautifully painted blown glass ornamental balls hung from the five-point chandelier over the dining table.

Everything was so festive, Danie nearly forgot that Wally wouldn't be coming to spend Christmas with them.

A new couple arrived at the B&B just in time to miss the heaviest snowfall. Danie, the only one left at the inn, sat reading by the fire when they arrived. She answered the door: "Come on it in folks," she invited. "Welcome to the Laughing Bear B&B!"

The guests always entered the inn with widened eyes as they looked around to orient themselves. The scene before them was a wonderland of Christmas sparkle and adornment. Danie led the new guests to their room taking note of the collection of Nutcrackers that lined the stairway up to the rooms.

"Should I be afraid?" The woman asked.

"Only if you're a nut." Danie smiled.

The couple howled. "We are both nuts!" They laughed. The man held out his hand, "Hi, I'm David and this is my wife Maxine. I think we are going to have the best time here," he said as he looked around. "Don't you, honey?"

"Merry Christmas!" Maxine whooped. She entered the Pine Valley View room with the giant king-sized bed and said, "Let's get started!" She fell on the bed spread eagle and Danie slipped away to let the couple have some privacy. Merry Christmas she thought as she quietly descended the stairway.

CHAPTER 43

Wally

The table was set, the bacon had been fried, the hash-brown potatoes were done warming in the oven and the egg-whip concoction sat on the counter waiting the heat of the pan on the stove. The pan sizzled with melting butter. The coffee was brewed and warming in its perch. The smells were warm and inviting. Wally looked around him — what was missing? Eggs, bacon and hash browns weren't enough food for the men he had coming for Christmas breakfast. They would be hungry because they had little chow available to them most of the time. Toast! That was it! He needed to make a mound of toast. Wally grabbed the loaf of bread on top of the refrigerator and began the process of browning the bread in the toaster two pieces at a time. He worried that it wouldn't be done soon enough for his arriving guests. Orange juice would have to tide them over while he got the whole meal cooked. He might even add a little Vodka to the juice to lighten up the mood.

This must be what it is like at the Bed & Breakfast every day, he thought. He had to admire the work the Neumann's put into their business. It was hard to imagine how the two of them could keep up with all the chores and be sociable, too. They were remarkable people and he thought his mom was remarkable pitching in with chores when Rose or Darwin was ill. He hoped the two of them would never become ill at the same time. He couldn't imagine his mother doing the whole thing alone.

A knock at the door came at the same time the toaster coughed up its first batch of toast. Caught between the sounds, Wally, flying from one noise to the other, did his mother's 'kitchen dance' trying to stay on top of it all. When he opened the door, he found a straggler he didn't expect.

"Merry Christmas!" he intoned not expecting Sally. "Hey, I didn't expect you here today."

"And why not? Christmas is a great day to spend together."

He shifted gears. "Sally, my apologies. My mind was on helping some guys I know who don't have anywhere to go for today."

"I don't either." She wasn't exactly pouting but she came close. "It's really cold out here and by the way it is *snow*-ing," she sang.

"Well don't just stand there. Come on in. I can make room. Have you had breakfast yet?"

"You don't have much in the way of manners, do you?"

"What are you talking about? I invited you in and offered breakfast!" What more do you want?"

"I would have liked an invitation, that's what."

Wally was about to take offense then changed his mind. She handed him a package.

"A present," she said. "They're socks. Men always need new socks."

"Sally my girl, thank you. Look, you are here now and we can have a good time, okay?" He took her in his arms and held her tight. "Can I get a kiss?" He asked. "You are so cute when you're angry."

"They all say that." She snarled. "Don't patronize me Wally Wharton."

"You're right, I'm sorry." He kissed her briefly and let go. "My toast is getting cold and I need to butter it before it does."

"Good god, you sound like a housewife!" she said.

"To be entirely truthful, I'm looking for a job as a house-husband. I would be very good."

Sally couldn't help herself and laughed. "Okay, you got me."

"No really. I'm not kidding. I really do want to take care of someone who makes the money and brings home a pay check.

"You're serious?"

"Oh, yes!" He took the softened butter from the microwave and slathered it onto the toast as he threw another two pieces into the toaster.

"Haven't you noticed? I look truly eye-catching in an apron."

"Wally, I have never seen you in an apron."

He grabbed the apron hanging from a hook in the pantry and donned the garment to prove his point. "See how cute I am?" His freshly grown beard contrasted nicely with the yellow and white apron that said, 'Good Cook — Good Luck,' printed on the front.

"You look darling." She laughed.

Checking around she found a chair and sat down. "I'm beat. You don't mind if I sit here, do you? I'll try not to get in the way of your 'house chores.' "

"Sally, how can you be beat at this hour of the morning?"

"Well, honestly. I am glad to hear you want to be a house-husband. I could use one."

"What are you talking about?"

"There is no other way to say this. I'm pregnant and you're the father."

"What?!"

The next batch of bread exploded from the toaster as if to emphasize his astonishment. He ignored it.

"You heard me. I'm going to have our baby in about eight months — July to be exact. He or she will be a Cancer or maybe a Leo, a great sign to be born under."

He sank cross-legged to the floor. "My god. I thought we had been careful."

There was a knock at the door. "I'll get it," said Sally. "You don't look in any shape."

Wally folded into the fetal position. *Was it possible? Could it have happened now at this late date?* Wally had gotten lax over time when Shanna didn't get pregnant. He had become accustomed to having sex often and without consequences.

"Hey Buddy, what's up?" Wally's friend, Gary, the pot dealer had arrived.

Wally moaned. "Oh man, I can't believe it."

"Looks like you could use a little product."

"Don't mind him; he's just getting used to being a father." Sally interjected.

"Man. Sorry Dude. Who's pregnant?"

"Who the fuck do you think?" Sally stood with her hands on her hips daring him to scoff.

"Ohhhh, it's you?" Gary was truly taken-aback. "Man, I am sorry," he said to Wally with such emotion that Sally steamed.

"What the hell is there to be sorry for?" She bristled. "I'm happy. I've wanted a child for years! I just couldn't get far enough into the marriage thing," She mumbled. "It never happened."

Wally's head shot up. "How many times you been married Sally?"

"Just two; they didn't last long."

"Up here? Do I know them?"

"No, they happened before I came up here. Both are long-gone now and I don't expect to hear from either any time soon."

"Hey Gary, I'll take you up on some smoke." Wally got up from the floor and resumed toasting.

Sally said, "Yeah, I'll join you."

"Oh no you won't." Wally intoned astonished. "You only get contact highs from now until the baby is born!" He added.

"Wally," she whined. "Marijuana should be okay. It's the hard drugs that are harmful."

"No. That is my baby and he will not be exposed to any drugs!"

"Wow, Wally. I didn't think you'd feel that strongly."

Gary added, "Yeah man, what's the deal?"

"No dealing here anymore."

"Does that mean nothing for you either?"

"Yeah, that *is* what it means." Wally pronounced. "Starting now, I am not going to smoke anything until my boy is at least eighteen-years-old. It is my New Year resolution," he said with great intensity.

"How do you know it's going to be a boy?" Sally queried with a grin. "It isn't a girl, is it?"

"How the hell do I know? Would it make a difference?"

"Well, yeah Sally. Girls are feminine and boys aren't."

"Sometimes."

"What? He isn't going be gay, is he?"

"Oh, Wally; please don't go homophobic on me."

"Hey man, how about a hit on my pipe. It'll calm you down a little." Gary handed the pipe to Wally who shrugged and accepted.

"There goes that New Year's resolution." Sally murmured. "Didn't take long."

"It's for me. You can't. You know that, don't you?"

She stared at Wally as he went back to the toasting with the pipe in his hand. "Wally, it isn't fair that you can and I can't."

"Who said life was fair?"

"That's a lousy excuse…Here, let me help you with that. You toast and I'll butter. I'll starve waiting for you to finish! I am pregnant you know."

"Oh brother. Here we go…"

CHAPTER 44

Danie

"Daddy! Daddy!" The four-year-old whose name was Camilla, or Cami for short, ran down the steep stairway as fast as her little legs would carry her, knocking a nutcracker down on the way. Excited, she said, "I found him! I found him! He lives here, right here in…" then her language skills faltered because she wasn't certain where she was or how to pronounce it. Danie, replacing the nutcracker followed her.

"Who did you find, Cami?" Her father queried.

"Santa lives…here! I found… I found," she had to stop to catch her breath, "his suit!" the little girl was so thrilled she could barely get the words out. "Santa Claus! His suit is hanging…up there." She pointed up the stairway as her voice reached an exhilarated pitch.

The father looked to Danie behind her for clarification. "She did. She found Santa's suit. And it is true, he lives right here in Dancing Bear Springs," she added.

"But…I thought he lived at the North Pole." The child almost cried with bewilderment.

"Ho, Ho, Ho!" Darwin, who was in the kitchen preparing the Christmas breakfast meal, peeked out at her. "Ho, Ho, Hooo! His voice rang out just like Santa's and the girl squealed with delight.

"It's him! It's him!" She screamed at a higher pitch than she had before.

Her little brother who was two toddled into the room to see about the commotion. The two tykes were look-alikes with blonde curls and blue eyes. They could have been Danie's grandchildren, they looked so much like her.

"Santa!" The little girl nearly danced as she ran across the great room toward the kitchen. In fact, she was a little scared and her footwork showed it. She started and stopped a couple of times before she reached the kitchen and flew into Santa's arms.

Darwin wasn't wearing his beard and hat of course, but his natural hair, which flowed over his shoulders and his whiskers, which were short by Santa's standards, were ample enough to convince Cami that she had found the real thing. He bent down, his knees creaking with the strain, and gathered her up into his arms.

"Ho, Ho, Ho," he continued trying to satisfy the child's thrill. "You know, I came by here late last night and left something out on the front porch for you." He knew the parents had brought a small sleigh for the child's Christmas present and it was out on the front portico.

Cami screamed with elation and wiggled from his arms running toward the door. Her father followed her out as everyone present awaited the squeals of discovery when she found her new sleigh.

This is a real Christmas, Danie thought. Her heart warmed — *A joyous time.* Only one touch of sadness — Wally wasn't here to see this.

The room filled with guests who had braved the Christmas Eve snowfall that blessedly tumbled over them the night before. El Nino was fulfilling its promise giving them a White Christmas just like the song.

Los Angelinos were notoriously horrible drivers in bad weather. They were far too used to the dry desert air and roads, so part of Santa's job on the eve of the big day was rescuing pitiable drivers from the snow. He had gone out twice the night before to gather two different carloads of Laughing Bear visitors from the side of the only road that led into the Dancing Bear Valley. Why they came up here so unprepared for possible snow was a total mystery to all who lived in the stuff. They often drove in rear-wheel-drive cars and failed to get chains even though they had been warned not to come without them.

The child's screams of joy at the discovery of her new sled, jarred Danie from her thoughts. It was too early to go sledding and the child needed to eat and dress properly before she could go out and play. Breakfast was almost ready and the smell of sizzling bacon beckoned the revelers to the table. Even Cami, who had misgivings about leaving her new sled outside, and her little brother were drawn by the delectable smells.

Though Darwin was obviously trying to be joyful for the guests, his mood had turned sour since Lucy's arrival and departure. Danie noticed that he lacked the ability to joke around and make great breakfast conversation. He had been oddly quiet and somber. She wondered if something had happened and what the ramifications would be if that something had to do with her. He seemed preoccupied and out-of-sorts. She decided not to let his mood affect her and the good time she was having.

During breakfast, she spoke of a time years ago when she had taken Wally up to Lake Tahoe during the winter. He was only ten years old and into skateboarding full time. "It was a new sport and Wally's obsession with it went way beyond normal," Danie said. When they arrived in Tahoe, snow was piled high and Wally could not find a good spot to skateboard. "So, he did the only logical thing a smart boy could do and removed the ball-bearing wheels from the bottom of his skateboard to create a snowboard." At this point in time, no one had thought of the idea yet. "Wally's discovery went unnoticed, of course, but he was one of the originators of the new snowboarding sport." To Jason she added: "I think your mom told me you took up skateboarding, too."

"Yes, I did as a kid," the tall, good-looking son responded. As a child, he had lived in Venice Beach near the boardwalk, which was a cement-covered lane that snaked across the beachfront covering about three miles of sandy shoreline until it met the boats docked at Marina del Rey. There Jason had mastered the art of skateboarding just as Wally had on the streets of West Hollywood.

"Jason made his first skateboard himself with a wood plank and wheels from his roller-skates." Rose stated proudly.

The two mothers commiserated what it was like to look after boys hell-bent on speed. Wally had lost a tooth to the sport and Jason had broken an arm. He said it still hurt when the weather turned cold. That was one of the reasons he lived in Hawaii, to avoid the nagging ache.

Danie thought Jason fulfilled the potential Wally had as a boy. He was tall and tanned, handsome like his mom, and he was just a little older than Wally. He was bright, had a good mind. As she got to know him better, she found he shared a lot of her political ideas, too, something Wally would never deign to do. Jason was fun to talk to and they got along very well. Her only wish was that Wally could be there to share in the breakfast chatter. He would have liked Jason. Of this, she was sure.

After breakfast, Danie took Jason aside, "Can you help me for a moment? I need to bring Darwin's Christmas present in."

"Where is it?"

"My room." They headed down the stairs to her suite and got the small live Christmas tree that she had undecorated that morning. Jason brought the tree to the main room and placed it under the big tree. Darwin had disappeared for a few minutes and wearing his Santa Claus hat, he "Ho, Ho, Ho-ed" his way back into the great room to hand out presents.

The children were so overcome with excitement and anticipation that their screams became nearly unbearable. Danie cringed at the sharp sounds (they hurt her ears) but laughed with glee at the sight before her. Christmas wrapping flew and squeals pierced the air. Rose opened the Christmas envelope from Danie and felt truly grateful that she would have some cleaning help in the New Year. Darwin hugged Danie in thank you for the baby tree and they decided the potted plant would look good in the front of the house until he could place it in the ground in the spring.

After all the jocularity was over, Wally finally showed up carrying some tins filled with his homemade Christmas cookies. He gave them to Rose, Darwin and Danie and handed an envelope over to Danie. She hugged him in welcome though she still felt put out by his poor handling of the invitation to the inn. Both Rose and Darwin felt badly they hadn't returned the call from Wally when it was still time to divert the invitation catastrophe. They both knew that Danie had been deeply hurt by Wally's maneuvering.

Danie sat down in her chair while she opened the cookies Wally made. One on top had cracked; she took the broken piece and tasted it.

"A chip off the old block." he joked.

"This is really good Wally. You did a great job without my help."

Wally's chest grew and he blushed a little with the compliment.

The envelope Wally brought contained a pre-paid dinner coupon for two at the Singing Bear Bistro. Danie knew she would have to host Wally for the meal. At least, this time he got something they could both enjoy.

She noticed he was in an especially good mood and wondered if he was high on pot, although his generosity toward the homeless men could produce a good high too. The dog, Buddy, was given a huge bone to chew, which he took to a corner and began gnawing so the other animals couldn't get to it.

Then Rose said that she'd nearly forgotten something she intended to give to Darwin, who was out of his Santa hat and back to his normal self. She headed up the stairs to retrieve the forgotten Christmas present. The children had dressed in their snowsuits and had gone outside to play in the snow and to slide on the new sleigh while their parents watched.

When Rose descended the stairway, she was carrying a huge framed canvass covered with a bed sheet. She placed it before Darwin who was resting for a moment in his favorite chair. "What is this?" He queried. "You've already given me plenty of Christmas joy.

"I made this specially for you, Darwin. I think you will like it a lot."

With that, she removed the sheet and presented the nude portrait of Danie in living watercolor. It was beautiful, the paints softly revealing the aging body of the beautiful actress, licking an ice cream cone — as melting vanilla plunged between her breasts.

"GRRGLEGRUMBLE, GRRGLEGRUMBLE, GRRGLEGRUMBLE."

The startled intake of breath followed by a profound hush filled the room like a receding ocean wave. The silence bursting the seams of the room said it all. Rose had crossed a line. As if she had been sleeping and was now awake, she looked at the surprised expressions of the guests, and Jason, Danie and Wally. Was the stunned silence aimed at her? She turned to Darwin who couldn't speak either.

Then at last, a guest, David, who had arrived late the night before stated the obvious. "The painting is beautiful. Your choice doing a watercolor of an older woman is unusual and it is quite alluring."

"Danie spoke for Rose when she realized her friend had also been reduced to silence. "Thank you. That is a portrait of me."

"Yes, I guessed. You are a beautiful woman."

"Thank you."

He smiled. "The painting is bold; it dares you to look at it. I am an art historian by profession and I can honestly say this is an excellent painting."

Jason was mortified. "Yeah, Mom, you hit it out of the ballpark this time," he said flatly.

Rose and Darwin became the center of attention as the focus remained on the artwork. "Rose," Darwin said as gently as he could, "Can we go upstairs and have a chat?" He took the painting covering it again with the sheet.

"GRRGLEGRUMBLE, GRRGLEGRUMBLE, GRRGLEGRUMBLE."

Rose's attention went to the garbage disposal. Her voice, shrill with frustration, she said, "Heavens, Darwin. When are you going to fix that awful disposal?" Eyes grew wide in the room.

"Rose, please."

She looked around at the guests and became aware they were staring at her. Embarrassed, she ran from the room and darted up the stairway knocking some nutcrackers down along the way.

Darwin followed saying, "Excuse us folks," and disappeared.

Danie stood motionless until Wally wrapped his arm around her and led her to her room. "It's going to be okay, Mom," he said trying to be reassuring. "Let's go over to my place and have an eggnog. I bought some special for you because I know you like it so much."

Danie smiled feebly and allowed herself to be led away.

CHAPTER 45

Rose

"Rose, Rose...Please come out." She had locked herself in their bathroom.

"I'm busy, Darwin. Leave me alone."

"Rose, Honey, we need to talk."

"Don't remind me."

He waited a moment and then, "Honey, this isn't getting us anywhere. You have to come out and talk to me."

"Darwin, I am so embarrassed. I don't know what got into me." The door opened a crack but she stood blocking the entry. "I will never be able to face those people again. I don't know how I can face you, or Jason, or... or, Danie!" With each name, her voice became more alarmed.

"You can Sweetheart. I know you didn't mean to embarrass anyone especially not me or yourself."

"I love the painting and I wanted you to have something that I feel very proud of."

"Well, of course you did. That makes sense," he said lamely.

"I'm sorry Darwin." He could hear the tears in her voice.

"The painting is stunning. I love the colors you chose." He wisely said nothing about how Danie looked. "You know, I was really impressed with how you used them. The bold yellows, greens and lavenders were used not only in the objects of the painting but repeated in the shadows and crevasses as well. It was very daring and different from what you have done before. You are not shy about showing her face and body as it really is wrinkles and all."

Rose had been very careful when she chose the paints to use. The soft corals and peaches used for the skin contrasted skillfully with the blues, soft browns and beiges of the background and she had used some soft breezy greens, strong yellows and lavenders for the towel that draped the bottom of Danie's body; those colors emphasized the shadows in her face, hair and curves. With little splashes of yellow, gold and vanilla color — "Oh my god, the creamy vanilla white of the ice cream!" She whispered.

"I guess I'm having trouble understanding the cone and the dripping ice cream," he said.

She groaned into the door which made the cry sound hollow and ghostly.

"I can't tell you why."

"Don't you know why?"

"It was Danie's idea." She stopped herself. "No, it was mine. I can't blame anyone but myself." She groaned again. "We had such a good laugh over it. I asked her to think of something she could be doing in the painting and she came up with the idea of the ice cream cone. Then, we had a laugh over the notion of melting ice cream. I just couldn't resist using it in the work."

"Well, it is suggestive."

"I know," she groaned. Rose took a piece of toilette paper and blew her nose with it. "It was stupid. I don't know what got into me." She sobbed now.

"Come out Rose, please."

Slowly the door opened, creaking on its hinges. Rose emerged slowly while blowing her nose again. "I am stupid. I know that now. I like Danie. She has been nothing but good to me. She listens to all of my troubles so patiently and she never criticizes, even though she manages to let me know where I took a wrong turn," she added wryly. "Why would I do something that would embarrass her so?"

"Yeah, she even pitches in when you need help."

"Don't rub it in, Darwin."

He took her into his arms and enfolded her close to him. "I love you, Rose. Please don't ever forget that."

"I know you do, Darwin. I have no doubt." She stopped for a moment, then, "I admit I was jealous of Danie. I thought maybe she was doing things to you."

"Like what?" He asked startled.

"Oh, I don't know exactly. Maybe I was seeing things that weren't there."

"Ya think?"

"Well." She unlocked herself from his embrace hesitating to acknowledge him. "What about the fact that you notice Danie coming into a room before anyone else does?"

"I do?"

"Yes, I've noticed you do that. It's like you see her before she is even there. What is that about, Darwin?"

"I don't."

"You do."

"I notice all of the guests as soon as they come into the room."

"Not the way you notice Danie. Your mood always lightens when she arrives."

"Gosh, I hadn't noticed. Maybe it is because she always laughs at my jokes."

Rose walked away still crying, "Good point, which makes me wonder why you are so funny to her." She was regaining her pique.

"I can't answer that. I just know her amusement makes me feel good."

"I am amused by you too, Darwin," she whimpered. "I even come up with jokes of my own occasionally." She angrily dabbed the toilette paper at her eyes.

Darwin took her into his arms again and hugged her close. "You do. Good ones too. You can be just as funny as I am. And you know Danie laughs just as hard at your one-liners as she does at mine."

"How am I going to make it up to her?" Rose lamented.

"Rose, look at me."

She looked up the tears streaming back into her hair. He was the only man she could look up to because all the others were too short for her. She liked that about Darwin; he was a man to whom she could look up. Looking into his eyes, she was embarrassed to think about how foolish she had been.

"I love you. Period." Darwin said. "And you are going to find a way to talk to Danie. You and she are going to be fine. We all are."

CHAPTER 46

Danie

Taking Wally's borrowed truck, Danie and Wally made their way over to his place. "You are going to be a little surprised when you get to my house." He said.

"Why is that?" These were the first words she could speak since the awful scene in the living room of the B&B. Her throat was rough and she coughed to clear it. "If I remember correctly you have some homeless people there."

"No, that's not what I'm talking about. In fact, my homeless friends have left and only one person remains."

"Really? Well, I'm not a mind-reader, a fact I have tried to impress upon you from time to time."

Wally smiled. "I have a surprise for you that may turn out to be the best Christmas present you have ever received."

"My goodness. What could it be?"

"I'm not giving any hints."

"I know you can't afford big expensive gifts."

"Truth is, I can't afford this one either but it's coming nevertheless."

"Lord, that sounds more like an unwanted pregnancy," she remarked innocently.

He nearly ran off the side of the road. "You aren't supposed to be that good at guessing."

"Huh? I wasn't guessing. I was joking!" Danie turned to check the road for cars. "Watch where you're going Wally!"

He deftly straightened the truck. "Well, no use hiding it any longer."

"Wally, you aren't pregnant!"

"No, Mom, I'm not, of course."

"Who the hell is?"

"Sally."

"SALLY OLIVER? How did she get pregnant?"

"The usual way Mom."

"Wally! You got her that way?"

"Yup." He smiled proudly. "I'm going to be a dad." The tears began to flow as his voice cracked. This time, he wisely pulled over to the side of the road and parked. "I can't believe it but I am going to be a father." His face crumpled and his eyes glistened.

Danie's eyes burned with tears, too. "Wally, I can't believe it either. I thought it wasn't possible."

"Why?"

"You were so long with Shanna and she never got pregnant as far as I knew."

"No, she never did until she met that 'scumbag.'"

"My god Wally. You are going to be a daddy. I had given up on being a grandmother. I can't believe it." They hugged as the tears of joy flowed.

When they arrived at Wally's place, Danie hurried into the house to meet with Sally who awaited their arrival. She opened her arms when she saw the young woman. "You have made my day, and my week and my month and my year; My god, my life!" she said and grabbed the girl hugging her mightily. "You have no idea how happy you have made me."

"Gosh, Ms. Wharton — Danie."

"I have prayed for a grandchild for years and I had given up."

"I was kind of thinking of an abortion."

"What?" Wally entered the room in time to catch the word 'abortion'.

Danie stood with her arms outstretched holding Sally at arm's length. "You must be joking! There will be no abortion!"

Sally smiled. "No, you're right. There will be no abortion. I want this baby too. I was just kidding."

"Good Lord, Girl. You scared me. I hope you don't go around joking like that too often."

"Noooo. I'm sorry. I couldn't resist."

"Oh, so you like to see people squirm?"

"Kind'a." She smiled coyly.

"Please, leave me off your list of people to frighten. My heart can't take it."

"I'll keep that in mind."

The living room of the cabin was typically suited to men. Two old oversized chairs sat in front of the fireplace where two men could sit with their feet up on the hearth and jabber all night long if they wanted. Buddy curled up between the two chairs on a pillow.

Danie took advantage of the arrangement and sat down in front of the fireplace to warm herself. Tears of joy returned as she watched the flames lick at the air. She would have trouble waiting for the baby to arrive.

Her head swam with recollection of the day's events and her thoughts unwillingly returned to the painting. What would happen between Rose and Darwin now? She prayed the painting would not cause a rift between them, though she could not imagine that it wouldn't.

"Mom, here's the eggnog I promised." Wally handed Danie a cup filled with her favorite holiday drink. The smell of rum warmed her nostrils. She took a sip purposely leaving the foam covered with nutmeg on her upper lip; she quickly licked it away for the flavor.

"I will have to move." She said after a moment.

"Wait until the paint dries, Mom."

"Are you trying to be funny, Wally?"

The pun flew way over his head. "Huh?"

"Until the 'paint dries'?"

"Rose and Darwin will be okay." He added, untouched by his own humor.

"Oh Honey, I don't know. What happened back at the inn, they didn't look very happy."

"What happened?" Sally asked as she sat down in the other chair next to Danie by the hearth.

"You don't want to know." Danie demurred shaking her head. "It's an impossible situation."

"Rose did a nude painting of my mom and presented it to Darwin for Christmas."

"No way!"

"Way." He answered.

"Yeah, right there in front of everyone — Her son — The guests — Us." Danie added.

"Holy shit!" Sally's language said pretty much the way everyone felt though Danie took note of the girl's consistent use of profanity.

Danie was going to have to get used to a lot of things she hadn't thought of before. Sally was pretty enough — though her style of dress was far too flashy. She wondered if being a mother would cause Sally to change anything about herself. Sometimes it worked out that way.

Danie's hopes began to soar. It occurred to her that Wally too would grow up when faced with the responsibilities of fatherhood. Perhaps he would learn a little humility when faced with the challenges that would come with having a little one in his care. She hoped that Wally and Sally would marry and make a real family together. The odds were against her highest hopes but it felt good to have them anyway.

CHAPTER 47

Rose

Rose stayed in her room until the noise in the main room downstairs subsided. She could tell that Darwin had taken over. He had gotten the dishes off the table and into the dishwasher, had chatted with the guests and had taken their credit cards, run the charges, cleaned up the living area of wrapping paper putting the remaining gifts back under the tree. All this was accomplished while he answered the phone and responded to inane questions about the weather. "The sun is shining and yes, it did snow last night..." *No, he didn't know if it would ever snow again — he was not the weatherman after all.* Rose knew how frustrating it was to answer questions for which they had no answers. The people who called were often more interested in superficial information than renting a room. Those calls felt like a colossal waste of time.

The bedroom was getting cold and she felt the urge to get downstairs and check on things. Jason's voice drifted up asking Darwin a question she couldn't hear. The guests had been gathering their things for their respective outings and were leaving for the day. She was grateful that she would not have to face them until much later when they returned.

Her thoughts spun back to Danie. Even though Rose was certain that Darwin loved her, she still didn't feel very secure with Danie. She wondered if Eugenia's warning was worth listening to — Darwin was attractive and his manliness made him desirable. She always felt safe in his arms and she was certain that Danie felt that way too. She had spent enough time there of late.

After reading Danie's book, it was hardly surprising she would feel paranoid by the woman's behavior. She had lured many men away from other relationships. Danie didn't just commit adultery which would be bad enough; she broke hearts. She made men want to leave their wives. She could do it again maybe without realizing the effect she has on them.

Rose had an idea. Danie didn't seem to date anyone. Maybe she could find a man who would ask her out, get her mind off Darwin. In fact, she had met a man recently who said he was single — a widower. She had met him up the street at a 'block party' given by a neighbor, Karen, and he was attractive with white hair, a tall, thin build and a nice smile. He even knew how to dress, something rare here in Dancing Bear Springs where men usually dressed more like lumberjacks. She could ask her neighbor the man's name which she couldn't remember and maybe get a phone number. Rose happily mused that she could set up a blind date and see to it that Danie was too preoccupied with a new man to care about Darwin.

Having decided on this course of action, Rose felt relieved. She could go downstairs now and face whatever came her way. One thing that always made her feel better was a plan of action. She remembered the time she talked her mother into coming to America. Victor, her father-attacker, was upping the ante and she needed to get away from him or risk something much worse. Rose had pleaded with her mother to take her away to America where they would both be safe. It was a plan she could get behind just as she was positive now about this tactical diversion. She picked up the phone as soon as she reached the message well in the great room, dialed her neighbor's number and awaited the result.

It turned out that Clint Jackson lived in Dancing Bear and had been here for some twenty years. He had a nice house; he was not only unmarried but unattached; he had a little money; and he probably would love to meet Danie. Her neighbor said: "Who wouldn't?"

Karen said she would check with him and find out if he would be interested.

When Rose finished on the phone, Darwin came up behind her and gave her a hug. "I heard you talking to Karen. Fixing Danie up, huh?" He asked as he nuzzled Rose's neck. "I love the painting, Honey."

"Mmmm, that feels good."

"Do you want to go upstairs?" He asked.

"Where do you think we should hang it?"

"The painting? Oh, now…That is a very good question."

They hooked up arm in arm and headed upstairs. "Maybe we should hang it in our bedroom." Rose suggested.

"You're kidding, right?"

She laughed wickedly.

CHAPTER 48

Danie

Her cell phone rang that incessant so-called "rainfall" ring. Danie hated it. *I've got to change that — as soon as I'm through with this call,* she thought for the hundredth time.

"Hello, Daniella Wharton?" It was a strange voice to her.

"Yes, this is Daniella."

"I hope you don't mind that I have your phone number."

"That depends on who you are," she said dryly.

He laughed. "Yes, I suppose it would. My name is Clint Jackson. I met you at your book signing earlier this year at the library."

"Oh." She tried to sound warm and welcoming.

"I was the one with the ten-gallon hat and I wore a white dress suit."

My god, he remembers what he was wearing! She thought and said, "Sounds interesting, but sorry, I don't remember."

"We had a picture taken together."

"Good." Danie was trying her best not to become sarcastic. He was a fan and she wisely wouldn't make him feel diminished because of it. In the movie business the fan was the most prized, yet their adoration was often uncomfortable because it was so unnatural. They thought they adored her but in truth they adored the out-of-this-world image they had of her which had been created by the films she was in and the press surrounding the work. Those images were unreal and the fans loved the images, not the real person. Danie was sensitive though sometimes impatient with them.

"I'm wondering if you would meet me at the club for a drink sometime."

Thankfully, he was straight forward and not too ingratiating.

"I'm really a nice fellow. I promise," Clint continued.

"Well, I usually go to the club on Friday evenings." She sighed inwardly. Dating wasn't something she was interested in doing.

The last encounter she'd had with a man turned her off. They had dated each other three times when she noticed that each time he focused on sex as his favorite topic of conversation. Sex was great and she enjoyed it but she hated talking about it, especially with someone she barely knew.

One time, the last time she saw the man, they were having coffee and he brought up the subject yet again. "I love breasts — the little puppies sit right on top of your heart."

Her reaction had been a flash of anger. "Well," she said, "let me tell you about *my* 'puppies.' They are heavy, cumbersome, and they give me a backache. My mother had breast cancer so I asked a doctor once if I could have mine removed to avoid the disease. She said 'no,' it was too extreme a solution for me since I had yet to contract the illness. But honestly, I would like to be rid of them. Mine hang down and perspire underneath creating an opportunity for a science experiment every time. And it smells! Actually, *my* puppies don't reside near my heart so much as…next to my stomach." She never saw that man again. The incident made her smile now.

She had sworn off men some time ago and didn't want to get started in something that would inevitably end badly. Love relationships always did and she had made it a rule to stay away from intimacy.

"I'll call you closer to Friday and ask again. Is that okay?" His voice interrupted her thoughts.

"Sure." When she hung up, she tried to envision this man who claimed to wear ten-gallon hats and white dress suits. "Clint," she said to herself trying out the name. "Jackson?" It wasn't a name that felt familiar though she supposed she had met him as he said. Her curiosity was piqued and she probably would join him…just for a drink.

The mood at the inn had changed although not as expected. Rose was in exceptionally high spirits. She practically danced through the B&B as she cleaned, washed dishes and laundered. Darwin was understandably more circumspect. The guests came and went as usual but somehow the breakfasts had become less unguarded and jocular.

It was early one morning when Rose announced she was taking Jason to the airport for his flight home. Danie and Jason were left in the kitchen to say goodbye as Rose ran upstairs to find her car keys.

"It has been very special getting to know you Jason. I hope you can come back soon. You add a level of levity to the house that it sometimes needs. Especially lately."

"Thanks, Danie. I love coming here. It gives me a chance to sort things out in my home situation."

"Do you have problems at home? You've never mentioned them."

"Oh, I mention them but only to Mom. She is the most understanding person I know."

"You're right about that. She does seem to understand a lot of things and I am sure she's helpful." She stood back a moment to look at him more closely. "Give me a hug," she said putting out her arms. And he did. "I hope you will have a very uneventful trip home. That's the best way to fly, isn't it?"

Jason smiled that wonderfully warm smile he always gave. His blue eyes sparkled in a way that stopped her suddenly. She looked hard this time. They were...Was it possible?...*his eyes* — her baby's eyes. She recognized them instantly; her breath caught and she felt her heart burst open. Her head was swimming and she covered her mouth to keep the tears from forming; she tried to disguise her astonishment. What if she was wrong?

"Please, I am so sorry. You just reminded me of someone I know. It caught me unawares. Please forgive me; it must be a mistake."

"You are forgiven for what I don't know."

"Your eyes. They are so blue and distinctive."

"I get a lot of comments on them. But no one has ever said they recognized them."

"My mistake, I am sure."

"I appreciate that you noticed. Thank you."

"Yes, they are gorgeous and...memorable."

He smiled as he blushed.

Danie was in a spin. "When is your birthday? I love to send cards for people's birthdays." It was the only thing she could think to say.

"It's June 24th. I was born in 1968. But as you know I was adopted by Rose and my dad."

Her heart stopped. It *was* him. It had to be. Jason was hers.

"Are you alright? You look like you're going faint," he said startled.

"Gosh, I just got a dizzy spell. I'm sure I'll be okay." This was not the place or the time to announce her discovery. If she was right, she would have to talk to Rose immediately. Oh my God, she thought. Rose is worried I am taking her husband. What will she think when I tell her Jason is mine? *If...If...* She had to repeat to herself — *If* it was true.

Just then Rose appeared in the kitchen. "Aren't you envious that Jason will be in Hawaii later basking in the warm sun and riding the waves." A place in Hilo or on the island of Kauai, two out of many good choices there, would rival Danie's time here. The islands were the only place on earth she liked better. And now she wanted to board the plane along with Jason to renew their relationship. She wished he wasn't leaving. She wanted to do something but she didn't know what.

"I guess this is it then." She said. "One more hug and off you go." Jason and Danie hugged one last time and she let him go reluctantly. He was strong and his hug was warm and loving.

Danie's mind was reeling. She watched him go with Rose, desperately wanting to stop them and tell them everything. It just wasn't possible now. She had to do the research first to make sure. Now she just wanted something to do to keep her mind busy. The revelation was so troubling, she didn't want to do something stupid that would cause bad things to arise between her and Rose. At the same time, she didn't know how that could be avoided.

A visit to the post office produced the envelope Danie had been waiting for. Her partner's name, Gregg Alcindor Bradshaw, was printed proudly in the upper left-hand corner indicating the contents would be a royalty check. Anxiously, she opened it hoping it would be substantial. Happily, she was not disappointed. The check she found would put her over the amount she needed to buy a house. Elated, she headed back to the inn.

New Year's Eve was only two days away. "What are your plans for the night's festivities, Danie," Rose asked. The question was curious. It almost sounded like she wanted to invite Danie to go somewhere with them. Danie wondered if it would be a good time to reveal her news about Jason. She had done the research — had been in touch with the adoption agency — and she was certain he was her son.

"I'm supposed to do a New Year's greeting for a live radio show about seven in the evening. The host of the show has a weekend place up here and he's coming up to celebrate. We're supposed to do this Podcast interview at his house and he said he was taking me to dinner after." She added.

"Oh, that's great!" Rose sounded a little disappointed but Danie couldn't imagine that she wanted them to be together for New Year's Eve.

"Yes, I hope it works out." Danie continued. "The DJ isn't feeling very well right now and he's wondering if he is going to make it up here at all. He said he has shingles. That's awful, isn't it?"

"Yes, I get them sometimes. It is very painful."

"Yeah, that's what I thought."

"Well I hope it works out for you." Rose added and walked away.

At least, she wasn't hostile, Danie thought. Oh, but she is going to be very hostile when I tell her Jason is the son I gave up and she adopted. It was all she could think about.

The shingles won. Danie would not be going for dinner with the radio host after all. The evening looked like a bust when she said to Rose, "I am available New Year's Eve, as it turns out." She wondered if Rose would invite her to join them.

"Oh, too bad. Sorry." And she walked away. Danie felt weird. Rose's initial question about her plans sounded like she was inquiring for a reason. Now there didn't seem to be a reason at all. Odd.

Clint Jackson called again on New Year's Eve afternoon. "How about meeting me at the club tonight? We could have a drink and go from there."

How did he know she was available? "As it turns out, I am free tonight."

"Come out with me then."

She was becoming intrigued. He didn't give up easily. That was to his credit. "Okay, I'll be there at seven."

"I'll be wearing a white suit."

"I know, and a ten-gallon hat."

"No, not exactly. My hair is white though."

"Okay. See you then." She prayed she would not be sorry.

Her hip was bothering her badly and she limped like an old woman. She had a wooden cane that Darwin had lent her so she chose to use it especially because of the icy walkways. One thing she didn't want to do was waddle like her grandmother had all those years ago. Being old was fine with her; looking old was not. She thought a nice cane would take the onus off the limp.

She decided on a navy-blue sequined top over her black velvet slacks. Wanting to look more festive, she chose blue sparkling earrings that dangled down low enough to peek out from under her loosened hair. She had worn it tightly back in a bun or pony tail most of the time and took the gamble of wearing it down for the evening. She donned her black boots — good boots were important. Putting on black gloves and a dark blue scarf, she added her good black overcoat and headed out.

The car was colder than a 'witch's tit'; she smiled as she tried to start it. She was going to be late if she couldn't get the car going. Finally, the motor turned over and she noted the time. She would be fashionably late — which was her goal after all.

When Danie finally arrived, she removed her coat before entering the main dining area. Her top sparkled in the low lights and she happily greeted the wait staff, young men and women she knew well. She hoped this Clint fellow would find her; she didn't want to go looking for him.

And there he was, in his white diner jacket sporting a slim mask across his eyes. The mask came from the centers of the tables which were set elaborately for the New Year Eve's festivities. Clint Jackson sidled up to her and took her arm. "Good evening, Daniella." He said.

"Please, no one calls me that; I am Danie, okay?"

"Fine, 'Danie...' I like it. Is it spelled D-a-n-n-y?"

"No. I spell it D-a-n-i-e; just leave off the l-l-a and you've got Danie."

He led her to a table and ordered their drinks. He was attractive, tall and thin, and had white hair as promised. He even had good manners.

"Do you recognize me now?" he asked.

"Frankly no. You are playing masquerade — you are behind a mask," she clarified.

"Oh, right." He removed the mask and finally showed himself. "Now?"

"Yes, I do. Now that I see you, yes you are familiar to me." She couldn't say why but she did recognize him. His eyes, like her son's, were blue and distinctive.

"So, tell me, Danie, what keeps you up at night?"

"Wow, that's quite a come on." Danie was taken aback. "That's the kind of line you hear on the news these days!"

"Oh dear, I didn't mean for it to sound that way."

"Well, if you really want to know, my son, Wally, keeps me up at night."

"Does he live up here?"

"Yes, he does. And, I just got the best news on Christmas Day. I am going to be a grandmother for the first time."

"Congratulations! That's wonderful. I have three grandchildren. You wouldn't believe it but I am eighty years old." And from there he took off. He spoke of his marriages (there had been three of them), his children (four) and grandchildren (three). It was quite a family and he was proud. "I used to love Elvis. I dressed like him and did impersonations at parties. I still do when asked." He spoke of his various businesses and his dating life. "I have to admit I am a bit of a rounder."

"Really? Not too many people are willing to confess that, especially not right off."

"Well, I think you should know that I dated Marilyn Palmer up here for fifteen years." Marilyn and her husband of five years had entered just moments before. Clint apparently took note. She looked fabulous. Danie knew her as a physical therapist. She'd had an injury from falling and Marilyn was recommended. It was the time when Wally was strung out on drugs. Danie didn't know meth was the problem then, but he had been behaving so badly that she became fearful he would become physically violent. In addition to the physical therapy, Marilyn had given her good advice about how to defuse the situation with Wally. She was truly a healer. She not only helped Danie with Wally, she was also able to help some of the physical pain. Danie was very fond of her.

Clint's attention had clearly switched. "Do you mind if I go over and say 'hello' to her?"

Danie was not sure how she could say she minded even though she did, mildly. "No, of course. I'll just sip my drink." She held up her glass as if in a toast and smiled.

The moment gave her time to think about Jason. In fact, she had thought about very little else. It was uncanny that Clint's eyes were as blue as Jason's. She remembered that Rose's eyes were dark, a dark brown.

Danie was beginning to wonder if Clint would ever return when he finally did.

"They would like us to join them."

"Oh, yeah, right." She gathered her coat and scarf.

"Would you like to have dinner? He asked. "There is a buffet here tonight."

"Sure. That would be fine." She hadn't eaten thinking she would have to pick up some take-out on the way home.

Danie hugged Marilyn and greeted her husband. They all sat down and began chatting as dinner was served which beckoned them to the buffet table.

As they ate their meal, she noticed Clint's energy had gone solely to Marilyn. He doted on her. Danie thought she was very beautiful with a lovely white bob. Her dress, a soft blue silk, flowed around her like a smooth, icy skating pond and her sky-blue eyes sparkled with all the attention. It was hardly surprising that Clint was still enamored.

Marilyn's husband sat quietly by, watching his wife flirt with her former lover. Danie felt bad for him.

Finally, the meal was over and Danie gathered her things to leave.

"Where are you going? It isn't midnight yet." Clint asked startled.

It was far from midnight and she had no intention of spending the rest of the time watching him and Marilyn get it on. She was tired and wanted to go home.

"Sorry Clint."

"May I walk you to your car?"

"Of course. That would be nice." She grabbed her cane as she thought about his manners which were spurious. At least he had some.

Coming home to her cat made Danie feel lonely. She didn't usually but having an unsuccessful date on New Year's Eve only reminded her that her life was empty of affection and love.

CHAPTER 49

Darwin

His belly had disappeared. Uncharacteristically, he was losing weight. Normally there was little that bothered Darwin. Lately, everything did. He heard himself complaining constantly especially about Rose and the way she did things. She was too persnickety. Everything had to be perfect all the time and he felt stunted in his actions because of it. His feelings about the missed opportunity to be a dad had knocked him off his game big time and that bold nude painting of Danie hanging right there on the wall opposite the bed created reactions he couldn't deal with.

Wandering around the house late one afternoon he noticed the gleaming wood floors in the great room, polished to a breath of their planks. The next morning, he headed for the kitchen planning to grab a bowl from the cupboard and pour himself some cereal. The lights in the kitchen weren't on — *Danie isn't up yet,* he thought. He felt around in the mid-winter morning gloom for a bowl on the usual shelf. It wasn't there. Rose had rearranged the entire cupboard system.

The light switch should still be where it was last time, he thought. Thankfully, it still was and he switched it on. He opened another cupboard. No cups.

"Where the hell…?"

"What are you looking for?" Danie's sultry voice, heavy with the night's sleep, pierced the silence and startled him.

"Oh, hi," he said feebly. "Just a fucking cereal bowl."

"Cereal bowls fuck now?" She asked with a little sarcasm.

He couldn't help himself. He snickered and then snorted. "Danie, you are not supposed to be funnier than I am."

"Sorry, I didn't think it was that funny…"

"It's that Rose changes things all of the time. I never can find anything once she gets started."

"I think I heard her in here last night. So that's what she was doing."

"She couldn't sleep so she cleaned!" He grimaced.

Danie giggled and he glared.

"Sorry, I couldn't help it," she said. "So, what happened to the painting?"

This was Danie's first encounter with Darwin in several mornings. He had been very busy dealing with the needs at the inn, plus he was called upon to the run the plows when it snowed. He had been out until midnight the night before clearing the roads for unhappy drivers. Fortunately, he hadn't run into any stuck motorists with no place to stay. He would have hauled them home to sleep on couches if necessary. Rose had announced the night before she wasn't ready for any more guests.

"You want to know where she put it?" Darwin was surprised at Danie's question.

"Yes, I am curious. I mean, I can't imagine where you could hang it."

"You won't believe it; she hung it in our bedroom.

"You're kidding of course."

"No, I wouldn't kid about that."

"Wow! I'm not sure what to think. I'm speechless."

"It is beautiful and she did a very good job. That art historian seemed to know what he was talking about. And Rose is very proud of it. She says that's why she gave it to me."

"You believe her?"

"Danie, I don't know what to believe anymore. I only know that I feel perplexed, angry and out-of-sorts. Rose may not have told you but Lucy's visit brought news that has turned my life upside-down. I have a son with Lucy she never told me about."

"Darwin, that's so cool," she began and then noticed his frown. "You don't look happy."

"I'm trying to be happy about it, but I missed out on parenting my son. He is a middle–aged man now with a family. I feel cheated because I never knew him when he was a boy. I still don't know him. He looks like a stranger to me."

"Oh, I am sorry. That really sucks."

"I tried with my wives to have kids and it never worked. And now I find there was a boy who was mine all along and I didn't know." His eyes filled with tears; embarrassed he wiped them quickly with his sleeve and started again looking for a coffee cup.

"It's tearing you apart. I understand now why you've been so distant."

"Sorry, Danie; I try not to be rude. And then there is the thing with Rose and the painting. I've just been so irritable. I tried to make love to Rose the other night and somehow it didn't happen. I don't know why." He felt extremely distressed and he didn't have an answer.

"I should leave." Danie said.

"NO!"

"My, that was definitive." She remarked. "But Monday morning I'm going to start looking. I'm calling the real estate agent. I called already but got a message that he is waiting for the snow to melt. He probably needs to sober up from the holidays."

"You're going to move?"

"I really must," she replied.

Darwin's mood plummeted. She was the one person in his life who made him feel better about himself. She didn't have any judgment in her vocabulary for him. "We will still be neighbors, won't we?" His voice became like that of a lonely child and he was embarrassed.

"Nothing in Dancing Bear is more than ten minutes away. I'm sure we will see each other often." She offered. "So yes, that will be true.

"I'll miss you." This time his voice sounded more mature and he was relieved.

"Darwin, this has been the best thing that has happened to me in a long time. Living here has shown me that I am still human and I am still okay. I don't know why, but I wasn't very certain before." She opened a cupboard door and there were the cups; she handed him one.

"Well, Wally could have been a good deal of the reason." He wisely commented. It was true. He'd heard about Wally's drugging days, that he had been abusive in his language toward Danie and about her. He had diminished her self-confidence considerably and being at the B&B for these many months had been a respite from the abuse. Darwin had heard the stories from Danie and he had heard things from other folks as well. He had a hated brother who was like Wally. It was impossible to be around him because he thought he knew everything and everyone else were stupid sheep being led to the slaughter. Darwin and his brother had the worst arguments over the current primaries and he thought his sibling was being led to the slaughter dragging the rest of the country with him. Wally and his brother were alike. They were both 'true believers.' "I'm sorry but your son has issues, even now," he said filling the cup with coffee from the coffee service.

"I know. Here, I have felt protected. I find I can hold my head up and be proud of who I am. That hasn't always been so easy."

"Honestly Danie, I don't know what I would have done if he had been mine. He has consistently tried to recruit me for the Internet folly he believes in. Moreover, he can be very condescending. What does his dad say?"

"Not much. He didn't have to live with Wally so his attitude is different. I don't suppose he believes Wally is so bad. He hasn't had to put up with the abuse."

"Well, I'm happy to hear Wally will be a dad soon. That should straighten his short hairs some." He laughed. "Just wait until he realizes what he has created."

"I'm happy too. I have high hopes he will respond from his heart which is a very good heart when he is in his right mind." Hers was the smile of irony.

"And Darwin," she continued, "I have something to share if I can count on you to keep a very important secret."

"What could be that serious?"

"Oh, it's serious."

"Sure. I can keep a secret."

"I have realized recently that a child I gave up at birth is the son of someone I care a great deal about. I really don't know exactly what to do except I know it is something that can't remain secret forever."

"You haven't shared this with her?"

"No, I just confirmed what I already knew. I recognized his eyes. They are the most intense blue I've ever seen and they were like that at birth. I got to hold him for just a minute before he was taken from me. I shouldn't have looked; I shouldn't have held him, but I couldn't help myself."

"I can't imagine."

"When I saw his eyes this time, I absolutely recognized him and when I asked his birthday, he told me and I knew."

"Danie, where did you find him?"

"Right here. Right here under this very roof."

"My God. Don't tell me…Oh no, don't tell me. Is it? Is it Jason?"

Her silence said it all. Jason was Danie's biological son born in the middle of a thriving career.

"He was a child of rape, Darwin. That makes this all the worse. I don't know what to say to Rose. I just don't know how much she can take. This will feel like a theft to her."

"Do you regret giving him up?"

"Well yes, especially now that I know him. I just wasn't ready for a kid and under those circumstances, I thought it best."

"I guess we make our choices based on the circumstance we find ourselves in at the time. It's impossible to know the future and how we might feel about it."

"You know, speaking of that, you don't know what would have happened to you or your son had you been there as a dad. Life has a way of showing us that our best laid plans are sometimes unrealistic and for good reason, unrealizable. Lucy is black and I imagine your son is half-white like Obama."

"Yes, I've seen a few photos and he is lighter than his family."

"You don't know what it would have been like for you in a mixed family. Times have changed, but then it wasn't that easy. I would bet there are still a lot of folks who believe the races should never mix."

"We'll never know now. That's what makes me so angry, that it's too late."

CHAPTER 50

Rose

"Rose, did you really hang the painting in the bedroom?" Danie asked a day later in the kitchen.

Rose was washing some pots and pans in the sink. "I've joined the witness protection program and I am not saying." She turned to her and smiled sheepishly. "Danie, I am sorry for any embarrassment I may have caused you. It was never my intention to make you uncomfortable."

"Rose, I'm more worried about *your* embarrassment."

"Needless-to-say, I blew it. I didn't mean to cause anything other than appreciation. I don't know what I was thinking." She took a towel and dried her hands. "Darwin was so upset. He still is.

"Rose please, Darwin is a good man. He isn't perfect but he tries very hard to make you happy. I know sometimes he is baffled about what that is, but he means well."

"I suppose he does."

"Don't suppose it. Know it. You have no idea the stories I hear about some of the husbands who can be utterly useless. Sometimes worse than useless, they can cause more problems for their wives to solve. You are lucky. And Darwin only loves *you*."

Her heart sank into her stomach and tears enflamed Rose's eyes. "But Danie, he does make problems I end up having to solve. You should see the basement in this house! It is piled high with junk we will never use but he can't throw away!" She stopped herself and sat down. She could hear her mother's voice in her head screaming about her sloppy husband. "I am probably being too hard on him. I have never been very secure. I told you my first encounter with sex was with my adopted father, Victor. My real dad abandoned me right after I was born and then died a spy in the war. At every turn in my life I have been the one who was abused or used. There was Victor. And my mother used me to avoid war and poverty, then refused to admit she knew what was going on between me and her husband. When we came to America, she depended on me to make sure we ate. I had to steel food. My ex-husband used me to clean his house and take care of our baby and to make sure he was on time for his business appointments. I was not only his wife, sexual object, and childcare worker; I was his secretary too. Never got a penny for it either. Oh, and did I tell you about the books I had to keep, the finances I had to straighten out? Finally, I became his battering ram. Darwin has used me to run the inn. If it were not for me this place would fall apart!"

"You know; you may be right about that. However, I watch both of you. Truth is, when you complain about each other you are only complaining about the same things. You both work very hard. You can't fault Darwin about that, and he can't fault you."

"What does he say about me?" Rose asked startled.

"Only that you clean too much, move things so he can't find them..."

"He leaves the cupboard doors open! I am always running into them."

"He says you strip the tops off plastic packaging and throw them on the counter leaving them for someone else to pick up."

"He leaves the whole bag!"

"That's true. I end up having to clean up after him...And you."

She hadn't heard Danie's last remark. "I don't know Danie." Her tears told a different story and she couldn't hold them back. "I really can't help myself. I have to clean things out and organize things. It's an imperative to me.

Danie held out her arms to her friend. "You do know Rose."

She sobbed into Danie's shoulder. "I am sorry. I am getting you wet."

"Rose, take the painting out of the bedroom. Sell it. Get rid of it."

Rose stood back surprised. "You think so?"

"I know so. Darwin doesn't deserve to have to live with it. It is a gorgeous painting and I feel flattered that you see me in such a becoming light. You surprised me by keeping the feeling of age yet depicting a desirable woman. The painting is organic. You did a wonderful job. Sell it...It will be much more appreciated by strangers than by anyone here."

"You are probably right." She conceded.

They went back to their kitchen chores, both silently contemplating the recent events at the inn.

"Darwin says you are planning to leave."

"Yes, on Monday I intend to look at some properties. Already I have one in mind. I think it may be time for me to move on. Honestly, this time here has been a blessing. It has given me time to heal and to think more clearly about what I want in my future."

"Danie, I would miss you terribly if you left. I have thought that in time when Darwin is ready to retire and collect Social Security, we would sell the inn and find a place to accommodate all of us."

"You're serious?"

"I am. You have been a rock to both Darwin and me. I believe he would say the same and he has expressed the desire to keep you around. Danie, we love you. Don't even think you have to leave here."

"Rose, I am very grateful and surprised you want me to stay. But there is something I have to tell you that could change your mind about that."

"I can't imagine." Rose responded.

"It was his eyes. You see…"

Rose stopped her before she could say more. She smiled big, "You've fallen in love with Clint Jackson!" She exclaimed. "That's great!"

"Heavens no! Not that!" Danie was astonished that Rose would jump to that conclusion."

"Who has eyes that would be that important?"

"You won't believe the coincidence Rose. You just won't believe it."

"Will you get on with it? I can't wait forever. I am very impatient."

"Jason…" She hesitated. He is *my* son Rose. I recognized his eyes and then he said his birthday and it was the same. I researched it and…"

"No…You fell in love with Clint Jackson and you are kidding me, right?"

"I'm sorry Rose. But no. It is Jason. I haven't told him yet but I've been encouraged to tell you first so we could tell him together."

"You are a thief!" She screamed. "I was warned and I didn't listen. You do break homes! You break hearts. You are a thief of the first order. You are a family wrecker in every way possible!"

"No, Rose. That's not what I want."

"You walk around here always acting so innocent liked you love everyone and only care about us, but the truth is you aren't happy unless you've spoiled things for everyone."

"Rose, please don't say that." Danie's eyes filled with tears. "I didn't mean to do anything bad. I'm not stealing him; it is just the way it is and I needed to let you know."

"You whore!" Her voice carried a deep anger. "No, you are not just a whore, you are a murderer." She held her heart as she said it; she left the room with disgust and headed up the stairs.

CHAPTER 51

Danie

Danie stood near the giant, black wood stove staring into it. *Well, you've done it now, Danie girl. You've blown it big time.* Darwin had gotten a good fire going and the flames leapt here and there like dancing ballerinas.

There was no question about moving. She didn't know how to respond to Rose. Danie had never been as happy living anywhere as she had been here at the inn. But she could see this would not work out from this time on.

Danie cried. She had hoped that Rose and she could go to Hawaii and tell Jason together. It would be a shock to him too. Maybe he never wanted to know his birth mother. He had never said anything about searching for her. Well in any case, he would have to wait until either she or Rose told him. Who it should be was anybody's guess.

One thing she had not yet considered. How would Wally react to the news? This was something that neither of them was ready to face. Would he be willing to share his mother's love with this stranger? Or would he rebel?

There was a lot to think about. The baby was on the way. She had Wally and Sally to think of. Would they need a place to have the baby and to get started in their life together? In the few mornings since the holidays Danie had devised a plan to buy the Dutch Colonial house and have them move in with her. She had already started the process with the real estate agent and the loan officer. She hoped to influence the two to live with her so she could help them — and be close to her grandchild of course. The dormered house was perfect for the four of them. The two main bedrooms upstairs were the same size and the tiny room next to the second bedroom was ideal for the baby. One problem was the bathroom. There was only one upstairs and a half-bath on the main level. Danie figured she would spend a bit of time downstairs.

CHAPTER 52
Wally

He was truly happy for the first time in his life. Expecting a baby turned out to be an all-consuming hopefulness that would lead him into the rest of his days. Since Shanna left, this was the only time he could say he wanted to live. He had hope, something he hadn't had in such a long time that it felt foreign to him. Happiness had been fleeting in his life and he had come to think that he should never have been born. Now however he had something real to live for.

Happiness wasn't fleeting anymore. It was a constant state that was becoming more comfortable each day. At first, he was so happy he couldn't sleep. It felt like he was living in a dream terrified that when he awoke the feeling would disappear. After a while he could fall asleep and wake up happy again the next day, something that was completely unfamiliar to him. Expecting a baby was so new and made Wally feel complete in a way he didn't know was possible.

He had heard about Darwin's recent discovery — learning you were a parent after all that time must have been an indescribable shock. Wally knew he would be furious with the mother for not telling him. This wonderful anticipation, the curiosity about the baby, what it would be and what it would look like. Would it be perfect in every way?

He didn't want to call his baby an "it" but not knowing what the sex was meant he had to wait to say either "he" or "she." He knew the baby would be mostly its mother's charge at first with breast feeding and diaper changing but when his little boy became big enough to play, he would be a very active father. He couldn't wait for his son to play ball, being chased or wrestling, boxing, and general roughhousing. And skateboarding! Wally couldn't wait until he could teach his son skateboarding and snow-boarding. Even though he vaguely knew the child might be a girl, he was so convinced that he would have a son, thinking about a girl wasn't possible. He supposed she would wear pink because the color was a favorite of Sally's. Beyond that, thinking about a girl, especially a baby girl, fell in there with thinking about black holes and nuclear physics. You knew they existed but they were incomprehensible.

The snow had been falling for several days; El Nino was so needed in the American Southwest that no one complained about the inconveniences of the white stuff. His mom was stir-crazy being cooped up for days on end. People called it cabin fever, an apt description here in the mountains.

The gift certificate he had bought for his mother to the Singing Bear Bistro was burning a hole in her brain. She wanted to go out for dinner. Tonight. Wally thought about the snow — and how uncertain it was to drive in. Nevertheless, his mother was on her way over to his house to share a 'bowl' and a glass of wine. She must have something on her mind. Sally was busy with her sister helping her to clean up the house from a tirade the sister's inebriated husband had staged over the New Year holiday. It was a good evening to spend with his mom and he was looking forward to their time together.

The knock at the door was her. He opened it with a glass of wine in his hand. There she stood leaning on a cane. After a hug in which he held the wine away so it wouldn't spill, he handed Danie the glass and escorted her into the house to sit by the fireplace. "Welcome to my humble but happy home." He said.

"Putting on the charm, are you? So, what is it you want?"

"Nothing Mom. I'm just really happy for a change."

"I like it…I like it." She smiled in response.

"It feels really good."

"So, becoming a daddy feels good to you?"

"Mom, why didn't you tell me this would happen?"

"Sweetheart, not everyone gets happy when they're expecting. To some people pregnancy means trouble. In fact, I have something to tell you about that."

"Really? I guess not everyone gets what they want."

"Sometimes they get something they didn't want and need to give away."

"A baby?"

"You do know there are unwanted pregnancies."

"Yes, but they don't make sense to me especially now. I mean, how could anyone be unhappy about a new child in their lives."

"You are happy and I am happy about Sally's pregnancy. I think Sally is happy too. But I was not happy the first time I got pregnant."

"I thought I was your only child."

"In a way you are. But in truth the first baby I had was a boy and I had to give him up to adoption.

"Gosh Mom why haven't you told me about this before?"

"I know I've waited too long. However, I didn't have a reason to. That child was the child of a rape."

"Oh no. Mom. I'm so sorry to hear this. It is hard for me to believe you could do that."

"I didn't do anything wrong Wally. I was taken by surprise. Overtaken really."

Tears stirred in Wally's eyes in a way he didn't expect. "Mom, I can't think of what that would be like."

"I'm glad it is unthinkable to you." She paused to take a sip of the wine. "As it turns out, it's more unthinkable than any of us could imagine. You have a brother or a half-brother to be more exact."

"Wait a minute. You know this person?"

"I've discovered him. He is someone we know."

"We?" Wally was so astonished he felt like the earth had opened up to swallow him. "Who?"

"It's Rose's adopted son, Jason."

"Oh. My. God." This sat Wally back on his heals. It was such a shock he didn't have a way to cope. What could he say? How did he feel? He had a brother, a man he knew but didn't really know. Jason? This was his half-brother? "I'm not hearing this well. You are telling me that you've been living with the mother of a boy you gave birth to and gave away? How did you find out he was yours?"

"I suddenly recognized his eyes! It was astonishing really. I couldn't believe it either. But his birthday is the same and I've done the research. He is definitely mine."

An anger was growing in his heart. It was an anger he never knew before and it felt like it was exploding inside him like a nuclear bomb — hot, molten, filled with fiery sparks, a mushroom cloud that threatened to swallow up everything he knew. Suddenly he hated Jason with everything he had in him.

"Wally, honey, are you alright? This is a shock I know. It is a shock to me as well. I can't imagine how we are all going to cope…Please, I need you to understand. Now that I know, I can't abandon him again."

Wally's mind was in a tangle. He was having trouble trying to see Jason as someone so close as to be a half-brother. He knew the man had been a skateboarder as a kid like he had, but that was where the similarities stopped. Jason had gone on to marry and though he had not produced a child that Wally was aware of, he had participated in rearing his wife's son. Wally thought he could be a good dad too, but this Jason seemed a little too perfect. Wally was instantly jealous of a man he barely knew. He didn't even know what the guy did for a living.

Wally decided to change the subject; it was just too hot and scary a topic, and to keep himself from exploding, he felt the need to forget about Jason. "Well, Richard is up north visiting his daughter." Richard was Wally's new 'BFF.' He had invited Wally to live there with him a few months back and they were getting along well enough.

"Nice for you that he is away, huh?"

"Yeah, it's very nice. I like the solitude. I like Richard but there are things…"

"He seems like such a mother. I've noticed he is over-protective with his daughter."

Wally nodded in agreement.

"When we were here for dinner that one night and she was too, he seemed very motherly toward her. How old is she?" Danie asked.

"I think she's nineteen."

"She's old enough to think for herself and to take care of herself."

"I guess old habits die hard."

"Well I think he should lay off her. My guess is she would appreciate that."

"How the hell do you know what she would appreciate?"

She gave him that look that said 'Whaaaat?!!!' "I don't. I said it was my guess."

The anger he had stuffed down came roaring back to life like a monster wave overcoming a ship.

"Mother! You always have an opinion, don't you?" He resented her opinions and his angry mood was overwhelming. "The girl is young and he *should* help her."

"Maybe. Although, she has to make her own mistakes so she can learn."

"Mom, what do you know about it?"

"I don't, not really…But I can speculate. I am old enough to know a few things."

Freakin', fucking, stupid bitch, he thought. "You are so stupid, Mom. Richard is doing his best to get her started in life."

"I'm sure he is. I just noticed the 'helicopter' aspect. I mean, when she announced she had changed her political party he nearly choked. I remember, he told her she couldn't make that kind of decision yet." Danie laughed. "Good god, she's old enough to vote; she can make her own decisions."

"I know you think you're perfect and you think you know everything, Mother, but…"

"I don't think that, Wally. Please, don't…"

"You always think you know what is best for everyone else."

"Honey, I don't know, but I do have opinions. And I think…"

"You don't know what you're talking about!" It wasn't exactly a conscious thought, but Wally had believed for years his mother should have helped him a lot more than she did when he was young and just starting out. Now he wondered if this other son of hers wasn't the real reason he'd received poor treatment from his mom. Maybe giving up the other boy made her resent him. "Mother, I am just trying to help you realize how wrong you can be." He said trying to change his tone and to sound reasonable.

"But he bought her a new car!"

"Sure, why not?"

"And a trip to Europe? You told me about that last…"

"Yeah. I wouldn't have minded a trip to Europe when I was her age."

"Wally, you know I couldn't afford that."

At this point he lost it. This was the one thing he hated most about her. "Why not?!" He screamed. "You were a fucking movie star! Freakin' grow up! Why *couldn't* you send me to Europe?" He was screaming at the top of his voice. "My friends always made fun of me because you were a *poor* movie star! Do you know how stupid that is?"

"No one knows that better than I do Wally." She admitted. "It was a long time since I'd made any 'movie star' money. You…"

"Maybe you were giving it away to this other son of yours! In any case, it was embarrassing when my friends made fun of me. A 'poor white boy,' is what they called me! His brain was burning with rage. "Dumb whore, you think you know it all! Well you don't! You are way behind!"

"Wally! I am not a whore! And I am certainly not dumb. I think I did fine with…"

"You got raped Mom. How does that happen?! I can't see it happening without some cooperation."

His Mom reached up and slapped him soundly.

He raised his arm and she ducked. Suddenly caught by his rage and wanting to run, he slammed his fist into the wall making a huge hole. It was the most satisfying thing he had done so far. Rubbing his fist, he looked over at her. She was regarding him with horror.

"And you never invested, Mom! You were asinine about money. Now I think I know why. Jason got it all. He got it all because you felt guilty. It's a damned good thing you were pretty you know. You never would have made it otherwise."

"That is a low blow Wally." She countered. "I did not cooperate with my rapist. I did not send money to Jason. I cut off all ties to my baby and stuck to my career. And I did not invest because there was never enough!"

Wally didn't care. He knew his dad hadn't been much help but nothing mattered now.

"There were a lot of reasons why I couldn't afford to send you to Europe."

"You went to China!"

"That was paid for by the institute that sponsored trip."

"You are so naïve Mom. That trip was paid for by the government. You were a propaganda tool. They used you!"

"Wally, I could say the same about you. You are being propagandized by the people you listen to on those Podcasts. They are not telling you the truth. They want you to believe things that have no relevance to reality. I don't know why but those people want you to believe your government is out to get you! Why do you believe that crap?!"

"I believe it because it's true."

"When I went to China, I was working in a private situation. That had nothing to do with our government."

He didn't see any difference between a private institute, whatever that was, and government tricks. "YOU ARE A TOOL MOTHER!" He was outraged by his mother's stupidity. She didn't know how culpable she was. "It's all big business and the government! Why can't you understand that? All of those people are criminals no matter what party they belong to or what business they're in!"

"Wally, I resent it when you accuse me like that! I do not work for the government and I don't like big business any more than you do. I never have."

"You wrote the screenplay about that Chinese massacre. You must have done that for the government! Who else would care?"

"That was my idea, dammit! It was never produced and our government doesn't..."

"Yeah I know your politics; you and your kind are killing people and you vote for it!" He screamed.

"Where in god's name do you get these ideas?!"

Now she was yelling too. She picked up her purse, jacket and cane and headed for the door. "I don't have an appetite anymore. Get your own damned dinner."

She walked out into the cold blinding snow. Wally knew it was a long perilous walk down to the car. He was still furious but he watched her go from the deck hoping he wouldn't have to go down there to rescue her.

CHAPTER 53

Danie

The biting wind brought the icy snow straight into her face. She hiked the hood of her jacket up over her head and marched plodding heavily with her boots hoping to gain enough traction to make it to the car. Using her cane for balance, she made her way carefully along the icy walkway. Falling would be hazardous at her age. She could break something and couldn't be sure Wally would know she had fallen. Danie was terrified. She could lie there for hours before being discovered and she knew she would not be able to get Wally's attention from where she was located now, not down the hill and beyond some bushes. Then she realized she'd left her cell phone in the car. She couldn't even make a call. The dense snowpack absorbed every sound and yelling, even with her ability to project her voice, would go unnoticed. The cane was helping; then it slipped out from under her and went flying. She caught herself grabbing a bush full of snow. The snow flew into her face — but the bush kept her from falling.

Finally, practically crawling, she arrived at the car and got in. It was an enormous relief. The snow was coming down in torrents producing whiteout conditions. Danie worried that she would run into trouble trying to get back to the inn. However, she wasn't going to get stuck just sitting here.

Starting the car, she eased out onto the road. All she could see was snow coming down around her. Slowly, she made her way down the street from the house where Wally lived with his friend.

Tears filled her eyes blurring her vision. She dabbed at them quickly with a tissue. "How can I be killing people?" She wept. Wally's words had cut deeply. They were like machetes cutting through all of the love and affection she had for him. It hurt as if the knives were real.

Richard, 'Helicopter Dad.' She had noticed the man was over-wrought about his daughter. She hoped he wouldn't make some of the mistakes she had made with Wally. Turning him into her best friend was clearly a big mistake. Now Wally felt like he could say any terrible thing to her. How could he call her stupid and naïve? And a whore! A killer?! How could he say she was at fault getting raped? At one point he implied she was "a baby" in her thinking. He certainly thought she was a dupe for the government! It was amazing the things he could come up with. Her trip to China had been paid for by her friend's self-made institute designed to open doors for Chinese and American business people, especially movie people. The trip had taken them everywhere interesting in the country. They had visited the Chinese movie studios in Shanghai.

While in China, she had taken private mental notes for a screenplay she had been writing about the Tiananmen Square Massacre. She hadn't been certain what the US government would think about her efforts, but the story she wrote had not been friendly to the Chinese. The story had been honest and not favorable to any government.

She had watched the massacre from the uncomfortable comfort of her living room in West Hollywood. The tragedy had followed months of student protests in Beijing lasting from early April to June 4th, 1989. Americans had watched the slaughter of thousands of Chinese students in horror. The Tiananmen Square Massacre had enraged her and she had concluded that the story had to be told. The trip to China had been a clandestine effort to get information that was not available to Americans at the time. What she had seen, heard and written was important and she hoped someday the screenplay she had created could be produced so that the Chinese people, who had been kept in the dark since, could know what had happened on that horrible night of the student bloodbath in Tiananmen Square. That knowledge among the general Chinese population could change things.

In fact, a lot had changed in China since that trip. Conversations she and her trip partner had about democracy and the free-enterprise system with high up officials could have influenced things in some small way. They may have had a hand in the changes they were seeing now. There was that saying that the flutter of a butterfly wing will affect the weather on the other side of the planet. How accurate that was she didn't know, but she felt they had brought good ideas and thinking and had been a positive influence on the people they'd met. She had entitled the screenplay: "West Wind." She thought it was an apt designate given that democracy was more likely now in China than ever.

And Wally had implied she was vane. She felt confident in herself but that didn't mean she thought she was special in any way. She had never thought she was better than others were. Or had she? She had been a "movie star" after all, adored by people she didn't even know. Fawned over by fans, hair dressers, make up people, wardrobe designers, dressers, craft table people, chauffeurs, publicity heads, the ADs (assistant directors), the men who couldn't seem to put their eyes back into their heads. She wondered if she came off vane. Did she walk around with undo pride without realizing how snooty she could be? It was something she had felt strongly about early in life when she realized as a young star, she had been too cool and distant with people. It had been a strategy she'd adopted because she was shy. And it was this shyness she was trying to overcome when she boldly accepted an invitation to go to Las Vegas with a man she should never have considered going with. He had been difficult to deal with but she had managed to get away from him before anything too awful happened. At the time, she thought she was being brave and a little reckless which is something she thought she should be since her parents had never allowed recklessness. But if you didn't take risks, where would you go? Well, she learned quickly not to take too many chances.

For god's sake, she had been raped! Wally thought she welcomed being raped! How could he have such opinions about her?

Of course, she hadn't been careful enough. She had ended up on the bad end of date rape a short few years after the Vegas trip. She should have known better than to let that man into her house. He'd been doing drugs on their date, and she'd found him naked in her bed after he excused himself to the restroom. He'd been fast and had caught her running down the stairs. When she fell, she'd knocked her head on the bannister which had rendered her helpless to resist the man's strength. She shuddered now remembering the harsh thrusts of him inside her.

Everything Wally had said to her, all the vitriol, cut deeply into her heart and felt like the thrusts of the rape. These attacks stopped her in her tracks every time. She froze when he spoke to her this way. She didn't know why exactly, except she felt if she did say anything, she would get a blowback that could be devastating. Wally could be vicious with his words, demeaning and harsh as a rape.

There had been a time when they were living at the dormered house, a time when he was still on meth, though she wasn't aware at the time the drugs were the problem. She had been ill and camped out on her favored couch in the living room. She knew she looked awful. Her face was pale and her hair hadn't been touched in days and it looked like a pile of hay. She looked truly awful and felt every bit as ugly on the inside. What he had said that day she couldn't remember but she remembered lashing out at him with some nasty things she probably shouldn't have said. Or, maybe they needed to be said. She didn't know but the blowback was serious. He had taped her on his new I-phone while she unleashed a verbal tirade, then emailed it to his friends and to hers. Horrified at what he had done, she swore she would never respond like that again. In fact, that was the day she decided to cut off all communication other than the very necessary things that had to be said like what's for dinner or who's driving. It had been hard to keep silent but she had worked at it…And failed often.

Sally was right; Wally was a 'piece of work'. It was hard for Danie to understand the source of his extraordinary wrath but she had reached the conclusion that Wally was a rage-a-holic. It was one holdover from his drugging days. He'd raged at her and torn up her house more than once. Many times, in fact. He would rage at his friends and friends of hers too. She remembered one time when he came within an inch of her friend's face screaming at him with threats that would make a Rhinoceros cringe. Her friend, much smaller than Wally, stood up to him without flinching and she thought he was very brave. Wally appeared as though he would trounce the man, but her friend didn't back away. Wally made an enemy that day; the man never forgot the encounter and never believed her when she said that Wally had changed since then.

Maybe he hadn't. He was better able to hold his temper with his friends but Danie was another matter. He still raged at her and she realized that she had become a willing victim. She always crumbled in the face of his first vicious salvo.

He was a 'rage-aholic' — the idea fit like a glove. Having a name for his behavior felt better too. It made it seem more manageable. Truth was, she had no idea what she could do about him; she never had.

Unwanted tears again gathered in her eyes making it harder to see through the blinding snow. She stuffed them down. No, there will no crying about this, she thought. It was his problem and she knew she would separate herself from him in every way possible. His behavior would never again bring a moment of despair. She may have to forget knowing her grandchild, but this had to stop. She could no longer avail herself to him and his rages.

Ice formed on the windshield and on the road. Danie's car hit a patch of black ice, the dreaded kind you couldn't see. Despite the 'all-wheel-drive' automobile, the car lost traction and began slipping down the hill picking up speed.

She applied the brakes and the car only spun around so that it was sliding uncontrollably down the hill toward another street. On the other side of the 'T' were a telephone poll and an embankment that headed down to a house and the large propane tank that serviced the property. Her car was headed straight for it. Danie couldn't see anything but she knew the area well and she knew what lay beyond the telephone pole. She had worried before about stopping in time at the bottom of the street. However, she also knew that the telephone pole was off to the side of the house and the tank. She prayed she would hit the pole — it might stop her trajectory and keep her from landing on what would become a fiery grave or worse, hitting the house and killing someone inside.

She closed her eyes in dread while the car kept spinning…Until…

It stopped.

Danie sat there stunned. She had been so certain she would go careening into the pole and then into the propane tank that she wondered if the stop was only temporary. Slowly, she opened her eyes and realized the Subaru was parked right next to the telephone pole by the side of the road. The relief was so huge she could barely get her breath.

Then, she cried. The overwhelming emotions she had been harboring gushed forth with heaving sobs. Everything came bearing down. Her son, *her* son, the boy for whom she had struggled so. The baby she had married the wrong man to have just to make sure she could have him. Wally named after her dad, Walton George Wharton, had become a monster. She didn't know him. How could he have thought for all these years that she was holding back from him in his youth. He thought she should have sent him to Europe, all expenses paid of course, bought him a car, sent him to college no doubt. She surely would have done all those things had she had the means to do so. The star money didn't last long enough, and yes, she had been a poor investor, always investing at the wrong moment and regretting the losses so much that investing became anathema to her. Money had never been that important but it was obviously the only thing her son valued. He had expected her to come forth with movie-star benefits even knowing how broke she always was.

The sobs began to subside as her resolve grew. As painful as it would be, she would separate from Wally, leave him to be with his woman and child. She would not contribute a sou to the situation. She would divorce herself from him as surely as she had divorced his father. It would even feel satisfying knowing she had done the right thing.

CHAPTER 54

Darwin

Darwin was clearing the roads. The snow was pouring down and he didn't expect to see anyone out on the highway. He had narrowed his plowing to the side streets. The thickness of the white stuff was unbelievable. Darwin had never seen California snowfall look so dense. Back in Wisconsin where he came from, the snow was sometimes so copious, the road, cars, trees, houses, buildings of any kind became nothing but big white mounds like glaciers rising out of the northern sea. Tonight, it was the same in Dancing Bear and Darwin could only watch in amazement and try to clear the roads well enough to help folks get home.

The crunch was so sudden, he wasn't sure of what he heard. But he was certain of what he felt. The snow plow had hit something metallic and Darwin hoped it wasn't a car though he couldn't imagine anything else. Slamming on the brakes, he pulled up the main handbrake hard. Hoping out of the large truck, slamming his knee on the door too hard so it hurt like hell, he popped out of the warm cabin.

Danie's car was white and blended with the snow. He was on her hood not realizing he had breached it. "What?" He couldn't imagine he had not seen the car before. He bent down to move the snow from the windshield. Inside, Danie sat crying, her face red with tears streaming down her face.

"Danie! Are you alright?" Slogging through the heavy snow, he found the door handle and tried with all his might to open it but his efforts were hindered by mounds of ice cushioning the car like a glove. Finally, he was able to move enough of the snow away to gain some purchase on the door. It took all his strength but he got the door open enough to see Danie. She looked up at him with the pain of child who had been abandoned.

"Are you okay Danie?" he asked startled. "What's the matter?"

"I want to go home." And she started crying all over again. Tears were not Darwin's forte; he hoped he wouldn't make things worse whatever the problem was.

"He called me a baby. He thinks it was a good thing I was pretty!"

"Who thinks that?" He asked not sure how to react to this not very horrible news.

"Wally!"

"Why am I not surprised?" He was trying to be sympathetic she looked so distraught.

Danie gazed up into his face and blubbered again reaching up to him as a child might an adult. Darwin could almost hear her say "up".

"You know you may be too sensitive. I mean, he only called you a baby." He reached in and grabbed her waist hauling her into his arms and marched to the cab of the snow plow. "Why did he call you that?"

"We had an argument about…Jason. I told him about Jason and he didn't take it well. Anyway, it is always about his 'horrible childhood'." She grabbed the door handle and hauled herself from his arms and into the passenger side of the cab. "I must have been the most horrible mother the way he tells it. I know I wasn't perfect and I was doing it all on my own without a dad to back me up. So, I guess that wasn't good enough."

Darwin wanted to hear all she had to say but he was freezing his ass off standing there listening. He slammed the door shut and climbed to the other side of the plow and got in.

"My car!" Danie was crying all over again. "You smashed my car!"

Darwin started the engine. "Sorry, I didn't see it. I didn't know you were there until I felt the crunch."

Danie's tears made him feel so inadequate he couldn't manage anything more. "Let me get you home and we'll worry about your car tomorrow. It's too late to call the tow truck over here."

"But how will I get around?" She whined.

"Danie please. We will work it out. You need to get some sleep before you deal with any of this again. The car will be fine and we'll get it fixed. Okay?" He was talking to her like he would a seven-year-old at school.

She started to laugh. Danie's tears turned to hysterical laughing. "Oh my god!" she cackled. In fact, the cackle sounded like the heights of hysteria.

Her laugh was so radical and infectious that Darwin joined in. "I don't know what's so funny but what the hell?!"

They sat there and laughed until neither had the strength to continue.

"Are you ready to go home?" He asked.

"I don't really have a home." Danie's eyes teared up again as she looked at him. "I really don't have a home!" She repeated, as if this was the first she realized how homeless she really was."

"Danie. Please don't worry. You will always have a home with us no matter what."

"No, you don't understand. Rose didn't take it well either. She's furious and says I am stealing Jason from her. I don't want to take anything away. Wally's right. I am a complete failure. I failed at my career, I failed at marriage, I failed in my finances and I certainly failed him as a mother! Now I am failing as a dear friend — and my god, I am a person who gave her baby away!"

"Danie, come on. You aren't a complete failure any more than anyone else is. We all fail at things."

"Don't make excuses for me," she demanded. "If I am a complete failure, then I should face up to it and learn to live with it."

The snow plow turned into their street and he applied the brakes in front of her door.

"I'd say you've already done that."

CHAPTER 55

Rose

Thankfully, no one had come to the Laughing Bear for a room this evening and Rose was glad because she didn't feel well. She would have had to make up a room to accommodate a new client and she was too tired after the long day. She stood in the doorway of the inn because she was worried about Darwin out so late clearing the roads. It was cold and the snow was amazing, like nothing she had ever seen before.

She thought about the day and how it had shaped up. The news about Danie and Jason was overwhelming in a way she couldn't fathom. It felt like her entire life had been a lie. Then, she heard the plow pull up to Danie's doorway.

Worried that something must be wrong she closed the front door and headed for Danie's room. Rose couldn't help herself; her curiosity drove her. She met her just as she was entering from outside, the snow and wind virtually blowing Danie in. Her face was red and swollen. Rose couldn't help but feel glad the woman was suffering. She deserved it.

Danie regarded her with suspicion. They hadn't spoken since Danie's unfortunate news.

"Danie. What's the matter? Why have you been crying?" When she didn't get an answer, she continued. "I thought you were having dinner with Wally."

Danie, shrugging said, "Yes, that was the idea."

"What happened?"

"I am divorcing him."

"What? He is your son; how can you divorce him?"

"Oh, I'll figure out a way. I simply don't want him in my life anymore. I want out just like when I wanted out with his father."

"What about the baby?"

"He called *me* a baby tonight!"

"How could he say that to you? You're his mother!"

"He called me a baby, a whore, a killer, stupid, naïve, a *'poor'* movie star and any number of other things that were just as insulting. He said it was a good thing I was pretty or I would have been sunk as if I didn't have brain in my head."

Knowing there were no good answers Rose asked, "Why would he say those things to you?"

"He thinks I am a total failure in every possible way. He made that very clear. I didn't send him to college or to Europe and I didn't buy him a car; made him get his own." Like a mower clears grass, she was pacing the room nearly cutting a strip out of the shag carpet. "I thought I was doing the right thing by making him be responsible for his own life. In any case, I didn't have the money. He thinks because I could send myself to college, I could send him. He thinks because I went to China, I should have sent him to Europe like all his friends who went on their parent's dime."

Not feeling very charitable toward Danie, Rose asked bluntly, "Well, why didn't you?"

I had to borrow money to go to college and pay it back. The China trip was paid for by the private institute that sent us. And Wally thinks I was sent by the US government as a dupe of some sort." At this point Danie's outrage had risen to the top of the proverbial thermometer. "I didn't have money when he became of age. I was broke paying student loans and never getting a decent gig going." She gathered a new breath. "I went on auditions until I was blue in the face and never got a bite. It was a real come-down too, having to audition at all. When I was in the money, I never had to audition. It was unheard of!" She threw down her coat after wrestling it off, her fury so intense she couldn't do anything right.

Rose watched her from the steps, slightly amused by her 'performance'. She was doing her best not to laugh. It was hard but she knew if she did, it would be a disaster. Danie was out of her mind with rage.

"Divorce is pretty serious. Are you going to formalize it in any way?"

"I don't know if that's a possibility but I might try. I'll call a lawyer tomorrow and see what's possible."

"You are kidding, aren't you?"

"Maybe about divorcing but no, I am not kidding about staying away from Wally."

He is your son, Danie. How can you do that?"

"I never want to see him again! I realized that I am the one letting him insult me. I don't fight back and I don't know why. I can't. He attacks with viciousness and a slew of weaponized words. I can't. I don't have such things in my arsenal. I can never say what I want to say because I made this stupid promise to myself when he was born. So, if I don't avail myself to him, he can never injure me again!"

Rose could see this was self-preservation and gave Danie a pass. Otherwise, she couldn't think of anything worse than "divorcing" your son. That was a love that did not go away. In fact, it was something that stayed with a woman for the rest of her life.

CHAPTER 56

Wally

He had eaten a frozen dinner not at all like the meal he had anticipated at the Singing Bear Bistro. He was still riled by his mother. He was certain she had held out on him all along. She could afford to buy a house now if she wanted. But would she? He didn't think so.

It had been his intention at the Bistro tonight to talk her into buying a house mostly for him, Sally and the baby, but a place for his mom, too. She had always backed away from buying a house. They had looked around Dancing Bear on many occasions trying to find something affordable. He had encouraged her to make the leap and had promised to help when she needed it, but she hadn't budged. She always rented.

He needed a home for his baby and Sally too. He resented his mother for being such a footdragger. His mother knew he couldn't buy anything on his own. He'd been foreclosed on more than once. No one was going to loan him anything for a home. His credit was crap.

Living in with other single men was no longer going to work. He needed a place to live without having to worry about eviction all the time. She knew that yet she wouldn't buy. The last time it came up, just recently, she had made the old excuse that she didn't have enough for the down payment. He knew she could get past that if she would just take the first step. There were loans available for first-time home buyers covered by the government. It had been years since she had owned anything substantial and he felt positive she could qualify. He conveniently ignored that the government would be involved, an association he would normally avoid.

And what about those royalties she should be getting for the book? She was holding out on him he felt sure. Thinking about it, he had to wonder if that dude, her partner, had anything to do with the lack of funds in her bank account.

Gregg Alcindor Bradshaw was a gay man who had partnered with his mom to help promote her book and was working to get the book made into a movie. He was acting like an agent collecting her royalties and paying some publishing debts then sending the balance to her. He paid himself too. Wally figured he was getting ten to twenty-five percent.

Whatever he was getting, it was too much. His mom didn't have much going into the project and she didn't seem to have that much more coming out of it either. He was certain the man was pilfering money from her. How would she know what he was stealing? Wally only knew one thing; she was terrible with money and it was a shoe-in that she had no idea what she should be making on the book. Wally thought it might be a lot more.

The book. He had never read it. He wasn't much of a reader. He'd cheated enough as a kid to never learn very much and still ace tests taking answers from his school mates' papers. He'd become very good at it and was never caught. But his knowledge had suffered. He was better able to read the scrolling on the Internet than turning pages in a book. So that was where he spent his time checking up on the latest news from his favorite sources. But reading her book was something he had avoided. He didn't like reading books.

"Okay I'll do it," he said to himself. "It won't kill me." He picked up the copy she had signed to him — "To my favorite son. With enormous love, Mom." She had signed it right under the title page where her name as the author was printed under a stunning photograph. He had to wonder who would be her "favorite" son now. The book looked smart — her partner, Gregg Alcindor had chosen the cover; the photograph of his mom was movie-star-beautiful and pensive at the same time. She had wanted something else, a painting she had done, but Gregg Alcindor had insisted against her judgment. Wally thought the guy was right about the cover but he still didn't trust him.

Settling down into his bed with the pillows propped up against his back he delved into the read with determination. He didn't want the page turning to keep him from continuing the book. There was no other way; he had to keep the thoughts straight as he turned the pages. Connecting the paragraphs was a problem too, though it was hard to understand why. They had tested him as a boy and his form of dyslexia made it difficult to connect one sentence to the next. 'Sequencing' they had called it. He had developed a method once when he had a computer and then with his I-phone because of the scrolling. Why his brain reacted differently to scrolling he couldn't say. He'd never asked those questions. They didn't have computers then.

The reading became easier as he went along. After a while, he gained a kind of rhythm he was unused to. The first few chapters startled him. She had begun with the tragedy of being raped and moved on to a time when she had a spiritual awakening. This was something he had never heard about. Now the fact of a pregnancy carried to term and a baby given up at birth, Wally was nonplussed by her choice. How could she give him up? Then, Wally had to wonder if he would exist had she not given up the other son. It was odd that she hadn't included the fact of Jason's birth in her book even though she seemed to tell every other secret. She wrote about the rape that produced him. The details surprised him.

It took a while for him to get to the part about her marriage to his dad. He had to stop a couple of times to get a beer and to pee. At last, there was the wedding. He had seen the pictures in her scrapbook but he didn't know much about that day. Someone had stepped on her gown and ripped it. She said it was a bad omen. And, of course, he knew nothing about the honeymoon.

At last the story turned to her family life and his, along with her career struggles, which he had learned little about back then. After a period, the book was easy to read and he decided his mother was a good writer.

Now she was going on about all the details. It embarrassed him to read about his parent's intimate relationship. Before he could get too off balance by the intimacy, she came to the time after they had made love when their conversation turned toward the future and what would be expected in their marriage. His mom had average expectations. She wanted two children, a boy and a girl naturally. She hoped his dad could get a better job and worried she would be the better wage-earner. His dad thought it was great that she could make so much money for doing so little. She had been piqued by his assessment of the work she did and said so. She was also adamant that she wanted him to be the major bread-winner, or at least equal to her, and that her work was not as easy as it looked.

Not to be outdone, his dad had countered with his vision of their future together. He'd had an insight into their prospects during one of his meditations. He had perceived that he would be president one day and she would be first lady. Wally could see how well that vision turned out…Not.

His mom had never been enthusiastic about her husband's immersion into Buddhism. She thought he spent far too much time "contemplating his navel" which she characterized as contemplating his ego. Wally had to smile at the memory — his mom, dressed in her workout sweats dripping with perspiration, standing in the middle of the living room with her hands on her hips pontificating about how people's egos could be counted on to make them feel better — about themselves. It was the only uncomplimentary belief about his dad she had expressed but it incensed him that her depiction had been so cruel. In the book, she had made his dad look a fool and his dad's mother a crazy woman which he supposed she must have been since she had spent the better part of her life in a mental institution. He remembered going to visit her there.

She made Wally feel like a fool a lot too. It wasn't fair how she treated him or his dad. She had walked out on his dad while he was on a trip with his Buddhist friends. They called it a pilgrimage and his devotion had made it important to him. His dad had told Wally about the separation when he became an adult: "I came home from the long weekend in San Diego to a house stripped of all the furniture. The house was empty and I realized with shock that she'd walked out on me!"

Wally didn't know much about his dad's religion except it had taken him away more than he liked. That made it bad and his mom's religion took her away from him more than he liked too. Wally hated all religions even though he knew nothing about religion except what people said, which was never very flattering.

When he turned thirteen, his mom had made him get baptized because she said it was the right thing to do.

That day had been miserable. It was a hot August day in Los Angeles which was overwhelmingly heavy when the smog bore down and the air refused to move like a stubborn grey mule that smelled bad. He had been forced to wear hot clothes — a dress shirt with a tie choking him around his neck and his pants were a cotton corduroy but heavy nevertheless. He hated her for the chore she had put him to, going up in front of all those people and letting the guy in the dress pour water over his head. Then they handed him a candle and told him from that day forward he would be Christ's own. What that meant exactly he couldn't fathom. He hadn't promised anything; he'd just nodded silently whenever they asked him something. He was so unattached to the whole incident he didn't remember some details. They were just too unimportant to him.

He did remember the afterwards part because he was so furious when she forced him to keep the hot tie wrapped around his neck for photos. Wally swore to himself he would never do what *that bitch* told him to do again for as long as he lived. He had kept that promise too.

Coincidentally, his mom had snapped a picture of him at just that moment when he made the resolution and she'd shown him the photo and pointed out his expression. From the look on her face he had to believe she knew what he was thinking when she snapped the picture. She'd framed it and placed it on the front desk, a visible reminder of his obstinacy.

He was only thirteen at the time but the moment she took that picture turned out to be emancipation from his mom. He had become very independent after that never following her instructions, entreaties, or briberies.

He molded himself the exact opposite of her in every possible way. If she was on time for appointments and other engagements, he would always be late; if she had table manners, he would eat like a hog. Whenever she had an opinion, he would take the opposite assertion always countering her with utter nonsense if he could think of nothing else. Often, he had frozen his butt off refusing to put on a jacket when she suggested it. Recently, she argued that the dude he supported in the primaries was a narcissist and that he could be just as bad. She hadn't really said that but he figured that's what she meant. It was an insult and he knew that what he had seen about the politics in the country he was right to support the man, especially against that woman.

His mom had made some points. On the other hand, he had developed a way to argue that was extremely effective. He would immediately put her down in some way, overwhelming her with exaggerations that would make her feel stupid. When he did this, she would waver every time, forgetting what she was going to say because he would make her feel less than the perfect. When he'd first succeeded at this tactic, it was awesome that he could so confound her with nonsense. She didn't know how to argue. He was glad he did.

As he contemplated the scenario that had played out in his parent's honeymoon bed, he grew more and more enraged. Her description of his dad made him look silly. How could his dad admit such a sensitive thing to her without knowing how cruel she could be? How could he not know she would use it to make herself look good in her *memoir* — a snooty sounding word that made Wally feel creepy.

The more he thought about it, the more infuriated he became. His anger grew as enormous as the beanstalk in that *Jack and the Beanstalk* fairytale, all the way to the sky where the giant lived. *Fee-fi-fo-fum! I smell the blood of an Englishman. Be he alive or be he dead, I'll grind his bones to make my bread."* The fairytale had been one his mother used to distract him as a child when they were in the car.

The memory made him cringe and he wanted to avenge his dad and he wanted to be the only son. He wanted to crush the bones of everyone who had ever made him or his dad feel bad. He wanted to crush his mom.

He realized that would be a big mistake. But he could crush her ego and that is exactly what he decided to do.

CHAPTER 57

Darwin

The snow was melting creating streams ambitious to be rivers running down the streets and through the rivulets of soil leading into the roads and byways of Dancing Bear Springs. For a change the town was a *spring* of gushing water everywhere and not a dry wasteland. If not for the drought that had plagued the whole state and many others in the region of the US for years, there would have been many more complaints about Dancing Bear being washed away. The hillsides had produced a ton of gravel on the roads causing slippery conditions. As it was, most people took it in stride placing sand bags along the peripheries of their homes to keep the water and rocks out while praying for relief.

Darwin was out planting sand bags along the outside areas of his property when he noticed the truck Wally borrowed regularly from his house mate. It pulled up into the driveway grinding the gravel heavily with its tires. Darwin had an odd feeling he didn't like; he didn't want to be seen and he backed behind the fence as Wally got out of the vehicle marching up the portico that led to the house. There he stood at the front door, not knocking but wrestling with a book that Darwin now noticed in his hands.

"What the hell?" Darwin marveled under his breath. He moved quickly toward Wally forgetting he didn't want to be seen and ignoring the pain in his knee.

Then as suddenly as he had appeared, Wally took off down the portico to his truck. Only now his hands were empty. There was no book.

Through the windshield, Darwin caught sight of Wally, his eyes blazing. He grabbed the torn book from where it had landed in front of the door and ran down the portico toward the parking area, the ripped pages fluttering in his hands. Their eyes met as Darwin came toward the truck to stop Wally in his tracks.

"Hey you!" He yelled and pounded the hood, wondering if Wally heard him as he scurried away. The gravel popped from under his tires, backing the car so fast to get out of there.

"What in god's name?" Darwin couldn't wrap his mind around this action Wally had taken. "Why would he rip it apart?"

"What did he rip apart? And who are you talking about?" Rose stood on the porch watching him.

"Wally. He stood here at the front door and ripped this book to pieces and then ran away like a scared rabbit."

Rose took the book. "It's Danie's memoir. My guess is he found something in here he didn't like."

"Okay. But why now?"

"Danie has said he doesn't read anything if it isn't on the Internet. Perhaps he never got around to it until now."

"Okay, but *why* now?"

"You're repeating yourself. It's cold out here. Can we go in the house and talk about this?"

As they entered, they found Danie coming from her room. "What's all the ruckus? I heard an engine and the sound of tires screeching up the road. What's up?"

Rose and Darwin looked at the each other wishing the other would come up with an answer.

"It was Wally and he left this behind." Rose handed the torn-up pages to Danie.

"Oh, I see. Wally didn't like my story. That isn't surprising. He doesn't like anything about me and has demonstrated that without hesitation whenever possible," she said nonchalantly.

Rose stepped forward. "Danie, did you ever hit him or abuse him in any way? I am sorry to question you, but this is an extreme reaction."

"I am quite certain that Wally has taken much of what I did as abuse though I never laid a hand on him except once when he was extremely disrespectful to my friend's daughter. He hit her in anger and I lashed out hitting him. I told him he had reached my limit but I don't think he ever forgave me."

"Was that the only time?"

"Yep, it was. Well, there was the other night when I slapped him for suggesting I was complicit in being rapped. But I swore when he was born, I would never call him names, I would never hit him and I would never make him feel bad about himself. I hit him that once and regretted it forever after. I don't regret the slap."

"Maybe you were too nice to him."

"Too nice? How is that possible?" Danie's frustration was clearly marked in her face.

"Well, with Jason, I often had to correct him. He wasn't perfect and I let him know when I was displeased, big time."

"Did you ever hit him?"

"No; I spanked him when he was a toddler, just a little swat on his diapered bottom. But as he was growing up, I would often take him aside and tell him I was displeased about his words or actions."

"You didn't worry he would lose his self-esteem?"

"I loved him and he knew that."

"I loved Wally, too. How is it that he didn't know that?"

Darwin, taking this all in, "There was a time not so long ago when parents were told to never hit their children, that it was violent and could only teach a child to be violent, too. We heard a lot of lectures about it at the school where I was teaching. We were admonished to never make a child feel bad. In fact, it got so serious for a while that we gave every student a gold star for showing up that day. No matter how badly they did in school, they were always praised as if they were the smartest kid in there. They all noticed the hypocrisy, of course. But they didn't feel bad about themselves so it was a practice that persisted for a couple of decades. They are stricter now, though you still can't lay a hand on the 'little dears' for any reason whatsoever."

"You don't believe in corporal punishment, Darwin. You never have." Rose pled.

"No, I don't, but if you can't touch a child, well it removes all authority from the teacher and makes it really hard to discipline the 'little darlings.'"

"I remember that time," Danie responded. "I was afraid I would ruin my child's self-esteem if I only looked at him cross-eyed. And I never had a man to back me up when I did discipline him."

"Does that really make a difference?" Asked Darwin.

"I suppose it could have been a woman. Without another voice in the mix they soon learn how to manipulate a single parent. I could see it happening and there was nothing I could do about it. I tried splitting my personality to be fatherly, then I'd be motherly to soothe the bad feelings. It never worked, of course. I was not a dad. Wally was never stupid. He was always two city blocks ahead of me."

"He is behaving stupidly now. I am furious he would destroy your book and throw it on our porch to make a point. Who the hell does he think he is?" Darwin was very angry. Danie had obviously tried to be a good parent and the boy was obviously a juvenile delinquent. Even at this age; Darwin guessed Wally was over forty.

The situation caught him up. Learning he was a dad at this late date had turned Darwin inside out. What would he have done given the chance? Would he have been a good father always understanding his son and knowing what to do or what not to do? Would he have always supported Lucy and have been fair and wise in his dealings with his boy? Would he have become so infuriated that he would want to hit his child? Would his son have become a juvenile delinquent if he had been unable to stay with Lucy for the duration? Having children was complicated in a way Darwin didn't understand. Not being there when his son was young made him feel completely inadequate as a human being. He should have been there! He was enraged that he had been cheated out of becoming a father. He knew he would have been a great dad. Why had it happened that way? Had it been race? Really? Had the whole debacle been only because of the color of their skins? These thoughts made him madder than ever.

CHAPTER 58

Wally

Now that he had accomplished his first task and it had gone so well, he began to devise a way to approach the partner, Gregg Alcindor, to get the money he was certain the man had stolen from his mom. Checking the email roster, he was happy to learn there had been one communication with Mr. Bradshaw from his computer. He guessed it was about the same time the book was published. Wally couldn't think of another opportunity he may have had since he got Internet service. Checking the date, he saw he was right. Gregg Alcindor was not the sort of guy he communicated with on a regular basis. But there it was. His access to the man. He didn't have a phone number which was what he wanted and he didn't think an email would be effective. He wanted to confront this Bradshaw dude directly and wanted to see the man flinch when he realized he'd been caught. Wally didn't have any proof either. He didn't have records of transactions; that was something his mom would have. He couldn't be sure her records would reflect the truth of those transactions.

He wondered if he could get into her room and find the income records when she wasn't there. It would be a coup if he could, then he could confront the man directly. In truth, it would be easy to get into his mom's room since she often left the door unlocked. Dancing Bear Springs wasn't the kind of place that attracted thieves, so she was casual about security. This was a good thing for Wally who determined he would find an opportunity soon to invade her space and find the file. She was thorough about storing things and keeping records. In fact, he had noticed a portable file case in her room just under the daybed and figured that would be where to look first. He needed to be nearby when she left in her car at some point. He hoped it would be soon. The job would be easy and fast — perfect.

Wally felt stoked now. He had a good plan and was certain he could pull it off with expertise. He had stolen some meth from a friend with the same strategy and had found that job to be a cinch. This one would be too.

Access was the only problem. He didn't want to be around his mom any time soon. In fact, he wanted to avoid her at all costs. Hanging around the B&B wasn't something he could do anymore with freedom. He had to be tricky. He decided to pass by the parking lot occasionally to see if her car was there or not. If not, he would take advantage of the moment and sneak into her room via her private entrance.

It didn't take long. In fact, Wally was surprised how easy it was to steal her records. One day soon after he had devised his plan, she left for LA; she went to the city once a month to a book club she belonged to there. It was a Sunday morning and he was out for a drive in Richard's truck when he went by the B&B to find she was gone. He remembered it was Sunday and she would be gone for the day. Perfect timing. Just in case Darwin might be around, he parked the truck up the street and snuck down to her door and walked right in as he expected. The portable filing case was located under her daybed. Opening it, he discovered a file marked 'Income Receipts.' There they were, the royalty receipts she'd received from the Alcindor guy. He slipped the file out and put the case back. Just then, he heard a noise coming from the kitchen. It was Darwin's voice and he panicked. Quickly, he moved out the private door and ran to his vehicle. His heart was pounding as hard this time as it had when he'd stolen the meth and when he left the ripped-up memoir. It was a feeling he hated more than anything else. Even though he had promised Sally not to smoke weed until the baby was eighteen, he decided to smoke a joint now. It had been several days since his last.

When he arrived back at the house, he took out his papers and a baggie of weed. Rolling a perfect joint, he lit up and began riffling through the receipts his mom kept in the file. It didn't take long — there they were, royalty receipts from Gregg Alcindor Bradshaw with the info regarding his payments to himself, a hefty sum Wally thought and other vendors she supposedly owed money to. It all looked good. He expected it to. She would not have any evidence of wrong-doing. Oh well, he had the address now where Alcindor could be found. He had the phone number too. He decided not to give the man any warning with an email or a phone call. Wally would go to the address in Beverly Hills, the famous Los Angeles suburb, and face the man directly. He knew he would be able to tell if he was lying.

CHAPTER 59

Rose

Rose was sure the vitriol between Danie and Wally would dissipate as quickly as it had arisen. They loved each other after all. It was possible the situation with Jason was causing a lot of the rift between them. Danie's relationship with her son was perplexing. Rose knew there was great love between them, yet she could see disagreements abounded. Certainly, love would draw them back together again. She wondered if the love Danie had for Jason would outdo the love she had for Wally.

Rose was taking her morning coffee break on the couch watching clips from the presidential debate the night before. Her cup of brew warmed her two hands as she couched it between them. She hated the contempt that flew between the candidates. There was so much going on in the country as well — the same kinds of misunderstandings seemed to be everywhere. It was a confusing time in just about every way. Poor Darwin was in a funk because of his missed opportunity to be a dad, Danie was clearly angry about everything these days and she herself felt confused about the overall reaction to her painting. She felt truly proud of it, but everyone else seemed put off by it. Surely nudity wasn't the unacceptable thing it had been before. Was it because of her age? An older woman could be beautiful and Danie certainly was.

The most confusion began with Jason. He still didn't know his birth mother was Danie. Rose wondered just how he would take this news. Danie had mentioned she wanted to go with her to Hawaii to tell Jason together. She had to admit telling him together would be the best way. She hoped Jason might come their way again soon, so a trip to Hawaii wasn't necessary. She didn't like to leave the B&B in Darwin's care.

And Wally. What was in his mind when he tore up his mother's memoir? Did he really think the story against him was that bad? Or his dad? She hadn't thought so. Danie had been honest about everything. The only thing she left out was the fact of her pregnancy with Jason. Apparently, the shame of the rape kept her from making such a revelation. Giving the baby away was likely something she felt some shame about. Danie had been very frank about how she raised Wally. To her credit, she had admitted that she was far from perfect and it seemed she didn't want anyone to see her as something faultless or special. She had talked about her parents and how they taught her that beauty came from the inside, from the soul, not from the outside. Beauty on the outside faded with time but the beauty on the inside stayed with you forever. It was that revelation Rose had liked most about Danie's story.

The televised debate had taken on a nasty tone; the people on the stage were too self-involved, too narcissistic, too uninvolved in the lives of the people they were wanting to represent. She grew weary of the hatefulness that possessed nearly every candidate.

Her coffee cup was empty and just as she got started putting the clean dishes away, Danie burst into the kitchen. "I can't believe it!" She pointed at the cell-phone she held to her ear. "Why would he do that?"

She was silent listening to the person on the other end while she stared at Rose in puzzlement. "But what does he know about my business?" A pause. "Gregg please, consider the source. He is angry with me and he isn't thinking straight."

Rose began to link the information discerning the gist of their conversation. Hadn't Danie mentioned the name Gregg as the person who helped her with the publishing of the book? She was sure that was the name. There was another name too that sounded different.

Just about that moment the phone conversation ended. "I'm furious with him!" She screamed. "Who the hell does he think he is? You won't believe what he has done now."

"What on earth?"

"Wally. He went to Gregg's office and confronted him about my finances. He claimed Gregg was stealing royalty money from me. He was certain it was in prodigious amounts, that I would be rich by now if he wasn't embezzling my royalties. Can you believe that?"

"You mean he went down there and confronted the man directly?"

"Yes, that's exactly what he did. The nerve! Now I'm embarrassed. Gregg has been extremely supportive and he would never do what Wally says he did."

"I am sure he realizes that."

"Oh, I'm not so sure. He was really pissed off and told me so. Told me he would not be doing business with someone who has crazy relatives. He said it wasn't worth it."

"You will see, he will cool down and it will get straightened out."

"I wish I could be that positive. I can't lose Gregg's help. He's too valuable to me. How could Wally be so careless? He sure can ruin things."

"Has he ruined things before?"

"Once he took a phone video of me when I was deathly ill and passed it on so it became what they call 'viral.' I guess it went all over the Internet on Face Book. It was really embarrassing. You can't imagine. I was truly ugly as I was raging at him for taking the pictures, and that's what people saw!"

"Gosh, Danie. That is bad. Was he doing drugs then?"

"Yeah he was. Wally was awful back then. I thought he'd gotten better since. Maybe not."

"He's angry. The news about Jason was probably difficult."

"Why wouldn't he be happy to know he has a brother? I'd be thrilled if I discovered I had a sister or brother. I just don't understand Wally sometimes. "Oh," she hesitated, "and, he believes I stole his childhood because I divorced his dad, I was never smart about investing my money, and I threw away my career because I wasn't as attentive to it as I should have been."

"You did the best you could. You were a single mom."

"Yeah," she said sarcastically, "he really should take that into consideration."

Rose smiled.

"You know Rose, he complains that I never made enough money; that I am a 'poor movie star'. He doesn't realize I made considerably less money than my male co-stars and the pensions and social security I have now are much less than they should be because there was no parity between our contracts." She sighed. "Guild rules prohibit too much of a difference between contracts on the same project but the differences were ignored when it came to women.

"I remember that I couldn't make as much money as the men in my position — this was when I worked in a bank. It was different back then. Men were paid more because they were supposed to be the only wage-earners. Women weren't supposed to work. I remember when I first came here, there was a lot of talk about 'Rosie the Riveter,' how she was a symbol for women working in jobs that were untraditional for females. Some girls I know went into jobs like firemen, excuse me — they were called something else because they were women. That's right; they were called 'firefighters'! Women did plumbing jobs and construction, too. I never understood wanting to do a man's job or what was traditionally a man's job, but a lot of women swarmed to those jobs as soon as they were available.

Danie smiled ruefully. "I'm sorry, Rose. I'm just surprised Wally is being so resentful. Isn't he old enough to realize that no one is perfect, least of all me?"

"No, I don't think children ever get over the idea that their parents are to be unassailable."

"Your son is reasonable and they are about the same age." She put her hand to her mouth. "I just said 'your' son. I'm not used to this new relationship." Then, "Rose, I am very sorry about this thing with Jason."

"I've come to terms with it."

"Have you?"

"There always had to be a birth mother; it was just such a shock that it was you."

"You are being very reasonable. Thank you. I hated it when you were mad at me."

"You've been very reasonable too. So, we're even." She smiled.

"Our son is a reasonable man. He is very different from Wally. I don't know Rose. I am completely perplexed by Wally. He seems to see nothing but negative forces operating in our world. The way he talks, I suppose he thinks the whole world is against him, including his own mom."

"I know you aren't against him, Danie. You love him and that's obvious."

"Why can't he see that? Why does he continue to blame me for everything?"

"I don't know the answers. But I am certain this will blow over soon."

"No Rose. It won't because I won't let it. I won't continue to offer him a target to endlessly ram like a bullfighter without a prayer. This time, there is no forgiving and no forgetting."

CHAPTER 60

Danie

Spring, 2016

Months passed. Danie stuck to her guns and refused to see Wally. He apparently stuck to his guns and refused to see her. They were like strangers and worse he had talked Sally into his point of view. He had convinced her that she would have to give up the idea of help from his mom. There would be no house; there would be no extra money; there would be no grandmotherly attention to her or the baby.

Richard, 'Helicopter Dad,' of course refused to have them at his house. He didn't want some baby keeping him up nights. He had stopped Danie at the grocery store and asked if she would be providing shelter for the couple and the baby when it came. When she told him how she felt, he decided the couple would have to fend for themselves. He wasn't providing shelter.

Danie didn't flinch when she heard the news. She'd heard about tough love and decided there must be something to it. There would be no dormered house for them to live in either. She avoided both whenever they met or occupied similar space in the small village. They seemed to avoid her too, so it worked out just fine.

She was naturally curious about the baby and Sally's pregnancy. She wondered if the girl was taking proper care of herself by seeing a doctor regularly. She worried about the birth and how the couple would afford proper prenatal and postnatal care. Worry would have to occupy her life because she was not about to offer help unless of course there was an undeserved emergency. She would have to trust that Wally would do the right thing and take care of Sally and the baby.

What to do about Jason was the other problem that hadn't yet resolved. Rose was reluctant to tell Jason and Danie didn't feel she could do it alone with the best result.

These thoughts tended to nag at her and she was determined to get rid of them. A trip up north, maybe to Yosemite, would clear her mind. She made arrangements.

Warm early spring air cushioned her mood as she drove the distance between Dancing Bear Springs and Yosemite. Her mind was filled with thoughts about how she had gotten into this situation. When she married her husband, she was older for a woman to start a family. She went ahead and fought hard to get pregnant with Wally. She felt strongly about family and she missed hers more than she was willing to admit. Her poor mother had died so young of breast cancer metastasized to her liver. It was wrong. Just wrong. But Danie had frozen up over it. She was too angry at a fate that could take her mother that way so early. She refused to let such an arbitrary twist in space and time touch her. She would not let life get the best of her no matter what. Not like that.

Yosemite was as beautiful and magnificent as she remembered it. She had visited there with her parents and two grandmothers when just a girl of six or seven. That had been close to seventy years ago. When she was little, Half Dome had seemed just a little bit bigger. It was a geological wonder; the site of the giant rock rose nearly 5000 feet straight up from the valley floor. People actually climbed it. The whole place had been carved out by receding glaciers. Magnificent. The sights were enough to take her mind off Wally and Jason for a few minutes.

She decided to stay one night in a cabin. It was sparsely furnished and had a potbelly stove which was the central focal point of the room. She made a small fire and sat down at the functional kitchen table. Engulfed with loneliness she decided to make a list of all the things that had hampered her relationship with Wally. In her dire efforts to spare him pain, guilt and embarrassment from his misdeeds, she had withheld every negative criticism she'd had of him. Remembering how she had screamed at him in her mind never opening her mouth to allow the words to surface taking those words back into herself and securing them for good like the crazy relative locked up in the basement. It was no wonder she suffered from stomach problems and headaches today. They were stuffed with unsaid criticisms and censures that gnawed at her insides.

The list was long. She loved Wally immeasurably but wondered if she had made a mistake by forcing the marriage and pregnancy. Danie had to admit to herself that she had married her husband only to have a small family. She had gotten pregnant at the first possible opportunity and was pleased with herself that she had conquered fate and created what she wanted even though the marriage was far from perfect and easily torn apart. She did regret making something that couldn't hold.

In fact, her regrets were numerous. If only she could go back and retrace those steps, change the dynamics and make a better life for her son. She knew so much more now than she did then. She wondered if other mothers felt the same. They were all young when they had their families while she had waited until she was in her early thirties. She should have done better as a mom than her cohort. Yet, it seemed she had done all the wrong things. What if she had said all those things she thought about Wally? Would it have made a difference?

A deep depression came over her as she contemplated her mistakes. In one tearful breath, she felt herself slip from solid ground to a feeling of falling into dark space. She landed on a dead and murky planet billions of miles away from home and earth. She was utterly alone and felt infinitely small, smaller than the tiniest nucleus. She wondered if there was something more minuscule than that, but could think of nothing tinier. In the whole of the universe, her importance was so insignificant that she could no longer trust her existence. In this deep state, she came to understand how truly unimportant she was. She was utterly alone and utterly insignificant. This depression was the lowest she had ever experienced and she knew somehow it was significant. "Heal my son!" She demanded of a deity she hoped existed but to whom she rarely prayed anymore.

The night had been a long one. She barely got any sleep with her mind working madly on the past, a past that was irretrievable and irreversible. When she finally caught a little sleep, it was fraught with nightmares, the last of which she was in a deep, dark cave and something or someone was stuffing rocks down her throat.

Early in the morning, she headed back to Dancing Bear Springs. She felt oddly refreshed by the short trip and ready to confront the problems awaiting her. She only wished there were such things as do-overs, a chance to do it right. "Heal me," she cried.

She decided to put an offer on the dormered house. It had been on her mind for a while and now was the time to act. She couldn't know what the future had for her, the baby, Wally or Sally, but having a home was a good thing. Danie knew she had to do something positive or she would fall into a very sad place and likely stay there.

CHAPTER 61

Darwin

With springtime waning and summer just on the horizon, Darwin was in a fixing mood. He wanted to fix the yard, repaint the sunny side of the house and plant some flower pots. It was impossible to grow anything other than trees in the mountain soil. Pine trees discouraged flowering plants and the ground squirrels ate everything from underneath the ground. Not even bulbs stood much of a chance.

But he had to wait until after Mother's Day to start the plantings. They had learned the hard way that Dancing Bear could freeze over, even in the springtime, occasionally into the month of June.

Instead of planting, he started on painting the side of the house. First, he had to sand the old sun-peeled paint away. He placed the ladder up the side of the house and climbed with his electric sander clenched in his fist. He was just getting a good handle on it when he heard the alarmed barking of Heidi. Her howl stripped the air of oxygen as she ran down the ramp toward his ladder which was propped up against the wall. He looked down to see what was causing the ruckus and found *he* was the center of attention cornered up the ladder by a bear. Dancing Bear Springs had gotten its name because of the yearly visits by the hungry Black bears. Hibernation was clearly over.

She was a pretty thing, blond, or as blond as a Black bear could be. And small. She was probably only about 300 pounds. Pepper was having none of it. Foolish or brave, she was at top voice and fury as she headed toward the bear. Darwin was horrified. He thought the bear would tear his beloved dog apart. She aimed at the bear's butt and screeched her displeasure at the animal's presence. Taking a moment of consideration, the bear apparently decided it wasn't worth the effort and took off. Darwin breathed a sigh of relief as Heidi finished off her job of protecting him roaring after the bear nipping at her butt. The bear with her butt tucked carefully beneath her, scurried away. Darwin was grateful she didn't turn on Heidi. She could have swiped the dog from here to the freeway at the bottom the hill.

His relief that Heidi could scare the bear away was palpable. She had been fierce, surprisingly so. He got off the ladder and hugged Heidi from the bottom of his heart. The dog loved the attention and nuzzled up to him just as Danie's car, the Subaru he had smashed in the nose with his snow-clearing machine and repaired months ago, appeared in the driveway. She had been out shopping with lots of heavy bags in the back that needed to be carried inside. Darwin, always helpful when it came to heavy objects was right on-hand.

"Good looking legs," he said. Darwin took note of the shorts Danie was wearing. Even though her legs had a little damage from varicose veins, broken capillaries that surfaced to just under her skin, he had to admit they were shapely.

"Thanks," she said looking down, "I guess they're not too bad for a woman my age."

As he gathered the bags up and headed toward the house, he couldn't help but brag about what had been on his mind the whole morning. He had gotten the call the night before.

"Guess what?" he asked with pride in his voice.

Danie gathered up a couple of bags and follow him. "I give up!" She laughed. "What?"

"Rose and I are travelling to Washington D.C. Do you know why?"

"Oh gosh, let me guess. You are going to meet your son and the boy who is dating the president's daughter."

"You've been talking to Rose."

"I have to admit, I do keep up with your life by asking Rose. She is the one who knows."

"Rose who knows! You're a poet and don't know it."

"Oh my god, please don't take that old tired joke out of the closet. It is entirely too trite."

"You're right; it is trite!"

She laughed. "You are sounding like Doctor Seuss.

So, the Johnson's are aware of the family mix-up?" She continued. "Mr. Johnson is okay with it?"

"He is a little miffed with Lucy for the same reason I am; she failed to say anything about it until now. I know she's very sorry for holding it in for so long, but it is what she did and we all have to deal with it."

"Oh gosh." Danie said as she sashayed through the front door. "What?"

"Well, I have recently discovered or should I say recovered the reason Wally and I have so much trouble."

"Good. What is it?"

"I failed to tell him everything I was thinking when he was a kid. He did a lot of things that were unacceptable as all kids do. But I feared that I would spoil his self-confidence if I spoke to him about his failings. So, I didn't. I'm afraid my angry thoughts somehow bled through and made themselves known even without my saying a word."

"Come on, Danie. That isn't possible. If you didn't say those things, he didn't hear them."

"Yeah, you think?"

"I do think. How could he?"

"I'll make a bet. I'll bet you know what Rose is thinking at least half the time even when she says nothing."

"She never says nothing!"

Danie giggled as she entered the kitchen and placed a grocery bag on the counter, "You are proving my point Darwin. In fact, it is my bet that Wally managed to get everything I thought no matter what.

"Wally has a terrible self-worth problem. He may try to cover it up but I can see how insecure he is." She paused briefly. "I really think his religious devotion to that fake news is his way of trying to be smarter than everyone else."

"He knows something they don't know."

"Yeah. Knowing stuff others don't gives him a sense of power, even if it isn't true. The people he hangs with believe everything he says because he is decidedly more intelligent than they are." I had him tested when he was sixteen. He came in with a 136 I.Q. So, he is no dummy."

"He's filled his mind with a lot of false information. That is not what I call intelligent." Darwin added.

"No, I don't either. He has treated his mind like a garbage dump and filled with it with junk."

"Did he ever finish school?"

"He never completed high school. Refused to do it. I think he was opposing what I did. I finished my education by going back to college as an adult. He didn't get his GED either. And when he turned eighteen, I lost what little power I had in his life."

"Danie. I'm sorry."

"Oh, but I am so happy to hear that you are going to meet your beautiful son! That is so exciting. Is he really dating the president's daughter?"

"No, that's my son's son. I am a grandfather too believe it or not."

"Remember everything because I want to know all the details when you come back. When are you going?"

"A month from now. July. We plan to be in Washington DC for the Fourth of July. We hope to see some amazing fireworks and the president's daughter's birthday is on the fourth. She was smart to be born on that day, don't you think?"

"Yes," Danie smiled. "Very smart."

CHAPTER 62

Wally

After selling his pickup truck to Wally who paid top dollar for it, Richard kicked Wally out and Sally's place, a small living space with a kitchenette, a bedroom and a tiny bathroom, was too undersized for the two of them (the cat and dog) much less the three they would become. Sally was huge and had quit her job two months before unable to complete even simple tasks because of her size and distress. This pregnancy had not been easy. She had been sick most of the time. Without an income to pay for it, she gave up the apartment and the two of them became homeless.

Wally was at a loss of what to do. He had no money to speak of especially after paying for the truck; just some left over from his last job making a bed frame from pine logs. The thing had been so heavy, they'd had a time just getting it up to the bedroom it was to occupy. In fact, Wally had to take it apart to get it up the stairs in sections. Then of course, he had to put it back together again. The whole thing had been such a chore, Wally didn't feel he'd been paid nearly enough. He decided in the future he would have to charge more for extras like delivery problems.

Gary the pot dealer had a connection. His grower had a place out on the Carrizo Plain where he grew and stored weed. It was an hour and a half from Dancing Bear Springs and the grower was antsy wanting to take some time off from his task of growing for a while. He wanted a long vacation maybe in Hawaii or the Bahamas. Wally agreed to grow the weed in the man's absence. And of course, he would sell to Gary and to some folks in Dancing Bear so he could make some money.

Sally was stunned. She didn't want Wally smoking weed much less growing and selling it. She wanted him to get as far away from the drug as possible until their child was at least 18 years old, maybe even as old as 25 since that was the age when scientists said the human brain was completed in its growth. People were said to make better decisions about their lives after the age of 25 with a completed prefrontal lobe.

It made sense to her but not to Wally who believed the scientists were telling the public what the Rockefellers and the Free Mason's wanted them to say. The Free Masons was the organization that was supposedly surreptitiously offering the public "true" knowledge to create a society that depended entirely on them for information. He believed the Rockefellers were behind it all with their money and the money they could get from like-minded people. Wally firmly believed the organization was super-secret and had most elected officials firmly in their grasp with promises to murder their wives and children if they didn't cooperate.

Sally told Wally what she thought — the Rockefellers were old and no longer active; most were dead. These days, it was the Koch brothers or the Mercers that had enough money to influence elections, elected officials and things like that. She told him so and he became sullen and uncommunicative after that. These were the kinds of arguments his mother made and he hated her for it. He hoped Sally would not become more like his mom. That would be a deal-breaker for sure.

Wally had made a deal with the pot grower and he and Sally, the cat and the dog, were on their way out to the Carrizo Plain where they would occupy the property and keep it safe. California was voting to make recreational pot legal so she could make little argument with Wally over his plan.

The drive out was horrendous. Much of the road had been dirt and deep ruts that bounced the light truck around like a beach ball. The cat in her carrier cried and hissed every time they hit another rut. Buddy the dog was making the best of it snoozing between Wally and Sally. It was nighttime and long-eared Jack-rabbits, attracted by the headlights, ran toward them and got hit flying here and there.

"There you go Sally. Road Kill — dinner. We'll never starve out here."

Sally screamed every time Wally hit another rabbit without even slowing down.

"Sally for god's sake, please. I can't stand your screaming!"

"I can't help it. What's wrong with those rabbits? It's awful. They are running right in front of us." Buddy who had been sleeping on the seat of the truck, awakened and barked displeasure at all the noise.

"They see the headlights and they are curious maybe."

"They have no sense."

"Well yeah Sally, that would be true. Rabbits are not known for their good sense."

"It would help if you didn't hit every pothole with full force. You're driving this thing like a racing car. If you aren't careful, I'll have this baby right here and now."

"You're not. Right?"

"No, not yet anyway."

After screaming over a couple more rabbits, a tiny mouse and a huge tarantula that literally bit the dust under Wally's tires, Sally quieted down. "So, what is this place we are going to?" Sally asked. "It sure is out in the middle of nowhere."

"We haven't gotten there yet and there are people…I'm sure." He took out the directions and checked a wooden sign that emerged out of the dark. "We're good." He said confidently.

"What about the pot farm? Will it be nice?"

"Sure. It'll probably have a small house."

"Probably? Didn't you ask about the accommodations?"

"No, not really. I wasn't thinking about anything nice. I was just thinking about a place to stay for a while."

"Oh Brother." She said quietly.

"Are you implying I won't be able to take care of you?"

"What about when the baby comes?"

"I'll call an ambulance."

"Is there cell phone service out here?"

"Yeah. My phone will be good anywhere."

"How will we pay for the ambulance Wally?"

"I'll figure that out when the time comes."

"Wally, I hate to remind you that I am nine months along."

"That's fine. We'll have a baby soon then."

"You're not thinking Wally."

Buddy barked as another rabbit leapt in front of the truck.

"Damn, another rabbit. Sorry." Wally was struggling to keep a lid on his frustration with Sally. Her constant chatter was getting to him. He figured he'd have to give her a pass since she was due and big as a house. She took to wearing jersey tops that hugged her belly snuggly. She seemed happy to show off her growing stomach.

Wally had grown to love Sally because she had made it easy this time. She had mellowed a lot and he found he had, too, in matters of love and being lovable. He found it easier all around to just be lovable even when he didn't feel like it. It felt phony to him and he didn't like phoniness. At least it put the brakes on arguments.

At last, they arrived at the address marked on the directions. There was a large chain link fence surrounding the place with small solar lights placed evenly around on top of the fence poles. They were just enough to give off some light at night. The fence was molded with dark green plastic tarp to keep prying eyes away.

Wally stopped the truck and got out. He had keys on his ring that would open the gate. Next to the gate hung a tightly framed glassed-enclosed paper, the license they needed to grow pot legally. When Wally opened the gate, to the side there was a blue outhouse just like the ones at public events.

"We have to pee in an outhouse!" Sally's alarm was as big as her belly. Wally knew this would be difficult for her so he remained silent hoping she would accept it as she would have to accept every little inconvenience they would find here.

As the gate opened wider it exposed the 'house' they would live in. Set toward the back of the property was an Airstream, a shiny and tiny place to live. Next to the Airstream there was a Quonset-hut-style tent which was where the weed was grown.

"Wally, I don't mean to complain but that Airstream is tinier than my apartment. How are we going to fit with the baby and all?"

"Let's look inside and see." She hesitated. "Come on get out." Wally urged, "We are here."

"Where are all the people you said would be out here? This place is as isolated as anything I've ever seen."

"No worries. We don't need people."

Suddenly, her voice gained an edge of panic. "Wally, I am going to have a baby and I need someone to help me!"

"It does no good to worry. I'll think of something. Tomorrow morning, I'll take a look around and see where the people are. Okay?"

"I don't know how okay that is. I only know this baby is due and I am beginning to believe you don't have a prayer."

His temper was being challenged like never before. He just wanted Sally to shut up before he lost it.

"Well," she said, "I'll get to work. My guess is the inside is filthy. A pot grower isn't likely to be a clean person or a neat person."

"What do you know about it?" his pique was getting challenged.

"Nothing really. I said I was guessing."

She was sounding like his mom and he wanted her to put a lid on it. Wally opened the door and standing aside with his arm in an exaggerated welcoming pose, he invited her in. It was dark and he shone his flashlight inside. When he looked in, he saw that Sally had been right. The place was a mess. Piles of dirty pots and pans filled the sink; used cups and dishes with dried food stuck to their surfaces adorned the entire counter space which was small to begin with. The trash was full of plastic and paper dishes the pot grower had used when all the others were dirty. There was a small table against the other wall under a window. A built-in seating arrangement surrounded the table. It too, was piled high with clothing, dirty dishes and used soda cans. Clothes, bed sheets and blankets were strewn across the only bed in the back. There were some pillows which looked inviting. Beneath the built-in bed were two large drawers that held more junk. The expression on Sally's face was worth a ticket to the front row seat of a *Grateful Dead* concert.

Wally wanted to escape, made an excuse about looking the property over for problems and took his exit. Buddy followed Wally while Sally got the cat in her carrier. "I don't want to let her out of the carrier. I'm afraid she'll run away."

"Leave her in there then. She'll be fine." The cat meowed her displeasure at being trapped.

"Maybe she has to go to the bathroom. I have to let her out for that, at least."

"Sally, you will have to figure it out; I'm looking inside the tent."

The tent, off to the side of the airstream, was where the pot was to be grown. He set aside the flap and when he entered, he was surprised to see one full-grown plant. "Ah, good," he said to himself and Buddy who stood at his side. "We have something to smoke." He was happy to see the Quonset-hut was amply large with huge barrels filled with soil lining each side of the space. There had to be at least twenty of the containers — he counted — yep, there were twenty.

Her scream nearly knocked him off his feet. "Water! We don't have water!"

Wally ran to the trailer wondering if Sally had hurt herself. When he got to the Airstream and look in, she was standing at the sink full of pots and pans, crying. "We don't have any water, Wally! What are we going to do?"

"We have water Sally. I have it in the back of the truck. I brought several gallons just in case." Wally was getting frustrated with Sally's inability to solve problems herself. "Sally, you must be more self-sufficient. I can't do everything!"

She sighed. "I can't imagine where I would have found water if I had been more 'self-sufficient.' Dig into the ground maybe?" Her voice carried a certain disdain. "Please get me water Wally. I need it to get this place cleaned up."

"Oh sure; no problem," he replied with the same condescension.

When he returned with the water, he made a seat for himself on one of the benches at the table. As he watched her scrub the dishes, he wondered about her. He realized he didn't know much about Sally and soon she would have his baby and they would probably get married. He wondered if he'd have to go to a church to get the deed done. "You believe in God, Sally?"

"Sure. Don't you?"

"No. My mother does but I don't."

"What about your dad?"

"He's a Buddhist. They don't believe in a god."

"He's religious, isn't he."

"Oh yeah, he's religious alright. It's hard to get him away from it."

"Well, I don't consider myself to be strictly Christian. If anyone asks, I tell them I'm a heretical Christian." Sally smiled a wide mischievous grin.

"What's that supposed to mean?"

"I just think the religious people today have turned Christianity into a right or wrong religion. It's a set of rules you have to follow to be okay."

"You don't believe that?"

"No, I believe in the spirit of love."

"I've heard that Christianity believes in love although they seem to believe in hate mostly."

She smiled. "Well, they don't exactly believe in hate but I think they have issues with the poor and disenfranchised. Jesus taught us to embrace those who are outcasts. Christians don't seem to do that very much anymore."

"Yeah, like my mom."

"Oh Wally, I don't know. Your mom seems okay to me."

"I'm more worried about the end of the world."

"There are a whole bunch of Christians who believe that Revelations means we, the ones who are heretics like me, and the non-believers like you, are going to get left behind soon. They believe they will be the only ones who will be 'raptured' into heaven. You know, like the end of the world."

"Yeah, exactly."

"There have been these predictions many, many times, and they have not come true. So, I don't believe that anymore."

"Well, it isn't difficult to believe in nuclear war, is it? That's why I like it here away from the bad folks."

"You think they're all bad?"

"Yeah, pretty much. Everybody is greedy or they're stupid and just follow along."

"Yeah, the "right or wrong" philosophy will always make for enemies."

"Some things are just wrong Sally."

"I guess it's how you look at it."

"No, Sally. Some things are just wrong!"

CHAPTER 63

Darwin

It was the plan to leave for Washington, D.C. as soon as they packed the car with their suitcases and themselves. Their plane reservations would put them in D.C. at about dinner time. Rose was leaving Danie in charge of the house while they were gone. They didn't plan any guests so it would be a simple job just keeping up with the dogs, laundry, dusting and kitchen duties. She would answer the phone and make reservations for when they returned in two weeks after they had toured the entire capitol and met all the relatives.

Darwin was nervous. He couldn't sleep for several nights before the trip, so he was slogging around on too little shut-eye. He knew Rose was becoming frustrated with him because of everything he didn't do that she had to add to her chores.

At last they were ready. Danie drove them down to the "Fly Away," a bus stop for the conveyances that would take them to the airport. Once on their way, Darwin's nerves calmed and Rose's frustration died as she went over the details and decided that everything on her list had been accomplished. They both let out a sigh of relief when Danie took off leaving them aboard the airport bus.

"Well, we are on our way." He said trying to open a conversation with Rose who sat quietly contemplating whatever was on her mind.

"Yes," she said. And that was it.

"I'm really excited about meeting my son." He said feebly.

"I am sure you are." She said flatly.

"Rose, are you okay with this? You're uncharacteristically silent."

"I am not. I've been answering your questions."

"But you aren't elaborating which is unlike you most of the time."

"I will elaborate when we get there. Right now, I am tired and want to sleep." She turned her back to him in her seat and promptly closed her eyes. "You might want to catch a cat nap too. It would do you some good."

"I don't know if I can sleep now. I'm too excited."

"You will be unhappy when you get there if you don't try. You will be even more tired than you are now." She peeked at him out the corner of her eye to see what he was thinking.

"We'll be at the airport in no time and I don't want to sleep right now. You go ahead though; don't mind me."

"Okay you got me. What is it?" She turned around to face him. "What's the matter?"

With that, he burst into tears. He couldn't help himself. "Oh shit. I didn't mean to start blubbering."

Rose took him into her arms. "It's okay. I understand. This is a very big deal for you Darwin and you are a little scared that it won't turn out well."

"How did you know?"

"I am a mind-reader of course." She smiled ruefully. "It is natural for you to feel unsure. I would too, and it is utterly human to cry."

"Oh yeah. Crying is good for you, right?"

"Right."

"Well, I am a man. I don't cry."

"You know how silly that is. The new generation will cry at the drop of a woe."

"I cry at sad movies."

"Darwin, this is not going to be a sad movie. It is going to be a joyous experience for you to see your son for the first time."

"I want to get to know him and I don't know if we will have enough time — or enough in-common."

"You will get to know him a little now and better on the phone or in emails later when you get home. We do have the technology you know, to get acquainted with someone without having to be there in person. You can even share pictures. Don't forget, we have Skype."

"Thank you Rose. I knew you would make me feel better. You always do."

CHAPTER 64

Danie

Danie had been left alone in the house and it felt terribly empty. The rooms sounded hollow. She almost wished there would be guests. At least, the place would feel normal. The week of the fourth didn't draw folks looking for fun and fireworks. In fire country no one would light a match outdoors much less set off fireworks. The entire forest would go up in smoke. She was grateful Rose and Darwin had chosen this time to go east. There was no doubt she would be terrible taking care of a bunch of people in the house.

And she was very excited for both Darwin and Rose. Their trip to D.C. was going to be wonderful. They would see all the sites and Darwin would get to know his son. They had promised to send back photos taken while they were there, especially of the fireworks, so she could keep up. And Rose had promised they would take a trip to Hawaii as soon as it was possible.

When her cell phone rang, she was sure it would be Darwin or Rose checking in. It was not. She hadn't spoken to Wally for months. When his name appeared on the display of her cell phone, she was unsure whether to answer it. But her curiosity overwhelmed her and she answered just in time before the call went to voicemail. "Wally, I am surprised to hear from…"

"Mom," he cut her off. "I'm out here on the Carrizo and Sally is having her baby. I don't know what to do."

"Can't you get her to an emergency room? Call an ambulance?"

"Mom, I can't afford it. I was hoping the baby would take its time but Sally has been in labor for a most of the day and she is screaming like she might have the baby now. I thought it took a lot longer." There was panic in his voice.

"Isn't there anyone out there to help?" She was trying to stay calm and trying not to alarm him. "How about paramedics? There must be a place out there to help people."

"I called and no one answered. I left a message but I haven't heard back and Sally is screaming in pain like she's having this baby now!" Clearly, he was alarmed. I've looked around the area and all I can find are solar farms. They're huge."

Danie was becoming alarmed. What kind of a place was this, she wondered? "Give me directions. I'll come out."

"Oh Mom, could you?" His voice had tears in it. He was truly worried. "I wouldn't have asked but I don't know what else to do."

After gathering the directions, she dressed and made her way to the car. The sciatica that had dogged her during the winter months had abated and she gratefully didn't need the cane. There was enough gas in the car and she was thankful for that too, since she didn't think there would be any stations between here and where Wally was. This was one time when she wished above all that Darwin was here to go with her. Even Rose would have been better than no one, but that was out of the question too. Oh well, she thought, I've been in strange places before. I'm sure I can do it again. Shoring up her courage, she stuck the key in the ignition and started off.

The drive out was as horrendous as she thought it would be. She passed Soda Lake fed by Wallace Creek, a small stream that was dry most of the year. The Lake, thankfully, had water in it because of relief from the California drought. She got lost a couple of times. Getting lost was one thing that terrified her. She hated the feeling of being in a place that didn't make sense and not knowing if she could find her way back. It was so dark; no street lighting and street signs made of wood — the lettering nearly faded in every case. She was stunned by the amount of rabbits that dogged her car. They seemed attracted by the car lights. It was horrifying to hit rabbits right and left, flying at her out of the black moonless night. One sprang up and bloodied her windshield. "Oh, my God," she groaned. The windshield was surreal. Disorienting was a good way to describe it. The trip that should have taken an hour and a half, took two.

By the time she got there, Sally's contractions were coming one minute apart. She could hear the girl screaming all the way out by the gate. Wally was standing at the entrance waiting for her looking like an old man. She felt bad finding him in such dire straits. He was obviously stressed to his max and wishing he could disappear.

He yelled to her in the car. "She's in the Airstream." Parking the car, she jumped out and headed past the gate to the Airstream, dreading what she would find there. "You know I have never birthed a baby before, Wally. All I know is you're supposed to boil water. I've seen that in the movies"

"Okay, I'll boil some water."

"Oh good, you have some?"

"Of course, Mom."

"Do you have clean blankets; how about towels? They have to be clean though." Her voice had taken on the tone of authority. Wally snapped to and began gathering what he could.

"How long has she been in labor?"

"I don't know. She's been complaining about pain all day long."

"All day? And you only just called me a couple of hours ago?"

"I didn't know." He said sheepishly. For once Wally was way out of his league and feeling helpless, something Danie had never seen.

"Okay, let's see what Sally has to say."

Danie entered first and Wally followed.

Sally screamed once more. "I can't stand it, the pain is too awful," she cried. She was in the bed on her side holding her belly.

"Sally, would you mind if I looked to see what is happening down there?" Danie asked quietly.

"Oh gosh, I guess it's okay. I want to know too." She turned over and spread her legs wide enough for Danie to look. The girl was quite unambiguous about it. Danie would have hesitated for some time before allowing a non-medical person to look at her privates. She figured it was a generational thing. Since the time of Wally's generation, young women were raised with far less shame about their bodies and about sex than her peer group had been.

Instinctively, she backed away from the sweaty crotch stench. Aware she had reacted so viscerally to the odor, she tried to cover. "Oh dear, the head is crowning. I'm calling an ambulance."

"Mom I told you, I can't afford an ambulance or a hospital bill!"

"There's Medical; both of you are eligible. And then there is me. I'll foot the bill for now and you can pay me back when your Medical kicks in."

"I didn't know you had money, Mother."

"I got a good royalty check recently and I can share it."

"Oh, so Alcindor decided to pay you what he should have all along!"

Danie didn't want this to turn into an argument, "Wally, did you try 9-1-1?

"No Mom. You know I don't like government stuff."

"It's a service."

"And, it is paid for by tax payers."

"Yes, you and I when we earn enough money to pay something."

"I haven't paid taxes since Shana. I haven't made enough to pay. So, I have no right to the service."

"Well I do, Wally Wharton!" Sally's voice, shrill will pain, cut in. "I've been working and I've paid plenty of taxes."

"Frankly, this is a ludicrous conversation." Danie took her cell phone out of her pocket and dialed 911.

Sally's contractions were closer together and she was chewing on a rag so she wouldn't scream. The baby was pushing harder and harder. Danie had washed herself up but she didn't have any rubber gloves so she was going to take this as it came since it seemed the baby was on its way, with or without a paramedic to help. At least she had found a bottle of isopropyl alcohol in the cupboard.

Wally and Buddy had gone outside unable to handle the scene. The cat was nowhere to be seen.

Sally cried quietly between the contractions.

Danie held her hand even when she squeezed it with pain. "It'll be okay. You're a healthy woman and babies have been born this way far more often in history than have been born in hospitals or with paramedics."

"That's very reassuring. Not."

"I'm here and you're a lot better off now than before he called me."

"Yeah." Sally replied somewhat mollified.

"What made him decide?"

"To call you? It was a big step but he couldn't stand my screaming at him anymore."

"Well, it is a step in the right direction; I suppose…I hope."

Another contraction took hold of Sally and she bolted straight up and jumped into a crouched position as if she was going to defecate. "The baby's coming! I can feel it," she screamed. I can't help it; I have to push."

Sally pushed with everything she had. The sound coming from inside her throat was like a wounded animal. Then, there was a blubbering sound and suddenly there was a baby girl on the bed kicking her little legs like mad.

"Oh my god! It's a girl." Danie shrieked. You've given birth to a baby girl!

She was blue and the umbilical cord was hanging from Sally still attached.

"Oh my god, oh my god, oh my god!" She cried. Danie was horrified with what she faced. The infant wasn't breathing and she knew that had to happened or the baby would die. But she remembered that the umbilical cord would pump oxygen to the baby while it was still attached. Danie took her up into her arms and marveled at the little face but noticed the baby's mouth was filled with guck. It didn't appear the child could cry and breath without choking until the guck was gone.

"Wally," she screamed out the door. I need something to suction this baby's mouth!"

"You mean, the baby's born already?" Wally shouted back as he ran toward the door.

"I don't know what to do." Danie implored. "Her little mouth is stuffed with guck and it has to come out or she won't be able to breathe!" Her voice was panicky.

"Oh shit. I don't know! Wally was looking around the cabin of the Airstream wondering if anything could be found to do the job. Sally had spent days cleaning it up and putting things away but he didn't know where things were yet, since she'd just finished the day before.

Sally had fallen back into the bed exhausted. "I'm pretty sure there is a straw around here somewhere. I just can't remember where I put it."

"A straw?"

"Yeah, to suck the fluids. I used one at the office once when we couldn't find the regular suction device."

"Great idea!" Wally said and began searching in drawers and cupboards to find it. "Was there only one?"

"Yeah Wally, and I'm sure I put it in a drawer."

He opened several drawers, "Ah, here it is!" He shouted. "I've got it."

He took the straw and inserted it into the baby's mouth gently drawing the fluids out, some of them ominously dark. As soon as her air passages were free the baby made a couple of gurgling sounds as she gained her first breath, then screamed at the top of her little lungs.

"Ah, scissors!" Danie yelled as she drew the scissors from the same drawer. "I'm sure this is the next step." She cut the umbilical cord and tied the end. The baby finally began to get color.

Danie still clutching the infant said, "Congratulations Wally. You're the proud father of a baby girl." She handed the child over to her son as the baby cried wildly. The expressions that crossed Wally's face conveyed everything. He had taken in a deep breath, but had yet to release it, he was so overcome. "Mom," he said astonished. "Look, she just opened her eyes and they are the most stunning color of blue."

Danie, through her tears managed to see the blue eyes. They were the same color Jason's had been.

Finally bringing her close to his chest, slowly exhaling, he cuddled his baby like he'd been doing this his entire life. "Hello, Little One. I don't know your name yet but I'm sure glad to meet you after all this time."

The baby continued to cry. "It's okay Little One. It looks like you're going to live." Wally was crying like the baby as he clutched his "Little One" to his chest.

"Something else is coming! Oh my god it hurts." Sally shrieked. Out plopped the afterbirth and the delivery was finally done.

Wally wanted to hand the baby over to Sally who couldn't take her just yet.

Danie took charge, "Sally, I'll wash her up first." Then to Wally, "Wally, get some warm water. Gracious, there is a lot of slime. And Sally, you'll want to bag that afterbirth. We can bury it under a plant or something. That's a tradition if I remember right. I'm not sure whose."

Wally had filled a small plastic tub with warm water from a pan on the stove that had been heating it and placed it on the counter where Danie stood. "She is so tiny. I thought she'd be huge by the way Sally looked."

"I can't tell how much she weighs. I don't suppose there's a scale to weigh her with."

"Yes, I have a scale to gauge product. It should be big enough." He ran out to the tent to get the scale while Danie immersed the baby into the tepid water. The newborn had such a startled expression, Danie had to laugh. "It's okay Little One," she said softly. "You are going to be clean in no time. She poured dish soap into a small towel and removed the slime and the light film that covered her beautiful granddaughter. Swaddling her into a clean towel, she handed the baby over to her mother.

"She looks really healthy, Sally. Congratulations. You did a great job." As soon as the infant was in her mother's arms, Danie began to weep happy tears. "Oh my God, I was holding a lot in," she blubbered. Danie felt a relief and an enormous joy she didn't know she deserved.

Sirens could be heard in the distance. "Just in time!" Sally sobbed. "Just in time."

CHAPTER 65

Rose

The trip to D.C. had been uneventful which was a relief to Rose who had grown weary of the current state of passenger airlines. They had been stuffed into tiny seats. Poor Darwin's knees had been jammed into the small seat space and he was in pain. He tried not to complain but it was obvious the cramped area between his seat and the seat in front of him had taken a toll.

The airport had been crowded on top of the uncomfortable seating arrangement and the folks who were to meet them seemed to be either late or lost. Finally, Rose got a bead on the sign with their names on it. "I see it!"

"What?"

"A sign with our name on it."

"Thank God. I was about to request a wheelchair."

At that moment, a tiny black woman with a wheelchair stopped by. "Did I hea' somebody need help?"

"Yeah, I do." Darwin reiterated.

He sat down in the chair with a big sigh. "That's better."

"Honey, do you really want to use this chair?"

"Why not?"

Rose wanted to be discreet and whispered in her husband's ear. "The woman driving this chair is very small, Darwin. She may not be able to haul your huge hulk anywhere."

"Oh," he replied. "You're right," he said looking back to take in the tiny woman's frame.

"You folks thinking I can't take you to pick u' you bags?" The woman asked. "You be surprise' how well I kin do this."

With that, she started to roll the chair toward the baggage area. Darwin who had barely managed to settle into the seat, found himself hanging on for dear life, his jacket and take-on bag flying. The person with the sign noticed them and waving the poster followed the tiny woman and the wheelchair, running, as was Rose trying to keep up.

Darwin laughed. The ride was a hoot and he was totally taken by the small woman. When they got to the baggage area, he took out a twenty and handed it to her. "Great job! Thank you."

"You look like Santa Clause." She replied.

"I've been accused on occasion."

"Well, thank you, Sir Santa." With that, she took off looking for another customer leaving the pair breathless.

The greeter person caught up at last, also a little winded, and took them and their luggage to the car. It was a government car which was a total surprise.

On their way to the hotel they passed the Watergate which looked just like it did in the pictures and, after a bit of traffic, landed at a small lodge which appeared to have every possible amenity.

"When will we meet the Hayes?" Rose inquired of the greeter whose name turned out to be Dan Grover. He was a very respectable young fellow dressed in a black suit and tie.

"Tomorrow morning. You'll have breakfast with the whole family. They thought you should have a night to rest and catch up on your sleep."

"That's very nice of them. We could use the time to get settled." Rose realized they were now three hours ahead of California and would need to solve the jetlag problem. They would be getting up three long hours before they were used to getting out of bed. "We are looking forward to meeting everyone," she replied.

After the check-in, Dan Grover took them to their room with their bags. He waited patiently for his gratuity. "I'll pick you up in the morning at 9:00 a.m. We'll go over to the Hayes' residence for breakfast." Darwin tipped him and he was about to leave, then said, "There is time to get room service for dinner if you haven't eaten yet." With that, the man disappeared.

Until the next morning when he reappeared with startling promptness. They were only barely ready, Darwin as usual lagging behind.

"Mr. Grover, you will have to be patient as I have become patient with years of practice. I hope you can do it now without any practice."

"Don't worry, Ma'am. I am used to people who can't seem to keep up. It seems they are usually married to a person who is always on time."

Rose had to laugh. Of course, she was the one who had to be on time. It was how she was able to avoid disaster. For a moment, she stopped herself and thought about how she used perfectionism as a way of control. She insisted that Darwin be on top of everything, as a military sergeant might insist his trainee be perfect. It was an unreasonable expectation and she knew it. The force of her emotions in this area, driven by her need to follow mother's orders, drove her to act unreasonably. Why? While thinking about this overpowering need, she had to admit she had sought her mother's protection from the beginning — the Nazis, death, homelessness, alcoholism, and Victor, were all dangers she should have been protected from…And there had never been the help she needed. She continued unreasonably to seek security by doing what her mother wanted — perfectionism, hoping unreasonably to be safe.

"Rose! Rose!" her husband's voice broke into her thoughts with such force, she almost lost what it was she had been thinking. "It's time to leave, Honey." Darwin's voice softened when he realized she had been reflecting. "Let's go. I am anxious to meet my son."

Everything seemed to happen so fast. First, they were hauled into a waiting black SUV and driven across town to a residential district. Rose was certain they were on the way to the Hayes' residence and indeed she was exactly right. It was a lovely two-story house of red brick and white balustrades. When they entered, they were faced with an open view of the whole downstairs area and a spiral stairway up to the second floor. The floors nearly sparkled and the ceilings were so high their voices echoed.

"It is so beautiful," Rose exclaimed almost in a whisper. "What does your son do, Darwin? Has anyone ever said?"

"I think he is an attorney."

"Oh. I suppose that explains this beautiful house."

As they marveled at the incredible surroundings, a voice interrupted.

"Hello," the voice said, "Are you the Neumanns?"

"Yes," Rose answered twirling around to see who was asking. There he stood, a light-skinned black man, tall, broad shouldered just like his dad and very handsome. He actually had a broad forehead and a nose just like the man who was his real father. Rose felt the need to take the man's hand and move him to Darwin who stood stunned and unable to move. "Darwin, congratulations, you are the proud father of a very handsome young man."

Darwin was overwhelmed with emotion. The man came forward and took him into his arms. "Hello, Dad. "I've waited a long time to meet you."

CHAPTER 66

Wally

The baby girl born at a solid eight pounds was healthy and looked happy. Wally was so proud he couldn't stand himself. He and Sally bragged their baby never cried. "You know sometimes I wonder if something might be wrong, because she never lets me know when she is unhappy." Sally said.

Danie smiled knowingly. "My mother told me that I never cried either. She would put me down for a nap and a couple of hours later remember that she hadn't heard from me in a while. She would peek into my crib and find me cooing and playing with my toes."

Present were Wally, Sally, Danie and the infant. The idea of a baby quietly playing with her toes made the group chuckle.

The doorbell of the dormered house rang. Wally's mom grabbed her cane — the sciatica was back — and went to the door. "Hi you two," she said before anyone else could see who was there. Darwin and Rose were at the door. "Come on in." Partially hidden behind them was Jason.

"We've come to see the baby." Rose was excited and showed it. "And the new house." They all entered the living room and said their hellos. When Jason entered, Danie let out a small yelp. "Jason! What are you doing here?" Danie cried.

"Well Mom, I was told I have a birth mother to meet."

Danie's eyes filled with tears.

The mood in the two-story Dutch Colonial changed from calm and happy to stoked.

"Oh my God!" Danie reached out her arms and Jason hugged her.

"Hi Mom." He couldn't help himself either. Jason's eyes filled with tears too. "I'm really thrilled to have two moms," he said as he took Rose and Danie into his embrace. "Always knew it was possible but never had an inkling about how it would turn out." He looked at them both with such warmth and love that Wally's heart succumbed to the circumstances. After all that had happened in the last few months, how could he remain angry and cold? He had a new baby and a new brother and that was worth a lot. Even he could see that.

Rose and Darwin had been unhappy and missed Danie after she left the inn. But a new person came along and took Danie's place in the Tea Rose Room. She was a younger professional woman and she worked most of the time. However, when she was at the B & B, they enjoyed her company enormously. Lots of lively laughter returned to the breakfast table and all the guests were delighted.

His mom had actually bought the dormered house, at a bargain price no less. She loved the little abode and she had decorated it perfectly using her beloved couch as the living room centerpiece. Instead of the sexy lady in red, the wall above the couch was adorned with one of Danie's Landscape quilts of a beautiful lake filled with Lotus blossoms. It was summertime and the fireplace lay dormant with potted flowers dressing the hearth. The dark oaken paneling complimented the warm colors and Wally felt truly comfortable here. Sally said she was happy to live here too. Now, with Jason in the mix, all seemed to be well. Wally had wondered how his mom had managed to buy this particular house. But he wasn't about to question her motives. He knew she loved the place.

They learned that the original owners Evilyn Seward and her husband had separated. No reason was ever given but they divorced, sold the house and moved on. Bernadine, while in residence, had done a good job upgrading the kitchen — no more Formica counter tops. Rumor had it she had moved on, too. Neither Danie nor Wally ever learned the real reason for the divorce but Danie was sure that Evilyn and Bernadine had been discovered by the hapless husband. It was a secret she would keep, except from Wally and Sally; there didn't seem to be any joy in outing people who were unwilling, and gay marriage was becoming something almost ordinary. Bernadine and Evilyn could have married and they would never know about it.

Spotting the baby, Rose grabbed Darwin's hand and dragged him toward the basinet. "Come on Darwin. I want to see the baby."

Wally came over to them and shook Darwin's hand. "Welcome to our home." He said. "I am very glad to see you both." Sally was making sure his manners were getting better and he was grateful. It felt better to him knowing he was making people comfortable.

"Can I get you anything?" Danie asked. "We have coffee, tea, wine, sparkling water, plain water, and champagne. The champagne is for celebrating," she added. "I can add orange juice for Mimosas."

"Thanks," said Darwin. "It's kind of warm out. Make mine iced coffee. Would that be too much trouble?"

"Of course not. Nothing is too much trouble for you." She answered. "Rose?"

"Me, too. I haven't changed any of my habits. Make it iced coffee… with a teaspoon of sugar." She added.

Jason was up for that champagne.

Danie left to get the drinks hobbling away on her cane. Wally remembered what his mother had said about the stiffness: "I find myself feeling very envious of the babies in diaper commercials. Have you ever noticed how supple their backs and limbs are?" He laughed.

His "Little One" was bundled in pink of course which made her pink all over. Rose and Darwin cooed and awed over her until the champagne and coffees arrived delivered by Sally.

"So, tell us, what is her name?" Darwin inquired. "Names are very important to kids you know. School children can be brutal if you have a funny name."

Sally felt challenged. "Tiramisu is her name!" She said in a defensive tone.

"You call her by the name of a dessert?" He was incredulous.

"Yeah, well, she is our dessert. We decided that between the two of us, life has been more like the main course — you know, meat and potatoes, the hated vegetables; our baby is the dessert. We couldn't call her 'chocolate cake,' which is our favorite, so it's Tiramisu."

Danie smiled. "It makes sense don't you think?" People call their children by very different names now. I guess it is the fashion."

"We didn't do it because it is the fashion." Sally added. Her voice had the edge of defensiveness. "We like the name."

"It is also a great name for a little girl," Wally said. "There's no end to the possible nick-names she can choose from."

"Like what? Suzie?" Darwin scoffed.

Wally ignored the implied disdain. The baby fussed and he gently picked her up. "Yeah, that's a possibility. We might call her Tara, or Terra, or we could call her Missy or Misu." He nuzzled Tiramisu's head and she cooed.

"I see your point." Darwin grumbled.

"Tiramisu. It's a beautiful name for a beautiful baby." Rose declared.

"It is." Danie shifted her weight as the pain in her joints urged her to do.

"Oh, oh. I feel a wet diaper." Wally was checking the wetness as he held his baby girl. "I better change her."

"Mind if I watch?!" Danie asked.

"Of course not, Mom. Come on upstairs with me."

They aimed for the stairway and climbed up to the little baby room. Danie sat in a small comfy chair. "My bones ache a lot you know."

Wally deftly took Tiramisu to the changing table and got to work. Danie watched as he expertly took over the changing operation. "You've got this thing handled, don't you Wally?" Tiramisu's legs kicked joyfully, happy to be free of a diaper for a moment.

"As you know, I'm getting lots of practice." The baby gurgled happily. "Mom, I know I have been a bastard and I want to apologize to you."

"Huh? You're kidding!"

"No. I mean it. He put Tiramisu into her crib and settled her. "I want to tell you how happy I am and I want to tell you that we could not have done any of this without you. I am truly grateful."

Danie was so stunned, she didn't know what to do. "I heard you were apologizing to everyone in the village that you've offended. Even Richard. But I didn't think…"

"You didn't think I would apologize to you?"

"No. I really didn't. I thought you hated me and were covering. I thought you were so desperate to have a place to live for you, Sally and the baby that you would say or do anything. I realize that wasn't very charitable of me, but…"

"It's my fault." He interrupted. "I saved you for last. I should have made you first."

"I would have appreciated that. I do love you, Wally. I even love you a little more than Jason, if that's possible. We've been through a lot together and that is a bond that Jason and I will never have."

This time is was Wally who was crying. "I'm sorry, Mom. I was so jealous that I couldn't see straight."

Danie stood and took him into her arms. "I too am sorry that I didn't stay with your dad and try to make it work. It would have been better for you and I didn't see that." It was a while before the tears stopped.

He held her strong and made sure she was okay. "Sit down while I get her bottle." He stepped out and ran to get Tiramisu's nighttime bottle. He bound back up the stairway and when he got to the room, he had a big question on his mind. "We've been so busy with the house and everything, I haven't had a chance to ask you something."

"Sure," she said.

"When you were pregnant with Jason, how did you hide it from the cameras?"

"I didn't even try. I claimed exhaustion as soon as I began to show and took a five-month hiatus until Jason was born. It worked out okay. I had been filming non-stop, going from project to project up till that time, so it was plausible that I would be tired and needed a time out. I've always been very lucky, Wally. That doesn't mean I didn't run into trouble at times but I always rose up from disaster with good things happening. Like now. I am very happy in a way I have never been before.

The baby would be more of a challenge as she grew, Wally knew, but he felt he was up to the job. His mom had told him he would be a good dad but it would not be easy for him. Tiramisu was bound to make life hectic and more taxing as time wore on. The demands of child rearing would place a strain on his emotional resources. He knew. He had been told by practically everyone he ran into. He was determined to be a good dad anyway, and the sleep deprived nights proved it.

Wally was working hard on himself making sure not to lose his temper again. He was learning to stop and think about the possible consequences of his rage. He couldn't afford to indulge again and he didn't need a twelve-step program to tell him so. He sobered up; made amends to all the people he had ever frightened with his rage and became a father. His only desire was that he would be a reliable dad.

Wedding bells were not ringing for the couple just yet, so Sally and Wally decided to wait until they were sure about each other and maybe long enough to have 'Misu' be the flower girl. They talked about two or three years testing the waters and finding out how steady they would be. His mom said she thought it was a good idea and, though she hoped they would marry, she also hoped she would be a fulltime grandmother to her beautiful little Tiramisu no matter what happened to the couple.

"So, what's new?" Danie asked Rose and Darwin as they gathered together on the couch. Jason sat between his two moms hugging them both. Wally was surprised he didn't feel jealous at all.

"I sold the painting." Rose said proudly. "It fetched a good price!" She bragged.

"Oh, great Rose," Danie said. "Who did you sell it to? Anyone here?"

"Yes," Rose's smile was big. "I sold it to Clint Jackson."

The stunned look on his mother's face was priceless. Wally laughed a big guffaw. He knew Clint Jackson and he knew the man was a player. "I can guess where he hung it."

"Wally, you can't know where he hung it."

"Maybe not, Mom. But I can 'guess' exactly where it is."

Darwin smiled big as he filled in with his own good news. "We travelled to D.C. where Lucy and her husband, Ted, live. I met my son. His name is Clarence. He and his wife live close by — their kids do too. I got to meet my grandkids." The familiar glint of emotion appeared in the corners of his eyes. "One grandson, the oldest, is dating the president's daughter! Can you imagine?"

"Darwin, I am so thrilled for you!" Danie cooed. "You must be very proud and happy."

Wally felt the pride too and considered the future to be positive. He knew it was very fortunate to know your own children and he thanked God he would know his. Life would be good to his little family. He would make sure of it.

"Not only that, I sold one of my screenplays — the one about the zombies and Santa Clause," Darwin added. Wally laughed at the concept. This was the first he'd heard it.

"Oh, and I fixed the garbage disposal!" Darwin looked proud.

"That GRRGLEGRUMBLE noise that came from the inner workings of your house?" Wally asked still chuckling.

"Darwin finally accomplished the abominable deed." Rose exclaimed.

"Sweet." Said Wally.

Wally grabbed a foot stool and sat down with the others. "Hey everybody, have I ever told you about the time a bear kissed my toe?"

Three months later, in November 2016, the blond business man was elected to become President of the United States of America.

CHAPTER 67

Danie

Summertime, Five Years Later

Her arthritis hurt more than usual. It couldn't be the weather. It was a beautiful day. And, the headache. Danie hadn't been feeling all that well of late. But Misu was pulling on her arm dragging her out to the front porch of the house she intended to live in for the rest of her days. The child had a bunch of her favorite 'dollies' gathered in her limbs and she intended to have a visit with them, maybe a cup of tea and some 'grown-up' conversation. Danie was always willing to play the games her beautiful granddaughter had in mind.

Now just five, the girl had a tassel of blond curls atop her head and blue eyes that sparkled in the same way her Uncle Jason's did. She loved to provide the various voices and characters her dollies lent to the array of nationalities and ethnicities they represented. Her "Uncle" Darwin had spent a good deal of time playing the parts of each with his amazing talent for voices and accents. He had modeled the array she presented now as she sat each one on the bench and the chairs available to sit on. Danie could see the creativity, the actor, developing in her grandchild with great pride.

All settled now in their respective places, each with a cup of tea, the conversation got started. "Do you think the lection will be good?" The little black doll-baby asked with great authority. "Grammy. What is a lection?" Misu's curiosity was enormous. She heard things on TV as she sat with her mom in the evenings and repeated them without really understanding the implications her words represented.

"Well, an election is a very grownup thing. It means that we choose who our leaders will be in the next few years."

"You mean like the preshitent?"

"Yes, and we have senators and congress people to lead us too." Danie answered not knowing whether her charge could grasp her meaning but hoping something would stick in the child's mind for the future. "There are a lot of people to vote for and it is a little complicated."

"What's copicated?"

These were big words for such a little one but Danie patiently tried her best to explain — "It means it is difficult to decide about."

"Oh," the child replied as if Danie had cleared up the mystery. "Sometimes it is copicated to decide what I want for breakest."

"Yes," Danie answered. "I have trouble sometimes deciding about cereal or pancakes in the morning."

"Oh yes!" Misu squealed. "I love pancakes! But mommy says they are too much trouble sometimes so I have to eat ceral."

"Your mommy works very hard and pancakes are hard too."

"I sappose," Misu replied trying to sound very grownup. "But daddy makes the best pancakes! I like it when he cooks breakest."

"I like it, too."

"Grammy, why do mommy and daddy argu all the time?"

"Oh, I don't know," she replied wearily. "I guess they sometimes find it hard to decide what is real and what isn't."

"Real?"

The perplexity in Misu's voice caught Danie up. How could she explain all of these complicated issues to her curious granddaughter? "Well…" she hesitated. "Sometimes real is hard to know. It is what we can't deny because we can see it, touch it, smell it, feel it and hear it right there in front of us."

The child looked up at her with such perplexity she felt she had to start over.

"You know when you watch TV sometimes, you can tell what is real and what isn't. Like the characters you like to watch on 'Child's Play.' And, 'Sesame Street.' "

"I love 'Sesame Street.' " She said with great earnestness.

"I love it too." Danie replied. But not everything on TV is like that. Sometimes we watch the news and that is what is real — or we think it is." Danie said suddenly not sure she could say the news was really real. So many people thought it was fake these days.

"I can see and hear Sesame Street. Doesn't that make it real?"

"The characters like your dollies aren't really real. When you play you make the sound of the voices for your dollies and Sesame Street characters get their voices from people like Uncle Darwin."

"He's an actor. Like that?"

"Yes. And Grammy was an actor too."

"Did you make the voices for the chacters like Uncle Darwin?"

"Sometimes we watch dramas and comedies on the TV too. I pretended to be people who were not real but I wanted to make seem real."

"Grammy, it is very copicated." Misu replied with distress.

"Yes, it is. But when you grow up you will understand."

"Then why doesn't daddy or mommy unnerstand?"

"Your daddy only watches his 'toy'." Danie referred to her son's device, his so-called 'smart phone.' "He doesn't watch TV like we do."

"Why not?"

"That is a very good question, my darling." Danie didn't know how to explain her daddy to Misu. She didn't understand him herself. "He believes that all TV is lying and that his toy is telling him the truth."

"The trut?" Misu asked perplexed. "What is the trut?"

Danie smiled. "It is what is real."

"Oh, the trut is real and my dollies and the chacters on TV are lies?"

Gosh, Misu was smart Danie mused. "In a way. Your dollies and the characters on TV are pretend. It is very complicated." Danie said hoping to end this inquiry. It was taxing her brain and she was feeling tired and dizzy.

"Grammy! The girl said excitedly. "There's a bear walking down the street!"

Danie looked up from her lap where her tea sat untouched. Indeed, there was an enormous Black Bear ambling down the street. Alarmed, she didn't know if she should herd her granddaughter into the house. The bear looked peaceful and unaware of their presence. He was loping down the paved street as though on an afternoon stroll. "Shush Misu. Be *very* quiet and still. We can watch the bear as long as he doesn't know we are here." Danie prayed she was right, but her instinct told her they were safe.

"Is the bear real?" Misu whispered.

"Oh yes, the bear is very real." Danie softly replied. She knew Black Bears were safe as long as you didn't scare them or threaten their cubs. They weren't the same as the Grizzlies or the Polar Bears who liked meat. They were mostly herbivores and almost never ate humans. She had heard of a Black Bear that had eaten a man who had died of a heart attack and was laying there undefended. That was the only instance she had known about here in California.

This bear was probably a male; there weren't any cubs trailing behind. It was a very magnificent looking animal. Soon, he was out of sight and Danie could relax. As she did so, she took her last breath. She collapsed in the chair and the teacup fell from her lap.

"Grammy!" The child thought her Grammy had fallen asleep. It was so unexpected she felt startled and ran into the house. "Daddy! Daddy! Grammy fell aseep!"

Thank You

My deepest thanks go to those who provided the most inspiration: (in alphabetical order) my son, Evan Andrew Burke; Francis Burras; Butch, the cat; Luba Croenthall; Vera Desmond; Peter Dunne and The Grey Quill Writing Workshop; Julie Given; Patric Hedlund; Heidi, the dog; Dale Jones; Jeet Kaur; Brenda Martin; Canda McCaulley; Mary McDevitt; Gary Meyer; Michael Gregg Michaud; Pepper, the dog; Mar Preston; Laura Quinn; Toni Scharf; Kim Selvert; Dan Silva; Sally Sloan; Maxine and David Stenstrom; Stix, the dog; Deborah Waynesmith; Kathy and Mel Weinstein; and James Weinstock. And, special thank you to the publisher, Ben Ohmart.

Every one of these wonderful people deserve to be honored as the number one person on my list. So, enormous thanks to all for being superb inspirations and such good friends, partners and neighbors.

CPSIA information can be obtained
at www.ICGtesting.com
Printed in the USA
FSHW020839031120
75402FS